The Archaeological Adventures of I. V. Jones

Barb,
Hope your knee is
all better. So enjoyed
our week together —
until next time...
Heidi

THE
Archaeological
ADVENTURES
OF I. V. Jones

Heidi Roberts

Bonneville | *Books*
Salt Lake City

Bonneville Books is a joint imprint of The University of Utah Press
and the J. Willard Marriott Library at The University of Utah.

This novel is a work of fiction. Names, characters, places, and incidents are either the product of the author's imagination or are used fictitiously, and any resemblance to actual persons, living or dead, events, or locales is entirely coincidental.

14 13 12 11 10   1 2 3 4 5

Bonneville Books
Salt Lake City

The Bonneville Books colophon depicts a Quetzalcoatlus, a giant pterosaur with a fifty-foot wingspan, and is courtesy of Frank DeCourten.

Bonneville Books is a joint imprint of The University of Utah Press and the J. Willard Marriott Library at The University of Utah.

LIBRARY OF CONGRESS CATALOGING-IN-PUBLICATION DATA

Roberts, Heidi.
  The archaeological adventures of I. V. Jones / Heidi Roberts.
    p. cm.
  "Bonneville Books."
  Includes bibliographical references.
  Summary: This new novel is a fictional retelling of the complicated world of Utah archaeology in the 1970s, a period out of which came field-changing cultural resource management (CRM). This entertaining book also presents a woman's perspective on the decisions involved in an archaeologist's life and the true-to-life adventures of a "dig bum."
  ISBN 978-1-60781-009-4 (pbk. : alk. paper)
  1. Archaeology—Utah—Fiction. 2. Women archaeologists—Utah—Fiction. 3. Utah—Fiction. I. Title.
  PS3618.O315741 5 2010
  813'.6—dc22
                                          2009053812

Cover painting, *In the Field*, by Bradley Giles Reproduced by permission.

For Matt and Christie

Contents

Acknowledgments

Many people helped me see this book through to publication. My sister, Emily Statham, was the first to exclaim, "I think you finally did it!" She read each chapter, and my dad, Earl Roberts, read and edited several chapters. My husband, my two children, and my friend Suzy Eskenazi offered constant encouragement and support. I'd especially like to thank Suzy for editing and formatting several versions of the book. I'd also like to thank Alexis Mills for her superb job with the copy editing.

Without Steve Simms, Don Fowler, Kay Fowler, and Reba Rauch this book never would have made it into print. Steve offered numerous helpful suggestions, and he forwarded the book onto Reba. Don read at least two drafts, spent a weekend helping me with character development, and provided lots of encouragement. Together, Kay and Don "talked me down" when I panicked from publication angst. Reba has been my biggest supporter, and she encouraged me to rewrite and improve the book at least twice—thanks Reba, thanks everyone!

Most of the places in this book are real. I have experienced archaeology much as Ivy does; however, all of the characters are fictional. When I started working on this book I left the world of science behind me and moved into the creative realm of fiction. In the words of Margaret Mead's teenage informants, I made it all up.

Please note that the term "Anasazi," which is used throughout, has generally been replaced with "Ancestral Puebloan." For the sake of authenticity I decided to use "Anasazi"; however, in future adventures you can expect Ivy to abandon this word.

The Dark Lord

Trudging up the hill to the anthropology building, I realized that summer was almost here and final exams were just a week away. The Anthropology Department at Utah College was housed in an eighty-year-old structure that reminded me of my childhood drawing of home: a rectangle with large square windows and a triangle roof. The only thing missing was a curlicue of smoke snaking out the chimney. I loved the ivy vines clinging to the building's limestone facade. They added an aura of academic legitimacy to an otherwise plain-Jane building. It was almost time for the landscapers to wage their annual war on the vines. In early summer they would spend a week cutting and taming them, pulling tentacles from windows and walls. But by fall, when classes started, the vines would have grown back, undaunted and relentless, climbing skyward as if the pruning only strengthened them.

When I was seven I decided I wanted to be an archaeologist. Now, fourteen years later, I was just one class away from graduating with a bachelor's degree in anthropology. So far I'd learned about ancient cultures and concepts like polyandry, ethnocentrism, and cultural ecology. I'd mastered the history of North American archaeology and memorized all the bones in the human body. But no one had taught me how to find an archaeological site or, better yet, how to dig one. Everyone told me field school was not only the place where I'd learn how to survey and excavate, but also a rite of passage for all aspiring archaeologists.

Pulling open one of the large double doors leading into the foyer, I timidly sniffed the air, my nose wrinkling like a rabbit's. Thank goodness the archaeologists weren't boiling roadkill again. Last month a graduate student had decided to expand the department's comparative collection of animal bones. He'd scoured the highways for dead animals and deposited them in an aquarium full of flesh-eating beetles. After the writhing swarm ate their fill, the bones were boiled to remove ligaments and grease. For weeks the building reeked of decayed flesh. I'd promised myself that next time they boiled a carcass, I'd sneak into the lab and add a few onions and bay leaves. Maybe herbs and spices would convert the smell of death to something more like bad soup.

For four years this building had been my second home. I loved its light, airy halls, the antique woodwork, and the seriousness of academia. Most days I'd feel relaxed and content there, but not this afternoon. My stomach was churning like that time I played Becky in my fifth-grade play, Huckleberry Finn. In the last scene I completely missed Huckleberry's face in a scripted slap. I silently prayed that my appointment with the professor in charge of field school would turn out better than my acting debut.

No one could get into field school without the director's stamp of approval, and the director wasn't just anyone, he was Dr. Maxwell Johnson—a world-renowned archaeologist and a legendary curmudgeon. He was arguably one of the most powerful men in American archaeology and, hands down, the meanest.

Johnson was an intense lecturer and an even more devoted chain-smoker. After lighting a cigarette, he'd leave it in his mouth while he talked. Mesmerized, I'd watch him smoke and talk, the ash becoming longer and longer as the cigarette moved up and down. The lecture forgotten, I'd count the seconds until the growing ash dropped. When his cigarette finally burned down to the filter, he'd throw it on the floor and crush it with the toe of his shoe.

He treated his students with about as much respect. Max, as his colleagues called him, had ruled the Anthropology Department with an iron fist for thirty years. In my Primate Studies class I realized that Johnson was just like a silverback gorilla—typically the dominant, or alpha, male of a group. Silverbacks gather mates and control the group through physical intimidation. In the same way, Dr. Johnson intimidated and dominated every archaeologist within a wide radius. Students were terrified of him, and awed by his power and connections. His tyranny was so all-encompassing that after the Lord of the Rings became popular in the mid-1960s, Johnson's students began openly calling him "The Dark Lord."

Successful completion of Johnson's field school was the equivalent of an archaeological pass directly to GO. Earning a Ph.D. under Johnson assured you a university teaching position. Unfortunately, his approval came with a price: ulcers, divorce, depression, nervous breakdowns, and alcoholism. Few made it out unscathed. Rumor had it that Johnson didn't approve of female archaeologists. In fact, he had only started accepting women into field school in the late sixties, after students had staged a protest march. That was just ten years ago.

I didn't understand why Johnson felt that women shouldn't be archaeologists. I grew up in the era of women's liberation, believing that women can do everything men can do. We have the pill, we burned our bras, and we expect to be treated equally in the workplace and in the educational system. Even Barbie dolls had abandoned their traditional roles as nurses, airline stewardesses, and teachers. Now they come fresh out of the box as lawyers, doctors, astronauts, and scientists. Although I'd known very few career women, I was raised to believe that I could succeed at any career I chose as long as I worked hard enough. If my Barbie could be a scientist, why couldn't I?

The problem with wanting to be an archaeologist was that I couldn't figure out how you actually become one. Lawyers and doctors follow a rigorous educational and on-the-job training program, and then, voilá, they go into practice. It seemed that archaeologists have only one career path: college professor. In order to become a professor I would have to go to graduate school and earn a doctorate. What if I wasn't smart enough, or couldn't attract a mentor? Would Johnson even give me a recommendation for grad school if deep down he didn't believe that women can be competent archaeologists? Could I even make it in academia if he didn't think I was cut out for a career in archaeology? He was my ticket to grad school, and I needed to show him that I had the right stuff. Up until now my only contact with Johnson had been in my North American archaeology class, and the class had been so large that I'd escaped notice. I'd flown under the radar, and that wasn't going to get me a recommendation. Field school would be my big chance to make an impression, but how would I do that?

I could hear Johnson's booming voice as I climbed the stairs to his lair. His office was on the second floor in a prime location next to the stairs. I couldn't resist snooping so I peeked in. A tall, skinny guy wearing a white leotard and baggy black sweatpants was sitting next to Johnson's desk. A hooked nose dominated his thin face, and his long, black, wavy hair was securely tied in a ponytail, high up on his head. The image of an exotic pigeon popped into mind. Randy, as I would later come to know him, was asking permission to attend field school.

"Why do you want to come to my field school?" demanded Johnson.

"Well, I need the credits for my minor in anthropology. My major is dance, but I love the Tarzan movies with those hunky archaeologists raiding the lost cities hidden in the jungle."

Johnson raised his eyebrows and frowned. He paused and stared. His eyes were hot points of light, and disgust framed his mouth.

"That stereotype is totally wrong. Those so-called archaeologists are nothing but goddamn pothunters. Don't mention them again, and save your gay stuff for someone else. If you attend field school, you'll need to act like a man. I don't buy into all this gay nonsense. It used to be a good word until you guys got a hold of it. You understand?"

Randy nodded vigorously. "Yes, sir. Um, one other thing. I'm a vegetarian. Is that going to be a problem?"

"Not for me. I don't care what you eat, but you won't get any special treatment. You eat what's served or don't bother to come. I am not running a hippie health food camp." He handed Randy a few sheets of paper and dismissed him with a wave.

Johnson looked up and saw me standing just outside the doorway. His eyes bore into me, and my heart raced. Randy scooped up his books and scurried past.

"What do you want?" Johnson demanded.

Johnson reminded me of a gargoyle perched on the edge of a medieval cathedral. Up close he was physically intimidating—at least six feet tall and solid. His face was deeply lined from years of smoking and digging in the desert sun. His thinning hair was streaked with gray. An arthritic stoop told me he was probably at least sixty. A few times in class I'd caught him wincing when he straightened his back.

He held my gaze and looked deep into my eyes. For a second I felt like a Mayan princess staring into the black waters of a steep-sided sacrificial pool just before being tossed in. I felt panicky and tongue-tied. Calm down, I told myself. Tread water. He can't be that bad.

"I would like to sign up for your field school."

"Who are you?"

"My name is Iva Veronica Jones, but everyone calls me Ivy. I took your prehistory class last fall. Um, I think I'm your next appointment."

Wire-rimmed glasses magnified his intense eyes. A trim mustache covered his upper lip, but not enough to hide his sneer.

He motioned for me to enter. His hands were veined and muscular, like God's hands on the Sistine Chapel. Dr. Johnson pointed to a hard wooden chair next to his desk, and I sat down obediently. Sit, Spot, sit!

Before he could say anything, his phone rang. He grabbed it and I watched him morph into a charming gentleman, witty and charismatic. He was even smiling. From his side of the conversation it sounded like he was discussing a graduate student's qualifications for a job at Harvard.

While he ignored me, I reviewed what I knew about him. Maybe that would help me focus. Cave sites had made Johnson one of America's most famous archaeologists. His careful excavation and radiocarbon dating of three huge caves' stratigraphic deposits had enabled him to reconstruct Native American lifeways across the Great Basin and Colorado Plateau for the last ten thousand years. Those caves were the American Rosetta stone, and Johnson's detailed analyses of the basketry, tools, clothing, food, and even the human waste recovered from these rock shelters had earned him his peers' respect. If that wasn't enough, he had also helped to define Utah's prehistoric farming cultures, the Fremont and Virgin Anasazi. His latest claim to fame was the major part he played in the archaeological survey of the Lake Powell area before Glen Canyon Dam was built. His students had gone on to establish important archaeology programs on both coasts.

Abruptly ending his telephone conversation, he turned to me. The gargoyle was back.

"So you took my archaeology class. That's a good start. Why do you want to go to field school?"

"I want to be an archaeologist," I answered in a shaky voice. I avoided making eye contact because it was just too scary.

"It's hard work. You don't look like you really know what that is." He paused and searched his desk for something. "From the looks of you, I doubt that you're cut out for hard physical labor."

"I've already participated in one excavation, and I know archaeology is what I want to study." I was aggravated that he'd already pegged me as a wimp. Yes, I'm skinny and small, but I come from a long line of tough women. "I know how difficult and tedious the work is."

"Oh, you think so? What makes you so sure?"

"I went on a dig in high school." I flashed back to my first excavation. It was by far the hardest thing I had ever done, working ten-hour days in humid ninety-degree heat in central Illinois.

He sneered. "Who was in charge?"

"The dig was under the direction of Bill Hodges. I spent one summer excavating a Late Mississippian period village near Cahokia, Illinois. Dr. Hodges was studying settlement patterns and…"

Johnson cleared his throat, interrupting me midsentence. "Never heard of him, and if I don't know him, I doubt he's competent." He pulled a cigarette out of the pack in his upper pocket and lit it. The smoke made him blink fast. "Against my better judgment, you can attend my field school. But you'll need to forget everything you learned from Hodges. You think you can do that?"

He reached across his desk, grabbed some stapled papers, and thrust them toward me. Then he gave me a dismissive wave. I walked out feeling shell-shocked, like one of the bodies laid out in my grandmother's funeral home. What the hell was I doing committing eight weeks of my life to the complete control of this man?

The first few days of field school were taught by Johnson's grad students in the anthropology building. Johnson showed up periodically, but he didn't seem very interested. Three of the grad students—Penny Van Ness, Jeff Davies, and Fred Smith—took charge of our initial training, which included the project's research design, excavation techniques, and local prehistory. We learned how to read a map and use a compass, how to map a site with a transit and alidade, and how to use the cameras.

Penny, our first instructor, could be described with one word: gorgeous. In junior high I had been the last one to hit puberty. I watched patiently as each of my friends matured. Short, skinny, and cursed with crooked teeth and big ears, I prayed for a lush figure. Penny got the figure I'd dreamed of, and she epitomized the swan that I'd never be.

Her thick golden hair flowed straight down her back to a tiny waist. Her breasts were not too big and not too small, but just right. She had a firm round butt, perfectly symmetrical facial features—and she was smart too. She spent the first morning teaching us about the prehistory of central Utah and describing the sites we would be digging. I noticed that all the guys except Randy were mesmerized. For our project we would be excavating Fremont habitation sites along a small drainage in central Utah called Pint Creek. Johnson's research design proposed that increasingly dry conditions had forced the farming hamlets to be located closer and closer to the source of the water, which was upstream at the base of a small mountain range.

In the afternoon Fred taught us how to map a site using a transit. He had just defended his Ph.D. dissertation and was applying for teaching jobs, so Johnson's telephone conversation during my interview had probably been about him. I guessed he was about thirty years old, just under six feet tall, and sort of preppy in an aging way. His attire suggested that he was working overtime to acquire that dignified professor look. I wondered if Johnson's recommendation would manage to land him that teaching job. Penny told us that Fred would only be at the dig for the first week.

Fred's lecture might as well have been in Greek. I'm math-challenged and equally unskilled with any kind of machinery. More than one person has accused me of possessing an electromagnetic field that interferes with all types of gadgets. Since archaeology's main tools are trowels, shovels, and notebooks, I'd figured up until now that I could avoid the two dreaded Ms: math and machinery. Hopefully no one really expected me to learn how to use the transit.

The second day Jeff lectured us on photography and note taking. Jeff was tall, blond, and buff—we are talking the Mr. Universe of archaeology. Everything about him screamed conservative: his posture, his personality, and probably his politics. I decided that the only thing he lacked was a sense of humor. I wouldn't see him smile until the fifth week of field school.

Johnson appeared at 3 p.m. to deliver a lecture on logistics. His talk can be summed up as follows: "You forget your digging tools, you will get an F; you forget your mosquito repellent, you will be eaten; you forget your sleeping bag, you will freeze; you forget your sunscreen, your skin will burn." And he really didn't care. I believed him. After his lecture he pronounced us ready for field school. We were to meet the next morning.

At 6 a.m. sharp my friend Pam dropped me off in front of the anthropology building. She helped me unload my gear and stack it on the sidewalk, then waved good-bye and drove away. Since no one else was there yet, I had a momentary panic attack. Had I screwed up the meeting time and place? I dug around in my purse for the "Things You Should Know" list. Nope, I had it right.

Looking up, I was relieved to see Betty walking toward me. Betty Fleishman was tall and thin, and she exuded strength and intelligence. Her huge mane of short brown hair dwarfed her head, and wire-rimmed glasses framed her brown eyes. Johnson had accepted Betty into the master's program in archaeology for the fall, but he had convinced her to attend the summer field school too.

As soon as she had made it over to me with her pile of gear, another car pulled up with Tom Hooper, a recently returned Mormon missionary. Tall, dark, and slightly overweight, Tom unloaded his stuff from the trunk of a huge Buick. He said good-bye to someone, probably his mother, and walked over to join us. Tom's face was an open Book of Mormon, but his eyes hinted at a natural skepticism.

Susan Walker showed up next, materializing out of nowhere. Short, sturdy, and tanned, Susan had long, shiny auburn hair and a pretty oval face. She seemed trusting and easygoing. I envied her self-confidence and sincerity. She walked over to us with a smile on her face.

Joe Lohan was the oldest student among us. He drove up in a station wagon and kissed his pretty wife good-bye. I had heard from Penny that Joe had decided in his thirties to return to college and study archaeology. His thick, black hair was streaked with gray, he wore a gold wedding ring, and he looked good in jeans. I wondered how he was paying for his return to college. Did he have children? Maybe he could give me some advice on how to afford grad school. My parents had made it pretty clear that they weren't going to pay for it.

The next to appear was Lynn, who popped out of a Volkswagen Bug driven by an older woman. She proceeded to unload mountains of stuff. How had it all fit in there? Lynn was cute with a capital C, complete with perky figure, tiny nose, and short blond hair. She reminded me of the high school cheerleaders I'd known who had all joined sororities in college— you know, the cute, smiling, happy girls with big boobs. Jealous of her looks and quick wit, I convinced myself that she was probably my intellectual inferior.

Craig, a tall, blond surfer dude, arrived at about the same time. He was the best-looking guy at field school—thin, tanned, and very fit. He looked perfect in jeans and a T-shirt. Having watched Craig and Lynn spend the last two days making eyes at each other, I gave them about one week until they started sharing a sleeping bag. They stood next to each other, talking quietly.

After a few minutes Penny and Jeff came walking toward us from the anthropology building. Jeff was grim faced, like he was heading to war instead of field school. Penny looked rested and, as always, beautiful.

Walking from the direction of the fine arts building was Kurt, who looked twenty-something and had his bright red hair tied in a ponytail. He strolled down the hill with no gear other than a backpack and a toolbox. Like Betty, Kurt had just moved to Salt Lake to attend graduate school in the fall. He was already shamelessly brown-nosing Johnson and the other supervisors. Rodent-like eyes and a thin, twitchy nose weren't the only clues that Kurt was ambitious and probably untrustworthy. For some reason I instantly disliked him.

"Are we all here?" Jeff yelled, examining the growing mound of sleeping bags, suitcases, and other personal gear.

Penny had just started a roll call as two huge white Suburbans rounded the corner. Fred and an older guy, Jacob, were driving. Jacob was Johnson's "cowboy" archaeologist and general handyman. They parked the vehicles and opened the back doors for our gear.

"Everyone is here but Randy," announced Penny. "Anyone know where Randy is?"

As if on cue, a red Mustang appeared, top down, driven by an Adonis-like figure. Randy, whose hair was flying in a million directions, was in the passenger seat. He opened the door, unfolded his long, skinny legs, and grabbed a mountain of stuff out of the back seat. I could tell he was resisting kissing his boyfriend in front of us. They traded endearments while everyone pretended not to notice. Randy walked over to me.

"I'm sure I forgot something. Am I the last one here? We overslept. I must look like a mess."

"Your hair could use a little work but no one is going to notice where we're going," I assured him.

"That's it. We're all here. Load up!" Penny yelled.

It would take about five hours to drive to Pint Creek, located about a hundred miles southeast of Richfield, fifty miles southwest of Green

River, and ten miles north of Hanksville—or smack dab in the middle of nowhere. I'd been living in Utah for almost four years and had come to believe that it was one of the most beautiful states in the country. I'd spent summers hiking in remote mountain ranges, and winter vacations in Canyonlands, Zion, Bryce, and Arches national parks. My hope that Pint Creek would be nestled in one of the beautiful red rock canyons dimmed as we drew closer and closer to Hanksville.

About an hour south of Salt Lake we crossed the Wasatch Mountains and began our descent to the Green River. Wildflowers and thick stands of pines gave way to steep limestone cliffs. Near the town of Green River the landscape turned tan and stark. A ribbon of bright green followed the swollen river south to its confluence with the Colorado. From Green River we headed west and then south again. Vegetation thinned from an occasional sage bush to patches of thirsty, emaciated grass and then nothing but gray as far as the eye could see.

When I saw a few cottonwood trees off in the distance, I suspected we had arrived in Hanksville. The tiny town had two gas stations, an RV park, two motels resembling the set of a low-budget horror movie, a small general store with a laundromat, and a single restaurant advertising chicken-fried steak for $5.99. I also counted five dilapidated one-story houses and six mobile homes. At most of the homes, broken-down cars and field machinery substituted for landscaping. There were only five trees in the entire town, all in various stages of decay. The trees were ancient cottonwoods that had probably thrived on springs that no longer flowed to the surface. Ground-water pumping in many arid towns had lowered the water table and changed the native vegetation. It seemed the town was fading away to nothing, blending in with the gray Mancos shale that surrounded it, and just barely alive.

We stopped to gas up and I learned that our camp was only fifteen miles to the south, off a dirt road in the foothills of the James Mountains. Last year's camp had been in a Forest Service campground, complete with outhouses and picnic tables in a lush stand of aspens. Unfortunately, Johnson had decided that it was too cold for his arthritis, so this year's camp was at an elevation of 5,500 feet in a thick forest of scraggly pinyon pines and juniper trees.

Conversation had come to a standstill during the last leg of our drive. I was riding with Randy, Tom, Susan, Betty, and Kurt. Fred was driving and Penny was copilot. During the drive Fred told us that camp had already been set up by a cadre of graduate students. I stared out the window, feeling lonely and anxious, as we left the modest civilization of Hanksville and turned off on an unmarked dirt road. It was rutted and rocky, but we made good time. The terrain was bleak and gray for several miles, but as we climbed in elevation, I began to see patches of green. Short, stubby pine trees and junipers filled the horizon, and the grade became steeper. Suddenly the mountains that had loomed in the distance were towering over us, dominating the landscape. About two miles into a thick stand of pines we turned off the dirt road and stopped.

"Here we are," announced Fred. "Home, sweet home. Wander around a little and then when the other group arrives, we'll give you your tent assignments and let you unpack."

I left the vehicle and followed a small path through a dense stand of pinyons to a cluster of tents. This was it? After a little more wandering I had figured out the organization of the camp. In the center was a cook tent, containing a gas refrigerator and stove. Next to it was a large mess tent with tables to seat all of us at once. There was an outside sitting area with a circle of chairs for heaven only knows what purpose. A few hundred yards away from this gathering area was a curious contraption consisting of a wooden frame with a fifty-gallon drum balanced on the top. The latrine was just a hole in the ground with a wooden frame and a toilet seat suspended over it. Jeez, I thought. How am I ever going to go to the bathroom on that? There aren't even any walls for privacy.

A short walk from the rest of the camp I found an old-fashioned trailer shaped like a silver bullet. Who gets to sleep in that? I wondered. Surrounding the camp core were several green military tents, each containing two canvas army cots. Like the cots, the tents were army surplus, made of canvas and wood. The last war they had seen was probably Korea, before I was born, in the early 1950s.

After my brief exploratory foray, I returned to the vehicles. Everyone else was gathered there, some unloading their gear while others stood in small groups. Penny was reading from a list.

"Ivy, where did you go? You missed your tent assignment. You'll be rooming with Susan in the tent that's southeast of the mess tent. Susan took her first load of stuff to your tent already." Penny pointed in the general direction, and I caught a glimpse of Susan through the trees.

Susan would be okay, I thought to myself. At least it wasn't Lynn, who was way too happy in an annoying way. Susan, who like Johnson was a chain-smoker, seemed more mellow and pensive, but when her smile lit up her face, she reminded me of a child getting her first look under the Christmas tree. She wore her lush hair in braids most of the time, and by the end of field school her skin had turned a shade darker than her hair. Susan seemed content with life, and I figured we would probably get along pretty well.

I hate to admit it, but in groups of women I'm not too happy unless I can be the alpha female. I like being in charge, and subconsciously compete for it. Unfortunately, here I was physically the smallest, one of the youngest, and, I suspected, far from being the most intelligent. Get used to it, Ivy, I told myself. You're low woman on the totem pole.

After collecting my duffle bag and suitcase, I headed toward the tent. Susan was just leaving to retrieve the rest of her equipment. I laid my sleeping bag on the canvas army cot, then found my flashlight and put it next to my cot with my toothbrush and nightgown. Susan organized her things into two wooden crates that, when stacked, made a passable bureau. We hardly spoke, both preoccupied with our own thoughts.

"Do you know what the schedule is tonight, Susan?" I reached over and fluffed my pillow, then flopped down on my cot. It was narrow but surprisingly comfortable.

"We were told to assemble in the mess tent at five for dinner. Then after dinner there's supposed to be a volleyball game."

Great. Next to computers, volleyball was my least favorite thing. "Volleyball? I didn't see a net."

"Volleyball was a big thing at field school last year. Johnson thinks it's good for team building or some bullshit like that." Susan lit a cigarette and stacked her five-carton supply in the corner. Next to the cartons she piled up chips, granola bars, pop, and other essential junk food.

My corner looked bare in contrast. All I had brought with me were the required clothes and equipment. No food, no drinks, and definitely not enough smokes.

"Where did the time go?" said Susan, looking at her watch. "It's five of five. Let's go to the meeting."

The mess tent looked larger inside than it did from the outside. Like our tent, it was army surplus and decades old. The ceiling was at least eight feet high in the center, and four large rectangular tables easily fit underneath. Two of the side flaps were rolled up, and there was a nice cool breeze circulating. Johnson was in the center of everything, talking to

Jeff and Kurt. My first impression of Kurt as a brown-noser seemed to be proving correct. Randy, looking bored, was sitting by himself at one of the tables. I decided to join him.

In my limited experience—all twenty-one years—I had discovered that many people were born with a special talent or gift. In my family my oldest sister can read music, my middle sister can draw anything, and my baby sister can add and subtract large numbers in her head. As far as I could tell, my only talent was an uncanny ability to figure out status hierarchies in social situations. By observing people's interactions and nonverbal cues, I could sum up the structure of a group as soon as it developed. In the field school hierarchy, I was pretty certain that Randy and I were trying to avoid being the lowest rung on the ladder. Everyone else seemed to be a matriculated graduate student, male and burly, or related in some fashion to Dr. Johnson. I sat quietly, watching everyone joking and sparring for Johnson's attention. Johnson looked at his watch and cleared his throat.

"Take a seat, children. Let's begin. Now that we're all here and you've seen the setup, let's cover a few rules. First, every day one of you will help Jimmy, our camp cook, with chores. Penny has posted a schedule on the board over there. When you have mess duty, you will wash dishes, make lunch, and do whatever else Jimmy needs help with. My advice to you is to be good to Jimmy." Johnson looked around, his mean eyes narrowing into dark points of light. "Where's Jimmy?"

"He's in the kitchen tent. I think he's getting dinner ready," offered Penny.

"Okay, you can all meet him at dinner time. In case you didn't notice, our toilet facilities are primitive. We have no walls on the latrine. When you use the latrine, leave a pin flag on the path. That way everyone will know that it's occupied. After 'number two' sprinkle some of the lime from the gallon coffee can over the honey pot. The shower is also tricky. Water is scarce here."

Johnson took a minute to light a cigarette. "Where's Jacob? Jacob will teach you to survey, and his other duty is to keep the shower tank filled. Since it will only be done once a week, take brief showers." The cigarette smoke was going into Johnson's eyes, but he just blinked faster rather than remove the cigarette. "So, children, you will wet, wash, and then rinse. To make the water flow, you pull a string next to the showerhead. Thanks to Jacob's genius you can't soap up and pull the string. Water wasters will lose their shower privileges. Got it?"

My dad had been in the navy on an aircraft carrier during World War II so I knew exactly what Johnson was talking about.

"Ivy, you will help me with a special chore after dinner. Remind me before we leave the tent."

He picked me! Maybe my luck was changing, and he'd noticed me after all. The rest of the do's and don'ts were much the same. Don't litter, do participate in the evening volleyball game, do meet in the chair circle each night before dinner to discuss the day's events, and do tell someone if you are sick or hurt. I listened half-heartedly, bored and hungry.

Dinner was a huge surprise: steak, baked potatoes, homemade bread, salad, and dreamy chocolate cake for dessert. Johnson's abuse might just be worth it if this continued. I had been surviving for four years on the standard college fare of popcorn, pot pies, and boxed macaroni and cheese, so Jimmy's cooking was heaven. The crash to earth came abruptly, and hardly a minute after I'd swallowed my last bite of cake.

Dr. Johnson stood up, excused everyone, and told me to grab a shovel and meet him at the shower in ten minutes. After a fifteen-minute wait, Johnson appeared with nothing more than a towel around his waist. What was this about? Looking all serious, he instructed me to dig a drain for the water while he took his shower. Was this some kind of test of my abilities? A little voice told me that this didn't have anything to do with abilities, and was more about dirty old man behavior. But he was a famous archaeologist. Wasn't Johnson above that?

I mumbled something like "sure thing" and stood there feeling like an idiot as Dr. Johnson went into the shower.

The shower consisted of a frame of two-by-fours enclosing a space just large enough for two people. The fifty-gallon drum on top was filled with water. Gravity and a shower nozzle turned the contraption into a passable shower. Black paint covering the drum was Johnson's idea of a hot water heater. Flaps of canvas hanging from the frame formed makeshift walls, but large gaps between the flaps made privacy impossible.

I quickly realized that digging while Dr. Johnson showered meant I'd be able to see his old, naked body. Yuck. I tried to avoid a glimpse of his little Johnson by keeping my eyes to the ground and digging like a madwoman. With adrenaline flowing and dirt flying, I felt close to breaking the world record for shower-channel digging. The sandy soil was easy to dig, and in no time my trench was about six inches deep and running down the slight hill for a distance of ten feet. I was standing back, admiring my handiwork, just as Dr. Johnson emerged with the towel back in place. He stared briefly at my trench and grumbled.

"I suspected as much. You'll be digging real trenches before this field school is over."

Shaking his head, he walked back to his trailer, leaving me feeling like a failure and convinced that my archaeological career was doomed.

Luckily Susan was off playing volleyball with everyone else, so I slunk back to the tent and called it a day. Tomorrow would probably be even worse.

Digging at Last

To beat the heat, our day started at dawn, which in June was about 5 a.m. The mess helper walked around camp at 4:30 yelling at everyone to wake up. I pulled on my jeans and a T-shirt, and brushed my teeth just outside our tent using water from a bottle and spitting on the ground. I checked out the latrine but the flag was up, so I headed to the mess tent for breakfast.

As I walked in, Jimmy set a plate of pancakes, bacon, and scrambled eggs in front of Dr. Johnson. Coffee steamed in his cup, sending out a delicious aroma of home and security. After I sat down, Craig, who was the helper of the day, placed a plate in front of me. I mumbled a surprised thanks and dove into the food. The pancakes were light and fluffy, and the eggs were cooked just right. The crispy bacon crumbled easily in my mouth, and the coffee was perfect, not too strong or too weak. Randy stumbled in soon after me, looking tired and worn.

"Did you sleep at all?" he asked. "I had a mosquito buzzing in my ears and trying to suck my blood all night."

"Did you hear what Johnson had me do last night?"

"No, honey. What?"

"I dug a trench for the shower while he took one."

"You lucky duck. He should have asked me." Lowering his voice to a whisper, he asked, "Does his Johnson live up to his first name?"

I couldn't help but laugh and glanced around to make sure no one was listening to our conversation.

"I didn't look. Why did he pick me? Do you think he's just a dirty old man who likes sweet young things?"

Randy added sugar to his steaming cup of coffee. "Silly girl. You should have looked. And you're probably right about the sweet young thing stuff. You look like you're just barely starting puberty."

"Thanks, same to you."

As Craig set Randy's plate down, Randy gave him the once over and I noticed a gleam in his eyes. After Craig walked away, Randy shook his head and focused on breakfast, but under his breath he mumbled, "What a waste."

"You want my bacon?" asked Randy, removing it from his plate and setting it on mine. He then delicately picked up a fork and cut his pancakes into little squares.

After breakfast we were instructed to collect our excavation kits, hats, sunscreen and other personal items and meet at the vehicles for the drive to the first site. I was told I'd been assigned to Penny's crew, which I soon found out also included Tom, Craig, and Randy. Since Craig had mess duty, we would be one person short.

Although it was probably too early to engage people in conversation, I decided to learn more about everyone during the hour drive. Tom seemed the most awake, and I thought he seemed nice.

"So, Tom, why did you decide to study anthropology and attend field school?"

He was sitting next to me, staring out the window at the thinning trees. He looked over at me casually, appearing slightly annoyed, like I was a bug buzzing around his head.

"I got curious about anthropology on my mission. For some reason I was sent to the Navajo reservation in New Mexico." He yawned. "It was an education living for two years in such a remote area and trying to learn enough of the Navajo ways to convince people to convert. When I got back I figured it would be interesting to learn more about Native American cultures. Why are you here, Ivy?"

"I've always wanted to be an archaeologist, and everyone has told me that this is where I'll learn the nuts and bolts of it. Did you convert anyone to Mormonism?" I had a lot of questions about the whole conversion process, but I'd been so afraid that the missionaries would try to convert me that I'd never asked.

"A few. We helped people in need and sometimes they became interested. I made some good friends there." Tom looked pensive and continued staring out the window.

"I hear New Mexico is beautiful." I couldn't think of much else to say, and we both became lost in our thoughts. The faint two-track road was so rough that once or twice the ruts bounced me out of my seat and into Tom's shoulder.

Finally we stopped.

"Here we are," announced Penny.

I got out of the Suburban expecting to see an exciting ruin. At the very least I pictured a small pueblo nestled in a snug alcove overlooking a vast landscape.

"Where's the site?" I asked of no one in particular. Penny pointed to a small mound of rocks. "This is it. You're looking at her."

"What? That pile of rocks doesn't look like anything. How can we spend weeks digging that?" I walked over to get a closer look. Randy followed me but everyone else just kind of stood around.

"Okay, relax everyone. This is a crappy site, but someone has to dig it. Come on over here and I'll explain." Penny put on her cowboy hat and walked toward the rock pile.

The so-called site's pathetic appearance confirmed my suspicion that I had been placed on the loser crew. While the other crews were excavating pithouses and masonry rooms, we'd be working on an enigmatic mound of fist-sized rocks that was circular and measured about ten feet across. I called it a mound, but it was really one or two layers of piled rocks rising less than a foot above the surrounding floodplain. Mixed in between the rocks were flakes of chert and bits of broken pottery. I hadn't noticed the pottery at first because it blended in perfectly with the soil. As far as the eye could see, everything took on the gray color of the Mancos shale. I had a nagging premonition that after eight weeks of digging here, I would turn that same gray color and begin to disappear into the landscape.

"Okay. Everyone see this pile of rocks? We have located several of these in this floodplain and we really don't know what they are. Johnson has decided that we need to figure out their function. So we'll dig this one first thing. Since none of you have ever excavated, just consider this site your training wheels."

"But Penny," I blurted, "I have excavated before. I spent a summer digging in a Mississippian site in Illinois." Out loud my words sounded really stupid.

Penny looked over at me but didn't say anything. She bent over and picked up one of the rocks and looked at a few pieces of pottery. "You can see there are quite a few artifacts mixed in with the cobbles. Any ideas what this could be?"

"How about a shrine?" Tom asked. "The Navajos leave rocks in places like this to mark an important event or a place along a trail."

Penny stared at him for a minute. "Interesting. Anyone else?"

Randy climbed on the pile. "There's a better view up here and, wait, there's a slight breeze. Maybe it was a platform to see how to escape."

We all laughed.

"Let's get started. It's not going to get any cooler, and we have a lot to do. Randy, you and Ivy unload the equipment. Tom, come with me. We're going to lay out the grid and set up some excavation units."

What was I doing here? And more important, why had Native Americans lived in this desolate place a thousand years ago? As far as I could tell the area was almost devoid of any living or growing thing. A few hundred feet to the south a large cottonwood tree, only partially green, was the only visible living plant. The landscape faded into an endless sea of gray, broken only by small knolls covered with slabs of shale. Most of the smaller plants appeared dead or dormant.

Randy and I headed back to the Suburban and unloaded shovels, wheelbarrows, coolers, pails, and toolboxes. After being out of the vehicle for less than an hour, I realized that I was wrong about the absence of living things. Invisible bugs buzzed in my ears. Like tiny vampires, gnats quenched their hunger by sucking my blood. They were worse than mosquitoes because their bites itched more intensely and lasted longer. I had ignored the other crewmembers' grumblings about the gnats because I had had no idea how bad they could be. My eyes started watering when I realized that I would have to work here for weeks with the bugs, heat, and gray landscape. I decided that my best strategy would be to ignore the discomfort as best I could. No whining, I reminded myself. Focus on your work.

Before any actual digging happens at an archaeological site, many different types of tasks, including mapping, photography, and artifact collection, must be completed. We started out our morning photographing the rock mound, making a map of the site, and creating a detailed drawing of the mound. We drew the map using an ancient surveying instrument called an alidade, which is nothing more than a scope connected to a ruler. The instrument was resting on a large drawing board covered with drafting paper and set on a tripod in the center of the site. We were told that the map should show the location and dimensions of the rock pile, the artifact scatter, and the nearby drainage. We accomplished this by extending a measuring tape from the alidade to several points on the rock pile and in the drainage. Then we sighted in the point, calculated the scaled-down distance on the drafting paper, and marked each point.

The map started to take shape. Elevation contours would later be added with a transit. As the day got hotter, a truck appeared in the distance. The good doctor had arrived.

While Penny and Dr. Johnson toured the site and discussed digging strategies, we took a brief break, huddling in a sliver of shade next to the vehicle and taking turns gulping water out of a canvas bag. Tom dug a bandanna out of his daypack and covered his ears to keep the gnats from biting. Randy sat primly on an upturned bucket looking grim-faced. I rifled through my pack and purse looking for something to cover my ears with. When I failed to find anything, I decided to braid my hair over them. Maybe that would help.

After our break we laid out the excavation grid with a compass and tape measures. Wooden stakes were pounded in at five-meter intervals across the site, and the coordinates were marked on each one to show its distance north, south, east, or west from the datum, or central point. This coordinate system enables archaeologists to keep track of the original locations of all artifacts from the moment they're spotted until the day they're curated in the museum.

By 10 a.m. I had three gnat bites on each ear, sweat was dripping into my eyes and making them sting, and I was covered with a fine layer of gray dust. The air was still and the heat stifling. Dr. Johnson left Penny and headed over to Randy and me. He looked us up and down and lit a cigarette.

"You two need practice using your arm muscles. You're going to dig a latrine. Follow me."

Great. Last night was a shower and today a toilet. I am so glad I paid money to learn how to dig crude bathroom facilities. I grabbed a shovel and joined Dr. Johnson, who was walking fast to the west. I looked back at Randy. Ever the ballet dancer, all legs and arms, Randy was somehow managing to look graceful with a shovel in one hand and a toilet seat in the other.

Out of sight of the others, Dr. Johnson stopped walking.

"This will do. Now I want you two to dig a hole about four feet deep and two feet across. When you finish, come and get me and we'll set up the seat." Johnson turned and walked away.

We dug and dug. My gnat bites had turned into big, inflamed welts, and the rivulets of sweat were now torrents running down every inch of my graying body. We took turns drinking water out of the canvas bag, kept mercifully cool by evaporation. About two hours into digging, Randy broke into song in a loud, clear voice.

"Nobody knows the troubles I've seen..."

I joined in, and giddy from fatigue and hunger, we suddenly began laughing as if there were no tomorrow. Let's face it. This was an absurd situation. Randy started throwing dirt on me, and I reciprocated until we were both on the ground, completely covered and laughing hysterically. Johnson's booming voice quickly brought us back to reality.

"Aren't you two done yet?" He leaned over to examine the hole. "That will have to do. It's lunchtime."

Johnson laid the wooden frame over the hole and pronounced the toilet officially open for service. After last night's shower experience, I half expected him to whip it out and give the toilet a trial run, but instead he motioned us to leave.

If the heat, bugs, and moonscape weren't enough, I soon learned that lunch took the cake. Penny explained that the heat made it impossible to keep meat or fish safe so we'd have to get by with peanut butter and jelly sandwiches—a.k.a "death wads"—every day. Oranges, cookies, and a daily salt tablet to prevent heat stroke accompanied the sandwiches.

I looked over our motley crew. Everyone seemed about as tired and hot as I felt. A small breeze, fueled by the thermal currents, thinned the haze of gnats. We ate in the shade of the only cottonwood tree for miles. After filling my stomach, I lay down and stared at the puffy clouds. It was deathly still, and with Johnson gone, we all felt relaxed and sleepy. Penny and Fred talked quietly, and after a while they headed back to the site to "strategize." We lay in the dirt and rested. Would this day never end? It seemed to go on and on. The heat was making the horizon shimmer in the distance, and nothing seemed to live in this forgotten place. I wondered what the Native Americans could possibly have eaten. The soil didn't look fertile, and water was scarce.

After lunch we started digging. Each of us was assigned a one-by-one-meter square excavation unit. We were told to use our trowels to carefully strip the dirt from the square a few centimeters at a time. Archaeologists use the metric system, where 1 inch is equal to 2.54 centimeters. I knew from my earlier dig that you drag your trowel toward you across the unit to evenly scrape the soil. Changes in the color or feel of the soil can signal the presence of a hearth or house. Charcoal from fires or decomposing organic material stain the natural soil color. Decomposing organic material from trash and human waste turns soil brown, and fire hearths can be black with red oxidation in places. It appeared to me that the soil I was digging lacked any cultural modification, consisting only of thin layers of water-lain gray clay.

Penny, appearing shower fresh and untouched by sweat or soil, planted her slim butt down on the edge of the mound. Her blond hair was woven into a single braid, and not a strand was out of place. She looked rested and happy. With delicacy and poise, she hoisted a three-ring binder onto her lap and began the supervisor's primary duty, note taking. Dr. Johnson believed that supervisors should spend their day telling the crew what to do, making sure they did it right, and then committing it all to writing. So Penny began writing. She occasionally looked up to offer comments or advice, but for the most part she seemed lost in her work.

"Randy," I whispered. "How does she stay so neat and fresh? I look like a pig that's been wet down and rolled in mud."

"Maybe she has magic underpants that deflect dirt."

We laughed and Penny looked over at us. "Seriously, Randy, how does she do it? There isn't a speck of dirt on her."

"She is pretty perfect looking considering this heat and dirt. That's it, I christen her 'Perfect Penny.'" We laughed and looked over at her again to make sure she hadn't heard us.

The day dragged on. By 3 p.m. it was almost 110 degrees, but thankfully it was also quitting time. I had managed to excavate my square down two levels, to a depth of twenty centimeters. I was proud that the walls of my unit were fairly straight, and the floor as flat as my chest—that is, only a couple of tiny bumps. Penny, still morning fresh, complimented my work. Then she collected her notes and instructed us to gather the equipment and load up.

I climbed into the third seat of the Suburban and realized for the first time that every muscle in my body hurt, my head was pounding, and the gnat bites itched like crazy. One day down, forty-eight to go.

Field Notes and Burned Baskets

The first two weeks of field school passed in a blur of routine, pain, and gray. Every day seemed hotter and more boring than the day before. Randy and the daily cold beer were my saving grace. Jimmy's dinners weren't half bad either, and Susan turned out to be a great tentmate. The downside of the daily beer was that we had to listen to Dr. Johnson's lecture and daily humiliation while we drank. Dinner immediately followed, and then we could choose between artifact washing or volleyball. Since I felt the same way about volleyball as I did about cheerleading, I washed artifacts. At least I got to see the ones that the other crews had collected.

Each evening after dinner Johnson would review the field notebooks of one lucky student. It was my turn today, and I was dreading the interrogation. I dragged my feet as I headed over to Johnson's trailer. He was sitting on a chair, reading my notebook, as I approached. On the table was a glass half full of something amber-colored, probably whisky. His godlike hand motioned for me to sit across from him. Then he pulled a cigarette out of his shirt pocket, lit it with a wooden match drawn from a large box, and handed the notebook back to me.

"Look over my comments, Ivy."

I opened my small notebook to the first page and saw that my words were hemorrhaging in a sea of red. What?! Johnson had asked us the first day to describe the site, and I'd thought that I'd done a decent job. The marked-up pages made it look like everything I'd written was wrong. I swallowed and tried to focus on his comments as Johnson started lecturing me.

"Your description missed the point. When I read it, I can't visualize the site at all. Your writing is also disorganized. Next time begin with the site's environmental setting. State what kind of site it is, then summarize the topography, the soils, the vegetation, and anything else in the setting that may be important. Next you should describe the artifacts and features. Lastly, you say what the site might represent and why it is important." He leaned over and took a big swig of his drink.

What could I say? I felt tongue-tied. "Okay." What a stupid remark. Couldn't I come up with something better than that?

"I want you to keep working on this until you get it right. Try again tomorrow, and then show it to me after dinner."

I reached out for my notebook and stammered my customary "sure thing." Then I stood up and headed back to my tent. Why was I so quiet around this man? He was never going to give me a good recommendation if I couldn't say anything around him. He'd probably already decided that I was an idiot. I promised myself that I'd think of some questions to ask tomorrow. Why not ask him about graduate schools and pursuing a career in archaeology?

At the site the next morning I tried my best to write a perfect description, this time following Johnson's outline. I reread what I had written, made a few corrections, and decided it was much better this time around. Maybe I could have Tom check it for spelling and grammar. During our lunch break I asked him if he could look over my site description. He agreed and I sat next to him while he read. He didn't seem to mind, and I watched him out of the corner of my eye. Was it my imagination, or had he lost a few pounds? I also noticed that his hair was lighter, and that he looked good with a tan. He didn't even smell sweaty like the rest of the guys. He finished reading and looked up at me.

"Ivy, you need to add something about the vegetation changes that occur on the site, but otherwise it looks pretty good. I like it."

"Thanks, I appreciate your help. I'm a bad speller and I never have figured out where the commas go. By vegetation changes do you mean the extra plants that seem to grow right around the site?"

"Yeah, it is kind of strange."

I read my description over again and made the corrections he'd suggested. I secretly hoped that Johnson would compliment me.

After dinner I headed toward Johnson's trailer, notebook in hand. This time he was watching me intently as I approached. He had a lit cigarette in one hand and a glass of booze in the other. Under his scrutiny my mind went blank again, and I totally forgot the questions I'd rehearsed. I offered him my notebook and mumbled, "Here you go."

He set down his drink, took the notebook, and reached in his pocket for a red pen. I sat down, relieved that I'd have some time to collect my thoughts while he read. After a few minutes I remembered one of my questions.

"I'm thinking of applying to graduate schools in the fall. I heard that it's a good idea to go to a different graduate school than where you went for your undergraduate degree. Can you recommend a good school with a good North American archaeology program?" There. I got it just right.

He looked up at me for a minute and then returned to his reading.

"My program is the best," said Johnson, "but I'm not sure you're suited for a career in archaeology."

"Why not?" I blurted without thinking.

"You look like the type of girl who will just get married and start a family. Why should I put all the energy into training you and then watch you go off and get pregnant?" He scribbled with his red pen, then looked at me for a minute—eyes like ice.

"Why can't I do both? Don't male professors have families?"

He looked up from his reading and stared hard at me. "Ivy, men have wives to raise their kids. Who will raise yours? Do you think your husband will stay home and do it?"

"No, but we'll figure something out. Maybe I don't want to have kids," I said without too much conviction.

He ignored my comment and went back to his reading. The red pencil continued to stab at my words.

"This is better, but it isn't there yet. Try again after your field trip."

Fortunately, I had plenty of time after that encounter to think about Johnson's discouraging observations regarding my chosen career: a three-day field trip to south-central Utah. Our destinations were Lake Powell, Escalante, the Coombs site, and the Boulder Mountains. A second trip was planned for the end of field school, a four-day trip to Canyon de Chelly and Chaco Canyon. We would also be going to the

Pecos Conference, which was going to be held at Mesa Verde National Park. Penny was helping plan this trip because she seemed to know everyone at the park. I had finally learned what her connection was to Dr. Johnson. Her father had been Mesa Verde's chief archaeologist, and she practically grew up there. Her father, like Susan's, was a friend of Johnson's.

During our daily beer lectures I had noticed that people were beginning to pair up. Susan was usually sitting next to Kurt, Craig and Lynn were sneaking away together after dinner, and Betty was like a lovesick puppy, following Jeff everywhere he went. Jeff rarely noticed anything beyond his own angst, but Betty was persistent. They both liked music and played their guitars together most nights. Tom was chasing Penny, but I figured that it was in vain because she was definitely out of his league. Randy had become my best friend and my only confidant, and we passed much of the time comparing notes on the others and talking about our lives back home.

The last day of fieldwork before our road trip started out the same as every other day. The ride to the site was so bumpy that I hit my head twice on the roof of the Suburban, the day dawned clear and buggy, and it took half an hour to get my stiff and sore fingers moving. Gripping a trowel or shovel for eight hours a day had made my arm and hand muscles stiff and sore. My back and knees also hurt from kneeling all day in a small hole. But though the day had started out boring, what happened later made me remember why I loved archaeology.

After the first week of digging the rock pile, Dr. Johnson had decided that it was an "enigmatic" site—in other words, there was no evidence that might tell us what the function of the rock pile had been. There was no charcoal, no trash-filled pits, no artifact concentrations—nothing but rocks and a few potsherds. Our crew was then moved to a more promising site, although on the surface it appeared to be nothing more than a scatter of waste flakes from tool making and a few pieces of pottery surrounding a slight depression.

On the first day at the new site we excavated a trench through the center of the depression. Bingo! We'd hit pay dirt. Apparently a compacted layer of clay buried under nearly two feet of water-borne soil was the floor of a thousand-year-old house. You could have fooled me. When I looked at the dirt in the wall, or profile, of the trench, I saw layers of soil shaped like a bowl. Imagine a glass bowl filled with alternating colors of sand and then buried in soil with its rim only a few inches below the surface.

A pithouse is an earthen lodge built in a hand-dug pit so that the pit forms the structure's lower walls. Posts lining the perimeter of the pit were covered with mats and soil. People who lived in extreme climates—those with severe winters or hot summers—often inhabited this type of structure because the pit insulates the house from both cold winds and desert heat. Pithouses come in all shapes and sizes, but the one we were digging appeared to be round and measured five meters across, or about fifteen feet. In the exploratory trench, near the center, we also encountered the edge of a clay-rimmed fireplace still filled with ash and charcoal. The only artifacts we found on the house floor in the test trench were a few potsherds and a mano. The Southwest's prehistoric Indians ground their corn and other seeds into flour with a mano and metate. Women would hold a flat oval or elongated mano, and moving it back and forth across the larger, concave metate, they would grind seeds between the two tools.

Today I was going to dig a unit from the trench to the wall of the pithouse. Penny had told me to remove the soil, or pithouse fill, in gradual levels until I was about five centimeters above the floor. The artifacts from the floor level would be bagged separately, and the unit would be excavated with extra care. Since the floor was a slightly tan-colored, compacted level of clay, it looked a lot to me like all the other clay. I suspected that the floor would be easy to miss if not for a thin layer of blow sand just over the top. The gray and charcoal mottled color of the soil just above the floor, mixed with the large chunks of charcoal, indicated that the pithouse had probably burned. I learned from Penny that most pithouses had been burned, either intentionally or because they had become dry and caught fire accidentally. Intentional fires were also set, often when a family member died or death was somehow associated with the house. Prehistoric Puebloan people sometimes buried their dead in the house and then burned the structure.

Let's hope no one is buried here, I thought as I started digging. The soil in the upper fill of the house was dense, compacted clay. It was hard as rock, so I switched from digging with my trowel to a small mattock, which looks like a pickaxe but has a wide flat end and an opposite pointed end. The flat blade chopped right through the hard clay. I then scooped the soil into a dustpan with my trowel and poured the contents into a bucket. We had convinced Dr. Johnson that we should screen some of the soil from the structures to see if we were missing small objects such as beads and bones. Although he thought it would slow us down too much, we'd finally convinced him that it wouldn't be too bad if we only screened the soil above the pithouse floor.

Randy was in charge of picking up my bucket when it was full and pouring it into a screen that was mounted in a frame attached to legs. Handles on the frame allow the entire contraption to be shaken back and forth, and as the dirt falls away through the holes, artifacts become visible. Everything is labeled and bagged according to unit and level, then given a control number. All of these field specimen, or FS, numbers are tracked in a logbook to make sure they're not lost or misplaced. Back at the lab, after the excavation, each bag would be checked in and stored for analysis.

The compacted clay was slowing my progress, and my arms were aching after I'd dug through the first level, but then the digging got a little easier. Late in the morning I was getting close to the floor of the pithouse, so I stopped using the mattock. Just above the floor I hit a thin layer of fine yellow sand, then lots of charcoal. I noticed small burned twigs that were coiled into a circle, so I switched to my fine brush and dental picks to carefully remove the soil from around the charcoal. I couldn't believe my eyes, but it looked like a burned basket was emerging from the surface of the pithouse floor.

"Penny!" I yelled excitedly. "I think I have a burned basket here."

"What? No one ever finds baskets in settings like this. Let me see." She put down her notebook and headed over. Everyone working at the site followed. Excitement filled the air.

"Move away a minute," commanded Penny.

I stepped out of the trench and let everyone else crowd around. Silently Penny bent over my find and began blowing some of the dirt off of the basket.

"I don't believe this, Ivy. It is a basket. It's totally burned but I can clearly see the coils. It looks like there's more of it buried under the floor fill." Penny began to carefully remove the soil covering the rest of the basket.

We all looked on with amazement. This was the first truly interesting artifact we had found in two weeks.

As Penny and I removed the rest of the soil, the basket took shape. It appeared to be not one but two nested bowls lying upside down on the floor. Penny thought that they might have been hanging from the roof of the house when the structure burned and collapsed. After closer examination Penny explained to me that the basket had been coiled with one rod and welt, and an interlocking stitch. She had never seen this type before. After fully exposing the basket, we covered it with plastic and left it in place until Dr. Johnson could examine it. Penny praised my sharp eye and careful excavation. I was the hero of the day.

About an hour after lunch Johnson arrived to check out our find. He slowly worked his way into the trench and looked closely at the basket. We all made believe we were working, but we were listening closely.

"Ivy was digging this unit when she discovered the basket," explained Penny, who was standing behind Dr. Johnson.

"Hmmm…surprise, surprise," Johnson mumbled without removing his cigarette.

Was he really smoking in the pithouse? I knew just enough about radiocarbon dating to understand that cigarette ash could contaminate the basket and make it impossible to determine its date. I noticed that Penny was staring at his cigarette too, likely thinking the same thing.

With everyone staring, Johnson smiled and said, "Don't worry, children." He finished the last puff, removed the cigarette, and stomped it out in the trench.

"Okay," he said. "I see what you mean. That does look like coiled basketry. How should we remove it? Any suggestions?"

Johnson was constantly testing everyone. His grad students were his favorite victims, but he also liked to play cat-and-mouse with us. Sometimes I think he laid traps just to make us feel stupid. Was he setting Penny up with the question?

"I would slip a flat clipboard under it, cover it with cotton and paper, and then place it in a box," offered Penny.

Johnson stood up, straightened his back, and slowly climbed out of the trench. "You need to put something over it to keep it from falling apart. What do you think that should be?"

Penny looked momentarily confused. Then her face lit up and she blurted out, "Wax! We need to treat it like a dendrochronology sample. We should cover it with melted wax before we remove it."

Johnson patted Penny on her shoulder. "Good girl. You got it." Then he lit another cigarette and walked toward his truck. I noticed that he'd winced when he stood up. I guess after forty years of archaeology work,

I'd be in pain too. I tried not to imagine what his lungs must look like after smoking all that time too.

"Penny," I asked, "what is dendrochronology?"

"Didn't you learn that in your prehistory class?"

I slapped my forehead. "Oh yeah, the tree-ring dating method. I guess it's hotter out here than I thought."

Penny continued to answer my question for the benefit of the rest of the crew. "The rings of pine trees provide a record of good and bad water years," she explained. "The rings form a pattern that can be tied to a master ring history. If a burned post can be dated, we'll know exactly what calendar years the tree lived and died. Dendrochronology is the most accurate method of dating a site."

Everyone was listening. All the guys were in love with her, and even Randy was entranced. Her voice was just as beautiful as the rest of her.

It was quitting time, and we didn't have any wax, so Penny said that she'd come back to the site later to remove the basket.

As usually happens when the temperatures are over 105 degrees for any length of time, my brain had slowed down. It felt like pond sludge, and when I tried to think, nothing happened. Sometimes my thoughts were like flies caught in cotton candy, and it seemed that as the day wore on, connections got harder and harder to make. Packing up, I realized for the first time in two weeks that I actually felt happy. I had found something unique, and we were getting away from this place for three whole days. I'd even forgotten about the heat and gnats.

Road Trip

The next morning we woke up even earlier than usual to pack and hit the road. Jimmy had gone home, so we made do with doughnuts. After a quick bite and three cups of coffee, I headed to the Suburban carrying my daypack, my sleeping bag, and two quarts of beer. We all planned to party on this trip, and beer in quarts was all I could afford. I was riding with Randy, Tom, Craig, Lynn, and Penny. For some reason, probably because of their Y chromosomes, Tom and Craig had been anointed the "qualified drivers" by Dr. Johnson. With Penny and Lynn in our vehicle, I would be rendered virtually invisible. All male attention would be focused on them. That suited me, though, because I had Randy to talk to. Anyway, I felt bone tired and had a good book to read. I could catch up on my sleep, watch everyone flirting, and lose myself in my novel.

As it turned out, being invisible never bothered me because I spent three days totally mesmerized by the beauty, grandeur, and isolation of south-central Utah. Everywhere we went was eye candy. Even better than that, it was food for my soul. After two weeks in shades of gray, the brilliant blue of the sky contrasting with the red sandstone and pale green of the sand sage was a Thanksgiving feast. The aspen groves and fields of multicolored flowers at the higher elevations were pie and ice cream.

By mid-morning we had arrived in a real town, Escalante. In rural Utah in the 1970s, that meant it had a dozen or so two-story brick or clapboard houses with lawns, a centrally located Mormon church, a gas station, and a general store. In some of the larger towns you could find a small hardware store, a drugstore, and once in a while a burger or taco stand. We made a quick stop to buy gas, more beer, and food, and then we headed into the desert. For the first time I realized that our only supervisors were Penny and Jeff. It seemed Dr. Johnson felt that we didn't need him, but I later found out he usually went home over breaks.

The plan was to spend the first night near Lake Powell. We would get there via an eighty-mile-long dirt road running parallel to the Escalante River. The Escalante is a perennial river, a tributary of the Colorado, that flows through some of the most remote and beautiful terrain in the country. The river had carved its way through several sandstone formations varying in color from bright red to orange, tan, and even shades of gold. The resulting canyon is wide enough to house a thick stand of cottonwood trees. Puebloan farmers also inhabited it prehistorically, growing corn, squash, and beans that were stored in small storage rooms made of sandstone and mud. Today you can still see many of these rooms fairly high up the vertical canyon wall. Since they blend in perfectly with their surroundings, the best way to see them is to look for the dark round entryway.

Our destination was a place called Hole-in-the-Rock, a narrow and very steep canyon that some of the first Mormon explorers used to cross the Colorado River. In the late 1800s the first Mormon settlers decided to find a shortcut to Arizona but lost their way. Without enough food or water to retrace their steps, they had decided that this narrow canyon was their best hope. The only problem was that they had had to widen it in places to accommodate their wagons. When the canyon got too steep, they used ropes to lower not just the wagons, but the livestock. In the 1960s, however, the Hole-in-the-Rock crossing had become part of Lake Powell.

After our long and dusty journey we were crazed to explore, hike the canyon, and, best of all, swim in the lake. We camped high up on the mesa above, without tents, under the open sky. Dinner was hot dogs and beans cooked over our campfire. After a quart of beer and a blissful day of hiking and swimming, I fell asleep early under a sky sparkling with more stars than I had ever seen in my life. Everyone else was still partying, and as I drifted off to sleep I could hear Jeff and Betty singing and playing their guitars.

I woke the next day to see Betty's sleeping bag joined with Jeff's. Kurt and Susan were also sleeping next to each other. Craig and Lynn were nowhere to be seen.

After leaving the desert at an elevation of 3,000 feet, we drove 150 miles of dirt road to the top of the 10,000-foot-high Aquarius Plateau. Known as the Burr Trail, the route is famous for its beauty but also for the steep, treacherous stretch between Capitol Reef and Boulder, Utah. Most people who have never been out west are terrified when they encounter their first road that seems to end at a steep cliff but, in fact, continues up the side. Often the road is narrow, with nothing beyond the edge but hundreds of feet of air, and it seems to continue forever. One slip and you'd be airborne. After climbing the escarpment, the road continues a hundred miles through the desert, winding through canyons between giant sandstone mesas and monoliths.

The road eventually leads to a wide valley surrounded by mountains to the north and west, and a labyrinth carved in sandstone to the south and east. Only the road to Escalante is paved. It's an understatement to say Boulder is isolated. When we arrived, dirty and hot, we found no more than a general store, a gas station, a Mormon church, and a dozen or so houses and ranches. Neat fields of corn and alfalfa lined the streets. Plump horses and cattle grazed under towering canyon walls. The bright green fields contrasted against a thousand shades of red sandstone.

During the drive I had done some thinking about Dr. Johnson's assumption that I would probably just get married and have babies. How would I juggle motherhood and a career? Would I just give up on archaeology to take care of my family? Someday I wanted to get married, have a family, and live in suburbia, but could I have a career too? Johnson had a point: who would take care of my children when I was off in the field? I wasn't attracted to the kind of guy who would be content to stay home and raise our family.

The more I thought about it, the more I realized I'd never met a woman who had successfully balanced family and career. All of my mother's friends and relatives were homemakers. None of my friends' moms worked either. The only career women I'd known growing up were my old-maid aunt, who was vice president of a bank, and my grandmother, who took over the family mortuary business after her husband died. In the Anthropology Department there had been two female professors, ethnographers, both divorced and childless. I guess I'd never really thought much about it before. Was it possible to do both? There didn't seem to be any easy answers.

Meanwhile, we had arranged to visit Boulder to tour the Coombs archaeological site. Coombs was one of the hundreds of ruins excavated by Johnson's Utah College team and the Museum of Northern Arizona's archaeologists prior to Lake Powell's inundation of the Colorado River's side canyons. The Coombs site wasn't located in the flooded area, but it had been excavated because it was one of the region's largest villages, and Dr. Johnson had decided that it held the key to understanding the region's prehistory. We learned during our tour that the site was a Puebloan village built and occupied by Native American farmers a thousand years ago. The village looked a lot like the larger sites at Pint Creek. Square-shaped rooms made of sandstone blocks were linked together to form linear room blocks. In the center of each room block was a plaza area with semisubterranean rooms that resembled pithouses, like the one I was currently excavating. The pithouses at Coombs contained features in the floors that resemble kivas, which are men's clubs that are still built by Puebloan people today. Kivas provide space for the men of the village to perform religious ceremonies and hold meetings. Most kivas have foot drum platforms and small holes known as sipapus. These holes, measuring less than a foot in diameter, are spiritual connections to the underworld. Although we had excavated room blocks and pithouses in Pint Creek, we had yet to discover any structures that would qualify as kivas.

The museum displays at Coombs identified the site's Puebloan farmers as Kayenta Anasazi, yet Penny and Jeff were telling us that the site's residents were part of the Virgin branch of Anasazi. Archaeologists group prehistoric sites into different "cultures" based on similar artifact assemblages. For example, the different groups of Anasazi in the Southwest were not real cultures in the sense that they shared similar languages and religions. Since archaeologists have no way of knowing what languages prehistoric people spoke, or details about their religions or governments, culture relatedness is defined on the basis of similar lifeways and artifact styles.

Pottery decorations are considered distinctive cultural traits by most archaeologists. The Anasazi, or Puebloan, prehistoric groups made gray pottery that was covered with a white slip and then decorated with geometric patterns painted in black. Through time, different types of pottery were developed, including different colors. In the Puebloan areas of the Southwest, first there were gray wares, then red wares, and finally yellow pottery. The yellow wares were being made by the Hopi when the first

Europeans traveled through the Four Corners region. Since pottery styles are time sensitive, and pieces from broken vessels last centuries, fragments from pots, also known as sherds, tell archaeologists when the site was occupied and by whom. The only problem is that archaeologists don't always agree on regional differences in pottery styles. The pottery from the Coombs site looked very much like Kayenta and Virgin Anasazi varieties, so there was disagreement about how to classify the site.

After our tour of the museum and ruins, we loaded up the Suburbans and headed north to the Boulder Mountains. We climbed and climbed. Tom drove our vehicle along the curvy dirt roads until we reached wide-open meadows surrounded by thick stands of aspens. I had noticed that Tom was paying closer attention to me on this trip. Maybe he had given up on Penny. Before we settled on a camping spot, we drove to the top of the mountain to see the view. It was a clear day, and I am positive I could see a hundred miles in all directions. I had never experienced anything like those incredible, expansive vistas. Tom followed me to an overlook and we admired the view together.

We camped under the stars again, no tents, and had a simple dinner of hamburgers over an open fire. With everyone getting low on beer, conversation turned serious. Penny sauntered over to the fire and sat down next to Jeff and Betty, flipping her gorgeous long hair out of her face.

"I'm beginning to wonder if Johnson is wrong to call some of our sites Fremont," she said. "The sites with stone walls have a lot of Kayenta Anasazi pottery as far as I can tell."

"Did you hear that Bob Vrey actually had the balls to tell Johnson those sites were Kayenta, not Fremont?" Lynn asked. "I heard them arguing over it. It was ugly."

Jeff stood up and grabbed a marshmallow from the open bag. "Bob's leaving the department because he stood up to Johnson, and now Johnson won't accept him into the Ph.D. program. He's going to have to go somewhere else." Jeff shrugged his broad shoulders and lowered his marshmallow over the fire. "He gets his master's degree next semester, and then he's out of here. He told me he thinks Johnson is full of shit."

"I have to agree with Bob," said Penny. "The two sites with masonry walls look Anasazi rather than Fremont. And the pottery sure looks Kayentan to me. The Fremont sites have the pithouses without storage rooms and masonry, like the one Ivy just found the basket in."

"Why won't Johnson admit that some of the sites are Anasazi and some are Fremont?" asked Betty.

Jeff's marshmallow caught on fire. "Shit." He threw it away and grabbed another. "I have a theory. If Johnson agrees that the Anasazi occupied the same region as the Fremont, then he has to throw out his research design and admit that the culture area boundaries that he has in about fifteen publications and reports are wrong. It's easier for him to bully his students into believing the sites are Fremont."

"But that is such bad science," said Betty, shaking her head. "How can he lie to himself like that? And how can I believe anything he says? As far as I'm concerned, he's lost his credibility. I'm out of the department after I get my M.A."

Penny, always the picture of poise and elegance, stood up and stretched. "Don't kid yourself, Betty. He's never allowed a woman to earn a doctorate anyway. Johnson won't admit that his Fremont and Anasazi boundaries are wrong. I think he should have changed his research design and focused on the nature of the Fremont and Kayenta occupations. That's what is really interesting about Pint Creek."

"Yeah," said Jeff. "He should be asking if the Fremont and Kayenta sites were occupied at the same time, or at different times. Perhaps the boundary between the two regions moved through time."

I sat quietly by the fire, listening, thinking, and consuming marshmallows. Could the great and powerful Johnson actually be wrong? My mind was racing. Do archaeologists just make it up as they go along? My favorite professor in the department, Dr. Adams, was one of the new breed of archaeologists who felt archaeology should become more scientific and less historical. Rumor had it that he'd been hired by the department to replace Johnson, but that Johnson thinks Adams is a wimp, and that his brand of archaeology is a waste of time. But Dr. Adams took me seriously, and his classes were a breath of fresh air. The conversation continued.

"What if the Fremont lived in Pint Creek and they were driven out by the Anasazi? Isn't there new evidence that the Anasazi were aggressive?" asked Betty.

Jeff, finally managing to toast his marshmallow to perfection, popped it into his mouth. Talking with his mouth full, he said, "Or how about the two groups had a symbiotic relationship? The Fremont were hunters and the Kayenta were farmers. They traded after the harvest and the hunting season."

"Perhaps Pint Creek was that meeting place," added Tom.

I liked Jeff's idea and realized that he was much smarter than I had at first given him credit for.

"I can think of a thousand scenarios that would explain why some sites are Fremont and some are Anasazi," Penny said. "But I can't imagine why Johnson is ignoring the facts. It makes you wonder about the guy. He's a great archaeologist, but maybe he's losing it." She decided to have a marshmallow too. I watched her toast her marshmallow to perfection, then nibble it around the edges—no muss or fuss.

Jeff and Betty decided to call it a night and walked off holding hands. Since Craig and Lynn had long ago retreated to their love nest, that left Penny, Tom, Randy, and me to continue the discussion.

Randy, who avoided sweets, asked if there were any burgers left.

"You're a vegetarian, remember?" I teased.

"I know, but I'm always hungry and there's nothing else to eat. Besides, I think I'm finally beginning to digest the stuff without emitting clouds of noxious gas from my entrails."

"Randy, what do you think of the Anasazi versus Fremont discussion?" I asked.

"Who cares? I'm done with archaeology after this. It's too messy and too macho. I'm going back to dancing and pretty boys." We all laughed, and he got up to get another burger.

"Tom, what about you?" I asked.

Each day Tom was looking more and more handsome to me. I'd been looking close to see what had changed, but I couldn't figure it out. I'd also noticed that he was paying closer attention to what I said and did.

He looked over at me and smiled. "You know, Ivy, when all is said and done, I think the boundaries are pretty silly. Look at the Hopi and Navajo. They share the same area but their houses are different. The Hopi live close together in pueblos and the Navajo pattern is to be spread out and isolated. Maybe what we have are two different groups in Pint Creek like the Navajo and Hopi. What do you think?"

"I don't really know. But I can tell you one thing. I'm learning that archaeology is a lot more subjective than I originally thought. It's not black and white, but often shades of gray. I don't understand why Johnson doesn't focus on the relationship between the Fremont and Anasazi. He's so smart. I just can't figure out why he insists that all the sites are Fremont."

A log snapped and fell out of the fire. I pushed it back in with my marshmallow stick. "Is it so bad to abandon a research design if it doesn't seem to work? This whole thing makes my head hurt. It's probably time for me to call it a night."

All the talk, beer, and quiet crackling of the fire had made me sleepy.

We were back in Hanksville by noon the next day and spent the afternoon washing clothes, buying supplies, and eating at the restaurant. Tomorrow we'd be digging again, I thought with dread.

Pithouses and Burials

Thunderheads had started gathering midway through our first day back at the site. I noticed with relief that the gnats had finally laid their eggs for next year's torture and flown on to bug heaven. Surprisingly, it felt pretty good to be back digging and eating Jimmy's meals. The site was a book still waiting to be read. The temperature felt warm and comfortable after camping in the higher elevations. The familiar cottonwood trees seemed like old lunch pals, and the air smelled clean and fresh. The clouds hovering over the mountains provided a welcome respite from the heat. Perhaps it would rain.

Randy and I were digging a trench to the edge of the pithouse. After the baskets had been removed, we'd been told to expose the pithouse wall. We did this by carefully following its eastern edge. All morning I scraped away and Randy screened. The only artifacts we found were a handful of chert flakes and a few pieces of pottery. The wall of the house was nothing more than a compacted layer of clay. I learned that the best way to find the contact between the fill and wall was to feel the soil compaction with my trowel. Near the wall my trowel clinked and the soil was slightly harder. The color of the soil also changed dramatically, from the gray clay of the wall to a tan yellow clay mottled with charcoal flecks.

I tried to ignore my stiff back and sore arm muscles and decided that conversation with Randy was a needed diversion. A large pile of soil from my digging was in my way, and I tossed shovelfuls directly onto the screen.

We had convinced Johnson to let us screen the soil covering the floors so that we wouldn't miss the small artifacts.

"So, Randy, tell me what it's like to be a gay dancer in one of the most conservative states in the country. I thought I had it tough being a feminist, but your position must be really difficult."

Randy smiled and looked over at me. With his dirty hand he pushed a lock of long black hair out of his eyes. "Salt Lake City is really no different than any place else, Ivy. I grew up in New Jersey and it was no better there. At least in Salt Lake we have all those gorgeous return missionaries. After two years of spending every waking minute with their partner, they're ready to party. It's truly a delicious treat."

"Huh? Gay Mormon missionaries? I thought that the church was against homosexuals of both sexes." I lobbed a shovelful of dirt up out of the pithouse and into Randy's screen.

"Oh, yes," cooed Randy in that special tone of his. "The church has a huge problem with homosexuals. But since missionaries are denied female companionship for two years, they often do more with each other than just preach the Book of Mormon."

I threw another shovelful of dirt. Half of it landed in the screen, some on the ground, and Randy took the rest in his chest.

"Hey! Careful, sweetie."

"I'm sorry. I just can't believe that. Do you mean that missions cause guys to turn gay, or some missionaries discover their homosexuality during their mission?" I aimed the dirt more carefully this time.

"Ivy, I was just born this way. I knew when I was nine that I was different from other guys. My mom says that she knew I was gay when I was even younger. I don't know about the missionaries, but the consensus among my gay friends is that we were born this way."

"You're my first real gay friend, Randy. Please pardon my ignorance." My shovel clinked on something.

I grabbed my trowel from my back pocket and bent over to examine the clink. "Oops! It looks like bone."

Penny looked up from her notebook. "Who said 'oops'?"

She had been taking notes for about an hour. "Never say 'oops' on a dig. It makes everyone nervous."

"Sorry about that," I said. "Maybe you should take a look at this. It looks sort of like a skull. Randy, could you find me a brush, one of those little soft ones?"

Randy went to retrieve one from the Suburban, but everyone else stopped working and looked in my direction. Penny put down her notebook and jumped into the pithouse.

"Randy, could you bring back the wooden tools, too? I think this is a skull. Looks like Ivy did it again. We have ourselves a burial."

As Penny and I carefully exposed the skull using flat and pointed wooden sticks, the white bone took on an oval shape.

"I think this burial is intentional. The head is on its side, which is typical for the Anasazi," Penny explained. "Fremont burials are less consistently placed." A hole, where a nose and eye had been, emerged, and I saw a flicker of color as I scraped around the chin.

"Is that a bead?" I pointed to a tiny blue-green ball with my brush.

Penny smiled and picked up the bead with her trowel to examine it more closely. "It looks like turquoise. I need to tell Dr. Johnson about this before we do any more. Cover up the burial with plastic sheeting, Ivy. It's time to quit anyway. Let's clean up and call it a day."

That evening, as we were waiting for the daily review, we sat in a circle sipping our frosty cold beers. I felt clean and relaxed from my quick shower. The shower worked amazingly well for a black-coated fifty-gallon drum. After showering I'd changed into my usual tank top and shorts, and the warm air and light breeze felt delicious against my almost bare skin. Tom had settled into the chair next to me and was trying to get my attention. He had the same look on his face as he did when he'd popped that s'more in his mouth.

The beer was giving me a slight buzz, and I felt good about having found something important today. But then Dr. Johnson walked over, looking at me like I was something at the dog park that he'd just accidentally stepped in. I smiled at him anyway and hoped he had forgotten his promise to edit my notebook one more time.

"How was your day, Dr. Johnson?" Maybe a little brown-nosing would help. I was feeling like a pretty good archaeologist in spite of his efforts to intimidate me. At least Penny seemed to take me seriously.

"It was good until you found the burial. Now I need to file a report and fill out more paperwork."

I tried to make myself smaller and looked at Tom to see his reaction.

As usual Dr. Johnson sat in the center seat. He cleared his throat and we all stopped talking. He inhaled deeply on his cigarette while looking at each of us in turn, then stopped at me.

"It looks like Ivy found a burial today," he announced. He took another deep drag and twitched his mustache. "I'll need to notify the State Historic Preservation Office. Luckily the site is on private land, so I don't think we'll have to deal with the feds."

"Ivy, why were you using the shovel rather than a trowel when you discovered the skull?"

"I was shoveling the fill that I'd removed from the wall into the screen."

"Well, you made a big, ugly gouge in the skull. Didn't think you'd be capable of such damage with those scrawny muscles of yours. Next time be more careful." Johnson opened his eyes wide and flicked his cigarette butt into a large can of water that served as an ashtray. "Kurt will take over the excavation of the burial. He has experience with these things." The dinner bell clanged and Johnson rose.

I just couldn't win. I slunk to the mess tent, trying to hide my disappointment and keep from crying. Randy put his arm around me. "Don't take him seriously, Ivy. He's just a nasty beast."

"Thanks, Randy. I am enjoying my time here, but I get so discouraged. Why me? Do you think he treats me worse than everyone else or is it just my imagination?"

"He's an equal opportunity asshole, Ivy. Don't be so hard on yourself. He's only one person. Besides, I think you're great."

"Thanks, Randy."

After dinner I decided to take a short walk to the creek flowing down the mountain slope nearby. The sound of a bubbling brook would soothe me. I needed to figure out how to get on Johnson's good side. I put on bug repellent and headed past the mess tent, where Susan and Kurt were lounging around. I couldn't figure out what Susan saw in him. Being my usual cynical self, I speculated that Kurt had realized that Susan had Johnson's stamp of approval, and she was easygoing and non-threatening. I had tried to talk sense into Susan, but she'd insisted she was in love.

I followed a well-worn trail to the creek. Dusk had fallen, and silence filled the space between day and night as the earth prepared for darkness. I could see why some cultures believe that ghosts come out at twilight, and for a moment I felt afraid. What if the skeleton I'd found was angry that I'd disturbed her or him? Glad to have something else to worry about besides Johnson, I picked up my pace.

I rounded a bend in the trail as it flattened at the bottom of a steep drainage and spotted someone sitting next to the water. It was Tom, and he looked deep in thought.

I decided to say something so that he wouldn't be startled.

"Hey, Tom."

"Ivy, what are you doing here?"

"I thought that the water might make me feel better. I don't seem to be having much luck with Johnson. He told me that he isn't interested in training me because I'll probably just go off and get married."

"He's probably spent too much time in Utah watching Mormon women. The church encourages them to marry young and have a large family. Maybe he's just seen it happen too many times. Ivy, you're so different from anyone I've ever met before. Where are you from?"

"Rhode Island."

"That might explain it. I've never met anyone from there. There were a few guys on my mission from back east, but they were typically LDS."

"Why are you here, Tom?"

"I guess you could say that I'm having a crisis of faith. After I got home from my mission, I decided I wasn't sure about the Book of Mormon. I don't really believe Joseph Smith's stories about the Lamanites."

"What are the Lamanites?" I asked, settling onto a large boulder near Tom.

"Mormons believe that Native Americans are the descendents of the Lost Tribes of Israel. The Book of Mormon explains how the Indians got to the New World and lost the grace of God. The problem is that after living with the Navajos for two years, I'm not sure I believe any of it anymore."

I picked up a small pebble and threw it in the creek. "Why not?"

"Their culture has nothing to do with Israel and Middle Eastern religions. I prefer the anthropologists' explanation, that they came across the Bering Strait between Alaska and Asia ten thousand years ago."

"What did you learn on the reservation that made you lose your faith?"

"I'm not really sure. I came here to think about it and try to figure it all out. It's so quiet and peaceful." Tom looked at me in a new way. "You're here, too, so you know what I mean."

We sat in silence for a while. Then Tom stood up. "Come on, Ivy, let's head back. It's getting dark." For some reason he took my hand, and his was so large and warm that it made mine feel like a loaf of bread in an oven.

After a few minutes we reached a rocky section of trail and he let go of my hand to hold a branch so that it wouldn't whip back into to me.

"You're smart, Ivy. Just keep at it and don't let anyone discourage you. Johnson may not be the mentor you need, but there will be someone else." Then he wrapped me into his arms and held me, making me realize how much I'd missed the comforts of a warm primate hug.

The morning broke clear and still. It was my turn to learn how to conduct a proper survey in order to find archaeological sites. Although I was disappointed that I wouldn't be around to see the burial exposed, I was looking forward to learning how to locate sites. Jacob was our teacher for the day, and we headed out in an old pickup truck that fit right in with his cowboy hat, boots, and Wrangler jeans. He was skinny as a teenager, yet with at least forty years' worth of wrinkles from the desert wind and sun. I didn't know all the details, but Johnson had told us that Jacob had recently retired as foreman of one of Nevada's largest ranches. Before that he had been a roper on the rodeo circuit. For some reason, he'd decided that archaeology was what he wanted to do in his retirement.

Randy, Jacob and I squeezed onto the pickup's ratty old front seat. Luckily the stick shift was on the steering column so I didn't have to straddle it. Our equipment—which consisted of our daypacks with water and lunch, compasses, maps, note paper, and hats—was stashed in the truck bed. I snuck a look over at Jacob as he drove. I couldn't figure out what a guy like that was doing with Dr. Johnson. He was at least fifty and looked like he'd spent his whole life mending fences and herding cattle from horseback. He always wore a mangled old Stetson that covered the small bald spot on top of his head. His eyebrows were dark and bushy. His demeanor was calm, but he always watched everyone and everything around him intently. A telltale lump in his cheek told me he chewed tobacco, but I never once saw him spit. He looked like the kind of person who might not need to spit. When he wasn't surveying, he maintained the camp, filled the shower tank, and made trips into town with Jimmy to buy groceries.

Randy, prim and proper with his hands on his knees, also looked over at Jacob, who was concentrating on the road. "So, Jacob, how do we find archaeological sites?"

Jacob glanced at Randy and then looked back at the road. It was impossible to read his face, but I thought I saw just a hint of disapproval.

"We walk and we look at the ground."

"Is there some special technique or strategy involved?" "Nope."

It was quiet for a while and then Randy decided to try again.

"Are we looking for artifacts while we walk? Is that the idea?" "Yup."

Randy gave up and decided to join me in silence. We drove about ten miles over some pretty rough roads. We didn't have seat belts, and twice I was thrown out of my seat with enough force that I hit the roof with my head. I had nothing to hold on to but Randy and Jacob, and that didn't seem like a good idea. All I could do was hope that Jacob would take the next bump a little slower.

We stopped about two miles north of the sites we were excavating, in a broad, open floodplain at the foot of the James Mountains. It was only 7 a.m. but already clouds were gathering, typical for July, which is monsoon season in the Southwest. Every afternoon the mountains would disappear in a tower of thunderheads. Some days we'd get a sprinkling of raindrops, but most days all we got was the wind. This morning, though, it was still, and the humidity made it feel much hotter. I squinted at the bright sunlight reflecting off the gray shale. My prescription sunglasses helped cut down on the glare, but on cloudless days the sun could feel like it was searing into my brain.

After parking the truck in an open area at the base of a small hill of clay, Jacob told us to put on our backpacks.

"We won't be back for a few hours so plan on having enough water and food. Ivy, have you got a hat?"

"I'll be fine without it," I assured him.

"If you say so." Jacob pointed to a small rocky mesa about a mile away. "That's our destination. All you have to do between here and there is search the ground surface for artifacts or other signs of ruins, like rock piles and rubble mounds. You two have both worked at a few sites so you know what the surface looks like before they're excavated. That's what we're looking for. Okay, let's line up and walk."

Jacob told me I was in the right spot to start, near the truck. Then he positioned Randy about fifty feet away, and himself fifty feet beyond that.

"You both ready? Just walk toward the east end of the mesa and stay this distance apart. Keep your eyes on the ground. Okay, let's go."

This seemed pretty easy—a lot easier than digging anyway. The first transect went quickly. We walked the mile to the mesa, took our new positions, and then walked back. After doing this three times, I was sweaty and tired, lost in daydreams, and forgetting to look for sites. At the end of the third transect Jacob broke the silence.

"You guys see anything yet?"

We both answered no.

"Well, you both missed two sites. On this transect back we'll stop and look them over. This isn't as easy as it seems at first, is it?"

"What? I didn't see anything. What did we miss?" I couldn't believe I'd walked right across two sites without noticing anything.

"You'll see," said Jacob.

This time back I really concentrated on the ground. The problem was that everything blended in with the gray. Perhaps I needed to focus on shapes rather than colors. Sharp-edged stones are flakes, and pottery sherds are angular and flat.

About halfway through the transect I saw a piece of obsidian sparkling in the sunlight. "I see a flake!" I yelled. "It's obsidian. There's another one!" Finally I'd found something.

As I slowed down and started looking more closely, I saw small, angular gray sherds. "There's pottery here too!"

Randy began seeing artifacts too. "Wow! I think I found an arrowhead."

Jacob came over to check out his find. "Sure enough, you get the prize," Jacob said. "The first arrowhead of the day gets you an extra beer tonight."

As walked back and forth over the site, Jacob took notes and sketched a map, pronouncing the site to be a prehistoric campsite. Then he told us to line back up.

We did this for six hours, and after all that walking in the baking heat, we had just two small artifact scatters, called "campsites" by Jacob, to show for our efforts. The day continued to drag, and we were already exhausted when Jacob announced that we needed to look around the edges of the small, flat-topped mesa, which was capped with sandstone or some type of conglomerate rock. Large boulders of this stone had tumbled down the slope, and in some places the massive rocks lay in jumbles, forming niches and overhangs with areas of shade. It looked like the perfect spot to sit and wait for the guys to return. Besides, I had a blister on my heel and the heat was beginning to make me dizzy. But no such luck.

The mesa was about a hundred feet tall. It looked circular from the angle we were at, and its flat top looked to be four to six hundred feet in diameter. The bottom was much wider.

"Ivy, you walk along the bottom," directed Jacob. "Randy, you walk halfway up the side of the slope, and I'll take the top. We'll meet back here. Holler if you find anything and remember to look under the overhanging rocks."

"All set?" he asked. "Okay, then, let's walk."

My route forced me to scramble from boulder to boulder, but Randy had it the worst. His transect was steep and there were twice as many boulders to look under. I stopped for a minute to take a drink. The water in my plastic bottle was now hot, but it was better than nothing. I wet my bandanna and draped it over my head. That felt better. I should have listened to Jacob and worn my hat.

Suddenly Randy, who was a little ways ahead of me, turned and waved, jumping up and down with excitement. "Ivy, come up here!" he yelled. "You won't believe what I just found!"

"This better be good," I thought, dragging my tired body up the treacherous slope. I yelled to Jacob, and he started down. Randy had disappeared.

"Randy, where are you?"

"Over here. Just keep coming."

"Okay, what did you find?" I asked, scrambling over one last rock.

Randy was crouched under a huge overhanging boulder. In the sand, wedged between two small rocks, sat a perfectly preserved ceramic pot. It was gray, which was no surprise, but its shape was that of an exotic gourd. Randy beamed with pride.

"I can't believe it! You found a whole pot! How cool is that?" I edged closer to get a better look. The jar had a narrow, elongated neck extending from three round sections forming the base.

"It's a trilobed vessel," said Jacob, ambling under the overhang. He was slightly out of breath but I could tell he was excited that we'd found something. "I'll be danged. I haven't seen one of these around here before. Looks like you found a rare one, Randy. I think it's Fremont, but the shape is unusual. I've only seen Anasazi pots shaped like this."

We spent the rest of the afternoon collecting the vessel, taking notes, and marking its location on a map. Jacob announced that we would finish surveying the mesa tomorrow.

Although I was bone tired, the discovery of the pot had made it all seem worthwhile. Randy was completely jazzed, ready to trade his dancing slippers for cowboy boots. We headed for home, the pot cradled in my lap.

The next day of survey was excruciating, and we found zip: nothing to show for a long day of hiking in the hot sun but a few flakes and sherds. Fortunately, that seemed to be it for our surveying education, and it was time for our final four-day field trip.

Four Corners

Our final road trip took us through the Four Corners region of Arizona, Utah, New Mexico, and Colorado—an experience that made me want to be an archaeologist more than ever. We camped in Chaco Canyon National Park the first night. Chaco had been the heart of the Puebloan world between AD 900 and 1200. Roads extended out from the three-story pueblos to remote corners of the Southwest. We toured so many ruins the next day that I inwardly groaned when, after we'd just looked at the tenth massive pueblo, Penny announced that there was just one more to see. Another field school associated with New Mexico University was excavating the last pueblo that we visited. After our tour there were endless discussions on the minute details of Chacoan construction methods, labor requirements, and ceramic types.

I finagled my way into Tom's vehicle and sat next to him most of the drive. We were enjoying each other's company more and more. From Chaco we headed west to the Navajo reservation. Having just spent his two-year mission on the reservation, Tom had lots of fascinating stories to share. He even coaxed two traditionally dressed Navajo women into letting us give them a ride. On the reservation, if you need a ride you just walk down the road until someone stops and asks where you're going. Most traditional Navajos would hesitate to get into a car full of white people, but Tom spoke to them in Navajo, so they reluctantly decided he was okay. We gave them a lift to the nearest trading post, and they thanked us timidly. Their language somehow fit the vast beauty of the region, vivid and dry, punctuated by strips of lush green.

Our next stop was Canyon de Chelly, a deep but narrow sandstone canyon with a small stream flowing in the bottom. We hiked five hundred feet down a steep side canyon to see a famous cliff dwelling called the White House, perched just above the canyon floor. It was spectacular—a perfect, straight-walled masonry structure built under a huge alcove.

Next we visited Aztec Ruins National Monument (which, despite its name, has nothing to do with Aztecs) and saw a giant kiva that had been reconstructed after it was excavated in the 1950s. From Aztec, in Farmington, New Mexico, we made a beeline for Mesa Verde National Park. Penny had made arrangements for us to camp there the next night. By the time we arrived, in late afternoon, the Pecos Conference was already underway. Since it had rained most of the day, everyone was crowded into a small room, and the smell of so many wet, sweaty archaeologists was like that of a shaggy dog that had just done laps in a pond.

I quickly reached the conclusion that the Pecos Conference was nothing more than a two-day binge of drinking and talking. The original purpose of the conference was for southwestern field school participants to discuss their excavation discoveries and compare notes. From what I observed, it appears to be all about alpha male chest pounding and ritualized feasting and alcohol consumption. In the 1970s, archaeologists seemed to be a pretty scruffy, smelly, loud group.

Tom and I watched several presentations and then retreated to the museum. We were both tired of archaeologists, ruins, and dirt.

"How can we escape this, Tom?"

"Let's see. I think there's a restaurant and bar. Let's go have a hot meal on me."

That seemed like the nicest thing anyone had said to me in a long time. For one thing he wanted to be with me, and for another he'd offered to buy my dinner.

I pushed some wet strands of hair out of my face and grabbed his arm. "Lead the way," I said, pulling him away from the crowd.

We found the restaurant, called the Sipapu Lounge, and settled into a dark corner. I ordered a beer and the cheapest thing on the menu, and Tom did the same. We were content to be warm, dry, and away from the conference. Tom held my hand while we waited for dinner and sipped our beers.

"So, Tom, are you really thinking about leaving the Mormon Church? After all, you survived a two-year mission, and your family is Mormon."

"I know. Maybe I just need a break. My family is upset that I haven't done the usual returning missionary thing."

I picked up my beer and drank deeply, wondering what he meant. "What would that be?"

"Getting married and settling down."

I noticed that Tom was watching people walking into the restaurant.

"See? I can't relax," he said. "It's almost like I expect someone to catch me drinking and having fun. They'd report me, you know."

"What?" I'd been watching a couple laughing next to us and hadn't been paying close attention to what he'd said. "Report you? To whom?"

"The bishop," he said, suddenly looking sad.

"What? The church keeps tabs on what you do?"

"Ivy, you don't get it, do you?"

"I guess not. What do you mean you'd be 'reported'?"

"Everyone keeps tabs on their friends, neighbors, and family to make sure they follow the rules. If you don't, there are consequences. I'm just not certain that I can be what they want me to be." Tom looked almost like he might cry.

I held his hand and looked closely at him. "Tom, they can't do that. You went on a mission. Doesn't that prove your loyalty?"

"Yes, they can," he insisted. "Unless you've lived with a religious group, it's hard to understand the hold they have over you."

"We're from such different worlds," I said quietly. "No one but my immediate family ever knows what I'm doing, and then most days I'm out here, so far away they don't have any idea what's up with me. I guess I like being out of everyone's range of vision. I never want everyone to know my business."

Our food arrived and we ate in silence. After dinner we found the rest of the crew and drank a few too many beers. We woke, like everyone else, with our sleeping bags joined.

The second afternoon at Mesa Verde we toured several more pueblos with Penny as a guide and everyone else looking hung over. We saw Cliff Palace up close and several other magnificent cliff dwellings from a distance before climbing into the vehicle and heading back to Pint Creek. We were all tired out from the trip, and no one felt like talking much. I sat next to Tom to help him stay awake while he drove. Then Craig took over and we slid into the back seat and slept the rest of the way back.

Kurt had not quite finished excavating the burial before we left on our road trip, but today it would be cleaned up and photographed before the sun got too high overhead. Although I was excited to see the burial, I was still feeling frustrated that I hadn't been allowed to participate in its excavation. According to Kurt, who had had osteology training, the burial was a young woman, probably childbearing age. I couldn't wait to see her.

When we got to the site, Kurt headed over to the pithouse and removed the tarp to reveal what had once been a living, breathing, feeling person. Her skull was still right where I had found it, and the rest of her had been exposed once again to sun and wind. Her small, white bones contrasted sharply with the gray soil. In death she seemed dignified and peaceful, but I wondered how she'd met her end. Had it been slow or sudden? Kurt explained his findings as we quietly stood and stared.

"She looks to me to have been in her late teens or early twenties. I can tell by the eruption of the third molars and the fusion of her bones. Her growth plates hadn't fused completely so that gives us an accurate age at death range." Kurt jumped into the pithouse and pointed.

"Here are the two bones that haven't completely fused. They're the exterior edges of her pelvis." Next he pointed to her upper torso and collarbone. "The medial end of her clavicle isn't fused. That's the last bone in the human body to stop growing."

Kurt stood up and looked at us. "She was placed on the floor on her left side. You can see her legs are bent at the knees and her arms are bent at the elbows. We call this a flexed position, and it's typical for Anasazi burials. We know less about Fremont burials. The two pottery vessels you see by her head are Fremont varieties. The bowl probably contained food that has been consumed by bugs and bacteria, but the jar still contains charred seeds. They look like amaranth seeds, or pigweed, to me. What do you think, Penny?"

"That sounds about right." Penny looked serious for a minute. She had been trained to identify different burnt seeds from soil samples and was currently the department's primary macrobotanical analyst. "I went through most of them and I didn't see any seeds from cultivated plants like corn and squash. They're all wild seeds, like amaranth and chenopods."

Kurt nodded and then continued. "Her head lies on a metate, and a mano was placed near her hand. The Anasazi are usually buried with their possessions, and these ground stone tools were probably hers. I can see no pathological conditions that would tell me why she died. She looks healthy. Her teeth are slightly worn, but there are no cavities or abscesses, and her bones are in excellent condition. I'll know more when I get her back to the lab and examine everything more carefully." Kurt put his hat on. "That's about it. Show's over. You can all go back to what you were doing yesterday."

Pointing at a shallow depression, Penny said, "Ivy and Randy, you'll dig a trench through there and look for another pithouse. I'll help you lay it out straight and in the correct spot. Follow me."

Great, I thought. I get to dig another trench with probably nothing in it while everyone else gets to dig in the pithouse. I find the good stuff, and then others get to wallow in it. Apparently Randy and I were still the bottom feeders in this crowd.

By noon my back was hurting from all the digging, but screening wasn't much better. As Randy continued throwing dirt into the screen, I continued shaking it and peering at what was left after the dirt fell through. Catching movement out of the corner of my eye, I looked more closely.

"Another scorpion!" I yelled, but no one seemed to care. I removed my trowel from my back pocket and smashed it, pushing first the tail and then the stinger through the screen. One more blow and the rest of the scorpion fell onto the dirt pile below the screen.

"Ready for more dirt, Ivy?" Randy was standing there, watching me, one hand on his hip and the other cradling the shovel. "Aren't you used to scorpions yet? We've only found like a dozen."

"Yeah, yeah, yeah, just throw me some dirt. Why should I be used to them? The only thing worse than scorpions are centipedes. I hate centipedes. Did you hear that Craig found one the other morning when he was putting his pants on and felt something crawling up his leg?"

"Lucky centipede. I'd like to crawl up Craig's leg."

"Randy, quiet." I shushed him with my finger across my lips.

"Well, it's been too long," Randy said, filling his shovel and lifting it to throw. "Even you're getting some. I guess that puts me officially last in the status hierarchy that you like to talk about."

"How many more days do we have left?"

"Ten days and five hours, and if you give me a minute, I can figure out how many minutes," Randy said with a grin.

"Has it really been that bad?" I shook the screen and went through its contents with my trowel in case there was another scorpion. I pulled out two flakes and a piece of gray pottery and threw them in separate bags labeled with the site and trench numbers.

We'd found nothing in the trench but a few artifacts, a scorpion, and several large, ugly grubs. The day had turned into a hot one. Was it quitting time? Kurt had removed the burial, and work on the pithouse was almost done. Tomorrow the pithouse would be photographed, and if we didn't find anything in our trench, we would probably move to another site. I daydreamed for a while about my growing relationship with Tom, wondering how long a Mormon boy could tolerate a Gentile.

"Quitting time!" Penny yelled. "Let's clean up and head for home."

I usually napped on the slow drive back to camp, but today I listened in as Penny and Kurt discussed the implications of the burial. When Kurt had moved to our site to excavate the burial, Tom had been transferred to Kurt's pueblo. Johnson had even allowed him to take notes once or twice. Why, I wondered, had Johnson let Tom have the honor when Tom didn't really even care that much about archaeology?

"I'm losing patience with Johnson's party line," Penny said, shaking her head for emphasis. "Someone has to confront him. Have you seen the site that Jeff's supervising? It's loaded with Kayenta Anasazi pottery, and the architecture is totally different from the sites with just pithouses and Fremont pottery." She ran her hand through her still-clean hair and shook her head again. "I'm going to suggest Jeff's idea during the beer hour tonight. What do you think, Kurt?"

"Do you really think you can change his mind? Or are you just committing career suicide?" Kurt looked over at Penny and then back at the road. Even if he was the worst kind of suck-up, he did seem pretty competent in his fieldwork and his driving.

"I doubt it, but I'm tired of the emperor's fine new clothes," Penny said. "Why don't we just tell him he's naked? This is crazy," she continued. "Prehistoric cultures are defined on the basis of ceramics, and when the ceramics and architecture are Kayenta, you can't just decide that all that evidence is irrelevant and call it Fremont."

Penny's voice had risen an octave and she was continuing to shake her head.

"You asked my opinion, so I'll give it," said Kurt. "Who cares what he says? Just go along with it so you can get through your master's program. Why rock the boat? He's not going to listen to you."

Penny sat back, resting her head on the seat and closing her eyes. She let out a big sigh. "I guess you're right. I just don't know if I have the strength to keep my mouth shut. I'll try."

I'd come to admire Penny's strength and determination, and after field school was over I planned to ask for her career advice. After all, her whole family was into archaeology.

The beer hour went smoothly. Johnson's daily lecture, or his latest "pearl of wisdom," as he liked to call it, went something like this: "If you don't figure out what it is in the field, you probably never will." Penny kept her cool and didn't say a word about the sites' cultural affiliation.

Unfortunately, the next day everything changed when Dr. Johnson paid us a visit to see the pithouse. As he and Penny were reviewing notes and quietly talking things over, I moved over to the truck so that I could eavesdrop. I fumbled around as if looking for equipment and listened in.

"Penny, you appear to be done here. I'm going to move you to Gnat Knoll. You know, the site that Bob worked on last year, with the small room block. It's almost finished and you should be able get it done before we leave for the summer."

"Will I be writing up the site notes as part of an independent study class next semester?" asked Penny. She looked closely at Johnson and moved closer—perhaps to try to intimidate him? Today she had on short shorts that showed off a great tan and a button-down red-checked shirt, complete with little creases down the sleeves. Her hair flowed down her back in a long ponytail, and a straw cowboy hat gave her a saucy edge.

Johnson didn't seem affected by either her nearness or her amazing looks. He fiddled with his cigarette for a minute, then started toward the truck. "It's likely. Bob started the write-up, but since he's leaving the department, someone will have to finish it."

Penny followed him. "You should know that I agree with Bob. I think the architecture and ceramics demonstrate that the site is Kayenta, not Fremont. If I write the site up, I'll have to say as much." Penny looked uncomfortable, and I imagined she was steeling herself for his reaction.

Johnson stopped, turned around, and glared at her, saying simply, "No, you won't." His eyes looked hard for a minute, and then with a sly smile he got in his truck and drove away.

"Shit!" Penny said, looking totally crushed. "He isn't going to listen." She blinked fast, probably to keep tears at bay.

I cleared my throat and Penny looked over at me. "For what it's worth," I said, "I think you did the right thing. Maybe he'll listen to you after you lay out a logical argument. He can be mean, but he's really smart, and he does know archaeology, right?"

Penny shook her head. "I'm beginning to think that this discipline is too subjective. Archaeology is not really science, it's history. It's nothing more than reconstructing the past from bits and pieces of information. At best, the story is incomplete. Johnson has blinders on about certain things and no one will ever change him. Maybe after this semester I'll just be a dig bum for a while. What do you say, Ivy? Is it quitting time?"

"Dig bum? What's that?"

"Quitting time!" yelled Penny, before turning back to explain.

"Since Congress passed the National Environment Policy Act, federal agencies have to take into account a project's impacts on archaeological and historical sites. There aren't enough federal archaeologists to do the work, so universities, museums, and even private companies are getting paid to do archaeological surveys. There are also some big projects going on. Have you heard about the Dolores project?"

"No." I shook my head.

"The Bureau of Reclamation is building a reservoir down by Durango, Colorado, and hundreds of prehistoric sites will be inundated. Pullman University was hired to conduct a multimillion dollar excavation project. I heard they were hiring."

We all wondered if Penny's career would survive a serious rift with Johnson. The drive home was quiet, like a career memorial in progress. Johnson was like an octopus with tentacles of power reaching in every direction. For almost a decade he had controlled the field of archaeology as editor of one of its most respected journals. On his word, people got or lost jobs. Given his stranglehold on the department, Penny might have trouble getting through the program now.

"Penny," I said quietly. "I've been meaning to ask your advice about the mix of archaeology and family. Do you think women can have both a career in archaeology and a normal family life?"

Penny looked sad for second and let out another big sigh. "I don't know, Ivy. I've been wondering that same thing. My dad and his dad were archaeologists, but their wives were homemakers. I guess I never thought about raising children and going into the field every summer. Then there's the problem with professors not taking us seriously. The most successful women archaeologists that I've met are married to archaeologists. Maybe the best strategy for a woman is to marry the most famous up-and-coming archaeologist she can attract."

"Are you kidding?" I asked, amazed that this advice was coming from a woman I respected.

I looked around to see what the guys thought. Tom was driving, and Craig and Randy were sleeping. Randy was snoring quietly, and I noticed he looked pretty cute in his sleep.

"I can't believe I just said that, but that's how it looks to me," said Penny sadly.

We drove the rest of the way in silence.

Things Are Not What They Seem

The next day dawned clear and cool. I was excited about moving to a new site. We had found zilch in our trench: no hearths, no features. We had nothing to show for yesterday's digging but a handful of potsherds and four blister-covered hands. With the temperature cooling, the air seemed fresher—in fact, was it my imagination, or did it actually smell great? I could smell a hint of sweet flowers along with the heavy scent of pine. The air was still, and the calm wrapped my soul in a security blanket of warmth.

With the Suburban loaded, we headed down the mountain. The sun rose, and the sky briefly exploded into gold and pink cotton candy. I'd grown used to the beauty of the outdoors, living each moment outside from dawn to dusk, watching the light and the dark change the landscape. From the second I woke till the moment my head hit the pillow, I was outside. I'd learned to enjoy the subtle changes in the smells, the sounds, and the feel of the air. For the first time in my life I had escaped walls to experience the freedom and joy of the outdoors. Maybe this was what it was like to be a Native American child growing up outside. It chilled me to remember that between 1930 and 1960 most Indian children were rounded up, taken from their families, and sent to Indian boarding schools to be raised. What would it have been like to be torn from this bond with the Earth and placed under the care of neglectful strangers?

The two-track road to the new site was pitted with holes the size of Rhode Island, and rocks carefully disguised under bushes. My head hit the roof of the vehicle three times in the hour it had taken to cover a mere ten miles. Penny gave us a brief tour and explained what we needed to do. My first impression of the site, after digging two pithouses, was that it was indeed very different. Unlike the pithouse sites, this one had masonry rooms made out of cobbles and boulders. There were three small, circular rooms and one larger room linked together to form a row: two small rooms, then the big one, and a small one. The walls had long since collapsed, leaving only stubby little foundations and rubble piles filling the rooms. Penny explained what we were looking at.

"Many of you have heard that Bob left the department after disagreeing with Johnson. This site is the reason why. The ceramics that Bob analyzed from last season's excavations were not Fremont. Over 70 percent of them were Kayenta. The rest were Fremont and Virgin Anasazi. The architecture is also more Anasazi-like."

Penny walked over to the smallest room. "See this linked row of storage rooms, and this larger room with a central hearth? This is more like Anasazi architecture than Fremont. The Fremont typically didn't link rooms together. What this site is missing is a kiva. If it's Anasazi, there should be one just to the south of the room block."

Penny walked over to where she thought a kiva might lie buried in a level area next to the midden. Then she headed to a room at the end of the pueblo and pointed to large sandstone slabs placed upright and forming a three-sided box. In the bottom of the box was a large metate. "And another thing, this mealing bin is a Kayenta Anasazi invention. It was used primarily for corn grinding. Now the reason we were sent here is because Johnson suspects that the masonry room has a second floor buried under this one. We're here to see if he's correct. Let's unload the vehicle. Tom and I will reestablish the grid, and while we're doing that, Randy and Ivy, you dig another trench from the midden to the level plaza area. Craig, you can help them. After we get the grid set up, Tom and Craig will start digging through the floor in the habitation room. I want to see if there's an earlier Fremont occupation under the Kayenta one. I think that's what's going on here, even if Johnson kicks me out of the department for believing it. So let's go. We only have seven days of digging left to prove I'm right."

Randy and I groaned at the thought of digging another trench until I remembered that burials were often placed in plazas and maybe we would find a kiva.

"Don't despair, Randy. Maybe we'll find another burial and this time we'll get to dig."

"Yeah, maybe it will just dig itself. I think I like surveying more than digging. Digging is just too macho."

We placed the trench so that it ran north to south through the edge of the midden and perpendicular to the room block. For Penny's sake I hoped we'd find a kiva.

We laid out the trench with string, making it fifty centimeters wide, or just under two feet, and two meters, or six feet, long. I felt like I was finally getting the hang of the metric system.

A few hours into digging, we hit something in the middle of the trench. The color and texture of the soil had changed dramatically from a grayish, hard, compacted tan clay to a brownish-gray, loosely compacted loam with charcoal flecks. We had also started to find more artifacts in the brown soil.

"Penny!" I called. "Could you please come and see this?"

Penny looked toward us, clean and fresh as always. Despite the recent argument with Johnson, she was smiling, and there was a spring in her step.

"Can it wait, Ivy?"

"No, this could be important."

Penny sauntered over to us and jumped down into the trench.

"Look here," I said, pointing to the charcoal flecks and two sherds lying in the brown soil. "There's a distinct color and texture change. What do you make of it?"

Penny asked to borrow my trowel, carefully scraped the upper layer of soil in the bottom of the trench, and nodded. "You're right, that is pretty obvious. Finish digging the entire unit down to this ten-centimeter level. Then if we can see a feature outline, we'll just dig into the feature, ten centimeters at a time. Okay?"

She returned to her work, and we kicked ass. The dirt flew. One of Johnson's "pearls of wisdom" came to mind and I started chanting it: "Dig faster, dig harder, and find more." Johnson may have been a mean S.O.B, but he definitely knew archaeology.

After two days of hard work we had doubled the width of our trench and excavated down to a hard, compacted clay surface—obviously a floor. Three feet of soil, chock-a-block with artifacts, covered the room. The northern wall was straight and lined with crude cobble masonry. There were big chunks of charcoal spread over the floor in a thick deposit of ashy soil. Pithouses and kivas were roofed with a combination of poles, brush matting, and dirt. The layer covering the floor looked just like that, except everything was burnt, just like the other pithouse we'd found.

Johnson had visited us soon after we'd discovered the structure and said we had probably uncovered another pithouse that would look just like the other two we had excavated: round, with straight walls, and a central fireplace. So far he was right. It also looked like we had gotten lucky and placed our trench right through the center, because we'd found a hearth. It was round and clay-lined, and we left it alone so that it could be excavated after we'd finished digging the entire structure. Beyond the hearth, we found something different: a wall made of cobbles that took a sharp, seventy-five-degree turn.

Penny thought it might be an antechamber, and knowing that only Anasazi sites had antechambers, similar to entryways, her excitement grew. With only five days left to prove we had found something other than a Fremont pithouse, Penny decided to get everyone working on our feature. Craig and Tom had already documented the second floor of the surface room, so they were able to help us excavate the possible kiva. Penny decided that the best way to prove that this structure was unique—and nothing like a Fremont pithouse—was to excavate the southern half completely and expose the antechamber and hearth. She talked about finding a sipapu, a small round hole near the hearth. Puebloan people still have sipapus in their kivas, believing them to be spiritual passageways to the underworld.

Since neither Randy nor I could dig as fast as Tom and Craig, we all agreed that they should dig, and Randy and I would screen. Penny wanted to get as much as possible exposed before Johnson returned. She suspected that he might make us move to another site rather than allow us to find a kiva. I disagreed, arguing that he was so convinced of his own viewpoints that he would just say the Fremont had borrowed the antechamber and kiva idea. He might acknowledge that it was a Kayenta trait, but he would say it was an example of one prehistoric culture emulating another, nothing more than an anomaly. We all placed bets on his reaction.

By noon we had exposed a small room extending from the end of the structure. Its shape resembled a triangle with a flat top. Together, the antechamber and main structure looked just like an old-fashioned keyhole. After our lunch break, we worked hard to completely clear the southern half. Luckily, Johnson never showed up, and by day's end we had only a small corner left to uncover.

Perfect Penny Takes a Stand

The drive to the site the next morning seemed short, perhaps because I was looking forward to my day. My muscles had become used to digging, and I felt rejuvenated from the deep sleep that followed my daily physical workouts. I loved waking each morning to the stars and moon fading in the growing light, soon replaced by a crisp blue sky. At first light, wispy clouds danced on the horizon—gray, then pink, and finally white. I savored the smell of pine trees and took great joy in the endless silence of the pinyon forests. At dusk I had started to take walks to the edge of the rocky cliffs. I'd found a perch high above camp where I could sit and watch. Sometimes Tom joined me, and the only sound we heard was blood racing in our ears. For some reason no birds sang, no crickets chirped, no jets roared; only an occasional shriek from the volleyball players in camp could be heard. I speculated that the birds were spending their summer in the higher elevations, and that noisy bugs like crickets preferred better-watered fields.

It was a perfect day, but the sun had just barely climbed over the horizon when everyone sensed a dark cloud approaching: Johnson had promised to visit the site at noon. Before he arrived, Randy and I were going to clean the floor, and Craig and Tom were going to finish excavating the final edge of the room. Find a sipapu, I chanted to myself.

"Randy, let's start at this end and work toward the other side. We don't want to walk over the clean area."

"What are you talking about? How do we clean a floor that's made of dirt?" With his hands on his hips and hair running wild, Randy wondered out loud, "How could we possibly know when it's clean?"

"You scrape off the top layer of soil with your trowel," I explained. "We're looking for discolored soil. Pits in the floor, even as small as a sipapu, will just look like a dark patch of soil. A posthole is dark because if the post burnt or just decomposed, the post leaves a dark stain from the decomposed organic matter."

"How do you know so much about this?" he asked.

"Remember the dig I went to in Illinois? It was all about brown stains in the yellow clay. We could see the house outlines because posts were placed in trenches to form the wall of a house, and when they decomposed, they stained the soil dark brown. Pits in the floor will look just like that. Right, Penny?"

I looked over but she was taking notes and hadn't been paying attention to our conversation. "Huh?"

"I was explaining to Randy that pits in the floor will look like discolored circles or shapes of brown soil."

"That's right," she said. Clearly distracted, Penny went right back to her note taking.

We worked side by side, carefully scraping the top layer of soil off the floor. Near the hearth we found an oval, grayish pit that Penny decided had probably been used for depositing ashes from the hearth. As I rounded the other side of the hearth, and with Penny looking over my shoulder, I hit pay dirt.

"Ivy, let me scrape that spot for a minute," Penny said, jumping into the structure and taking the trowel from my hand. She knelt down and carefully scraped over a brown circle of soil only slightly larger than the diameter of a beer can. "Do you see it?"

Randy and I were watching closely as she scraped. "Yes," I said. "I see it. Do you, Randy?"

Randy bent over and looked closer. "Sort of."

Craig and Tom stopped digging and came over for a look. "Wow," said Craig. "I see it too."

"I guess so," said Tom, not sounding too convinced.

Penny kept scraping over the spot, but it didn't change in shape or color. Instead, with each scrape it looked more and more obvious.

"Okay. Here is what we are going to do before Dr. Johnson arrives. Ivy, you have little hands. Use this spoon and just excavate half of the hole. That way Johnson can see the shape and the fill. Maybe that will convince him."

Penny drew a line across the stain with her trowel. "Dig this half, Ivy, and save some of the soil for a pollen sample."

I sat with my legs stretched out straight on either side of the hole. "Randy, could you get me a coin envelope for the pollen?"

"Why do we bother with these pollen samples?"

"Pollen can tell us a lot," I explained. "We can learn what plants were used in the house. For example, corn pollen and other cultigens like squash would suggest that the pithouse occupants were probably farmers. If the conditions were right, the pollen can also tell what plants were used to make the pithouse. Grasses or arrow weed bundles were generally tied to the outside of the structure to make walls. Then dirt was thrown over the grass to form a crude adobe."

I heard a car off in the distance. "Incoming!" I yelled.

"Looks like we have company. Johnson will be here any minute. I'll do the talking," cautioned Penny. "I want you to keep digging the sipapu, Ivy, and Randy, you keep cleaning the floor. Then get the photo board ready for pictures. After Johnson leaves, we'll take photos."

We heard the truck door slam and looked up to see Johnson heading toward us. He was dressed in his usual field clothes: khaki pants and a long-sleeved shirt. I thought he looked particularly grumpy today. His field hat was askew, and he was limping slightly.

He walked over to the edge of the structure, stared, walked over to the other side, and lit a cigarette. He then sat on the edge of the excavated area before lowering himself onto the floor.

"How are you today, Dr. Johnson?" asked Penny as tactfully as possible.

"Dandy. What have you got here, Penny? Why didn't you tell me about this last night?"

"I wasn't sure what we had till today. I wanted to wait and see. It looks like a classic Mesa Verde type keyhole-shaped kiva to me."

Penny looked at Johnson as she talked, but he was staring at the floor. She walked over to the sipapu, which I had abandoned as Johnson came over.

"It even has a sipapu." She pointed down to the small hole that I had just excavated. It was about eight inches deep and straight sided.

"See?" Penny asked, pointing to the remaining fill. "The fill is clearly cultural, and it's the right size and depth."

Johnson suddenly started pacing like a caged tiger, smoking and examining every angle. "You missed this pit over here, and this one too." Johnson pointed to two faint brown stains riddled with flecks of charcoal. The pits were oval shaped and along the edge of the wall.

"I saw them, but we haven't had time to excavate them yet."

Johnson looked at Penny and then kneeled. "Hand me your trowel." He scraped around the floor near the sipapu and said nothing. He stood and slapped Penny on the back. "Congrats, young lady, this just may be the first Fremont kiva ever discovered. Looks like the ties between the two groups were close. Good job."

Penny looked like someone had just told her there was no Santa Claus. Her mouth had dropped open, and she appeared too stunned to speak. As Johnson turned and walked to the truck, Penny shook her head and sat down in a daze.

"Can you believe that? How can he just ignore the pottery evidence? He'd rather believe that Fremont sites have kivas than agree that this is an Anasazi site? That's just too much. I give up."

Lunch was longer than usual, and the rest of the day no one felt much like talking or joking. Johnson had sucked the fun out of everything, like a receding tidal wave, leaving behind only anxiety and angst.

All afternoon Penny worked on her notes. She was pensive and at times seemed even angry. We gave her a wide berth while we continued locating and digging the floor pits.

When all the floor features were half excavated, and the floor was clean enough to eat lunch off of, Craig set up the camera and began taking pictures. He'd become quite proficient at using the old-fashioned large-format camera with black-and-white film that Johnson preferred. Photographs needed to be high-quality for the excavation report and possible journal articles. Without good photos, it's difficult to convince others of the validity of your finds, and Johnson considered them one of the most critical parts of fieldwork.

After we excavated the rest of the sipapu and the other two pits, Craig took a few more photos, and then we loaded up for the drive to camp.

Taking my seat in the Suburban, I was suddenly hit with a deep sadness. I dreaded my return to the city, full of noise and confusion—traffic signals, cars, dirty air, and harried faces. I realized that, for me,

Pint Creek had morphed from an ugly frog to a handsome prince. As the road climbed up into the trees and we neared camp, I took a deep breath of fresh air, trying to memorize the smell. Today there was a hint of sage mixed with the dominant scent of pine. It probably came from the higher elevations where fields of sage and grasses covered the open meadows, and hot thermals over the desert mixed with the cooler mountain air. Looking out the window, I saw a family of Harris hawks hunting together, probably for rodents and bunnies, and realized that once back in the city, I'd miss seeing wildlife every day too.

That evening, as we sat around sipping our afternoon beers, Johnson reminded us that the end was near.

"There are only two days left. So we all need to work extra hard to finish tomorrow. Then on the last day we'll backfill the sites. I promised the ranchers we wouldn't leave any open holes for cattle to break their legs."

As he spoke, Johnson glanced up and stared at Penny, who was looking pretty glum. Everyone was there except Jimmy and Jacob.

"Penny found what she thinks might be a kiva today," Johnson said. "What do you all think of that?"

Everyone shifted uncomfortably. I noticed Tom was squirming in his seat. I looked over at Randy, and it was pretty clear his mind was somewhere else. Jeff was picking the label off his beer bottle, and Betty had folded her arms protectively across her chest. I sank lower in my chair.

"No one has an opinion?" he asked. "How about you, Kurt?"

"I haven't looked that closely at the literature," Kurt said, "and I haven't seen Penny's site." That effectively tossed the ball right back in the court.

"Jeff?" Johnson asked.

"I need to see it," he said. "What have you got, Penny?"

Penny perked up, happy to have an opportunity to defend herself.

"Well, all of you know that the site is an L-shaped string of storage rooms with one habitation room sandwiched in the middle. The possible kiva is south of the masonry rooms. It looks like a classic Anasazi site to me. The kiva is semisubterranean, it's keyhole shaped, and it has an antechamber. There's a small hole next to the hearth that resembles a sipapu. We haven't found a ventilator shaft yet, but we have a few more floor features to excavate tomorrow. Taken together with the Kayenta pottery, I would say the site is not Fremont, although there may be an older Fremont component under the room block."

She had finally spoken her mind. I looked over at Johnson, and his face was red. He reminded me of a cartoon bull pawing the earth with smoke coming out of its nostrils, ready to charge. No one said a thing.

Johnson lit a cigarette and then threw his wrecking ball at Penny's argument. "There are many reasons why this is not an Anasazi site, and if you had more education and experience, Penny, you would understand this. First, your possible kiva looks totally different from an Anasazi kiva. It has no bench, it lacks a ventilator, and it's too shallow. The hearth is clay-rimmed instead of masonry, and the sipapu may be nothing more than a posthole or an entry ladder divit." He stared her down. "You didn't even think of that. It could be a posthole for the roof ladder. You haven't shown me yet how the roof was held up. There is no bench and no pilasters. Let me be clear on this, Penny. You've jumped to conclusions based on your biases, and your conclusions are wrong."

He stared at each of us as he was talking, almost daring us to defend Penny. We were all slumped in our chairs. I silently prayed that I was invisible and that he wouldn't call on me.

"You have to wait until all the artifacts are analyzed and then carefully weigh the evidence before making a functional determination. Penny, you have skipped that part and blindly come to your own biased conclusion. I suspect that once the artifacts are examined and we complete all the other studies, we'll decide that the feature is a pithouse, just like all the others. You let your biases get the best of you."

Johnson patted at his pocket and realized he was out of cigarettes. He walked over to Susan and grabbed the pack sticking out of her pocket. He lit a cigarette and blinked fast to clear the smoke from his eyes. He looked ready to continue his rant, but Penny just stood up and walked away. No one ever did that to Johnson.

Ignoring the snub, Johnson changed the subject to packing up the camp. All I heard was "do this, don't do that, blah, blah, blah." I wasn't listening. I was too mad that no one had defended Penny. We had just let her take the beating without saying a word. I felt horrible and everyone else was looking sheepish too.

"Dr. Johnson," I said.

He looked over at me but said nothing.

"Perhaps Penny has a point. I learned in your class that ceramic types define the region's prehistoric cultures. I don't know my types all that well, but I heard that Bob Vrey thought that the ceramics from this site were predominately Kayenta."

"Bob is an incompetent ceramic analyst," Johnson said. "He confused the types."

Off in the distance I heard Jimmy yell, "Dinner!" Johnson stood up. I was saved by the bell, but I felt a little better for backing Penny up. Maybe he would never forgive me for taking sides, but I really didn't care. It was clear that I would never be one of his chosen golden boys: I had the wrong plumbing. He had already decided that I wasn't worth his time, and I didn't need the abuse. I'd heard Jeff and Joe talking about a private company that had started doing archaeological surveys for the government and oil companies. Perhaps I could get a job with them when I got back to Salt Lake City.

Last Chance Creek
in Mussentouchit Flats

"You must be Ivy," said Jim, reaching over to shake my hand. "Are you ready for this? I hope Dr. Lockyear warned you. We're going to spend five days in the middle of nowhere. We start to smell pretty bad after five days."

One week after returning home, I had landed my first job as an archaeologist. No one at field school could remember the name of the new private archaeology company in town, but there was one listing in the Yellow Pages under archaeology: the Archaeological Science Company. Without thinking about what I would say should someone answer, I dialed the number. The company's founder, Dr. Lockyear, answered and asked me to come in for an interview the next day. After a fifteen-minute question and answer session he hired me as crewmember to start the following Monday. The company had been awarded a government contract to find and record archaeological sites on hundreds of acres of vacant land in the heart of central Utah's coal deposits. Unfortunately, the survey work was lagging behind schedule. The only way Dr. Lockyear was going to finish on time was to add another crew. I couldn't believe my luck.

Jim, so blond and pale he almost looked translucent, struck me as a decent guy. He stood nearly six feet tall and had that clean-cut ex-missionary look. Dr. Lockyear had gotten his Ph.D. in anthropology at Joseph Smith College, and I was pretty sure that Jim was a Mormon too. He wore stained khakis and a white dress shirt that was unbuttoned at the neck and slightly frayed around the collar. He covered his thinning hair with a "Caterpillar" ball cap.

"Dr. Lockyear told me the project area would be isolated and primitive—no bathrooms, no showers. I didn't really know what to pack so I just took all my backpacking gear—except for my tent." It was only six in the morning. I'd lain in bed most of the night worrying about heading into the middle of nowhere with three people I didn't know at all.

"Hi, I'm Ben."

He reached out his calloused hand. "Good to meet you." Ben was tall, skinny, and dark. His eyes twinkled when he smiled, and he was handsome in a country boy kind of way, although he'd gotten a bad haircut and his upper lip was hidden under a thin mustache. His jeans were baggy and worn, and his plain, gold T-shirt had a small tear in one sleeve. I couldn't guess if he was Mormon or not. I suspected he was a Jack Mormon, meaning he may have been raised as one, but didn't go to church every Sunday and sneaked a beer or cigarette now and then.

"I'll take your stuff for you." Ben grabbed my heavy duffle bag, then my backpack, and shoved them both into the back of a beat-up Blazer. My gear was the last to go in. The Blazer had thin scratches trailing along the sides like pinstripes. The dark blue paint was faded on the right door and left bumper, and the white vinyl roof was cracked and peeling. A thick layer of mud coated the undercarriage and wheel wells, and I noticed the front windshield was cracked on the passenger side.

"Is that it? You travel pretty light. What do you think of Blazo here?" Ben's eyes sparkled with mischief.

"Huh? Blazo?"

"Yup, this Blazer is a pretty fine field vehicle," Ben said, looking the vehicle over.

"I think I've got everything, but I didn't bring any food. Dr. Lockyear said food would be provided, right?"

"We'll stop in Salina and buy food." Ben turned and motioned for me to get in. "You should be okay. We have plenty of camping gear."

I pulled the front seat forward and looked into the back seat, where a young woman was already sitting. Thin, tall, and dark, she seemed overdressed for the field. Her short hair was cut fashionably, and she wore a pretty pink polo shirt. She wore jeans and flimsy flip-flops on her feet. I, on the other hand, wore thick, clunky hiking boots—solid leather with Vibram soles.

"I'm Marie. I guess we're in this together. This is my first week too."

I shook the hand that she reached out from the dark back seat as I scrambled inside. Marie's palm was cool, and her hand bony.

"Hi, I'm Ivy. To be honest, I'm relieved to see you. It's strange enough heading into the middle of nowhere with three people you've never met. It would have been even weirder if all three were men. I guess Dr. Lockyear figured that out."

"All aboard!" Jim squeezed behind the wheel, and Ben flopped into the passenger seat.

"I guess you two have met." Jim looked back at us and turned the ignition. "Here we go—another week of fun in the sun."

Jim and Ben talked quietly while we drove. About an hour south of Salt Lake, Ben fell asleep. Marie and I visited enough to learn that we had skiing in common but not much else. Small talk helped me relax. I hadn't slept well, worrying about my new job, and I was still feeling anxious and uncertain about my first week on the job. I kicked myself for not asking more questions about supplies, conditions, and the project when I had the chance on Friday. I was just so surprised and elated that I got the job that I forgot to ask about what I'd be doing. Oh well, I had my backpacking gear, so I was good for a week under any conditions.

"Have you been doing this long?" I asked Marie.

She stopped gazing out the window and smiled. "No, this is my first time. I just got married to Dan Roth. He's a supervisor of one of the other crews. His crew left a little earlier than us." Marie looked like she was in her early twenties; she was pretty in an understated, classic way. "I'm not really trained as an archaeologist, but I have done a bit of fieldwork. How about you?"

"This is my first week too. I just got back from Utah College's field school."

"Where was it? Dan went to field school last summer."

"Pint Creek." I noticed Marie's face lit up whenever she mentioned Dan.

"That was where Dan went. He's a graduate student at Utah College."

"Oh, now I remember hearing his name. He started the sweat lodge craze. We couldn't do that this year because camp was moved to a different spot and no fires were allowed." I was glad to have anything in common with Marie.

"Did you like field school? I had the feeling Dan didn't get along with what's his name, you know, the professor in charge."

"Dr. Johnson. No one gets along with Dr. Johnson. He's a first-class asshole." I said it softly, like the gods might hear me and strike us down.

"That's what Dan said." Marie returned her gaze out the window. "It is pretty here. Different than Colorado, where I'm from, but pretty."

We drove for three hours before stopping in Salina, the last town with a decent grocery store on the way to the project area. Salina is a farming town located close to the center of the state. It had the largest and most modern grocery store near the project area. The store seemed pretty deserted as we pushed shopping carts through, throwing in the food we would need for a week.

"Do you guys want steaks or pork chops?" Ben asked.

"I like both," I said.

Ben selected large T-bone steaks and several packages of pork chops. In the vegetable aisle, he threw in oranges, apples, lettuce, cucumbers, and tomatoes.

"What do you like for breakfast? We usually have cereal or oatmeal. If we get up early, we cook eggs and bacon. Does that sound okay?"

"Sure," I said. "I eat anything."

"How about lunch stuff? Why don't you go find some bread and peanut butter and jelly, and some hard sausage, cheese, and crackers." Jim waved toward the front of the store. "They're over there." He pointed in the opposite direction.

"Hey," yelled Ben, "get me some of those Vienna sausages. You know, the little ones in the can."

"Do people really eat those?" Marie asked as we headed away from them.

"I never have. They look disgusting, like obese grubs. I saw a movie in an anthropology class once about Australian Aborigines who ate large white grubs. They would dig the grubs from around the trunks of bushes. The movie showed a small child holding a grub that was as big as my thumb. It wiggled in her hand, then she popped it in her mouth. After chewing for a few minutes she looked at the camera with angelic smile, like she just ate the best candy in the store."

"I've seen that movie, too." Marie pointed at the picture of a row of sausages on the can. "You're right. They do look like those grubs." She shook her head. "I knew there was a reason I didn't like them."

We met the guys at the checkout counter, and they dumped several bags of ice and some butcher paper–wrapped packages of dry ice into the cart. It took at least half an hour to unpack the vehicle, load the coolers, and repack. Since we would be camping for five days, we packed the meat in a small cooler with the dried ice. We stored the vegetables and other perishables in a large cooler with two bags of ice.

"We usually run out of ice in two days. If we're lucky the meat will stay cold until Thursday night. We need to use the milk, cheese, and fresh stuff first. Then toward the end of the week, we'll eat the canned goods." Jim threw the last bags into the Blazer. "Good-bye civilization."

We took I-70, which crossed the Wasatch Plateau and then headed straight east to Green River. Near the top of the plateau Jim pointed out a rock shelter that had been excavated by Dr. Johnson in the sixties.

"There's Deep Shelter. The points from that site and two other deep caves were used by Fred Smith to create a projectile point typology for the entire region. I think it works well. Ivy, do you know Smith? He created a computer program that compares the points numerically."

I looked at a shallow overhang under a steep cliff. The opening was fenced and gated. "Fred helped get field school started this summer, and then he left. I didn't spend much time with him, but he seemed pretty smart. I hear he just got a teaching job at Montana State."

An hour east of Richfield we started losing elevation. The lush green mountains gave way to rocky foothills, thick with shrubby pinyon pines. We crossed a sluggish creek winding its way along the edge of the foothills, and then we began to climb. Ahead was an escarpment that signaled the western edge of the San Rafael Swell—one of the most isolated places on Earth. My ex-boyfriend had been a geology major, and we spent two camping trips exploring the region's geology. The Swell is a geologic anticline that formed 50 million years ago when 2,000 square miles of bedded sandstone were uplifted, creating steep escarpments along the Swell's edges. The result was a vast mesa that became deeply incised by the San Rafael River and its tributaries as it continued to uplift. In the millions of years since the dome formed, the river has carved its way through thick sandstone deposits, creating the Swell's colorful canyons.

We left the highway at an interchange labeled with a warning that there were no facilities. Then we turned onto a graded dirt road and headed southeast across a broad, open plain. We followed this road for almost another hour. The countryside was dotted with scruffy junipers and an occasional pinyon. Low stands of sage and thin patches of grass supported small herds of skinny cattle. As we traveled deeper into the Swell, the canyons narrowed, and the walls towered above us.

Ben drove and Jim navigated. Jim traced our route on a series of land management agency maps. I had used these maps in my adventures and found them to be accurate and detailed. They provided good information on topographic features, dirt roads, jeep trails, and even land ownership. Jim picked up a USGS topographic map and checked our location.

"Stop here. There should be a section marker, and I'd like to be sure that we are where I think we are." Jim scanned the side of the road. "Look for a pile of rocks or a capped pipe. The section marker should be right here on my side of the road."

Everyone took up the search. After ten minutes we realized we missed it.

"Turn around, Ben. Let's try that again, this time a little slower."

Halfway back, I noticed three rocks surrounding a pipe. "Could that be it?" I leaned forward between the two guys and pointed out the front window. "See over there. It's on the wrong side of the road."

"Yeah, that could be it. Pull over, Ben."

Jim jumped out to check out the rock pile. He tilted his head slightly to read the engraving on the cap of the pipe.

"This looks right—Sections 5 and 6, Township 12 South and Range 14 East. Okay, I know for sure where we are. Now we just need to follow some bad roads to our first survey area." He got back in the Blazer.

"Check the odometer, Ben, and tell me when it says we've gone two miles. There should be a road off to the east. We need to follow it for five miles, and then we have two miles on another road that takes us down a steep embankment. That should deliver us right to our 160-acre survey unit. Let's go."

"Jim," I timidly asked, "what are we surveying? No one has told me much about our project."

"We're surveying 160-acre square blocks randomly dotting the landscape. Each of those squares is a quarter mile on each side, or a quarter section. Do you know about township, range, and sections?"

"Sort of."

"The first surveyors out west divided the land into a grid based on 36 square miles per township, each of which contains 36 sections. Right now we're in T12S, R14E—or Township 12 South, Range 14 East. A section is a square mile, or 640 acres, and our units are one-quarter of a section, or 160 acres. We're surveying for archaeological sites in the region's coal deposits. In fact our survey will sample about 1 percent of the coal regions of central Utah, scattered over 300 quarter sections. The quarter sections were randomly selected so that the survey data will be statistically defensible. You got that?"

"I understand the township part, but you lost me on the random sampling. So our survey areas are 160-acre blocks located all over central Utah where coal deposits have been found?"

"Correct. We spend most of our time just finding each survey area. As you can see there are no signs, and most of the maps are out of date. There are usually new roads that confuse us if we aren't careful. I make sure we know where we are by locating the section markers. That way if we aren't exactly in the survey unit, at least we're real close. Most of our units don't have any section markers, so we have to figure out where we are by reading the topography. I'm getting pretty good at it. Are we at two miles, Ben?"

"Sorry, I was listening to you and forgot to check the mileage. Want me to turn around?"

"No, this is probably it." Jim was looking ahead at a two-track road running east down a narrow wash.

We turned onto it and Ben reset the odometer. The road continued for a few hundred yards but then disappeared at the edge of a steep slope.

I gasped out loud when we reached the edge of the cliff. The road continued down, but it was rutted and steep. I didn't like the looks of it.

"Whoa," said Ben about the exact same second as me. "What do you think, Jim? Let's check it out?"

Ben stopped the car, and the two sat for a minute staring at the road. Jim opened his door and Ben followed. They walked over to the edge, where they stood debating if we should continue.

Marie, who had been sleeping, woke up. "Are we there yet?"

"I don't think so. The guys are checking out the road. It looks really bad to me. I don't think we should drive it." I looked over at Marie, who picked up her purse and began rifling through her stuff. "I need Chapstick. This desert makes my lips so dry. Have you done much four-wheeling, Ivy?"

"My last boyfriend owned a Jeep and we drove it over some pretty horrible roads. Have you ever heard of the trail over Elephant Hill in Canyonlands Park? The road scales a steep-sided sandstone hill where in most places the only traces of road are patches of scrapes in the sandstone. Anyway, I don't like the looks of this one. It's steep and deeply rutted. If we lose traction, we could roll right over the edge."

Jim got behind the wheel, and Ben sat in the passenger seat.

"Looks like we're going for it," Jim said. "If we don't go down this road, we'll have to hike another two miles just to reach our survey area. This hill would be a death march at the end of a long day." He turned around and gripped the wheel, then looked over his shoulder at us. "Fasten your seat belts, ladies." He fiddled with the four-wheel controls for a minute, then we began the steep descent.

The narrow road hugged the edge of a cliff. To our right was a steep, jagged wall of sandstone, and to the left, only air. One slip and we'd be history. After about 200 yards, the road widened slightly, but it was bisected by a narrow gully. Looking farther ahead, I noticed the gully grew into a mini Grand Canyon. We'd be fine as long as Blazo managed to straddle the rut. Unfortunately, where the road curved up ahead, the gully looked too wide to straddle. I couldn't stop myself from speaking up.

"I don't know, guys. This looks really bad to me. Maybe we should back up while we still can. That gully gets too wide near the turn," I said, pointing ahead.

Jim and Ben smiled as they exchanged glances, and I could almost read their minds: "What does the cute chick from back east know about driving in the desert?" Ben turned to look at me, grinning, and his eyes did that twinkling thing again.

"Hey, little lady, nothing to worry about. Blazo and me have driven more of these roads than you can imagine. Right, Jim?" His western accent was exaggerated, and his smile really lit up his face.

Suddenly Jim turned the wheel hard to avoid a boulder on the right, and all I could see out Marie's window was air. One slip, I thought, and we are Blazer sandwiches. We straddled the gully as long as we could, but it was too wide, and finally the left front tire slipped in. Blazo lurched forward, and we stopped short. The right back tire was spinning.

Jim struggled with the wheel and then gave it the gas, hoping that the other tires would catch and move the Blazer forward. Instead the right rear tire continued to spin and the front sank deeper into the gully.

"Looks like we might be high centered," Jim said. He opened his door and Ben followed. They walked around the car for a few minutes, looking under Blazo and reviewing our predicament.

I rolled down my window, and Jim grinned at me. "Nothing to worry about that a shovel and jack can't fix."

"Sure," I said.

As he walked away, I looked over at Marie and whispered, "We may make it down the road, but I'm pretty sure we won't be going back up it."

I regretted opening my mouth and offering a warning. Maybe that had only spurred them on. Maybe they would have turned back if I hadn't said anything.

"Aren't we full of gloom and doom?" asked Ben, another devilish grin on his face.

"This road is starting to make me nervous," Marie said. She looked worried and began paying closer attention. "It never occurred to me that we could get stuck. I just thought that you two were experts with this kind of thing."

Ben opened the back of the Blazer. "Damn, the jack and shovel are buried."

Jim was in the front of the vehicle, examining the right tire. "Guess we have to unpack. How about if you two help Ben?" Jim stood up and motioned for us to get out and help.

Ben opened the back and we formed an impromptu bucket brigade: Ben to Marie, and Marie to me. In no time the back was half empty, and Ben had the shovel and jack.

"Should we reload?" I asked no one in particular.

"Nah, let's try to get out before we bother." Jim shoveled dirt under the left rear tire while Ben collected rocks to throw in the gully under the right tire.

I stood and watched. Perhaps they did know what they were doing.

"What can I do?" I asked.

"Go collect some more rocks," Ben said. He looked toward a slope a few dozen yards down the road.

Marie joined me and we carried rocks back and forth, throwing them into the hole. Jim had joined Ben, and the gully began to look less ominous.

"Okay, I think it's ready. Let's try again. I'll drive. Ben, you stand and guide me."

Jim got behind the wheel. Ben stood nearby, hands on hips and looking serious.

"Go easy on the gas, Jim. Let her out slow."

Marie and I watched from the sidelines. The engine turned over, and Jim eased the gas. As the back tires caught, the Blazer lurched forward a short distance. We cheered. But before we'd finished, the Blazer veered right, and the front and rear left tires sank back into the gully. This time it looked really bad. The left tires dove deep into the rut. Jim poured on the gas, hoping that the vehicle's momentum could pull it out. Blazo stalled, but he restarted it. After two starts and stalls, and spinning tires, I began to smell burning rubber.

Jim got out and examined Blazo's submerged tires. I noticed he looked less cocky and perhaps even a little worried.

Ben squatted down near the tires. "This is beginning to look pretty bad. Even if we get out of this, we're going to have a hard time keeping out of the gully. Let's have the gals fill in the gully down a length of the road while you and I dig out the tires.

"Where do you want me to begin?" I asked.

"Start here and work as far down as you can."

"Do we have another shovel?"

"Just collect rocks and throw them in the holes."

Marie and I started our road construction detail, but it felt pretty hopeless. The gully grew from two feet wide and two feet deep where the Blazer was stuck to nearly three feet wide where the road curved at the cliff's base.

An hour later the guys had removed the loose soil surrounding the front right tire, and they had placed sandstone slabs underneath it. They had also excavated and stabilized the roadbed in front of the tires. Below Blazo, Marie and I had filled about twenty feet of gully and reduced the depth of another ten feet by half. We had pretty much used up the close supply of rocks, and we were filthy and thirsty. Ben's face was streaked with dirt, and Jim was beginning to smell pretty ripe. Sweat dripped down his face. Marie looked fresh as a daisy, but then she wasn't really helping that much either. As usual, I had morphed into Pig Pen and was dirtier than everyone else by a factor of two. Marie and I moved out of the way, and Jim slipped behind the wheel. He turned the ignition and the engine coughed and stalled. It took three tries before Blazo decided to cooperate.

Jim gripped the wheel and eased the gas—nothing. He gave it a little more. The car lifted slightly and the rear tires caught, moving Blazo out of the gully and down the road. Jim steered so Blazo hugged the right side. We cheered and then held our breath. Jim turned into the curve. The

Blazer's left tires skirted the edge of the gully, but then it gave way and the tires fell in. Like a song's refrain, the getting-stuck sequence repeated itself. The Blazer stopped, and Jim poured on the gas trying to muscle out of the ditch. I smelled more rubber and heard the whir of tires without traction.

"Whoa!" called Ben, running over and waving his arms, staring at the left rear tire. He disappeared briefly in a cloud of smoke and dust. "Stop. Give it up. We've got a flat."

Jim swore under his breath as he got out of the car. The guys huddled by the flat tire, and I ran to get a closer look.

Sure enough, the left rear tire was pancake flat and buried deeper than ever. A sharp rock, hidden in the side of the gully, had punctured the sidewall.

Jim was definitely an optimist. "We're making progress. Look, we're almost down this hill. Let's change this tire and get to our survey area."

The spare tire was buried, of course, but we removed the rest of the gear in record time. I was stacking a Coleman stove on top of a folding table when I noticed everyone was very quiet. I turned and saw Jim shaking his head. The guys were staring at the spare. It was flat.

"Looks like we're stuck," said Jim, finally admitting the inevitable.

"Shoot, we were so close," said Ben, shaking his head. "That road was looking good with all the rocks thrown in."

"Guess we walk from here." Jim trained his gaze up the slope and in the general direction of civilization.

Marie, who had gone off to pee, returned looking like a bunny in the headlights. "Did I hear you guys right? Walk? It's twenty miles to the nearest paved road. What do you mean walk? It's your fault that we're stuck."

"Okay, relax. Let's have lunch and think about this."

We headed over to the gear and food. Blazo's contents formed a chaotic pile. I saw one cooler in the middle, under sleeping bags and tents. A second cooler was off to the side, sitting in the shade under a low bush. I walked over to that one to see if perhaps I would get lucky. Bingo! Cold pop! I searched two boxes and found peanut butter and jelly. After a few minutes Jim located the bread and some chips in another box. Ben uncovered a buried cooler and pulled out some oranges.

Grabbing a folding chair, Ben casually set it up, made himself a sandwich, and sat down for a rest. He looked relaxed and happy, clearly at home in the middle of nowhere. I wasn't feeling quite so nonchalant. I had absolutely no idea where we were, I was with two boneheads who had just managed to get us stuck without a spare tire, and it was almost a hundred degrees in the shade. Marie, who was still moving stuff around, didn't look like she'd last for five miles of hiking, never mind twenty. Since our present situation was not my doing, and I'd even tried to warn them, I decided to keep my mouth shut and let them figure out a solution.

Jim headed for a sliver of shade under an outcrop of sandstone, and I decided to join him. The day was clear, and as I sat down, I noticed the view was spectacular. To the east I could see for twenty miles. We were on the edge of the Swell, and a panoramic view of the valley below filled the eastern horizon.

"Guess it's been a pretty weird first day on the job," said Jim, looking like a whipped puppy. I felt bad for him. All that macho and bravado were gone. "We would have made it if the spare wasn't flat. I guess Ben and I will walk to the road. You two can stay with the stuff and take it easy."

"How long do you think it will take?"

"Well, if we have to walk the whole twenty miles to the main road it will take at least two days before we make it back. But I'm thinking we'll meet someone traveling on the dirt road. If that happens we could be back as early as tomorrow afternoon."

"I'd be happy to walk with you. Ben can stay with Marie," I offered. The sandwich tasted good, and there was a slight breeze in the shade. I was feeling better with food in my stomach and a cool breeze. A lone fly kept trying to land on my bread, which had stiffened already from the hot, dry air. I drank from my water bottle and looked over at Jim. He was covered in dirt. He had taken off his stained cowboy hat, and his hair was matted and sweaty.

Ben and Marie joined us, dragging along their chairs and a bag of chips. "I've got an idea," Ben said. "Let's walk cross-county." He pointed to the northeast. "That way, it will be five miles shorter if we head east instead of following the roads. We can bushwhack across the Swell."

Jim shook his head and laughed. "What do you think this is, Ben? One of your pot-hunting adventures gone wrong? What if we hit a cliff that can't be climbed? We don't even have a detailed map of that area."

Ben grinned. "You know I gave up digging in ruins." He poked his fingers into a can of Vienna sausages and popped one into his mouth. "And there's always a way over a cliff. I remember one time we hiked fifteen miles into a site so no one would see our vehicle sitting there. Then just two hours into digging, we heard a truck and realized it was a government ranger.

We took off into the desert and decided our best chance would be to hide out for a while. Then, when things cooled down we'd take a direct route cross-country. We had no maps and only a little water. All I had with me to eat was my lunch. I think I had two cans of peaches, a can of beans, and one can of Vienna sausages. We traveled farther and farther away from our truck. We spent the night in a cave and then hiked east in the general direction of the truck, wandering around for five days, living on snakes and water collected from green potholes and pockets of water in the dry creeks. This is nothing compared to that. We've got everything we need for a week or even two weeks."

"Ben, where are you from?" I asked.

"Monticello. I come from a long line of pinto bean farmers."

"You were a pot hunter?"

"Sure, everyone digs sites. It's a local pastime in southern Utah. An archaeologist named Mathers taught us how to find the good stuff. My grandfather was Mathers's guide on his Grand Gulch expedition. He worked for the Wetherill brothers before Mathers arrived on the scene. My whole family used to go pot hunting on Sundays. We would pack a lunch and head to our favorite ruined pueblo for a little recreational digging. Those were great times. I miss those days."

"Did you keep the stuff you found?"

"You should see our collection. It's better than a museum. We used to sell some of our better stuff, but those days are gone. We're too afraid of getting caught to sell anything now."

"What kind of things have you collected?"

"Well, my daddy has the best stuff. He has hundreds of whole pots, baskets, sandals, hafted arrows, feather and rabbit robes, axes—you name it, he's got it. I guess my favorite artifacts are an effigy pot of a duck and a prehistoric backpack filled with all kinds of stuff."

"Do people still dig for recreation?" I was amazed that people weren't more worried about getting caught.

"Nah, most people have stopped. They know it's illegal. I guess some sneak in a dig now and then, but most have retired their shovels. I was real good at finding baskets and pots. Guess that's why I decided to study archaeology at Joseph Smith College."

"How did you find whole pots? Aren't those usually in burials?"

"Yup, the good stuff is usually in the graves. What we would do is take a probe, which is a fancy name for a metal stick, and push it into the soil slowly until we could feel it hitting something hard. I can tell the difference between a rock and a pot just by the feel. I guess it's an art finding them and not breaking them. I used to be the best in my family with a probe."

"So, you don't dig sites illegally anymore?"

"Well…I'm learning in my classes that it's unethical to dig anything without permits, but I still don't see much difference between pot hunters and archaeologists. Both dig graves for the stuff."

Jim interrupted. "Ben, you swore to Dr. Lockyear that you were reformed."

"I guess. It just doesn't seem like Joseph Smith College writes anything about their field school digs. The one I went on two years ago still hasn't been written up." Ben looked over at Jim.

"The report is still being worked on," Jim said. "I was helping with the writing for a while. It often takes years to complete the artifact analysis, and then the people who did the analyses have to be coerced into finishing the reports."

I moved deeper into the shade and looked over at Jim. "Johnson is adamant about Utah College's field school sites being written up. Legend has it that Johnson never put a hole in a site that wasn't written up."

"Yeah, he has that reputation," Jim said. "I wish Joseph Smith College could say the same thing." He stood up and headed for the Blazer. "Guess we should start packing up some stuff for our hike. Ben, are you coming with me?"

"Wouldn't miss it," he said. "It's been a while since I was stranded."

They traveled light. Both of them filled small backpacks with food and water. They figured two gallons each would be enough, but I wasn't so sure. They skipped the camping gear since it would just slow them down. It was 1 p.m. and over 100 degrees when they hit the road.

"Ivy, I'm leaving you in charge," said Jim. "Stay within sight of the vehicle, okay? Don't wander away for any reason. We should be back in less than three days, so don't worry until around this time on Thursday. Drink plenty of fluids and try to keep the coolers in the shade. Relax and enjoy yourselves. Here are the keys to the vehicle. I guess I don't need them. Just don't lose them."

I caught the keys. "Good luck. We'll be fine. We have the easy job, just sitting here guarding the stuff, right?"

A Silence Too Deep

Marie waved to the guys as they began climbing up the road. She was uphill from me, perched on the edge of a huge boulder. She had changed into her swimsuit and was working on her tan. At the top of the hill I saw Ben turn around and check out Marie, then he waved and trudged on. I waved back, but no one noticed.

When they left I hadn't known if I was mad, scared, or just confused. It had all happened so fast. Yesterday I was spending a slow Sunday reading the newspaper in my cozy duplex, and the next day I'm stranded in the middle of Utah with a stranger in a bikini. I guess I was feeling more overwhelmed than anything else. Since I had nothing to do, and a whole afternoon before me, I decided I should follow Marie's lead and relax a little while taking stock of our situation. Maybe I'd hike around and enjoy the view. I looked over at Marie, who was now topless, lathered in sunscreen, and reading a book.

I checked the coolers to make sure they were still in the shade, then grabbed my daypack and headed up the road. My plan was to follow it to the top of the slope and then walk along the edge of the cliff until I could see the view to the south. The escarpment curved around to the southeast, so if I followed the edge, I figured I would still be able to see the car. Deciding I'd better explain what I was up to, I stopped by the tanning salon.

"Don't wander too far," Marie said. "I'll really freak out if you disappear."

Even though I grew up back east, in a land of green fields and lush forests, I knew from a young age that I belonged out west. Maybe it was from watching westerns, or perhaps the lure of vast uninhabited spaces, or the myth of the Wild West. I picked Utah for college because it took me west and the skiing was great. During my first spring vacation I went backpacking in Canyonlands and knew from the moment I laid my eyes on southern Utah that I was home. A sense of peace and belonging filled the nooks and crannies of my soul, and I felt certain windows in my mind opening for the first time. The closest I'd ever come to feeling this way before was probably on Rhode Island's beaches, where I spent most of my childhood. The vastness of the ocean resembles in many ways the open vistas of the West. But out west, the sky seems bluer, the quiet more peaceful, and the air fresher.

I hiked up the road and then followed the edge of the cliff as it veered south and then east. Below me Blazo had shrunk to a small cricket, and Marie an ant. I walked along the middle of a narrow spur projecting east, both sides dropping steeply, hundreds of feet down. But the spur seemed solid, and the view was worth the slight vertigo that I felt as it thinned. At the end of the spur I planted myself under the shade of a large boulder. I noticed Marie waving at me so I waved back. Then I drifted into my own thoughts, enjoying the view and wondering about Jim and Ben's hike. I took out some granola mixed with M&Ms and raisins. I'd munched down about half the bag when, out of the corner of my eye, I saw a flicker of movement and noticed a chipmunk skittering back and forth across the rocks. I tossed a few pieces of granola in his direction. He jerked away, scared for a minute, then ran forward to see what had dropped from the sky. Tail twitching with excitement, he grabbed the small piece of granola and ran to his hole, partially hidden under a sandstone slab.

After a few minutes the chipmunk returned and I threw him a raisin. He reacted the same, scurrying back to his den to eat or hide his snack. With nothing better to do, I decided to try to get him to take granola from my hand. After an hour of trying, I got bored and threw a handful to my furry friend. Watching him march back and forth to his hole, I noticed a marking on a nearby rock. Its shape was unnatural so I decided to investigate. The tip of the spur was a jumble of large sandstone slabs, and the exposed surfaces had blackened from weathering. Then I spotted a spiral carved into the black surface that covered the windward side of a flat boulder. The carving had exposed the red sandstone underneath, and the color contrast between the black varnish and red stone is what had caught my eye.

As I stood up and climbed onto the carved boulder, I was startled by a thunderous clicking, like the sound of a train racing across tracks. Instantly my body reacted. I jumped away from the sound, screeching as I jumped. I heard my pulse roar in my ears, and my heart was pounding so hard I thought it would leap out of my chest. What was that sound? Then my head cleared and I realized that there is only one thing that makes such a terrific racket: a rattlesnake.

I had never been afraid of snakes, but alone in the middle of nowhere, I felt terrified in some ancient primal way. After a few more seconds I decided I probably shouldn't make a sudden movement until I knew where the snake was hiding. I looked toward the sound and noticed movement a few yards away, close to where I had been standing near the spiral. Poking up over the edge of the boulder, I saw the rattler's tail shaking in a blur of movement. That was all I could see of him, but I was relieved that I had jumped out of striking range. The sound continued, and I realized his warning might have saved me. A few more steps, and I would have been an easy target.

So much for peace and quiet. My heartbeat slowed, and I looked toward Blazo to make sure that Marie hadn't heard my scream. She was still reading and apparently hadn't heard me. The rattling stopped, and quiet was restored. I was amazed for a minute at how such a small creature could make such a loud sound. Did the volume of the rattling correlate with the size of the snake? This was my first encounter with a rattlesnake in the wild, and I was curious. Perhaps if I climbed around the slab, staying out of striking range, I could actually see it. I grabbed my pack and inched around the rock. In a few minutes I could see under the rock, and there lay the largest snake I had ever seen in my life. It was coiled, so I couldn't estimate how long it was, but its size explained the volume of sound.

The rest of the day was uneventful. Thunderheads gathered, and it began to look like rain, so Marie suggested that we sleep in the back of Blazo. There was really nowhere to pitch a tent, so it sounded like a good plan. We collected all the gear, stowed it near the vehicle, and covered it with a tarp. Then we cooked a dinner of beans and hot dogs on the Coleman stove. Time slowed, and although the scenery was spectacular, I was beginning to get bored just sitting. As darkness fell, the stillness deepened, and I had no television, no stereo, no reading to turn to for distraction. Off in the distance we could see lightning, but the storm was too far away to hear the thunder. We watched the distant lightning for a while, but by 9 p.m., bored out of my mind, I decided to call it a night.

I collapsed the back seat to make a bed and laid out our sleeping bags. The sleeping surface was rock hard, but we'd be dry and warm if it rained. As soon as I'd settled into my bag, the wind kicked up and I caught the scent of rain. That strong, delicious smell of sage and damp earth meant the storm was close. About half an hour later we heard the first thunder. The storm drew closer. Lying there, waiting for the deluge, I wondered how Jim and Ben were doing. They had no tents or sleeping bags. I hoped they would find a rock shelter to wait out the storm. On the drive across the Swell we had seen plenty of shallow caves carved into the sandstone by wind and rain. They would probably spend the night in one of them, protected from lightning and flash floods.

While I was worrying about the guys, the storm was moving in. Raindrops at first pelted the vehicle, and then fell in torrents. I sat up and looked out the window. When lightning lit up the skies, I could see water pouring over the cliffs, creating small waterfalls where I had walked earlier that afternoon. The rain was also collecting in the road, filling the gully and racing downhill. Two lightning flashes later, I noticed the gully was now a creek, with water rushing down the road. Where we had repaired sections of the gully, the creek leapt out and spread across the road until it collected and resumed its race down the cliff. For a while the lightning stopped, and I couldn't see anything in the deep black of night, but I could hear the waterfalls and imagined them growing in strength and fury. Every now and then large rocks, loosened by the rain, came crashing down the steep slopes. We were glad to be safe and dry in Blazo, but it was impossible to relax and fall asleep.

The violence of the storm reminded me of something I learned in my class about Native American tribes in Arizona. The Pima and Papago, who lived near Tucson and Phoenix, considered the slow winter rains to be female, and the violent thunderstorms of summer to be male. Out in the desert, far from homes and cities, this dichotomy seemed fitting. Just as I was on the edge of sleep, I was startled by a tremendous boom. The earth shook, and both Marie and I sat up in our bags.

"What was that?" she asked, sounding as terrified as I felt.

"I have no idea." I strained to see out the window. "Perhaps it was one of those huge sandstone slabs just below the cliff breaking loose and falling down. It sure sounded close."

We sat quietly for a minute. My heart was pounding for the second time that day, and I had the urge to flee to safety, but there was nowhere to go. We had to stick it out in the vehicle. We listened. It sounded like the storm was slowing—the thunder and lightning had stopped—and I could no longer hear running water.

"I think the worst is over," I said, "but I don't know if I can sleep."

Marie lay back down. "I know what you mean. I wonder how far away that rockfall occurred. I've never heard anything like it before. What a huge crash."

I don't remember falling asleep. It seemed like I lay there forever—listening and thinking. But I must have fallen into a deep sleep because I awoke confused and disoriented. Marie was sound asleep next to me, snoring lightly. The sky was brightening to the east, and my bladder was full. I decided to get up and make a pot of coffee—coffee in, coffee out.

I'll always remember that magical morning, filled with so many sounds, smells, and colors, still vivid in my memory. The rain had cleared the air, now crisp and smelling of mountains and rich soil. As the horizon brightened, the sky burst with color—pinks, reds, and yellows, a painter's palette, a riot of color and light. I sat and watched the sky until the sun wiped the palette clean. Two chipmunks scurried around our covered gear. A small gray bird stood near a pool of water that had collected on the tarp. I watched him stretch down for a drink. He did this twice before jumping in for a quick bath. When he flew off, I lifted the tarp and rummaged around for coffee, matches, a pan, and the stove. When the water started boiling, Marie appeared. She was running a hand through her hair, which was knotted and matted in the back, and her eyes were bloated with sleep. She looked like a lost and confused child.

"How did you sleep, Ivy? I slept like the dead."

We talked and cooked, passing the morning quietly as the sun climbed and the day heated up. We cleaned the dishes, changed our clothes, put the sleeping bags away, and settled into the shade with our books. The day dragged. We felt isolated, forgotten by the world. When I closed my eyes, the silence was so complete it seemed the world had disappeared. In the desert, in the heat of the day, there is a silence like no other, but by afternoon, after the sun's heat has created thermal winds, the silence evaporates. We ate an early dinner in case the building thunderheads erupted. We wanted to have everything stowed and battened down. Neither the storm nor our rescuers arrived that night.

In the evening I remembered that I'd brought playing cards, so we played a few games and talked. We talked about relationships, and Marie told me she wanted to start a family. I realized that I wasn't close to being ready for that step, and I wondered again how I could be an archaeologist and mother. By nine the waning moon had risen, and a billion stars filled the skies. We turned in early and slept right through the night.

It was cooler in the morning than it had been the day before. We both slept late and woke only because it was getting too warm in the vehicle. The sun was already high in the sky.

"Let's turn the radio on and get some news. Do you realize, Ivy, that we haven't heard anything from the outside world for three days?"

I looked at my watch and saw that it was almost ten. "Good idea. I'll get the keys."

We listened to the news and turned the radio off. Nothing momentous had occurred in our brief time away. About an hour later, after we had finished breakfast and cleaned ourselves up, as best we could, Jim appeared at the top of the road. He was walking toward us with a tall, strong-looking man, who I found out later was the field director. Marie waved and started walking up the road. I followed her. It looked like the cavalry had arrived at last.

Fifty-Two and Counting

Three weeks after my fateful introduction to the job we were almost finished with the Utah Coal project. Marie quit after the second week, but I stuck it out. Dr. Lockyear replaced her with a Joseph Smith College student known strictly by her nickname, Patsy. She was tall, stocky, strong, and one of the funniest people I'd ever met. We had spent the last three weeks on Jim's crew, walking the vast expanses of central Utah, recording small lithic scatters and prehistoric camps. Patsy's humor broke the tedium and made it all bearable. We camped each week at a different location and worked from sunup to sundown. Temperatures rarely climbed over 90 degrees, and the weather remained clear.

I liked camping and living outdoors, but the work was physically demanding and mentally boring. I began to realize how much I depended on television for my evening entertainment. Most nights in the field we watched the fire, then climbed into the vehicle to listen to the evening news. By 8 p.m. we were ready for bed. My biggest challenge was keeping up with my six-feet-tall crewmembers. At just 5'1", my short little legs had to work double-time to keep up with Patsy and the men. Each night I fell into my sleeping bag exhausted, praying that tomorrow would be easier. Patsy prayed too, but it was for real. She was the first devout Mormon woman I had really gotten to know, and I liked her. She never pushed her religion on me, but she answered many questions I had about Mormons, women, and archaeologists.

Friday had been my last day on the Utah Coal survey. Dr. Lockyear decided that two crews could finish it up, so I was assigned to a new project in the Troutlake National Forest. Bob Vrey, the Utah College student who had dared to disagree with Dr. Johnson over the cultural affiliation of the Pint Creek sites, was going to be my new crew chief. I was looking forward to meeting Bob, but anxious about keeping up with a new crew.

I was at our meeting place early on Monday, waiting for the crews to assemble. Only two other people were there, two guys I didn't know very well. I introduced myself as a beat-up pickup truck drove up with Ben at the wheel. He handed the keys to the blond woman passenger and got out of the truck looking in my direction.

"Hey, Ivy, it looks like we're on the same crew again."

"We are? All I know is that I'm on Bob's crew, and we're starting a new project. Did you get moved too?"

Ben, happy-go-lucky as usual, unloaded his stuff from the back of the pick-up and said good-bye to his friend. "Yeah, you, a new guy named Stan, and I are on Bob's crew. I hear our project is in thick pinyon-juniper. Ever worked in thick PJ? It's a bitch."

"Great, a new form of archaeological torture. Do you know anything about Stan? I don't think I've heard anyone mention him."

"He was just hired. He recently finished a tour with the Marines and decided to see the West."

"You're kidding, right?"

Ben sat down on his duffle bag. "Nope."

"I am on an all-guy crew and one's an ex-marine?" I scowled and looked up to see a husky, dark-haired guy walking toward me. His hair was speckled with gray, and he wore John Lennon wire frames.

"The good news is you'll have your own tent," offered Ben in consolation.

"You must be Ivy. I don't think there could be two petite blonds with braids waiting around here for me." Bob had a deep voice and his smile was wide and heartfelt. "I hear you're from Utah College too."

"Are you Bob?" I was busy looking at his lips. Somehow they didn't move when he talked. He wore cowboy boots, a jean shirt, pressed jeans, and an expensive Stetson; he wasn't at all what I expected. His face exuded kindness and strength.

"Yup, I hear you went to Pint Creek this summer."

"It was hot and buggy. I guess I survived to tell."

Bob looked me up and down. "Well it's good to have you on my crew. I hear you have a pretty good eye for sites, and you can keep up." There, I did see his lips move.

"No one has told me that," I said, feeling a mixture of pride and annoyance. Bob headed over to a pumped-up GMC Scout. It was navy blue but very faded. Lot of miles on that baby, I thought.

I helped Bob and Ben load the field equipment. When we were about done, Stan appeared. He wasn't what I expected at all. He was short, at least for a guy, about 5'7", his face was round and bearded, his hairline had receded, his belly hung ever so slightly over his belt, and he wore glasses. About the only thing that connected him to the military were his clothes: green T-shirt, camouflage pants, and military issue boots. I breathed a sigh of relief, assuming I could probably keep up with this guy.

We were on the road by 7 a.m. and headed for the grocery store in Salina. The access to our project area was a dirt road intersecting I-70 at the eastern edge of the Wasatch Plateau. We would be working sixty miles from Salina, and thirty miles from the nearest small town. We planned to camp just on the edge of our survey area: a large block of 2,000 acres in the heart of coal country. The survey was for a mining company that wanted to strip mine the rich deposits, all on government land.

The area's low hills and ridges were covered with a thick forest of pinyon and juniper trees, but we camped in an open meadow, complete with a meandering creek, and a few ponderosa pines. It was early September, so early mornings would be cool. Since we would be camping at an elevation of 6,000 feet, I suspected it would get chilly at night too.

After unloading our camping gear and setting up our tents, we drove to the starting point of the survey, another open meadow. It was a beautiful blue-sky day. The temperature was perfect, and the edges of the meadow were lined with rabbitbrush in full, yellow bloom. Large, low shrubs with clusters of tiny yellow flowers, they reminded me of the goldenrod covering the fields in Rhode Island.

We took our places on line, fifteen meters apart, with Bob on one end and Ben on the other. Bob looked over our spacing and called out final instructions.

"We're walking due west. This transect goes about half a mile. Then we'll swing around and follow your line back, Ben, so watch where you walk. Stan, do you have your compass out? Keep us heading due west, and I'll count my paces and follow the map. Let's go."

Everyone moved forward together on Bob's signal. Being in the center, all I had to do was keep an even distance between Bob and Stan. We waded through the rabbitbrush for a short distance and then entered the forest. The trees were so thick that I had to concentrate to keep sight of Bob and Stan, and look for artifacts at the same time. I came to a shallow creek, walked down a steep slope, then up the other side. I couldn't see anyone, so I stopped to listen, but couldn't hear them. What now? I wondered. After a few more minutes I realized I had no choice but to yell for the guys.

"Hey, where is everyone?"

"Over here." I heard Bob to my left and caught a glimpse of him climbing up the side of the wash. Stan yelled too, from about fifty meters ahead of me. I headed toward Stan while trying to stay on my line and picked up my pace. Our transect ended at the edge of a deep, wide canyon. It was beautiful, but there was no time to appreciate the spectacular view. Bob was telling us to swing around to the other side of Ben, take our new spots, still fifteen meters apart, and walk due east. I grabbed my water bottle from my daypack and barely had enough time to get a drink before Bob motioned with his arm to start.

We did this, back and forth, all afternoon, stopping only long enough to record a prehistoric campsite that I found. All that was visible was a scatter of flaked stone and a few small pieces of broken pottery clustered on a wedge of land next to a small drainage. After walking over the site, Bob filled out the site form, Ben took pictures, and Stan and I sketched a location map. Among the artifacts were two arrowheads, a small side-notched arrow point that suggested use by Ute or Paiute Indians, and the base of a large spear point. There were also pieces of a broken grinding stone, a cobble that had been used for pounding, and a few pieces of thick brown pottery the exact same color of the soil. I would never have seen it if Bob hadn't pointed it out. He referred to it as brown utility ware, and he seemed to know a lot about ceramics.

In the afternoon I had started sneezing, which was no surprise since I had always suffered from fall allergies. For the rest of the day I sneezed on and off. My allergies got worse and worse, and like Bolero's crescendo, my sneezing attack ended in a glorious clash of man and nature. As we were walking across a field filled with blooming rabbitbrush, my sneezing worsened, then wouldn't stop. My nose ran and my eyes watered. On the last transect, I decided to count my sneezes until they stopped. One, two, three, four, five, six…they continued, and continued. At fifty my nose started bleeding, but I kept sneezing. I lost count at fifty-two because of my nosebleed and hunt for tissues. But I kept right on sneezing. I think I probably sneezed over seventy times in a row. Thank God we were done for the day. My head was pounding as we loaded the vehicle and drove back to camp.

By the time we got there, my headache was so bad that I went right to my tent, laid out my sleeping bag on my thin cot, and buried my face in my pillow. Blocking everything out helped the pounding. After a few minutes I got up and popped two aspirin, and held a clean tissue over my nose as an impromptu pollen filter. About an hour later, it was starting to get dark outside but I felt better. I was hungry and noticed that the guys were grilling steaks. A large can of beans sat, lid ajar, on the edge of the fire. All three guys were sitting in chairs, staring at the flames.

Bob looked my way. "How are you doing? That was some serious sneezing. We were just talking it over and decided that you did more sneezing this afternoon than we thought could be possible. Must be the rabbitbrush, which in Latin is *Chrysothamnus nauseosus*. The pollen is a well-known irritant."

Feeling a little better, I walked over to the fire. Ben stood up and got me a chair.

"I cooked you a steak. Here, have a seat."

I felt numb and slightly out of it. I was glad it was almost dark because my nose felt like one of those fake clown numbers. Damn, maybe it was glowing in the dark. I sat in the chair and mumbled thanks for dinner.

Except for the crackling of the fire, it was absolutely still. At first the stillness had bothered me, but I had grown used to the quiet of living hundreds of miles from civilization. The guys were staring at the coals; they were tired and quiet. The steak was tasteless and tough, and I considered throwing it away, but I knew I'd be starving all night if I didn't eat now. I fantasized about baked potatoes smothered in sour cream and butter as I stared at the coals and chewed. Bob and Ben were asking Stan questions about the Marines, but even though I was curious, I didn't have the strength to engage in conversation.

The rest of the week was much the same as the first day. The guys spoke maybe fifty words a day, my allergies were horrible, I was tired and sore from walking all day and struggling to keep up, and the food was terrible. When we packed up to leave on Friday morning, I realized that I was lonely. Without another woman on the crew, to talk to about everything and nothing, the quiet had become oppressive. I wasn't sure that I could handle too many more weeks like this one. I'd grown up in a family of four girls, and for the first time I realized how different women and men really are. But I couldn't give up. I needed the work, and how could I become an archaeologist if I couldn't do fieldwork? For that matter, how could I do this work if I didn't like working with men? After all, most archaeologists are male. If I couldn't turn them into gabby women, should I try to become more like them? Was that possible? I had my work cut out for me because I'd grown up around women and felt like I didn't understand men that well.

I thought about the times my dad took me on fishing trips with my Uncle Bill and three male cousins. I was astonished to observe that boys lived by different rules than girls. I had been taught that little girls should not swear, they should be obedient, clean, and, most important, pretty. After we left port on our small fishing boat, I discovered that boys were allowed to swear, pee over the side of the boat, and wipe fish guts on their clothes, with no one seeming to care. They'd just laugh, pat each other on the back, and try something even more outrageous. They especially liked to try one-upping each other, the cruder the better. At the time, being only ten years old, I was confused and grossed out, but I soon realized that there really were different standards of conduct for men and women. Maybe I needed to behave more like the men in the field if I wanted to fit in and belong.

I decided I'd give it a try, but my first order of business—that is, after a two-hour shower—was to buy allergy medicine. Maybe without the sneezing and sniffling, another week of surveying wouldn't be so bad. And it would give me a chance to observe the men on the crew more closely so I could learn how to fit in.

Gasoline in Paradise Valley

What an optimist I was. Just when I thought I had it all figured out, things got even worse. Monday morning dawned just like all the others. We loaded our gear, bought groceries in Salina, filled the gas tank, checked our spare, refilled our two extra five-gallon gas tanks, and then headed into the field. The first day of work was uneventful. My allergy medicine was working like a charm, and the weather was crisp and clear. On our drive I noticed that patches of aspens were beginning to turn to gold, their leaves trembling in the breeze, perhaps fearful of their demise. The rabbit-brush flowers had turned a tarnished shade of gold—they had passed their prime. Thank goodness.

After unloading gear and pitching our tents, we started surveying. I found a spectacular site that first afternoon, a small rock shelter on the edge of the canyon. Pottery and arrow points littered the charcoal-stained soil. The pothunters hadn't found the site yet, so its surface was smooth. In the back of the shelter were aligned slabs, suggesting that a cache of food, tools, or even a human burial lay undisturbed. A patch of the rear wall had been painted with red and black lines. The painted area was no bigger than a couple of feet in diameter, but the entire space was covered with thick, zigzag lines.

Even dinner that night was fine. Tired of the "same old, same old" meat on the grill, I convinced the guys to let me make shish kebabs out of beef wrapped in bacon, tomatoes, mushrooms, and onions. They were delicious, and the guys were grateful for a special meal. It wasn't until I went into my tent after dinner and smelled the strong odor of gasoline that I realized that all was not well in paradise.

After a few minutes of following my nose around the tent, I discovered that my duffle bag, with all of my clothes, was soaked in gasoline. Ben had set up my tent and thrown my duffel bag inside so I hadn't noticed the problem before. Then I realized that the extra five-gallon tanks must have spilled. I swore out loud and rifled through my bag, hoping that something had been spared. Panicky, I held each item to my nose, praying that the spill wasn't that bad, but everything—underwear, coat, socks, shirts, pants—reeked of gas. I swore and screamed, and the guys came running.

"What's wrong with you?" Bob asked, looking seriously concerned.

"The gas leaked on my clothes. Everything smells like gasoline. What am I going to do? How can I possibly wear this stuff?"

I could feel my eyes tearing, so I was glad it was dark. The guys crowded around, feigning concern. Ben tried to make a joke, but it fell flat. Then the tears really started flowing, and they realized they couldn't make me feel better.

"Why don't you hang them up and let them air out?" offered Ben.

Feeling equally helpless, Stan offered his condolences, then headed back to the fire.

"Let's hang 'em up in the trees overnight. That should help." Ben reached over to grab my empty bag and started stuffing my clothes back in.

I sat and cried, suddenly overwhelmed by loneliness and a sense of failure. Not only had I blown an opportunity to win Dr. Johnson over in field school, but I was having second thoughts about trying to work in a male-dominated field, and everything was starting to seem so hopeless. No matter how cheery I tried to be in the field, the fact was that I wasn't sure I could hack a career in archaeology. Randy had been right. It just seemed too macho, too physical, too lonely.

"Ivy, I think I have some rope," Bob offered. "I'll make you a clothesline."

The guys got busy trying to salvage my clothes, giving me some privacy so I could cry in peace. Eventually, I dried my eyes and carried the rest of my clothes outside. At least my sleeping bag was okay. I mumbled thanks to the guys for the help and finished hanging everything over the line.

As I stood there, the full moon rose slowly over the trees like a giant snowball, a reminder that some things never change and beauty is everywhere. I returned to my tent and unzipped the windows to let the crisp night air in and the gasoline fumes out. It was bright enough inside the tent to see without a flashlight. I picked up the book I was reading and found it was almost light enough to read.

The guys had returned to the fire. They sat and stared.

"Thanks for your help," I called out. "I'll be okay. I'm turning in. See you tomorrow."

I laid out my sleeping bag on the cot, took off my hiking boots and dirty jeans, and crawled into my sleeping bag wearing just underwear and a T-shirt. Taking stock of my uncontaminated supplies, I realized I had a sweater in my backpack and my flannel shirt was okay. Luckily I had worn it all day and then shoved it in my daypack. I had salvaged one pair of underwear from my duffel bag, two pairs of socks, and a T-shirt that might be okay after it aired out. I fell asleep imagining I was loading all my clothes into the washing machine and adding extra soap.

I woke at first light to the sound of coyotes howling. Then it turned to yipping and a frenzy of barks. They must be sharing the kill, I thought. I felt so cozy and warm in my sleeping bag that I didn't want to get out, but I could hear someone banging the coffee pot. It was probably time to get going. I sat up and looked outside. A thin frost covered the nearby meadow. Slivers of bright sunlight streaked through the trees. At least the frost would kill the rabbitbrush, I thought. Then I remembered that all my clothes stunk of gasoline. I put on my flannel shirt and sweater. My down coat was a lost cause, but it didn't seem like it was cold enough for me to need it. I stumbled out of the tent and sat down to put on my hiking boots.

Ben was cooking bacon over a smoky fire, and Stan was cracking eggs into a bowl. Bob stood outside the tent brushing his teeth. He spit on the ground and headed over to the fire. I noticed the coffee pot was on a grill over the fire, already perking. Another day in paradise, I thought, heading over to the guys.

"Morning. How are my clothes?" I walked over to the line and sniffed my favorite jeans. I didn't have to get too close to realize that Ben's plan had been a failure. "Phew! They still reek." I walked over to the fire to warm up. The smoke blew my way, reminding me that I'd smell like smoke and sweat for the rest of the week. My clothes wouldn't be wearable. I sat by the fire and resigned myself to a week of not having clean clothes. It would probably be best if I just pretended I was a mountain man, living far from civilization with only the clothes on my back.

Feeling like I was caught in a bad dream, I glanced over at the rest of the crew, all of them busy with breakfast. They already looked pretty scruffy. Ben's hair was matted and greasy. Bob's looked uncombed and knotted in the back from a restless night. What was left of Stan's hair was covered with a broad-brimmed hat. I usually wore my long hair in tight braids, which kept it from looking too dirty and greasy until the end of the week. The guys dealt with their filthy hair by wearing hats. Sometimes Ben wore a bandana under his. For the first time I noticed that they all seemed to be wearing the same clothes they had on yesterday. Stan was in his military green, Ben was wearing yesterday's faded red T-shirt, and even Bob looked like he was wearing the same light blue work shirt he had on yesterday. I had never noticed how often, or even if, the guys bothered to change their clothes.

On Fridays, when my friend Pam usually gave me a ride home from the rendezvous place, she would tease me that she could smell us about two blocks away, even with her car windows up. I knew she was exaggerating, but really, I didn't think we smelled that bad. I come from a long line of women whose nasal acuity is legendary, yet I couldn't smell my fellow crew members' body odor after a week without showers. After three weeks of her complaints, though, I started suspecting that some forgotten primate behavior was at work here. I hypothesized that living and working together for five days made us immune to each other's body odor. Since we ripened together in the sun and smoke, our smells became synchronized in some primitive way. I decided that I needed to take a more philosophical stance on cleanliness this week. With the smoke, hard labor, and lack of showers, who cares if I only had one change of clothes? Look at this motley crew. Did I really think it mattered? Maybe rule number one for succeeding in a man's world is that personal hygiene is optional.

I felt better after adopting this new outlook on cleanliness. Breakfast tasted wonderful. The bacon was crispy, the scrambled eggs fluffy, and Ben's toast was only slightly burned on one side. The coffee was hot and thick, and the orange juice sweet and cold.

Despite my positive outlook, by Thursday my philosophical pep talk seemed like a bunch of mumbo jumbo. I was filthy and smelly. I joked with the guys about having to lay my pants down after I took them off. My jeans were so thickly coated with dirt and grease that they almost stood up on their own.

Luckily, it was another beautiful fall day, and we'd be going home tomorrow. It was warming already as the sun climbed over the trees. The sky was deep blue, and there wasn't a single cloud. As usual, our conversations focused on the day's work. Bob explained that we were going to survey the deep canyon where our previous transects had stopped. We would climb over the edge of the canyon and place ourselves at fifteen meter intervals perpendicular to the canyon rim, and then traverse one side of the canyon and come back along the other side. Bob thought two transects on each side would probably do it.

"Make sure you take your time and check out all the alcoves for signs of fires, blackened roofs, or charcoal flecks in the soil. Look for rock art. Painted black lines are common in this area. I don't expect to find petroglyphs pecked into the rock. Any art should be painted on. Also, remember that seed caches are often in pots placed under boulders and small alcoves."

"I noticed a couple of places in the canyon with overhangs," added Ben. "I think we should find a couple of good rock shelters."

"The expert speaks," said Bob, starting the car.

Following a dirt road to the edge of the canyon, we arrived in fifteen minutes and looked over the rim. A hawk soared overhead and the air was still and clean. I noticed that the birds had finished their morning chorus and the heat was settling in. Indian summer, I thought—warm, clear, and perfect—lulling us into complacency before winter struck. Since I was an avid skier, I was looking forward to the winter, with its lengthening shadows and snowy winds, but I wondered what camping would be like in another month.

We lined up downslope, with Bob taking the spot just below the rim where it looked like most of the shelters would occur. Ben was next, then me, then Stan. We would return following Stan's transect, which should be easy given his uncanny sense of place. He seemed to remember exactly where his previous transect had gone and was able to follow it back with precision. Bob had recognized Stan's skill and kept putting him at the end of the line to take advantage of it.

I estimated that we would walk about a half a mile of canyon slope. Then I remembered that we had surveyed for two weeks, and we had covered a lot of terrain. On second thought, maybe it would be closer to a mile.

"Let's go!" yelled Bob.

I looked ahead and started walking. The slope was steep and dotted with boulders that had fallen down from the ever-widening rim. Most of the boulders on my transect were too small to hide rock shelters or caches. This isn't so bad, I thought, struggling through the middle of a manzanita thicket. At least the footing on the slope was firm, so I didn't have to worry about sliding downhill. Bob and Ben were moving slowly, taking time to check out several large overhangs. I gazed upslope and saw Bob disappear in a shallow rock shelter. Ben was looking under a huge boulder. Then I saw Bob emerge. He cupped his hands and yelled down to us.

"Hey, everyone! I found something. Come on up here so we can record it."

I hiked slowly up the steep slope to join the crew, thinking that it might be a long, slow day if we were going to find sites under every overhang. I fought my way through another thicket and pulled myself around a boulder. Right in front of me was a deep, narrow rock shelter. I felt the hair on my neck rise as the thought that this would make a good bear den popped into my head. I told myself that was ridiculous, especially since I know nothing about bears. Looking down at the floor of the shelter, instead of bear droppings I saw a large potsherd. It was the inside of a bowl that had been painted with bold black stripes. More pottery littered the floor, and then I spotted flakes of chert.

"Wow, this is amazing." I let my eyes adjust to the darkness while I removed my pack and set it down just outside the shelter.

"Ivy, come here," said Ben. He was way in the back of the shelter, looking at the ceiling. As I joined him, I saw several black parallel lines and two red ochre bighorn sheep painted on the wall. A stick figure man was throwing a spear aimed at the sheep.

"This is a different style than the stuff I usually see near home," Ben said. "If this site was in Monticello, I suspect that we'd be looking at a flute player."

Bob had finished examining the artifacts and had started filling out the site form. Stan, who had taken on the role of mapmaker, had spread a thirty-meter tape across the shelter's opening and was counting squares on the graph paper attached to the clipboard in his lap. I had been given the job of photographer, while Ben's main role was chief arrowhead finder. He was amazingly good at locating even the tiniest projectile point.

I removed one camera from my pack and asked Ben for the other, heavier one, which he had offered to carry for me. Two cameras are always used to record sites. That way, even if the photos from one camera don't come out, chances are the second set will be okay. The recording standards don't always require photos, but it's considered good science to record whatever you can. I waited until Stan finished with the tape measure and then moved it out of the way to take two pictures with each camera.

Bob was looking closely at the pottery, and I decided to break the silence and ask him a few questions. We had spoken so little that I almost felt like I should ask if it would be okay to ask a question or speak. I had become self-conscious about talking too much.

"What type of pottery is this, Bob?"

"Fremont," he said. "But the patterns are unusual. The decorations are poorly done, and the rims have these little balls of clay on them. See here?" He pointed to an oval-shaped bead of clay just beneath the rim of the vessel.

"I saw those in the Pint Creek pots. Jeff called them coffee bean appliqués, I think."

"You're right," said Bob, sounding impressed. "That's what they are, and we did have them in a some of the Pint Creek pottery. You never see these on Anasazi pots. The only other place that I've seen this type of decoration is in the Midwest."

"Oh, that's right," I said. "I remember this type of decoration on the pottery at the Wendorf site. I had totally forgotten about that." I thought back to my first dig in Illinois. It seemed like a long time ago, in a faraway place.

"You worked in Illinois?" asked Bob, looking at me with a little more respect.

"Yeah, I spent the summer after my last year of high school working at a Late Mississippian village, a satellite community of Cahokia."

"I've heard of it," Bob said. "I did some ceramic analysis for Northwestern University when they were working at the Foster site."

"Oh, I remember Foster. Wasn't it a stratified open site with 10,000 years of nearly continuous occupation?"

"That's the one." Bob returned to his form.

I put my cameras back and walked to the front of the shelter. Artifacts littered the apron of stained and mounded soil at the entrance. Some of the soil had eroded downslope, and I decided to take a closer look for artifacts. I scrambled around some boulders, scanning the ground. Flakes of gold, white, and red chert were scattered around, most of them small and probably the by-product of biface manufacture. Bifaces were used as cutting tools, knives, or projectile points, and sharpening the cutting surface made the bifaces thinner and smaller. In their final stages, they would be shaped into points for arrows or spears.

I kept walking back and forth across the slope, hoping to find a perfectly shaped projectile point—one of archaeology's great pleasures. Not only functional, some of them are beautiful works of art. Spotting one triangular flake, I stooped down for a closer look. Possibly, I thought. I picked it up. Bingo!

"I've got a point!" I called out. "It's a big one—a spear point."

Ben scurried down the slope for a closer look. I held the point in the palm of my hand. It was black obsidian, volcanic glass, as long as my palm and triangular shaped. The base was only slightly wider than the upper shoulder, where it began to narrow to a point. It had large notches on either side of the base.

"It looks Archaic to me," offered Ben. Taking it from my hand, he looked carefully at both sides. "I'm not sure what type it is. Let's ask Bob. We should also draw it."

Ben had the most talent for drawing and had become our official artist. Having good drawings was especially important because we generally didn't collect any artifacts. Instead we would draw them and put them back exactly where we'd found them.

After we finished recording the site, we returned to our designated places on the slope and continued surveying. Even though we recorded two more rock shelters and a pictograph of two handprints of red ochre ncxt to a wavy line, the day dragged.

By the time we were done, my legs ached and I was dirtier than I could ever remember being. Thank goodness tomorrow was our last day. We would finish the canyon in the morning and drive home around lunchtime.

Back at camp I longed to wash up a little and put on clean clothes. Oh well, there were no clean clothes, so what was the point? We all chipped in to fix dinner: green beans in a can, pork chops, and garlic bread cooked in tin foil over the fire. It smelled good. My stomach growled, and I realized I was very hungry for a change. The wind had picked up, and the flames roared. We drank the last of the beer and sat around the fire to eat. Perhaps I would ask Bob about his falling out with Johnson. But how should I bring it up? What the hell, why not just ask him straight out?

"So, Bob, I heard at field school that you and Johnson didn't agree on the cultural affiliation of the sites at Pint Creek. Penny got into an argument with Johnson toward the end of field school over the same topic."

Bob glanced at me and then stared into the coals of our hot fire. "I heard that you guys found a possible kiva."

"That's what Penny thought, which made her believe the site was Kayenta. Johnson said it was a Fremont kiva."

"He's so full of shit." Bob shook his head. "The guy just doesn't get it. The sherds at that site were 70 percent Kayenta. There may have been an earlier Fremont component, but the masonry structures were built by Puebloan folks from the Kayenta branch." Bob's lips weren't moving again, and I watched in fascination.

"You know," he said, "I've thought about this a lot, and I just don't understand why he has to believe that only the Fremont lived in Pint Creek. It's right on the border of the two culture areas, and it makes perfect sense that there were two different occupations. I just don't get it, but I refuse to be bullied by Dr. Johnson. To hell with him, anyway. I'm going to another graduate program."

"I heard that you were going to transfer to some school in Canada?"

"Yeah, I start at the University of Toronto in the fall. I got a graduate assistantship. I guess I'll work for Lockyear until I leave."

Silence returned. I finally got up and cleaned my dishes. There was just my plate and silverware. We cooked everything in cans, tin foil, or directly on the grill, and usually cleaned the breakfast dishes when we first got back to camp. The wind was really howling now, and it was getting cold. A few clouds covered the waning moon, and I suddenly felt bone tired.

"I guess that's it for me, guys. See you in the morning."

I heard them talk a little longer around the fire and then fell asleep. The wind continued most of the night. It whipped my tent around, and the loud flapping woke me several times during the night. It had finally quieted down at dawn when I heard Bob yelling to everyone to rise and shine. Then I heard some swearing and laughter. I pulled on my filthy jeans and headed out to see what was going on.

Ben and Bob were examining our camp chairs. They were aluminum with plastic woven netting, and the seats of two of them were melted blobs of blackened plastic.

"What happened to the chairs?" I asked.

"We left them standing and the wind must have blown them into the coals." Bob examined a third chair and it seemed okay. He picked up the fourth. It was still partially in the fire pit and barely recognizable. "Guess this one is a total loss. At least it's our last day and we can replace them next week. I don't think they're very expensive."

"Guess we should close them up next time and lay them on the ground," offered Ben, who had thrown his down and returned to making coffee.

"At least it isn't windy today," I said. "I slept pretty badly. How did you guys do?"

Ben shrugged, Stan looked at me and said nothing, and Bob was still checking out the charred ruins that were once our chairs. Looks like another day in Paradise, I thought.

A Feeling of Place

"Got a site here!" yelled Ben.

He sounded far away. When we had arrived at our new survey area about an hour ago, I'd suspected that we'd find lots of rock shelters and rock art. Most of our survey area was tucked inside a deep canyon, which would have been attractive to the Puebloan farmers who inhabited the region between AD 300 and 1200.

It was a cool, sunny fall day, and we were on our first transect of the week. I was struggling down a steep and slippery slope; one missed step and I would fall forty feet. Playing it safe, I inched down the slickrock on my butt with my knees bent and my Vibram-soled boots wedged firmly into the sandstone to keep from slipping. Moving one foot, then the other, I finished the descent and headed in the general direction of Ben's voice. The transect ended in a narrow canyon that had been carved by a small creek running through the middle. The water had created an oasis of cottonwood trees and bright green patches of horsetail and watercress.

"Where is everyone?" I yelled.

"Over here."

Rounding a corner I saw the crew in a narrow alcove on the edge of a side canyon. Stan, who had been promoted to supervisor, and Ben were examining a small masonry room tucked in the back of the alcove.

Rose, our new crew member, was petting her dog, Max. Rose was a sheepherder by trade, and Stan had told us that she'd spent the last summer, alone, herding three hundred sheep in the Boulder Mountains. Since many of ASC's employees had returned to school for the fall semester, Dr. Lockyear was desperate for people to work in the field. He had decided to hire Rose because she was used to living and working outdoors. She didn't have any formal training in archaeology, but she knew how to find arrowheads and pottery. On Monday we had taught her the basics of surveying, and today was her first day on the job.

I patted Max and was rewarded with a fierce tail wag. He appeared to be a golden retriever/blue heeler mix. Rose said he was an excellent sheep dog and came from a long line of herders.

The masonry structure, made out of mud and sandstone slabs, was about three feet high and four feet wide. There was no roof; presumably it had collapsed long ago. The room was too small to live in. Often small structures like this were perched on narrow ledges in a canyon wall and could be reached only with a ladder. I circled the alcove, looking for artifacts, but the soil was thin and eroded, and I didn't see any. Stan had taken out his notebook, and Ben, who had been assigned the task of taking photos, was removing the cameras from his pack. I sat down to begin sketching a map of the site.

"Did anyone see anything else?" I wanted to make sure that I recorded everything on the map.

"Nah, the only other thing I saw was a faded pictograph on the rear wall," answered Ben.

"Yeah, that's all I saw too." Stan said, returning to his notes.

"I must have missed that."

I headed to the rear of the shelter to figure out why I hadn't seen the rock art. Scanning the wall behind the room, I noticed something inside.

"Wow! Corn cobs!" The floor of the room was covered with a thick layer of cobs, indicating that the owners had never come back to recover the stored food. After the sealed opening had fallen away, the rodents had feasted on the forgotten corn, leaving only the cobs. As I looked over the wall above the door, I noticed a set of fingerprints. They looked exactly my size. I put my hand into the imprint and felt chills down my spine.

"My fingers fit perfectly." No one heard me. They were busy with their assigned tasks, and Rose was heading to the wash with Max.

Despite the hundreds of years that had passed since the room had been made, I felt a connection. It probably hadn't taken too long to build. Sandstone slabs were everywhere—I'd walked over several in the wash bottom—and mud could quickly be gathered from the creek. My thoughts drifted, and I imagined a small family gathering the ripened corn that they'd planted months earlier along the creek. The older family members, with knowledge of food storage, would have overseen the masonry room's construction. First a layer of thick wet mud would have been placed on the floor of the alcove to set the first sandstone slab, with successive layers built to form a wall.

After the harvest, the family would have feasted. What they couldn't eat, they would have sealed away in the room to see them through the lean spring months. After the corn was safely stored, the family probably traveled north, following the creek to their fall camp in the mountains. Deer would have been plentiful in the higher elevations, and the pinyon juniper forests would have provided abundant fuel for warming and cooking fires during the cold winter months. The family likely built a winter home, partially underground, for warmth. While the men focused on hunting, the women would have collected and stored pine nuts. Nuts and meat would have sustained the family through the winter, and in the early spring they would have headed back to the canyon to eat the stored corn and plant once again.

"Ivy! Did you hear me?" Stan yelled.

"What?" I was jolted back to the present.

Stan had walked over to where I was sitting. He was looking down at me, apparently amused.

"Where were you, Ivy? I have been trying to get your attention for five minutes."

"I guess I didn't hear you."

Stan's eyes twinkled. "Guess your mind was somewhere else. Now that I have your attention, would you please put the creek on your sketch map?"

"No problem." I headed over to a smooth spot on the back wall of the shelter. Yes, the rock art was there: two faded handprints in red ochre at about eye level. They looked like my size too. I placed my hand over one of the prints. Another perfect fit. They could have been my own, which gave me a creepy sensation of déjà vu.

I retrieved my clipboard and paced the opening of the shelter. It was six meters wide. I started drawing: first the shelter outline, then the storage room. I drew the slabs and mortar as best as I could. I also made a small sketch of the pictograph and showed its location on my map. I finished just as Stan put his clipboard down. Ben and Rose were throwing sticks for

Max down by the creek. Where did they get the energy to play? It was only 9 a.m. and I already felt like I'd put in a full day's work.

We spent the rest of the day surveying the canyon bottom. We found two other shelters, both with masonry habitation rooms and dense scatters of pottery and flakes. Rose became more enthusiastic about archaeology after she found her first site, a small knoll covered with artifacts. A shallow depression in the center hinted that a pithouse was buried there.

On our last transect of the day, everyone seemed to be lost in their thoughts, or maybe just tired. My legs ached from climbing in and out of the canyon.

"Okay, that's it for this survey area," said Stan. "Let's take a break and then hike out."

We assembled at the other end of the canyon, where we had started, by the first rock shelter. Walking past it again, I could almost feel it drawing me back in. This is really weird, I thought. Although I'd never been in the canyon before, I could swear that I knew this place.

"This is a good spot for a break." Stan took off his pack and sat down. He picked a grass stem and stuck it in his mouth.

Ben flopped down like a chicken with no bones. He was lying on his back, spread eagle, staring at the deep blue sky. I walked slightly past Ben and lay down too. Rose was nowhere to be found. She must have gone off to find "the ladies room." When breaks were announced, people would wander off to find a private spot to attend to their business. After six months of living in primitive campgrounds, I had learned to pee anywhere. In fact, I'd gotten so good at it that I no longer peed on my pants or shoes. I had also gotten over the need for toilet paper. Number two, however, was a different matter. For one thing, squatting was awkward, and flies would immediately appear, even landing on your butt. My biggest problem, though, was that it just never seemed private enough. Anyone could appear around the corner and catch you with your pants around your ankles and your ass hanging in the breeze. If we were staying in a campground, I usually tried to hold it until we got back at the end of the day. Even a smelly, fly-infested outhouse was better than nothing.

Lying on the ground, I had that great feeling of being tired but happy. The earth was cool and soft, and the slight breeze made me glad I had worn my flannel shirt. As usual no one spoke. I thought Rose might help conversation along, but in the two days she had been with us, it seemed that she was even less interested in talking than the guys. She was a sheepherder after all, and they were known to be loners. What was I thinking?

As I stared at the puffy white clouds and deep blue sky, my thoughts returned to the masonry structure. I imagined the eldest daughter, her mother, and grandmother finishing the walls and looking it over, satisfied that their corn would be safe and dry until spring. The rest of the family would have picked the ripened corn and squash in the narrow fields, emptying their baskets into two separate piles. Their summer home would have been a simple brush shelter made of willow branches joined at the top to form a round frame and then covered with brush and reeds. Such shelters let the breeze in, but keep the rain out during the summer thunderstorms. After roasting the corn, they would have sealed it in the masonry room, roofing it with poles, brush, and mud. The mud covering would have kept even the most diligent rodents out, and the corn would have stayed dry and fresh for months, even years.

Movement to my left brought me out of my daydream. Ben was returning his water bottle to his pack, and Rose was walking toward us. Stan had already reached the steep sandstone slope, which was as void of vegetation as Stan's head was of hair, and the only passable route back to the vehicle.

I scrambled out of the canyon and onto the slickrock. Ben followed, with Rose close behind him. As an expert skier I was no stranger to steep slopes, but the smooth sandstone, which is appropriately called slickrock, made me nervous. Near the top, where the slope was very steep, one slip could mean the end. Once you fell and started rolling, you'd fall hundreds of feet to the bottom. Since no one else seemed particularly concerned, I kept my fears to myself. Ben was bounding straight up. He seemed completely oblivious of the danger, and Max raced ahead to join him. Rose and I took our time picking separate routes.

Halfway up I found a deep crack where I could wedge one foot for a better grip. I climbed and climbed, moving one foot at a time. Near the top, I felt light-headed with vertigo and fatigue, so I sat backward on the rock and inched my way up on my butt, my Vibram soles pressed firmly on the rock. I was almost at the top when I saw a huge bird soaring overhead. I stopped and stared, thinking it must be an eagle. It flew higher and higher in a wide spiral.

Once again I felt myself traveling back in time. When the family was ready to leave their summer home for their winter camp, other families would have joined them to collect pine nuts and hunt the fattened deer. I felt a deep sense of peace and belonging.

"Ivy!" yelled Stan. "Are you okay?"

"I'm fine, just a little slow." The eagle soared north, off to the Boulder Mountains. I continued my slow, careful ascent. As the slope leveled, I was able to stand up. Everyone was staring at me, and Max headed over to give me a sniff.

"What is it with you today, Ivy? It's almost like you're somewhere else." Stan looked concerned.

"Yeah, where have you been?" Ben added.

"I know this is weird, but I keep having this strange feeling that I've been here before. I can almost see the people who made the storage rooms. It's kind of creepy."

Everyone looked at me funny. Ben joked that maybe I needed to drink more water. I felt tired and stupid. Thank goodness it was too late in the day to begin surveying the next area. The days were getting shorter, and so were our workdays. With the sun low on the horizon, the light just wasn't bright enough to see artifacts early or late in the day.

We climbed into the Blazer, and Stan drove the narrow road to our latest campsite.

"What's for dinner, Rose?"

Rose had offered to cook dinner in Dutch ovens, something every cowboy, sheepherder, hunter, and serious camper knows about. They're actually heavy cast-iron pots, and the larger models have short, stubby legs so they can be set above the hot coals. When coals are shoveled onto the flat lid, the heat from above and below turns the pot into an oven. A talented cook can bake anything in it, but my efforts had twice met with failure. A few months ago I had attempted to make biscuits. They were burned on the bottom and gooey on top. My second attempt, making corn bread, wasn't much better. It seemed that Dutch oven cooking was as much an art as a skill.

"How about beef stew and fresh bread?"

"That sounds great," I said, already imagining the wonderful aromas. "I'll help you. I haven't had much luck with Dutch oven cooking."

"You can wash and cut the vegetables. The meat is already cut. I'll mix and knead the bread. It'll take a few hours for it all to cook, but it should be worth the wait." Conversation over. Rose stared out the window again.

This week we were camped just south of Boulder, Utah, in a deep sandstone canyon called Half Creek. Just below our camping spot Half Creek joined the Escalante River, one of the main tributaries of the Colorado River. It cuts a wide swath through some of the most remote and beautiful terrain in Utah, if not the country.

I looked out the window. There was nothing but air on both sides of the paved road. Stan was a careful driver, but the road was treacherous, running down the center of a narrow ridge. A wrong turn off this road would send you eight hundred feet straight down to the canyon floor.

We were staying in a Land Management Agency campground complete with picnic tables and outhouses. There were no showers or running water, but just having a toilet seat seemed like a luxury. Because it was early November, we had the campground pretty much to ourselves. Half Creek was one of the most beautiful places that I'd ever seen. It was in the bottom of a deep canyon, with individual campsites hugging both sides of the clear, shallow stream. Such permanent streams are a rarity in southern Utah. When they do occur, they create a lush ribbon of vegetation and habitat for wildlife. The canyons were also a magnet for prehistoric people, and typically they're loaded with ruins and rock art. Although the leaves had fallen from the cottonwood trees, the canyon bottom was still very green, contrasting with the sandstone's countless hues of red, from deep red to pale pink and every imaginable shade in between.

This week I was sharing a tent with Rose and Max, and both had proven to be good tent mates. Rose looked to be in her late twenties. Tall and lanky, she kept her auburn hair in a single braid that fell almost to her waist. Her plain face was covered with freckles, and her nose was thick and crooked. Her straight, gleaming teeth and generous smile were her best features. She reminded me of the biker chicks I'd seen perched on the back of Harleys behind their muscle-bound boyfriends. Her eyes sparkled with intelligence, but I suspected that her education had ended with high school.

Max stuck his cold, wet nose under my hand, and I rubbed his neck to make him quit. He panted and wagged his tail, recognizing that we were back at camp.

"Stan," I asked, "do you have any idea how long this new project is going to continue? And what kind of project it is?"

Stan took the keys out of the ignition, cracked his door, and turned around to look at me in the back seat. He spoke with his usual slow southern drawl.

"The word from Dr. Lockyear is that this project is just like the Utah Coal project. I think he just barely won the contract, and we have about two hundred quarter sections to survey. I guess we'll be working into the new year."

"How many crews are working? Do you know?"

"Well, let's see. There's Russell's crew, Justin's, Bob's, and then me. That makes four. If we all average five quarter sections per week, that means we can do twenty all told. At that rate it will take us a while. The travel time to get down here is a killer. Dr. Locklear should let us work ten days and then stay home for four. That's what we always did at the other companies I've worked for. I guess he doesn't want people to miss church."

As soon as we'd all retrieved our gear from the Blazer, we headed for our tents. Hiking boots were replaced with sneakers or sandals, and hats and daypacks were put away. But Rose skipped this step. Instead she immediately built a fire using juniper logs and a splash of Coleman fuel to kick-start the process. After washing her hands, she poured flour, yeast, salt, and something from a jar into a large plastic bowl. She mixed it with a wooden spoon and then kneaded the white mass on a piece of wax paper. After ten minutes of kneading, she returned the bread to the bowl and covered it with the wax paper.

"Do you want me to cut up the vegetables now?" I asked.

"Sure, the bread is mixed and rising. I'll brown the meat in the Dutch oven. We should have everything ready to go in no time."

Rose stood the Dutch oven on the edge of the fire and dropped in two packages of stew meat. She stirred as it sizzled and sputtered until it was brown and the fat had turned crispy. Rose then added the onions and cooked them until they were golden. In the meantime, I finished cutting up the carrots, potatoes, turnips, and squash and carried them over to Rose. She mixed some flour in with the meat and onions, and then poured wine liberally over the mix before motioning for me to add the vegetables. She poured in enough water to cover everything and then stirred the mixture again. After adding salt and pepper, she put on the heavy lid.

"Okay, it's ready for the fire," Rose announced with pride.

"It smells great already. How long does it cook?"

"About two hours should do it."

Rose put the delicious mix over the coals, and using a small shovel, she scooped some of the glowing coals from the fire and put them in a pile before shoveling them onto the lid. She did the same with the second oven, filled with bread dough.

"There. Now we wait. I guess I'll go clean up and take a short rest." Rose walked to our tent with Max in tow.

While the food cooked, we sat around the fire and relaxed with a few beers. The smell of baking bread made my mouth water. Conversation was thin, but Ben was unusually talkative.

"Ben, tell the story of your hike when we were stranded. It was my first week on the job."

"Well, okay. So the Blazer was stuck—we had a flat tire and no spare. The only way we were going to get out of there was if we walked twenty miles to the nearest well-traveled road. Jim and I packed up as much water as we could hold and started hiking during the hottest part of the day." Ben got up and fished another beer from the cooler. He sat back down, pulled the pop-top, and took a long gulp.

While Ben enjoyed his beer, I added my side of the story. "I was left at the vehicle with our other crew member, Marie."

"So," Ben continued, "we walked and walked. Like the tortoise, slow and steady. Late in the afternoon it clouded up and the thunderheads got real mean. When we could smell rain, we searched for a shelter where we could rest and hole up until the storm passed." Ben took another long swig and shifted in his chair.

"The only place we could find was a shallow overhang on the edge of a deep gorge. We huddled under the shelter, drank water, and ate some oranges and raisins. The rain came down in buckets, cats and dogs. Off in the distance we heard what sounded like a freight train. I knew it was a flash flood, but Jim had never experienced one. We took a few minutes to make sure we were out of the way if the flood came down the canyon below us. When we looked over the edge, we saw trickles of water flowing down the canyon walls and collecting in the canyon bottom. The sound grew louder and louder. I can't explain it other than to say it is one of the loudest and scariest things you will ever hear. When we looked up the canyon, we saw a wall of red water churning with rocks and trees racing down the canyon. It must have been at least twenty feet high. We were way above it and could see huge boulders and trees rolled along like Tinkertoys. The flood lasted about an hour. Then it stopped, just as suddenly as it came. We decided to hike until we found a better shelter for the night."

Ben stopped, guzzled some more beer, and watched Rose checking the stew. She removed the cover, stirred for a minute, and then put the oven back on the fire and added more coals.

"I guess we made it about ten miles until it was way too dark to see where we were going. We spent the night in another rock shelter. It had a full-sized painting of a warrior on the back wall. You know, the Fremont guy, complete with headdress, shield, and bow.

"The night was pretty uneventful except Jim kept talking in his sleep about a kachina trying to suffocate him. When I told him in the morning that he'd kept me awake, he said he had a dream that a man dressed like the guy in the painting had tried to choke him. He had spoken to Jim in a language that sounded Indian. Jim said the dream seemed very real—and creepy with a capital C. He was tired and grumpy the whole next day."

Ben ran his fingers through his hair and took another swig. He shook his head.

"Anyway, we woke up at the first light, had a few more granola bars, and then hit the road. We got another five miles or so before a rancher picked us up. He gave us a ride to town after we helped him check on his cattle. That's it. End of story. We got back to the other crews camped at Green River and told everyone what happened. The field director, Allen, drove us back to rescue the girls and get the vehicle. Ivy, why don't you tell them about your part? You know, the dead battery and Allen's long hike."

"It wasn't me," I protested. "The battery was real worn down after all those attempts to get unstuck."

"That isn't what I hear," teased Ben. "I hear you killed it listening to the radio."

"Well, it's possible. I wonder if Allen will ever let me live that down. I've already taken a lot of teasing for it."

Rose got out of her chair to check the bread. She pronounced it done and moved it off the coals. The stew cooked for another hour. Dinner was every bit as delicious as Rose had promised, and the home-cooked meal rejuvenated our spirits. After dinner we watched the fire, its coals hot and red. It was cold now in the canyon, and the fire felt good.

"Looks like the moon is going to be full," said Ben, pointing to a giant spot of light peeking above the canyon wall.

We stared, transfixed, watching as the full moon rose over the rim of the canyon. The light poured over the steep walls, falling like a dream, spreading deep into the canyon bottom, like Ben's flash flood. The light streamed into the canyon, filling it with light and shadow. We sat silently, mesmerized, unable to break the spell of beauty. As the huge Harvest Moon continued to rise, the flood of light turned the canyon walls a thousand shades of gray. Tired, well fed, and filled with the wonder and beauty of nature, we shuffled off, one by one, to our tents.

Morning came too early. Stan usually woke first and did the human alarm thing. Sometimes it was a fake bugle call. Today it was a simple "GET UP you lazy bums!" I was swaddled in my down mummy bag and covered with a second, unzipped bag. It was freezing, and to conserve heat I'd pulled the drawstring around the top of my bag so that only my nose stuck out. I loosened the drawstring a little so I could see out. My breath was smoke in the still freezing air. Max jumped up and ran out of the tent. Rose was sitting up on her cot, half in and half out of her bag. She was gathering up her warm clothes and changing into them as best she could without leaving the lingering warmth of her sleeping bag.

I could hear Stan building a fire. Since our water was frozen in the morning, we had started making coffee the night before. That way we just put the frozen pot right onto the Coleman stove burner and then turned it on, full speed ahead. Rose finished dressing and grabbed a plastic container of baby butt wipes. As she pulled one out to wash her face and hands, she saw me watching her through my tiny peephole.

"Ivy, you really should try these wipes. They're loaded with lanolin, and they not only get you clean, but they help with the desert dry skin problem."

"Okay, I'll try one. The water is frozen so I can't wash anyway. I hope Stan melts some so that we can at least brush our teeth." I stuck my head completely out of my bag. "Damn, it's cold. Why do I do this?"

Rose offered me the wipes. "Here you go."

I grabbed one triangle of wipe but got two. They did feel good on my dirty face and hands. I looked at the wipe after I'd finished. "Wow, I can't believe how dirty I am. Guess I've kind of gotten out of the habit of washing."

"Feel free to use the wipes any time you'd like," said Rose as she slipped out of the tent.

I grabbed two more wipes and washed my hands and face again. Boy, did that ever feel good. My coat had doubled as a pillow, so I grabbed it and put it on. After it had warmed up, I got out of my sleeping bag and changed the lower half of my body: long johns off, clean underwear on. Jeans, already pretty dirty, clean socks, boots. I would change my upper half just before we left camp.

I headed over to the coffee pot, which was boiling away.

"Is it ready, Stan?"

"Give it a few more minutes."

Stan was standing near the fire with his backside toward the flames. Ben sat in his chair, fishing the last bits of oatmeal out of a disposable cereal bowl. He threw the bowl in the fire and retrieved his coffee cup. I did likewise. Rose finished feeding Max and grabbed a frying pan.

"Anyone want bacon and eggs?"

"Yes!" we all answered, almost in unison.

"Can I help?" I asked. Rose was putting bacon in a cast-iron frying pan that I guessed was hers because I didn't remember seeing one like it before.

"Why don't you crack the eggs into this bowl?" asked Rose, pointing to a pan that I guess you could call a bowl. We cooked in silence. The incredible aroma of bacon filled the air, and then Rose threw in the scrambled eggs, covering them with a layer of processed cheese slices and some salt and pepper. Over this mix she floated slices of bread. She then set the pan on the stove over a low flame and covered it with tin foil. Heading to the fire with her coffee cup, she said, "It should be ready in about fifteen minutes."

Ben was playing with the fire, and I sat and stared. Smoke was pouring out of the fire pit and wafting over me. I imagined that it had already filled my baby-wipe clean pores with new bits of crud. I looked over at Stan, who was sitting at the picnic table covered with maps and papers. This was part of his routine for planning our route each day. Curious about where we would work next, I walked over to take a look.

"So where are we surveying today?"

Stan ran his fingers over his bald scalp. "That's what I'm trying to figure out." He pointed to a square that had been drawn onto a USGS map.

"This is our area, but I don't see any roads nearby. It looks like we'll have to hike in a mile or so."

"Sounds like yesterday." I looked at the map and noticed that the contour lines both inside and outside the square were very close together. "That looks steep."

"Yeah, it'll be a tough one," Stan admitted. "It's just upstream from yesterday's survey. Actually, it should look a lot like the canyon we surveyed."

"Breakfast is ready!" called Rose.

We hit the road after our second great meal of the session. I wondered, hopefully, if Rose would keep cooking as long as we did the dishes.

The day's survey was long and hard. We hiked over a mile down a side canyon just to reach our starting point. The hike in wasn't nearly as dangerous as yesterday's, but the long, uphill climb to get back to the Blazer at the end of the day was a death march. A hard hike in the morning usually activates the endorphins and gives me a rush of euphoria, but by the end of the day my endorphins stop kicking in. Perhaps these natural painkillers were just plain worn out, like the rest of me. When I'm tired and the endorphins aren't helping me out, a hard hike at day's end usually discourages me.

Today I was not only worn out, but everyone else was way ahead of me and I could no longer see them. Usually someone would walk with me, but today I'd been abandoned. I guess they'd figured I wouldn't get lost since their tracks in the sand were obvious, but as I trudged along the canyon bottom, alone, I was annoyed that they'd left me behind.

Annoyance had turned to anger by the time I got back to the Blazer. As I walked up, the three of them were talking and laughing, and it made me even madder that they were having fun without me. Would it have killed them to slow down and wait for me along the trail? No matter how slow I am, they shouldn't have left me that far behind.

"Stan, what's the idea of not waiting for me?"

"Relax, Ivy. You were fine. I knew where you were."

"Well, what if I'd had a bimbo moment and gotten lost?"

Ben snickered, and I turned and glared at him with my best death-ray look. "Are you saying I AM a bimbo?"

"No! Not only no, but hell no!" Ben said, looking sheepish as he walked over to fill his water bottle.

I looked back at Stan, death-ray beams still on high. "I don't think it's safe to leave a crew member behind like that." Angry and tired, I almost started crying.

Seeing how upset I was, Stan decided to concede. "Okay. I won't let it happen again."

He fiddled with his boots to avoid looking at me, and I got into the back seat. Not only was I tired, mad, and frustrated, but even worse, I felt like the odd man out. Everyone else seemed to have a bond that I just didn't understand.

I really could have gotten lost, I thought. What if the wind had come up and their tracks had disappeared? What if I'd gotten disoriented and starting hiking the wrong way? What if I'd fallen and hurt myself? And then I asked myself the most important question of all: Why was I doing this? I loved the archaeology part, but most of the time surveying was just plain boring, with a capital B.

I looked out the window, wondering why no one else was getting into the vehicle. Ben was off somewhere, probably using the facilities, and Stan was flirting with Rose. I took my boots off and covered my eyes, feeling tired and sad. The next thing I knew, I was waking from a nap and we were back at camp. Rose was busy around the fire, and Ben had assumed "the position"—that is, he was sitting in his chair and drinking beer.

I got out of the Blazer and headed for the tent. I was still mad at everyone and intended to spend the night alone. I lit the Coleman lantern and lay down on my cot. It was already cooling off so I put on my coat. Never in my life could I remember feeling this alone. In high school I had been one of the popular (if not slightly mean) girls. In college I was the cute coed with the cool boyfriend, an excellent skier and a straight "A" student. For some reason I hadn't been popular at field school, but at least I'd had Randy and then Tom to keep me company.

The loneliness was really getting to me. I missed my family, who were always talking and laughing. We never ran out of things to discuss or plots to hatch. As my sisters had grown older and gone off to college, the house had become quieter, but I'd filled the empty times with lots of friends. I'd always been outgoing and never without companionship. But fieldwork forced me to associate day in and day out with people I normally wouldn't have chosen to spend time with. We had little in common, and in truth, I didn't feel like any of these people cared a rat's ass about me. I hid out in my tent, stewing and feeling sorry for myself. I stayed up for a couple hours, thinking and reading, then gagged down a few granola bars, brushed my teeth, and went to sleep.

My first thought when I woke up was that it was Thursday, meaning only one more day of surveying before I'd be back in my apartment with running water and electricity. I could meet my friends at a bar, go to a movie, maybe even call Tom to see what he was doing.

The day started out like all the others until I learned that everyone had walked in the moonlight to a waterfall without me. Hearing that, I became even more sullen and withdrawn.

We managed to survey two units that were close to the road, and I felt my mood improving slightly until we found a spectacular rock shelter that had been severely damaged by pothunters. It was ruined, violated; the secrets it could have revealed about prehistory were gone forever. Holes as deep as I was tall dotted the thick midden. Only a small area near the back of the shelter remained undisturbed. After we found a cache of tools, including a shovel and screen, we decided the pothunters probably returned to the site often and didn't want to be caught near the road with the tools of their trade. Ben had a guilty look, but swore it wasn't him. We were far from his former pot-hunting territory in San Juan County. By the end of the day I felt more lonely and disgusted than ever—with everything.

Despite my foul mood, I tried my best to be social that night. I figured it would just make everything worse if I kept to myself. Rose cooked an excellent chicken and rice casserole, and I helped as much as possible. Stan had obviously developed a crush on Rose and beamed whenever he talked to her. I figured it was either love, lust, or just his stomach doing the thinking. Seeing them having so much fun together made me feel even worse, but rather than wallow in self-pity, I focused my thoughts on how nice it would be to get home the next day.

As I lay in bed, waiting for my cold sleeping bag to warm up, I debated whether I could continue working in the field. It was October, and I'd been doing fieldwork since May. I had survived gnats, heat, allergies, filth, and hard labor, but the loneliness was pushing me over the edge. I had nothing in common with these people, and they didn't even seem to like me very much. As I drifted off to sleep, I decided that perhaps fieldwork wasn't for me after all. I just wasn't tough enough. Why torture myself endlessly? Maybe Dr. Johnson was right. I just wasn't cut out for archaeology.

Whenever I run a high fever, I have a recurring dream that I am being crushed under a heavy sheet of plywood piled with rocks—so many that I have trouble breathing. I didn't feel like I had a fever, but that night I had a similar dream, with one major difference: I was that girl who made the storage structure, and I was being crushed under rockfall. Somehow the roof of the shelter had collapsed, burying me beneath boulders and debris. Just as I was giving up, I was approached by a man-spirit decorated with body paint and wearing a headdress adorned with the horns of a bighorn sheep.

"You need to keep trying," he said. "Your journey is just beginning. Don't give up. Move your arms and legs. The rocks will fall away. Don't let them crush you. Fight."

As I struggled in my dream to free myself, I woke up. My main sleeping bag was all twisted, and the second one had fallen off. Despite the freezing cold, I was sweaty and alert. I fell back asleep without giving the dream much thought, but I realized the next morning that I wasn't ready to give up on archaeology just yet.

Are We Having Fun Yet?

The alarm jarred me awake. I opened one eye, looked at the time, and then snuggled deeper into Tom's embrace. I had called him when I'd gotten home on Friday, and he'd wanted to spend the weekend with me. I have no idea what he told his family. We had gotten in the habit of touching when we slept together, even if it was just his finger against my arm, or my foot pressed against his leg.

It was Monday morning, and I was dreading spending another week in the middle of nowhere with no boyfriend, no running water, no heat, no television, and probably no toilets. Tom and I had spent a perfect weekend together. Friday night, after my shower and an hour-long soak in the tub, we'd watched movies and made love. Saturday we drove up Little Cottonwood Canyon and hiked the trails at Snowbird. Sunday we had brunch with friends and a quiet afternoon at home together. That evening we cooked dinner, sipped wine, and went to bed early.

I realized it was getting harder and harder to pack every Sunday night and face leaving Monday morning. I really needed a break from camping. I didn't know how much longer I could stand it. I planted a wet kiss on Tom's neck.

"Tom, wake up."

Nothing, no movement, no moan, no protest.

I shook him lightly and whispered in his ear. "Remember last night? We have just enough time to do that again."

He rolled over and smiled. Parts of him were more awake than others, lending further proof to my theory that the little brain has a mind of its own. He grabbed me, and I temporarily forgot about camping—and everything else.

With a smile back on my face, I looked over at the clock. "We need to leave in fifteen minutes. I can be dressed in five and I'm already packed. Get up, Tom. It takes you longer."

We quickly dressed, and I grabbed a banana for breakfast, but there was no time for coffee. Tom threw something on and helped carry my stuff to his old, beat-up Volkswagen Bug. We roared off, making it to the meeting place with only a minute to spare. Still not fully awake, Tom kissed me and promised to pick me up on Friday. As he drove off, I felt the loneliness descend on me again.

I looked up and saw Stan, always a blur of military green. He motioned me to come over.

"Ivy, Dr. Lockyear wants you on Russell's crew this week. They lost one of their technicians, and we decided that my crew could get by with three people. Is that okay?"

It took me a minute to digest the news. "I don't know. I've never met Russell. Is he here yet? I suppose it's okay, though. I've been doing this so long that I guess it doesn't really matter which crew I'm on."

"My, aren't we gloom and doom today." Stan raised one eyebrow and looked at me more closely. "Bad weekend?"

"Actually it was a fine weekend."

Stan scanned the group. "I don't see Russell, but you can't miss him. He's tall and dark, with a short beard. I'm pretty sure he's a JSU student, but he doesn't look like one."

Stan touched my shoulder and looked closely at me. "Cheer up, Ivy. Change isn't always a bad thing."

Somehow, though, I knew that in this case he was wrong. I scanned the crowd for Russell and saw a guy that matched his description talking to a tall, skinny, clean-cut Mormon missionary type. He reminded me of a panther, with a cat's movement, and he was staring at one of the women like she was prey. His brooding eyes were deep set and partially concealed under bushy eyebrows and heavy lids. He had jet black hair, which was just a little too long for a Mormon elder, and he towered over me. He was at least 6'6".

I walked over to introduce myself, but Russell just mumbled hi before turning away and walking to our vehicle. Great, I thought. Another guy who's language-challenged. I groaned as I hauled my stuff over, threw in my bags, and climbed into the vehicle.

Our crew included a short, middle-aged guy named Tim and another blond returned Mormon missionary, Mitchell, who looked like all the other missionaries I'd ever met. His handshake pretty much summed him up: limp and sweaty. Imagine the Pillsbury Dough Boy, remove about thirty pounds, add a frayed shirt and worn out pants from a missionary suit, and voilá, you have Mitchell: all smiles and enthusiasm, but soft through and through. Tim was a JSU friend of Dr. Lockyear's who had recently lost his job and needed work. He had some background in archaeology, but I never figured out the details of his prior experience.

My gut was telling me that this could be bad. The good news was that I would have a tent to myself, and no one knew anything about my religious affiliation. Usually I could thwart conversion lectures by telling missionaries I was Jewish. Apparently Jews had such a low conversion rate that young missionaries were told to avoid them. One of my Jewish friends in Salt Lake City had let me in on this secret, and it had saved me countless knocks on my door. I suspected that I was listed in a church file somewhere as officially Jewish. Was I going to go to hell for that? I reminded myself not to talk about religion at all since I know very little about Judaism.

I slept through most of the drive, only waking up when we stopped to shop. We were going to stay in a state park campground—with flush toilets and flowing water—in the center of Escalante. Since all of the crews except Stan's were together in the same campground, I ended up sharing a tent after all, with a woman named Maureen. Also Mormon, she hadn't found anyone to marry her yet, so she'd gone on a mission and then gone back to school. I wasn't sure why she'd picked archaeology. Maureen was freckled everywhere. She was tall and robust, and very masculine. I wondered if she was gay. If so, she probably didn't know it, or perhaps she was still struggling to figure that out herself. After a brief conversation, I decided we had absolutely nothing in common.

Somehow, even after driving half the day and setting up camp, we managed to survey two-thirds of a unit the first afternoon. Since our survey area was located on the edge of town, we didn't have far to drive. We worked until it was too dark to see flakes.

The next day we finished that unit and then surveyed another one nearby. We didn't find sites in either. The guys were fast walkers, so once again I had to move pretty fast to keep up. In fact, I almost had to jog to keep up with this crew. We talked very little, but at least there were other people in our campground to talk to at night.

That was where I'd finally met Benton, one of the other supervisors. He was a hippie who had never grown up—and certainly never stopped smoking pot. His shoulder-length hair was tied back in a ponytail, he had an amazing handlebar mustache, and he wore a fringed leather jacket and leather hat that made him look like a mountain man. He looked around thirty-five, but it was hard to tell.

On Wednesday we were going to be surveying near the outskirts of Escalante in an open field next to a small drainage. In the center of the field were two low hills that looked like perfect places for Native Americans to have lived. After the first two days of working with Russell, I'd begun to suspect that he didn't know what he was doing. He took too long to read the map, and when I was able to get a peek over his shoulder, it never looked like we were where we were supposed to be. But the worst thing about working with Russell, Mitchell, and Tim was that they never found anything, and whenever I found something, Russell would come over and dismiss it as nothing. Even so, I was certain that some of the artifact scatters I'd found were sites.

Wednesday morning dawned freezing cold but sunny. We lined up and started walking across the grassy plain. The grass was sparse enough that artifacts were easily visible, but I still wanted to concentrate so as not to miss anything. After two transects we were lined up so that Mitchell walked right over the top of the hill. Curious to know if my intuition was correct, I called out to him.

"Do you see anything, Mitchell?"

"Nah, there's nothing here."

How could there be nothing there when I was so sure there would be a site?

"Wait a minute!" I yelled and walked up the hill. I could hear Russell telling me to stay on my transect, but I ignored him. Reaching the top of the hill, I immediately noticed a semicircle of rocks that didn't look natural. I walked over to take a closer look and, sure enough, saw a flake and then a potsherd.

"Ah, here's a sherd." I picked up a small, gray piece of pottery, showed it to Mitchell, and then pointed to a cluster of flakes. "And here are some lithics too." After a few more minutes I had found dozens of small sherds and noticed a place where the soil was black and charcoal-stained. Russell started walking toward us.

"What ya got, Ivy?"

"It's a site, Russell, and I think it's Fremont. That rock ring looks like a pithouse." I didn't bother to point out that Mitchell had walked right over it.

Russell walked around for a few minutes before agreeing. "Okay, it's a site. Let's record it."

I drew the map, Russell filled out the site form, and Mitchell took photographs. While walking over the site and sketching the map, I found a Fremont-type projectile point and a large basin metate. This was one of the only open Fremont habitations that I'd seen since I'd started working for ASC. The strange thing was that the site was well outside of what was currently considered Fremont territory. I examined the pottery more closely to make sure that the site wasn't Puebloan. The pottery had tiny bits of basalt, used as a temper to keep it from exploding when fired, so it was definitely Fremont. Russell seemed oblivious of the importance of our discovery, and I wished again that I was back on Bob Vrey's crew. He would have immediately recognized the site's significance.

Russell was rude and bossy to me the rest of the day, probably my punishment for finding the site. To make matters worse, I found two more sites by veering off my transect to check out spots that looked promising. When I found the third site, I could tell Russell was really annoyed. It was a large prehistoric hunting camp that was loaded with projectile points and other stone tools.

"Site!" I yelled. "I've got a lot of flakes here. Are you guys finding anything?"

No one said a word. We all stopped and circled around.

"I don't see anything," said Russell. He walked over to me. "Show me your artifacts."

"Okay." I pointed to three flakes of red glassy chert and several more flakes nearby. "I saw a biface just back a few meters, Russell. And, look, here's a mano." I held up a perfectly round cobble, about the size of my hand, that was smooth and ground on both sides.

Russell walked around, staring at the ground.

Mitchell was on the other side of me, and finally he spoke up. "Yeah, there's stuff here too. Wow! Here's an arrowhead." He held up a large corner-notched Elko point made of bright red chert. Elko arrowheads turned a wooden spear into a lethal hunting tool, and prehistoric people had used them throughout the West for thousands of years.

Tim continued to circle, staring at the ground, but he never said a word. I wondered if he could tell the difference between an arrowhead and a cow pie.

"Here's a projectile point!" yelled Russell, who seemed to be catching on. "Okay, let's record it."

We went through the recording drill again and then finished the survey unit before returning to camp. When we got there, Russell looked over at me.

"Ivy, I need to talk to you for a minute." Everyone else got out of the car and headed to their tents. My stomach turned as I realized he was going to give me the business for finding so much.

"Yes?"

"I don't appreciate you leaving your transect to check out anything that catches your eye. Stop doing it and mind your own business."

I noticed a muscle spasm under his eyelid, and I stared him down with the most defiant look I could muster. "Sure, I'll be happy to if everyone else quits missing so many sites."

I was already annoyed with Russell, and getting more so. I could hear my voice climbing higher with each word, which always happens when I'm mad. "Have you thought about why I'm the only one finding sites?"

"You need to follow the rules and stay on line. The others would find the sites if you didn't have to be first."

"That's bullshit and you know it. I walked over to their line because they had missed stuff, including sites."

Russell's Adam's apple started jumping up and down, and he pointed his finger at me. "Ivy, just don't ignore me when I tell you to do something in the field. Got it?" Then he got out of the vehicle, leaving me stewing in the back seat.

What an arrogant, incompetent prick! I thought. I needed to talk to someone about this. I was steaming mad. Looking out the window, I saw Benton heading toward the campfire and made up my mind to ask his advice. I was so out of place on Russell's crew that I didn't know if I could stand working with him for the rest of the week. He was missing too many sites, and now he was trying to intimidate me into not finding them. I went to my tent to clean up and then went looking for Benton. I found him cooking a can of stew over a Coleman stove.

"Hi, Benton." I walked over and watched him stirring brown glop in a saucepan. It looked bad but actually smelled pretty good. I was reminded of Rose's stew. "Have you been to the bar down the street? I want to check it out, but I don't want to go alone. I think we're the only two here who drink. You want to be my bodyguard tonight?"

Benton looked up at me, his eyes searching for my motive, as if it might be etched in my face. He stroked his mustache and broke into an almost dirty grin.

"Like a date, you mean?" His eyes twinkled with mischief. He reached into his cooler and grabbed another beer. "Want a beer?"

"No, thanks. Come on, Benton, you're married, and I have a serious boyfriend. Plus I think you might be too old for me," I explained with my most sincere look.

"You never know, you might like old guys," he said, smiling again like a dirty old man.

I gave myself a mental head slap for the "old guy" comment. Luckily, Benton had turned his attention back to his stew. "Damn, this looks good. I never seem to get enough to eat on these survey projects."

I sat down at the picnic table and watched Benton eat his stew right out of the pan.

"Want to try some?" he offered.

"No, thanks." After a brief pause, I said, "Okay, so I don't need a body-guard or a date. What I do need is your advice, and I thought we wouldn't be overheard if we talked in a bar. I don't think anyone else would be caught dead there."

"It's a good plan, but there's one problem. People in these parts hate long-haired hippies so you might have to protect me from the rednecks. Can you handle that?"

We made a plan to meet in an hour, so I cooked and ate my steak in record time, washing it down with a beer. I'd decided it was way too much trouble to try to organize meals and cook for everyone, so this had become my staple field diet. I wondered how long I could live without vegetables, salad, or fruit.

I went to my tent to prepare for my big night on the town. I took out my braids and brushed my hair, hoping that the dirt and grease would get mixed around and be less noticeable. I put on clean jeans, a slightly wrinkled shirt, and my old orange down ski jacket. It smelled like campfires and sweat, but it was the only coat I had with me, and the weather guys were predicting snow by morning.

When I walked out of my tent looking my best, Benton was standing next to the picnic table waiting for me. I made believe I didn't notice his approving look and sly smile. We started walking to the bar and crossed a field of dead grass and weeds that looked beaten down by the wind and frost. I'd forgotten my gloves and my hands were feeling numb, so I shoved them into my coat pockets.

"I appreciate this, Benton. I have kind of a problem, and I could use some advice."

"I'm honored. Not too many people want my advice these days." It was dark out, but if I were a betting woman, I'd wager he was smiling.

I didn't know what to say, so we walked the rest of the way in silence.

Our destination was the Waterhole #1, the one and only bar for a distance of at least sixty miles in any direction. I liked the name, and it looked rustic and homey. The exterior was covered with wood paneling, and a neon sign near the door simply said BEER. I was surprised to see that the parking lot was chock-a-block with pickups and four-wheel-drive vehicles.

"Isn't it Wednesday night? I didn't expect so many people here."

Benton stared at me and shook his head. "Don't you know what today is?"

I thought for a minute and shook my head. "No."

"Tomorrow is the first day of deer hunting season. Everyone and their brother are heading out to their favorite spot to kill Bambi. It should be hopping here tonight. Alcohol is a side dish to this killing feast. Maybe with all the out-of-town hunters no one will even notice an old hippie like me."

Benton opened the door and we were greeted with a blast of moist, warm air. The room was dark and smoke-filled. The jukebox was playing country western tunes, and two couples were line dancing on a small dance floor. I was momentarily stunned by the number of people wearing cowboy hats and tight Wrangler jeans. They all looked like ranchers except for a small group by the pool table. Two of them wore orange hats, and the others wore military-style camouflage coats and pants. Stan would fit right in, I thought. Benton, however, was like a swan trying to hide in a flock of

Canadian geese. We tried not to attract any attention by sitting in a booth tucked away in the back of the room.

I took off my dirty coat and set it on a coat rack. "Since this was my idea, I'll buy the first round. What do you want?"

"Any kind of draft, if they have it. Otherwise a Coors will be fine." Benton sat with his back to the wall and scanned the crowd.

I elbowed my way through the throngs of leering cowboys and secured two large mugs of draft beer. I placed them on the table and watched Benton for a minute. He lifted his beer and took a sip, delicately, like Hercule Poirot, the Belgian detective.

"Benton, I heard you got your M.A. in anthropology at Utah College. When did you graduate?"

"Two years ago." He took another long drink and set his glass down. His mustache was covered with beer foam, and I noticed for the first time that his skin was deeply lined from too much sun.

"Who was your adviser?"

"Thomas."

"Oh, you were one of the Middle East guys. Did you dig in Jordan?"

"For two seasons."

This conversation wasn't going as smoothly as I'd hoped. Perhaps more beer would help. We drank in silence and watched the crowd.

Everyone seemed to be having a good time—dancing, laughing at funny stories, and playing pool. I couldn't even remember the last time I'd gone out with a group and had fun like that. I felt a touch on my hand and looked over to see Benton staring at me with a slight smile.

"So, Ivy, what is it you want to ask me?"

"I guess it's time to spill the beans. Have you ever been on a crew that doesn't find sites, and worse, doesn't want to find sites?"

Benton thought for a minute. "Are we talking hypothetical or are you having trouble with anyone in particular?"

"I guess I may as well level with you. I don't know how I'm going to continue working with Russell's crew. Either they can't or don't want to find sites." I then told Benton about the Fremont site and Russell's lecture about not leaving my transect. He listened intently, and when our glasses were empty, I got up to buy two more.

When I came back, Benton was stroking his mustache and looking at me closely.

"I guess you're in a tough spot, Ivy. But I do have some advice. I've discovered over the years that some people can find sites and some can't. It's kind of like a sixth sense. You can teach some people, but others just never seem to get it."

"I guess I never thought about it," I said. "I've always been able to find sites. I found them in my high school athletic field even before I really knew what one was. Why do you think that is?"

"I have no idea. Maybe it's because some archaeologists don't concentrate on what they're doing, or maybe it's because they don't notice the subtle changes in the environment that a good archaeologist sees. I've never told anyone this, but sometimes I think there's a bit of mysticism involved. I swear there have been many times when I knew a site was in a certain spot because a little voice in my head told me it was there."

"You know, I've had that happen to me too. I just figured I had an overactive imagination. I never wanted to tell anyone that before."

"I don't know, Ivy, maybe it is just chance or imagination. But I do know one thing, and that is that you really can't teach some people to find sites. With that said, I'll tell you about an important rule I've developed over the years to help me keep my sanity: if you can't change something, there's no sense losing sleep over it. All you can do is keep on doing the right thing." Benton looked deep in my eyes for a minute and then looked away. "If I were you I'd keep finding as many sites as I could and I'd ignore any crap you get from Russell. It won't do any good to make a big deal out of the fact that Russell's crew sucks. You know what I mean?"

"I guess so, but it seems so wrong to ignore the fact that Russell and his boys are incompetent." I felt frustrated just thinking about it. I pushed my hair back behind my ear and noticed a couple kissing and holding hands.

"Suppose you tell Dr. Lockyear that Russell doesn't know what he's doing. Do you think he'll believe you? And actually do something about it? Maybe he already has his suspicions about Russell's abilities and that's why you were moved onto his crew. Did you think about that?"

"No," I replied. "I didn't." I felt a tap on my shoulder and looked up to see a tall, handsome cowboy.

"Care to dance?" He had a deep voice with a slight Utah twang.

I was too stunned to think of a reason not to, so I agreed. I sheepishly shrugged and smiled at Benton, then followed the cowboy onto the dance floor. By this time several other couples were dancing, and I actually had a good time. My dancing partner told me he lived in Escalante and worked on his family's ranch. He'd been smart enough to figure out that Benton and I were just friends, and his manners were perfect. After two dances I told him I needed a break and headed back to the table. Benton was watching me closely.

"You're pretty good at that western dancing. Didn't I hear you were from back east? Where did you learn to dance like that?"

"I've never done this kind of dancing before," I admitted. "I just followed my partner's lead. He's pretty cute. I think we made a fine couple. How did we look out there?"

"You looked great to me. But then I'm not a dancer myself."

"Benton," I asked, "why are you working on this project? Don't you have something better to do?"

"This *is* what I do. I'm an archaeologist, and I'm doing what I love."

"Don't you get tired of the camping, the dirt, the strangers that you have nothing in common with, and the bad food?"

"Ivy, I don't plan on doing this forever."

"What are you going to do?"

"Well, I'm hoping to get one of those cushy government archaeology jobs. My wife wants to start a family, and I guess it's time to settle. But I sure love being a gypsy archaeologist. I'll miss it."

"Don't you get lonely?"

Benton took out a cigarette and lit it. He inhaled deeply and looked pensive. "Ivy, you're still young, but I think you'll find that the older you get, the more alone you are. Archaeologists work in the middle of nowhere. It's always lonely, and if you want to do this, you'll just have to get used to it."

I sighed and chugged my beer. I had a slight buzz and was feeling pretty good.

"How about one on me?" asked Benton. "I guess everyone's too busy to bother an old hippie." I nodded and he headed to the bar.

I danced a few more times, but after the third beer, I'd had enough. It was midnight when we left to walk back. We crossed the parking lot okay, but then I tripped in a hole and fell down. Benton helped me up and put his arm around me since I was weaving badly. At the campground we said good night, and I stumbled into my tent. Maureen was asleep, but despite my efforts to be quiet, she woke up.

"Are you all right?" she asked.

"Just a little drunk, but it feels good."

"Well, you don't smell too good, and I doubt you'll feel good in the morning."

"I'll worry about that tomorrow," I said in my best Scarlett O'Hara southern belle voice.

The wind had picked up while we were in the bar, and the tent was flapping and swaying. I changed into my long johns, falling once in the process, then inched into my sleeping bag. As soon as I'd tightened the drawstring, though, I started spinning. My last thought before passing out was that I hoped the tent wouldn't blow over.

I dreamt that I was digging a deep pithouse when the wall collapsed. A wall of dirt engulfed me, and the world turned black. The dirt had filled my nose and mouth when I suddenly heard Maureen muttering and yelling at me to wake up.

"Ivy, are you okay? Wake up!" she commanded.

I tried to sit up but something was holding me down. I realized that our tent was covering us. It must have blown down after all.

"We need to fix the tent."

"Okay," I mumbled. My head was pounding and I still felt a little woozy. "Just let me get my coat on." Luckily I'd used my coat as a pillow so it was easy to find, and my boots were right under my cot.

The tent had become a giant, weighted blanket that made movement difficult. We crawled around looking for the entry, then unzipped the door and crawled out. The wind was so strong that we were almost knocked over. Frozen rain mixed with snow stung my face. We were in the middle of a blizzard, and we realized right away that it would be impossible to raise the tent. It was pitch black, and snow covered the ground.

"What should we do?" asked Maureen in a whiny voice.

I thought for two seconds. The beers weren't helping much. "We can sleep in the rest room. It's dry and pretty clean. Let's crawl back into the tent and get our sleeping bags."

We retrieved our bags and ran to the restroom, doing our best not to drag them in the snow. As the door closed behind us, my first thought was that the restroom felt warm and cozy. I was still too drunk to notice the urine smell, the large spider webs in the corners, and the muddy footprints covering the floor.

We laid out our sleeping bags on the cold concrete floor. There was barely enough room, but thanks to the beer, I was asleep in just seconds.

Morning was bad. I looked out the window and saw a white world; an inch of new snow had blanketed the campground. My head was still pounding, and the bright sunlight was causing stabs of pain. At least I was dry and warm. Looking outside, I saw a few people wander out of their tents and then quickly go back in. I decided to go back to sleep since we couldn't survey until the snow melted.

Eventually, hunger drew everyone out of their tents. I dragged my sleeping bag outside and put it in the collapsed tent. Since the Mormon Church did not approve of coffee, I wandered over to Benton's camp to bum a cup. Only two people on Benton's crew drank coffee, but they'd made a whole pot.

After two hours of drinking coffee next to the fire, the snow had melted, and Russell announced that it was time to go to work. The guys helped us raise and secure our tent before we headed out. All of the remaining survey units were located some distance away, so the drive to our new unit was blessedly long. Somewhere between Escalante and Bryce Canyon National Park, my head stopped pounding. Our survey unit was on the northern boundary of Bryce, and the closest road was the main road through the park. We were planning to hike down the edge of the plateau and through the colorful, carved formations that had made Bryce Canyon famous. Russell paid the park fee and drove to a trail that would take us close to our survey area.

"Here we are. We have about a mile hike into our unit, so pack plenty of water and food."

We filled our water bottles, checked our recording equipment, and donned our packs.

Russell headed toward the trail. "Come on, Ivy. Let's see if you can keep up today."

I tried to ignore his comment, but it really made me mad. I always worked hard not to slow everyone down. His legs were twice as long as mine, so I had to move that much faster to keep up. Why should I put up with his crap when he couldn't find a site if his life depended on it?

"I may be slow, but at least I find sites."

He stopped abruptly and glared at me.

"What do you mean by that?"

"You know what I mean. Let me ask you something, Russell. Do you ever find any sites, or is it all about surveying the most units?"

We all stopped walking.

"If I don't find sites it's because there aren't any there," Russell said. "At least I'm not slowing everyone down because I'm a drunk."

I've always had a bad temper, and when pushed too far, I sometimes lose it. This was one of those times.

"Having a couple of beers doesn't make me a drunk, Russell. Let's stick to the facts, which are that I've found all the sites this week. That means that without me your crew would have missed at least four sites, and only your God knows how many other sites you've missed this week."

"You've slowed us down all week because you drink every night," Russell shot back. "I have no idea why Dr. Lockyear hired you. You drink, swear, and are bossy. You have no standards of decency, and I'm tired of your uppity, 'only I can find sites' attitude. I'd fire you if I could."

"Well, you know what, Russell? You're a smalltown bigot, and I'm sick of you too. So FUCK YOU! I quit."

I turned around and headed back to the car. I was so mad I could not spend another minute with these guys.

"Good riddance!" Russell yelled back, before he and the crew continued down the trail.

I started walking down the road toward the park entrance. I had no idea where I was going, but I'd had enough of males judging me. I was sick of their rules and their close-mindedness. They were so self-righteous, it was sickening.

I'd walked about a mile before I was able to calm down and think straight. Should I return to the vehicle and wait for a ride back with the crew? That would be too much like admitting defeat. I didn't think I could stand being in the same vehicle with Russell ever again.

But Escalante was at least twenty miles away. Since that was too far to walk, I figured the only way I was going to get back was by hitchhiking. This was a national park, so there should be plenty of cars in an hour or so. When I was a college student I'd hitched to the ski slopes every weekend with my roommate. I knew it wasn't safe to hitchhike alone, but what choice did I have?

Fortunately, a nice couple from Germany who were on a cross-country tour gave me a ride in their Volkswagen van. They were curious about my circumstances, and even more interested that I was an archaeologist. I'd almost forgotten what a real conversation was like with educated, worldly people. Their English was good, and they wanted to know everything about my job and my life in Salt Lake City. They kept me talking nonstop until we reached Escalante and then invited me to join them for lunch in the town's only restaurant.

After they dropped me off, I spent the rest of the day reading and napping in my tent. It was strange to be alone in the campground.

By the time Russell and the crew got back, I was sitting with Benton, drinking beer in defiance of Russell's conservatism. After we finished eating and cleaning up, I noticed Russell heading our way.

"Benton, could I have a word with you?"

They moved a short distance from Benton's picnic table and discussed my situation. I could just barely hear their conversation.

"Ivy cannot come back on my crew. Did you hear what she did today?"

"Nope, but I figured it must have been good because she was already back in camp when I returned."

"She will not listen to directions, she told me to F-off, and she abandoned the crew."

Benton smiled. "Did she?"

"I don't want her on my crew anymore. Would you mind if we traded Ivy for Maureen?" Russell looked over at me and scowled. I stuck my tongue out at him and just barely stopped myself from flipping him off.

"Sure, that's fine by me. Do you want me to tell her about this plan?"

"You may as well. She doesn't listen to me." And with that Russell walked back to his table.

Benton walked toward me, shaking his head. "Ivy, you didn't tell me you swore at him."

"What does it matter? I'm sick of him and tired of these conditions. I can live with the hard work and camping, but I can't stand the self-righteous attitude of guys like Russell—especially when he's incompetent and won't accept my help. Screw him."

"Well, it seems you've won. He wants to trade you for Maureen tomorrow. I said yes." Benton shook his head and got another beer. He returned to the fire and we sat and stared at the flames.

"At least tomorrow is Friday. Do you think Dr. Lockyear will fire me for this?"

"I probably would if I was him. But then, I think he's pretty desperate for good archaeologists. He'll probably just keep you on my crew. You better be good or I'll put you over my knee." Benton's eyes twinkled and a smile crept back.

"I promise to be a good girl. I was raised that way, but it just doesn't seem to get me ahead. All it earns me are bosses who take advantage of my good behavior. Anyway, being bad is much more fun."

"You know, Ivy, if you weren't so darn cute you'd never get away with it."

I batted my eyebrows and did my Scarlett imitation. "Oh, Rhett, do you really think so?"

"Your boyfriend has his hands full, that's all I'm going to say."

Wind and Gnats
in the Moss Backs

"Bob, how long will it take us to get to our new project area?"

It was Monday, and we'd been driving south for four hours. Although it had been cool this morning, the temperature had risen quite a bit since we'd left Salt Lake.

"Ivy, you sound like my son. 'Are we there yet? How much longer? I'm thirsty!'"

"But I *am* tired, hungry, and thirsty—and I also have to go to the bathroom, so when will we get there?" I looked over at Bob and he was smiling. His hand was draped casually over the steering wheel, and he was staring ahead at the bleak terrain. "Are you going to answer me, or what?"

"Have you been good? No recent fights with crew chiefs? I still can't believe Dr. Lockyear didn't fire you for walking out on Russell's crew. I wouldn't have thought you had it in you."

"It wasn't one of my best moments, and if you didn't bring it up again that would be great with me." I still felt bad about losing my temper with Russell, but I reminded myself what a jerk he'd been.

"So why *didn't* Dr. Lockyear fire you?"

I stared vacantly out the window. "He told me he'd give me a second chance since this was my first offense. But I think the real reason he didn't fire me was because he can't afford to lose another warm body."

"Ivy, maybe he realized he needs your talent. You're being your own worst enemy. You do have a talent for finding sites. Give yourself a break."

I couldn't stop my favorite alter ego, Scarlett, from chiming in. "Why, Bob, I do believe you actually gave me a compliment."

"That was pretty good!" Bob laughed out loud, and it made him look years younger. But was his hair grayer than it had been in the fall? Or was that just my active imagination?

"Are you going to tell me where we're going, or do you want me to beg?"

"We're heading to a place near Cedar Mesa called the Moss Backs."

"That helps me a lot since I have no idea where Cedar Mesa is," I said.

"Haven't you ever heard of the ruins in Grand Gulch? Grand Gulch drains Cedar Mesa, and both places are loaded with pueblos. Grand Gulch is a deep canyon with cliff dwellings, like Mesa Verde. Have you had your head in the sand?"

"No, just in the field, where I've been treated like a mushroom—kept in the dark and fed a lot of shit. Will the Moss Backs have cliff dwellings?" I reached into my pocket for my Chapstick. Already the dry desert air was wreaking havoc on my lips.

"Probably not. The area where we'll be working is more like a mesa, covered with a thick pinyon juniper forest. The terrain looks pretty rugged from the maps." Bob slowed down because the road suddenly turned steep and curvy. We were traveling south in a fairly new Ford Bronco that Dr. Lockyear had leased.

I felt someone's breath on the back of my neck, and it scared me for a minute until I realized that it was just Martin, who was sitting behind me. After working at ASC for seven months, I now had enough seniority to sit in front and help with the navigation. Martin and Frank, our other new crew member, were brand new hires. Both had studied archaeology in college, but neither had field experience. They both seemed pretty weird to me. Martin wasn't bad looking, but seemed to have very little going on upstairs. Frank was another story. The best way to picture Frank is to imagine Ichabod Crane's ghost: tall and lanky with a bad complexion and a face that was completely dominated by his hawklike nose. His posture was bad and his pants were too short. He was also one of the most shy people I'd ever met. Martin was the opposite: tall, handsome, blond, and fit. He reminded me of a happy, faithful dog—head out the window, tongue flapping in the breeze, and too dumb not to be happy.

"Bob," asked Martin, "when do we get there?"

Bob looked over at me with a sly smile and then, to my surprise, answered, "About two more hours."

"Great. Then I can go back to sleep."

The amazing thing about Martin was that he did just that. In two minutes he was sound asleep.

"Can we continue our conversation now, Bob?" I asked.

"What did you want to know?"

"How many acres are we surveying and why?"

"Why can't you be like everyone else and not care?"

"Because I do care. That's just it. I want to be in charge some day, and the best way to get there is if I pay attention. Why does everyone assume I'll give up archaeology and have babies? Is there a sign on my forehead that says 'Baby Factory'? We have the pill now. I don't have to have babies."

"All right, relax. I don't need the whole women's lib drill. I'm married, remember? I get enough of that at home."

I noticed Bob tried to look very serious about driving.

"Then how about just answering my questions?" I asked.

Meeting my intense stare, he said, "Okay, okay. This is what I know. We're surveying two thousand acres for a uranium mine. The mine folks are being required by the LMA to write an environmental impact statement, an EIS. The survey is needed for the EIS."

"Huh? Go slower. Will the EIS explain what the mine will do to the archaeological sites?"

"Correct." Bob nodded. "The EIS will evaluate the impacts to the archaeological sites."

"So the sites won't be destroyed?"

"Well, the way the law reads, sites can be destroyed, but only after they're excavated."

We sat in silence for a while. I had to think about this. I really didn't know much about the laws that required these surveys; it was all a mystery. We were leaving the small town of Moab and the terrain had become spectacular. Moab straddles the Colorado River in a wide valley at the foot of the La Sal Mountains. To the north of Moab the landscape is dominated by the gray colors of Mancos shale. In Moab, where the river has carved a wide valley through sandstone formations, the landscape explodes with color. But ten miles south of Moab, you're back in no man's land. Sandstone canyons and forested mesas dominate the region. On occasion we drove past bald and wind-carved domes of sandstone. We were in Ancestral Puebloan, or

Anasazi, country. Major portions of the Four Corners area had been farmed prehistorically, but today most of southwestern Utah was sparsely populated. Ranching, mining, and tourism were the major industries.

Just south of another small town, Monticello, we turned east and traveled along a two-lane paved road for another hour. About an hour after lunch, Bob found the dirt road he was looking for and announced that we were there.

What he meant was we were nowhere. The dirt road led into a wide valley surrounded by mesas blanketed with pinyon pines and junipers.

Bob raised his hand and pointed out the window. "There are the Moss Backs."

"Do you mean those two mesas?" I asked.

"Yup, those are the ones. Our survey area begins at the base of that mesa on the left and extends south for a couple of miles. The project area is a swath of land about three miles long and a little over a mile wide."

I groaned inwardly, wondering how long it would take to walk over that entire area. "Are we the only ones surveying here?"

Bob stopped the car and looked over at me. "Nah, we'll have help next week, but this week it's just us." He looked into the back seat at the two sleeping beauties. "Wake up, you two. It's time to work."

The first two days were great. We walked and walked and walked. The weather was a pleasant 60 to 70 degrees and the sun shone brightly. Wednesday morning, though, the wind started to kick up. We were waiting in the car for Bob after a nutritious breakfast of Pop-Tarts and cold cereal. As I stared out the window, a strong gust blew all our chairs over and knocked over the tiny aluminum table that we used to prepare our meals. The stove, silverware, lanterns—everything on the table went flying.

I looked over my shoulder into the back seat. "Guys, let's batten down the hatches." I jumped out of the car and Frank followed.

"What happened?" Martin was never really awake until about noon. I wondered how many sites he missed walking the morning transects.

Frank ran over to collect the chairs and then helped me right the table. We gathered everything that the wind had scattered. The Coleman stove had fallen to the ground but looked none the worse for wear. The lantern was another story. Both the glass globe and the mantle were broken.

"I think we have extra mantles," I said to no one in particular.

"I saw a few in the green box," Frank said, gesturing with his head to a box by my tent. After he'd started talking, I'd discovered that Frank was not what I expected. He was articulate and very smart. I liked him more and more each day.

Bob emerged from his tent. "Looks like spring has come at last. Brace yourselves. These winds can last for weeks."

"What do you mean, 'weeks'? As in, windy all day and all night?" I asked, wondering just what was in store.

We did our best to make sure the tents weren't going to blow away by weighting them down with everything that was lying around outside. Bob checked the tent stakes and pronounced them secure. Then we loaded up and headed to a densely forested area about a half a mile away, stopping at a tree draped with bright orange surveyor's flagging.

"Okay," announced Bob. "We're walking long transects so bring plenty of water. We should be back to the vehicle for lunch."

In the trees the wind wasn't so bad. I was enjoying this survey more than the last project because the archaeology was more interesting.

We lined up and started walking. I was between Frank and Martin, and Bob was at the end, keeping us going the right direction with his compass. Both Frank and Martin had gotten the hang of walking in straight lines. In fact, Martin was a human compass with the route-finding ability of a migrating bird. He always seemed to know where north was. Frank, in contrast, wandered on his line, but he didn't miss a flake and had a talent for finding sites.

Once we were in the thick brush, we had to yell back and forth to stay in contact and avoid getting lost. As usual, everyone was a foot taller than me and I struggled to keep up. About a half a mile into our first transect I noticed a low mound of rocks just ahead of me. Looking around the linear pile, I spotted some bright red pottery and then a few white pieces with black decorations.

"Site!" I yelled, continuing to examine my find and hoping I'd see something really neat like a complete arrow point or a drill. Everyone straggled over and circled around the site, looking intently at the ground.

"Looks like late Pueblo I to me," announced Bob.

"What are the dates for Pueblo I again?" asked Martin, who had been told at least three times already about the Puebloan cultural sequence.

"AD 700 to 900," Bob responded like an automaton. "Hey, look at this. I haven't seen one of these here yet."

I walked over and Bob handed me a disk made out of a red potsherd with a hole punched through the center.

"What is it?"

"It's a spindle whorl, for spinning cotton into thread. It looks like we've got ourselves a good-sized room block. This mound of rocks probably represents three or four masonry-linked rooms, and this depression, to the south, is probably the kiva."

"How can you tell all that from this pile of rocks?" Martin asked, a confused puppy look on his face.

Bob pointed to linear rows of rocks in the rubble pile. "This alignment is the wall. See? Here's another. I don't see the end of this room, but the wall fell over, and you can see the five or so courses of masonry." Bob pointed to wall fall that, now that he'd pointed it out, did look like a wall that had fallen on the ground intact. Bob really knew this stuff, and I liked being on his crew because I learned so much.

"Okay, let's record the site. Ivy, you make the map. Frank, you take pictures. And Martin, you look for cool stuff. I'll fill out the form."

I wandered around for a few minutes and then ran a thirty-meter tape across the east-west axis of the rubble pile, using my compass to get the tape just right. After several months of making maps, Bob had taught me this method, and it worked much better. Masonry rooms, especially, took a long time to map without a tape as a grid reference.

Each transect that day took us closer and closer to a small but steep mesa right in the center of our survey area. By the end of the day, when we'd reached the base of the mesa, my back and feet hurt, and every exposed piece of skin felt sandblasted. My ears had little sand dunes building inside, and I'd somehow managed to get sand in between my teeth too. Talking was impossible, not only because of blowing sand, but because the wind carried away the sound. Looking up at the steep mesa that we'd have to climb tomorrow made my whole body ache. It would probably be even windier up there.

"Looks like tomorrow we climb to the top, but that's it for today!" Bob yelled.

We trudged to the car. The guys looked even worse than I felt. Frank's hair was going every which way, and his eyes were swollen from the dust and pollen. His face was streaked with dirt, and he had a large tear in his shirt. Even Martin, our happy dog, looked whipped.

Perhaps a few words of encouragement would help. "Hey, guys, it could be worse."

"This is pretty bad," said Frank. He sat down next to the vehicle and reached into his backpack. He found what he was looking for, a granola bar. He removed the wrapper and took a huge bite. Frank ate all day long, and more than anyone I'd ever known, yet he was impossibly thin.

"Well, let's see," I replied. "It could be 105 degrees, or it could be windy and really cold, or how about this? The gnats could be attacking."

"Don't say a word, Ivy. Gnat season will begin any day." Bob removed his glasses and attempted to clean them. "Let's load up and get to camp."

Lately I'd started giving myself mental pep talks, like Charlotte on her web. As she ripped out the old words and added the new, she'd talk quietly to herself as she spun Wilbur's future. In my pep talks I reminded myself how much I had learned, and how tough I'd become. I may have shorter legs than everyone else, but I'd been using them in extreme ways for almost a year. I was really in shape, and that mesa would be no problem. Plus I was doing what I loved most in the world. Wasn't I?

By the time we made it back to camp the wind was howling. Trying to cook and relax around the fire was going to be a challenge. Bob was able to get the fire going by using a common archaeologist's technique—namely, pouring Coleman fuel on a pile of logs and throwing a match on it. With a loud "whump," the fire caught.

I'd decided to make dinner for everyone: tamale pie casserole baked in a Dutch oven. No one offered to help, so I got busy. First I browned the hamburger and onions in a frying pan on the Coleman stove. After transferring the meat and onions to the Dutch oven, I piled on a can of creamed corn, a can of pinto beans, and a can of tomato sauce mixed with chili powder, cumin, and other spices. The final layer was a package mix of corn bread. By the time I finished assembling the casserole, the coals were ready, and I set the oven on to bake.

I grabbed a beer and sat down next to Frank, who was hunched down with his coat pulled up around his ears. He looked miserable.

He stared at me for a minute. "Ivy, how is it you can look so cheery? This wind is driving me crazy." He put his hands over his ears and stared blankly into the fire.

I stood up and pushed a few coals closer to the Dutch oven. "The trick to staying sane is to cover your ears. The wind isn't as annoying that way. I have this bandana on for a reason."

Frank raised his eyebrows and then disappeared into his tent. He returned with a winter ski hat that completely covered his ears. "I hope this helps."

Martin wandered over to the fire looking equally miserable. He held a beer can in one hand and a bag of chips in the other. "What is with this wind? My tent is flapping so loud I can't hear myself think."

I realized that we were yelling at each other to hear over the howling.

"As long as the sand keeps out of my food, I can stand it," said Bob. He threw another log on the fire. "Your dinner smells good, Ivy. When will it be ready?"

"About half an hour, I think. This is my first time trying this recipe."

The wind was relentless, gusting at what felt like forty to fifty miles per hour. The fire consumed wood about as fast as we added it. No one had the energy to talk, so we just sat and stared at the flames. For some reason I was glad for the silence. Maybe I was finally getting used to the loneliness. I tried to read a book, but the wind made it difficult to concentrate, seeming to blow the thoughts right out of my head.

"Do you think we could find a camping spot that's better sheltered from the wind, Bob?"

"I suppose there might be a better spot, but I haven't seen one. It was just as windy where we were working today. We just didn't notice it as much because we were moving."

"How about moving to the other side of the mesa that we need to climb tomorrow?" I asked. "The mesa may block the wind."

"Usually it doesn't help that much, but we can see tomorrow. It may not be worth the trouble since we only have one night left. This wind sure stinks though." We all nodded our agreement. Frank seemed to be having the worst time with the wind, but maybe his hat would help. He looked over at me with sad dog eyes and then stared at the fire again.

"How's the hat working, Frank?"

"I guess I feel a little better."

Bob looked over at us. "Yeah, covering your ears does help some. But after a couple of days of wind, nothing helps. Let's move into the Blazer. It'll be better in there."

One by one we shuffled inside the vehicle. Immediately I felt like a stone had been lifted from my chest. It was so quiet. We could still hear the wind howling, but it wasn't assaulting us physically.

The casserole was tasty—at least no one complained—and I thought it was good. We ate quietly in the car to avoid the inevitable sand flying into our food. After dinner it was too dark to read so I headed to my tent. At least I could light my lantern in there and read. I would just have to ignore the flapping and howling. My tent was securely staked, and the sides were tied to two large junipers standing as sentinels on either side of my tent. I climbed into my sleeping bag, secure in the knowledge that my tent wouldn't blow over. When I tired of reading, I turned off my lantern and blocked out the howling wind by burying my head inside my bag, sleeping that way through the night.

I woke as the sun was rising. I couldn't hear a thing; it was dead calm. I still packed my bandana, just in case.

Bob was a morning person and liked big breakfasts. He had already made the coffee and fried a pound of bacon. I filled my coffee cup.

"How are you this morning, Bob?" He always had the same answer, but I liked to hear it anyway.

"Every day's a holiday, and every meal's a feast."

I smiled at him and dragged my chair over to the fire. Bob was busy cracking eggs, and he didn't like help making breakfast, so I sat down to savor the smell of pine trees mixed with wood fire, coffee, and bacon. There's nothing better.

It was chilly out, but the hot coffee cup warmed my hands. Martin and Frank soon joined us, and we ate breakfast in silence. After washing the dishes, we loaded up and headed to the base of the mesa where we'd stopped yesterday. Just as we'd taken our places on line and were ready to start walking, we felt the first gust of wind. The plan was to climb the mesa on this first transect and survey the top. The slope was steep, but it looked like we could all safely climb it without veering too far from our transects. The going would be slow but manageable.

"Let's go!" yelled Bob. "Don't take any chances as you're climbing. If you're worried that something's not safe, don't do it."

I looked up the slope and picked my route. It looked like I'd be able to zigzag back and forth across the steepest sections, weaving between chunks of sandstone and the slippery talus slopes. I'd found arrowheads in places like this, so I wanted to scan carefully for artifacts. I looked over at Frank, who was squeezing around the edge of a huge boulder hanging precariously from the slope. One step at a time, I told myself. Don't look up or down; that just makes it worse. I paced myself to avoid running out of breath. Over the months I'd learned that the safest way to climb was to fully weight and straighten one leg before moving the next. It kept me from going too fast and also took some stress off of my knees. My daypack was heavy with the water and food I'd need for the day.

I inched up the slope until I could see the sky over the top. I'd lost sight of Frank, but Martin was over the top and walking on his transect. I gained the edge, adjusted my backpack, and started walking. On the mesa top was a thin stand of pinyons thriving in the thicker soils along the shallow drainages. Much of the mesa was slickrock, though, and I doubted that we'd find many sites. I looked carefully at the ground for flakes but saw none. By now we'd all made it to the top and were walking our transects again. It looked like we could finish surveying the mesa top in two or three passes.

I'd lost sight of Frank but had kept on walking until my transect ended abruptly at the edge of the mesa and a sheer cliff that dropped hundreds of feet to its base. A gust of wind reminded me to step back from the edge. I stared for a minute across the wide, empty space, taking in the spectacular scenery of red earth, green pines, and narrow canyons snaking their way to the Colorado River. There were no signs of humans for forty miles in any direction. I tore myself away from the view and headed in Frank's direction. Our return transect would follow his line. As I approached, I was surprised to see him sitting on the edge of the cliff reading a book.

"What's happening, Frank? Is it time for a break?"

Frank looked at me with fear in his eyes, and then his face went blank. "I got to the edge of the mesa, and I had this overpowering urge to jump. So I figured I'd better sit down and cool off." He smiled weakly and returned to his book.

I was too shocked to respond. I decided to take a pee break and think about this one. "Frank, tell the guys when they get here that I'm taking a pee break."

"Okay."

I headed back the way I'd come and found Bob. He had finished his transect and stood mesmerized on the edge. "Bob, I think you better let Frank take a little break. He said he had the urge to jump."

Bob looked at me funny and headed toward Frank.

Was Frank for real? Do people really think like that? The thought of jumping from the edge of a high place had never occurred to me. Frank was pretty strange, but was he suicidal? I found a tree that sheltered me from the wind and squatted to pee—downwind. Peeing for women is so undignified, I thought, especially with your pants pulled down around your ankles. I pulled my jeans back up and secured my belt. Then I grabbed my pack and fished out my water bottle, reminding myself to stay hydrated.

When I returned, Frank and Bob were sitting and quietly talking. Frank had put his book away and was explaining his fear of heights.

"It's not fear so much as the desire to jump that scares me. I have a lot of dreams where I jump off the edge and can fly. No, I guess it's more like floating."

"Yeah, I have that one too," said Bob. He shook his head. "Guess the desire to jump never occurred to me."

"It's strange, but I'm fine now. Reading is the best way for me to calm down."

Bob stood up. "Why don't you stay a good distance from the edge? We'll cover that last little bit of ground. And on the way down you can walk with me."

"Oh, don't worry, I'll be fine." Frank put his book away, put on his pack, and smiled weakly at me.

As we lined up, the wind seemed to calm, and the sun was darting in and out of the clouds. Its warmth on my back felt good, and I was glad I had no issues with heights.

The rest of the day was, fortunately, uneventful. True to his word, Bob kept a close eye on Frank, who did seem fine now. I found a large projectile point made of obsidian, and Frank found a grinding slick. Bob examined the point and decided that it had an impact fracture. Its shape told us that it had been made several thousand years ago. It had likely been hafted to a spear that had been thrown at an animal but had missed and hit the ground. The grinding slick was a sandstone boulder, partially embedded. I ran my fingers over the grinding surface, and it felt deliciously smooth, like a baby's butt. Native Americans had ground seeds on it, probably to make porridge.

"What would the Indians have been doing up here?" I asked Bob.

"I suspect they were hunting bighorn sheep. There were lots of bighorns before domesticated sheep were introduced from Europe. Now there aren't any."

"What happened?" I wondered aloud.

"Domesticated sheep brought diseases that the wild species had no immunities to. The diseases almost completely wiped them out."

We hiked slowly down the mesa after lunch. The wind had picked up again, and we all decided that there was no point in moving camp. The wind was everywhere, and the car was our only hope of respite.

Friday was just as windy as the previous two days, but we quit before noon for the long drive home. During the drive I looked forward to my bathtub and cozy bed like never before. As we got closer to Salt Lake City, I planned out my weekend. First I'd take a long shower—and then a bath. I'd eat a bowl of tomato soup and then climb into bed with a good book. Saturday I'd wake up late, take another long bath, watch television, and go to bed early with a good book. Maybe by Sunday I'd feel like doing something with my roommate, or maybe Tom. Nah, he'd be in church. Whatever I did couldn't involve hiking or camping. Football on TV actually sounded pretty good. I stopped at Sunday afternoon because I couldn't face the idea of coming back and camping for another week of torture.

It was Monday morning, and we were already halfway back to the Moss Backs project. The weekend had been perfect: just as I'd imagined, with long stretches of nothing but lounging around indoors. The weather had matched my mood, slightly overcast and gloomy. The skies had looked threatening when I'd woken up, but as we traveled farther south, the weather seemed to be improving. I was still glad I'd packed my best rain gear. I could see the sage and pinyons dancing in the wind. Would the winds never cease?

Bob was driving and I was copilot again. I was thinking about the first explorers—crossing the desert on horses, meeting frightened Indians, and seeing sights never imagined. They would have had to brave the winds without the benefit of a car for shelter. Just as I'd decided to take a nap, Bob asked me a question.

"Ivy, guess what I brought this week?"

I looked over at him. Bob seemed happy and relaxed after his weekend, and he was wearing the sly grin that usually means he's feeling pleased with himself. Since I had nothing better to do, I decided to play along with the guessing game.

"Let me see. How about a wind deflector shield?"

"Yeah, that would be nice, wouldn't it? Guess again."

"Hmmm...how about a special back massaging lounge chair? Or how about a bottle of Courvoisier?"

"Nope. Give up?"

"How about a site-finding robot that can walk my transects for me?"

"You may be a crummy guesser, but I'll give you one thing, you have a great imagination. Give up?"

"Yes, I give up. Just tell me."

"I brought my fishing gear, and I even brought an extra pole just in case you like to fish."

"Don't we need water to fish? I haven't seen a body of water big enough to fish in since we left Provo. Is this some new desert sport-fishing thing that requires no water? Or what?"

"Lake Powell is only about thirty miles away. We can be there in no time. Tomorrow afternoon we can pack some sandwiches and go fishing."

"What will we be fishing for—bass and trout?"

"That's right. I guess you are a fisherwoman."

"I have three sisters, and out of necessity I became my father's son. He took me fishing quite a bit with the boys. My sisters didn't like the worms, smells, and mess. I was happy anywhere with my dad, and I loved being outside."

"Okay, then, are you in? We go fishing tomorrow."

Bob looked really pleased with himself. Fishing did sound fun. It would break the boredom of the daily routine and remind me of many happy hours spent with my dad. I missed my family. They all lived back east, and I only got to see them on holidays or vacations. My sisters were married or busy with careers, and we were scattered across the country.

On Monday and Tuesday we recorded several small pueblos that looked more like piles of rocks—dense scatters of broken pottery and waste flakes surrounded the rubble piles. The pottery indicated that most of the sites were occupied during a narrow range of time between AD 700 and 900. All the pueblos were in the dense pinyon juniper forest, which sheltered us somewhat from the relentless winds. Bob explained that in prehistoric times these forests had been cut down for fuel, building materials, and to clear the land for crops.

We chose a better-sheltered spot to camp this time, in a canyon tucked around a protected corner. Strong gusts still found us, but it wasn't a continuous assault. Nights were still difficult because the tents flapped and shook. Eventually we all got used to the sounds, but I slept fitfully the first couple of nights.

During Tuesday's lunch break Bob announced that we were going fishing and everyone was invited. Frank and Martin declined. After work we packed some sandwiches, filled the cooler with beer, and headed toward Lake Powell. The drive took about an hour through some beautiful country. The days were getting longer, so we still had an hour left of sunlight. Bob parked the vehicle in a cove that we reached via a small two-track road.

"Now what?" I asked as Bob turned off the engine.

"Well, we grab our chairs, fishing gear, and the cooler and we find a good spot. I think I know where the fish will be biting. You get the chairs and poles, and I'll carry the cooler." Bob lifted the cooler as easily as if it were empty. I put the aluminum chairs over my shoulder and had two hands left to carry the poles and the tackle box.

We walked a few hundred yards to a steep ledge next to a deep, clear pool. We were sheltered from the wind by a high cliff and the view was spectacular.

"I don't have a fishing license."

"I thought of that and brought my ex-wife's license. She hates to fish, and now that she's rid of me, I'm sure she won't be fishing anymore." He said this with a touch of bitterness, like he had a dirty penny in his mouth.

"How long have you been divorced?" I asked, trying to sound sympathetic.

"It's only been a few months since the divorce was legal, but we've been separated for a year. We tried making it work again for our son, six months ago, but we both realized that it was hopeless. You see, my wife fell in love with a woman about two years ago. I guess she discovered she was gay or some damn thing…."

I stopped setting up the chair and looked at Bob, stunned. "Your wife left you for a woman?" The question came tumbling out before I took the time to think it over.

"Yeah," said Bob, shaking his head and looking out at the lake. "It hurts. Can it get any worse than having your wife dump you for a woman? She keeps telling me it doesn't have anything to do with me, that I've been a great husband. It's just that she's gay. It sounds even worse when I say it out loud."

"I'm sorry, Bob. That's really sad, especially if you still love her."

Bob blinked fast and shook his head. He reached for a beer and started to rig up a pole.

"I'll get your pole ready first. We're going to use lures I have that work great on bass. You need to cast out and reel it in nice and slow."

He worked in silence for a while. I drank a beer and ate half of a sandwich. Sitting in my chair and relaxing felt great after a long day of hiking. I had on my flip-flops and wiggled my toes with joyous abandon—free from hiking boot prison. I watched Bob as he added and removed tackle from each pole. I decided that you could tell a lot about a man from his tackle box. Bob's was clean, organized, and well stocked. So far that pretty much summed him up. He was also cheerful and a hopeless optimist. Bob had made these last few weeks of fieldwork bearable.

"So how is custody of your son going to work when you move to Canada?"

"I'll have Eddie during summer vacation and Christmas break. He'll live with his mom and her girlfriend the rest of the time. I can't believe my son is going to be raised by lesbians. Who would have thought?"

"My grandmother's cousin, Estelle, lived with another woman. They were elderly by the time I met them, and they lived together in a house next door to Gram. It turns out that Estelle was married and even had a daughter when she scandalized everyone by moving in with a woman. She lost custody of her daughter, but they stayed close. Her daughter turned out fine. She married a really nice guy and had eight kids. The grandkids would often visit Estelle and her girlfriend, and I used to play with them. The fact that their grandmother was a lesbian never seemed to be a big deal. I didn't know there was a stigma until I got older, and that seems to be a thing of the past. Don't worry. Your son will be fine."

Bob handed me my pole.

"I know it will be okay, it's just that the wounds are still open and painful. Anyway...let's fish."

And we did. The fish were biting, and we caught enough for breakfast before it got dark. I helped Bob clean them, and we headed for camp. I still had lots of questions for Bob about graduate school, and even the divorce process, but he seemed far away, and I decided not to pick at his wounded heart.

I noticed as I got out of the Blazer back at camp that the wind had stopped. The night was still and beautiful, the thin sliver of moon surrounded by a billion twinkling stars. "Guess I'll call it a night. I enjoyed fishing. Thanks."

"Good night, Ivy. Sleep tight and don't let the gnats bite."

His last words were like a prophecy. As soon as it began to warm up the next day, the tiny little no-see-um gnats appeared. The winds had given way to the gnats, and they were merciless. They buzzed in our ears, climbed in our hair, and even flew up our noses. My hands, neck, scalp, and ears were covered with tiny, itching welts. I covered up as best as I could, but the gnats even managed to crawl under the edge of my bandana and into my ears. Long pants and long-sleeved shirts helped some, but the gnats still managed to worm their way under the cuffs wherever my skin was exposed. Having grown up with gnats, Bob seemed the least bothered, but he was also the best prepared. He had managed to completely cover his body. He'd even sewn Velcro along the slits in his shirt cuffs. And to keep the gnats out of his ears, he wore a headscarf like an Arab sheik.

The rest of us didn't cope well with our latest tormentors. Martin swore loudly throughout the day, and Frank got quiet and sullen. Since the gnats were small enough to get through my tent screens, I hid in the vehicle when we were in camp. Cooking was out of the question, and I started living on granola bars and potato chips. By Friday I was a mass of welts. The only thing that kept me going was the thought of leaving on Friday and never coming back. Over the last eleven months of camping and working in the field I'd managed to survive loneliness, filth, allergies, gas fumes, bad supervisors, and constant wind, but there was no way I was going to manage two months of gnat hell. If I couldn't work in the office, I promised myself I would quit. Enough was enough.

From the Frying Pan into the Fire

After working as a landscaper over the summer, and barely making enough money to survive, I'd decided to look for another archaeology job. I double-checked the downtown address and the bus schedule. My interview was at 10 a.m. in downtown Salt Lake, and the bus ride would take about an hour. That left less than an hour to get ready. I decided that I should dress like an archaeologist: jeans, long-sleeve work shirt, and Frye boots.

I showered and let my hair dry naturally. It had gotten very blond from weeks in the sun, and it almost reached my waist. Most of the time I tied it back in a braid or a ponytail, but today I decided to wear it straight and parted just off center. Archaeologists generally don't wear makeup, so that was easy. I looked at my reflection and decided I looked pretty good, despite the lack of makeup and boring clothes. In my opinion, most female archaeologists dress incredibly frumpy. The older academic types shun makeup, hair dye, and flashy clothes. They wear blocky tweed suits to professional meetings—and never anything sexy.

Sitting on the bus, I reviewed what I knew about Ken Blink. He was the Land Management Agency's head archaeologist in the regional office, and he was in charge of the cultural resources budget for the agency's Utah program. I had never read about anything he'd done, and when I had asked a few other archaeologists if they had heard of him, no one seemed to know anything beyond his role as the agency's regional archaeologist.

When I spoke to him on the phone to set up the interview, I learned that ASC's southern and central coal surveys were under Ken's oversight.

The office building was easy to find, and I presented myself to the Resources Division secretary about ten minutes early. She called Ken to announce my arrival and led me to his office. The agency was housed in a fairly new twelve-story office building in the center of the city. The Resources Division occupied the west half of the ninth floor. The walk to Ken's office provided a spectacular view. It was a clear fall day, and the scrub oak on the Wasatch foothills had turned red. The city, steadily creeping from the valley bottom into the foothills, was surrounded by mountains. The steep, rocky Wasatch Front on the east side of the valley is home to world-famous ski areas renowned for their deep powder. The Oquirrh Range to the west cowers under the smokestack of the Kennecott Copper smelter, located at the northern tip of the range. I called this area the Valley of Mordor, as in *Lord of the Rings*. Toxic fumes spewing from the smelter's stack had killed the trees and natural vegetation along the northern third of the range. Scars from one of the world's largest open pit mines had consumed an entire mountain.

Everyone in the Resources Division shared a large, open space that was light and airy. Low partitions delineated the offices. When we walked up to Ken's office in the northwest corner, he was sitting at his desk watching me. The intensity of his gaze made me slightly uncomfortable, but I wrote it off to nerves.

As he stood, I reached out to shake his hand. "Hi, Ken, I'm Ivy Jones." His hand was large and warm, and he wore a plain gold wedding band and a cheap watch.

"I know. I asked around about you. They were right. Cute, petite, and blond."

"Really? I hope they said good things about my archaeological abilities, and not just my looks." I had a fleeting thought that maybe he didn't care about my abilities or intelligence, but I quickly reminded myself not to be paranoid.

"They said you can find sites, but you have some issues with authority. Tell me about that."

"You talked to Dr. Lockyear, didn't you?" Ken motioned for me to sit down and I relaxed a little. "I can explain."

"There's no need. Dr. Lockyear already described the circumstances and gave you a good recommendation overall."

I made a quick decision not to dwell on problems at ASC. "Why don't you tell me more about this job?"

I had learned that most people love to talk about themselves, so I decided my best strategy would be to get Ken to talk about himself. Instead he launched into a long discourse on the tasks he planned to have his assistant tackle.

"The Land Management Agency's cultural resource program is just being developed. I was the first state agency archaeologist hired, and I've been working closely with a team of other agency archaeologists to develop the cultural resource program. We've been meeting in Washington every month and have almost completed the program's design. I'm also working with the five regional offices here in Utah to hire archaeologists. We have one of the best cultural resource programs in the country."

Ken went on and on about how fantastic his program was—thanks to his great abilities. He was possibly the biggest braggart that I had ever encountered. He talked about his education, his previous jobs, his single-handed development of the Utah program, and he believed every word. I was too shocked to say anything, so I just observed him in action. He appeared to be in his late forties. He was average height, a bit under six feet, and was wearing jeans, a pinstriped shirt, and cowboy boots. His hair reminded me of the Ken doll's hair—that is, peach fuzz. Unlike Ken doll's, real Ken's hair was peppered with gray. A dark brown handlebar mustache added character to an otherwise plain face, and the lower half of his face melted into a short scruffy beard speckled with gray. He leaned back in his chair and put his feet on his desk. His bright blue eyes were probably his best feature, and couldn't be disguised even behind his horn-rimmed glasses.

Finally he paused, pushed his glasses up his nose, and sat back in his chair. "Did you get all that?"

No. I'd spaced out through most of it, but I had listened to the descriptions of the tasks he needed an assistant to perform.

"Yes, I think I've got it. If you hire me, I'll update your set of maps that show the locations of known archaeological sites and previous archaeological surveys, I'll develop a new site form for the agency's computer system, and I'll assist you with some of your tasks like permitting and contracts. I'm sure I can handle all of that."

Ken smiled. "Good. When can you start?"

"Does that mean I got the job?" How did this work? He'd asked me practically nothing about my background, education, career goals, and previous experience.

He chuckled. "Yes. My hiring decision will need to be approved by the department director, but he usually goes with my recommendation."

He looked me up and down again, and a little voice in my head sounded an alarm. I ignored it and reminded myself that jobs like this were few and far between. So what if he was a little lecherous? I could handle it. After all, I'd spent two summers fending off dirty old men as a waitress on Block Island in a Mafia-run restaurant. Playing dumb with their overtures and then getting the hell out of there had turned out to be my best defense. I needed this job.

"I can start immediately."

"Let's see. Your application will take at least a week to process, so why don't we plan on two weeks from today." Ken pulled out a small leather calendar and flipped the pages. "That will be September eighteenth. How does that sound?"

"That will be perfect."

Abruptly, Ken stood up and smiled. He offered his hand. "Welcome aboard. I need to head off to a meeting, but I'll call you after the paperwork is signed."

We shook hands and I thanked Ken for his time. I continued trying to convince myself that the little voice, which was now screaming at me, was ridiculous. I would just have to deal with Ken, even if he was kind of slimy.

I walked past the secretary, said good-bye, and left. Wait a minute, I thought. I'd forgotten to ask what time I should be at the office. I turned around and as I opened the door to the Resources Division, I overheard the secretaries talking.

"Looks like Ken found another cutie to torment."

"Just like a lamb going to slaughter. I don't know how he gets away with it."

I stuck my head inside and they both turned guilty eyes to me. "I forgot to ask what the office hours are."

"I guess that's kind of important," said the older secretary, a redhead in her fifties. "Most people drift in between 7:30 and 8:00, but our official starting time is 7:45. Aren't you working part-time?"

"Yes. Maybe I should call Ken and ask him what hours he wants me to work."

"That's a good idea. He's in a meeting or I'd call and ask for you."

I smiled, thanked her, and headed back to the elevator, wondering what I'd gotten myself into.

My two weeks of vacation zipped by. I'd been so busy working that I had a million little things I needed to do. I cleaned out shelves and painted my small bathroom bright white. I also decided to go through my clothes to see what would be acceptable for work. I had no money for new clothes. I spread my work-type clothes across the bed: two skirts, three blouses, a couple of shirts that would be marginally acceptable, one pair of good jeans, a pair of khaki slacks, and a single pair of shoes that were dressy enough for skirts. I would wear my boots with my pants. Until I made some money, I would just have to make do with what I had.

The phone rang and I raced across my small duplex to get it.

"Hello!"

"It's Ken. The paperwork was signed today. You start Monday."

"We forgot to talk about my hours. What schedule would you like me to work?"

"How about nine to three? My other line is ringing. See you at 9 a.m. on Monday."

I held the phone away from my ear and stared at it. "Okay," I said to no one in particular.

My first week on the job was a blur. I had to learn so much about the Land Management Agency, cultural resources, contract archaeology reports, and the regional archaeologists. My desk, which was next to Ken's cubicle, was stacked with survey reports, all of them to be plotted onto a set of maps of the entire state. It looked like I'd be working on them for months.

Ken was on the phone all the time, talking to what sounded like a million different people, most of them archaeologists. I perked up at the sound of my name.

"Ivy can help too. She's my new assistant. We can meet you down at the site. Yeah, in two weeks. You organize all the equipment and materials. Okay." Ken hung up the phone.

I looked over and he stood up and started walking toward me. "It's lunchtime. Want to join the gang today?"

"Where are you going?"

"The Mexican place down the street. Come on."

The "gang" consisted of Chuck, a range conservationist; Guy, a geologist; and Peter, a biologist. The professional staff in the Resources Division consisted entirely of middle-age white guys and me. Everyone was twice my age, and I was the only woman on the floor who was not a secretary. I had little in common with the guys and was too poor to be eating out. However, I was curious about what Ken had committed me to on the phone, and it was Friday. I threw caution to the wind and decided to join them.

We walked to the restaurant and were seated at a booth in the back. Most of the tables were filled with noisy customers who shoveled rice and beans into their mouths between sentences. A busboy arrived to fill our water glasses.

"Water, sir?" he asked Ken.

"Never drink it. Fish fuck in it," he responded, to my complete horror.

Speechless, the busboy stared at Ken and then moved over to Chuck and filled his glass. He filled everyone else's glass and quickly left. As I would quickly learn, eating a meal with Ken meant one rude, inappropriate comment after another. The other guys usually laughed, and Ken thought he was very witty, but I suspect that most people just thought he was a jerk. He even requested that the checks be separate because we didn't know each other.

"Ken," I asked, between mouthfuls, "what was that you were saying on the phone about me going with you somewhere?"

"I was talking to Gordon, the agency archaeologist in Washington City. We're going to help him stabilize the Slickrock site the week after next. We'll be gone for a week and will stay in St. George. Greg Lehman, the agency archaeologist in Hurricane, will help. The ruin needs to be stabilized, and there's no one else to do it."

"I've never done that kind of work before. What exactly does it require?"

"The site is a Virgin Anasazi habitation that Gordon excavated in the agency campground north of St. George. There are storage rooms and deep, slab-lined cists that with a little concrete, some signs, and a protective roof will make a good interpretive site. With all of us working on it, we should finish in a week."

We got up to leave. It would be great to work outside again. I still wasn't used to being indoors all day, and I was glad I didn't have to be in the office for forty hours a week. On the walk back to work, the guys talked about their weekend plans, most of which involved their kids' football or soccer games. I really didn't have anything in common with them.

Back in the office I plotted several more surveys and sites onto the base maps. The huge pile of reports had shrunk, but I still had a long way to go. Since the task was pretty boring, I decided to take a little more time and actually look at the survey reports to see what the various companies were doing. There were about five or so in Utah that were writing the reports as contract archaeologists. When I plotted the archaeological surveys, a pattern emerged. Most of the surveys in the northeastern part of the state, the Roosevelt region, were done for oil wells. The survey areas were roads and drill pads. In the central region of the state, coal mining was the force behind development. Surveys in central Utah surrounded coal mines, so they were large blocks. In the Green River region, in southeastern Utah, many of the surveys were for geophysical exploration, and a few were uranium mines. My former boyfriend, the geologist, had explained that geophysicists were searching for oil deposits using new mapping methods that tracked how sound waves traveled through rock. The archaeological surveys for these projects were straight lines because the geophysicists laid out strings of geophones, which tracked vibrations. To create vibrations along the lines, geophysical explorers use large trucks, called thumpers, that pound the ground or set off small explosions. The vibrations travel through subsurface rock, and the geophones record their movement.

As usual, Ken was on the phone talking to one of the regional archaeologists. He spent hours each day offering advice on how to deal with local managers or how to get a particular survey done. I was learning the six regional archaeologists' names from their survey reports, and from overhearing Ken talk to them. As far as I could tell, the regional archaeologists usually did only small surveys for fences, cattle tanks, campgrounds, or other cattle range improvement projects. Miners, drillers, and mineral explorers were told by the agency to hire contract archaeologists if they wanted to obtain an archaeological clearance for cultural resources.

Ken stood up and walked over to me. "I'm going to be out of the office Monday and Tuesday. You can answer my phone while I'm gone. I'll be in Vernal training our new archaeologist. A week from Monday we'll drive to St. George for the stabilization project."

"Will I need any special equipment for the field?"

"Nah, Gordon will have it all. Just pack some old clothes, sunscreen, and a hat. It will probably be pretty warm down there, and the motel we stay at has a great pool, so bring your swimsuit."

"I think I might be half finished with the map work by next Friday."

Ken smiled, like he knew something I didn't. "Except that I have another pile of projects to plot that you don't even know about."

I groaned and rolled my eyes. "I'll be ready to get away from this for a week in the sun. Are you sure it's okay that I've never done this before?"

"None of us have ever done this before." He walked away and then looked over his shoulder, smirking more than smiling.

Ken's lecherous expression and his greasy, slippery aura were giving me the creeps. I'd have to be on my toes. But even though I wasn't thrilled about spending a week in the field with him, I was looking forward to meeting Gordon and Greg. I'd spoken to Gordon on the phone, and he had a deep voice that rolled out of his mouth like a cresting wave. I had a mental image of him as tall, handsome, and tanned. I'd never spoken to Greg, but he was the only archaeologist working for the agency who was about my age.

The next week was hectic and busy. It seemed like Ken's phone never stopped ringing. I kept track of everyone who called in a logbook. Although I didn't know who many of the callers were, I recognized some of their names from my archaeological studies. The constant interruptions made it impossible for me to concentrate on the map work, but I managed to make another dent in the pile of reports.

The following Monday, we left the telephone behind in Salt Lake and headed for St. George, a small Mormon farming community in southwestern Utah. The economy depends on tourism, farming, and ranching. Recently, St. George had become a retirement community for wealthy Mormons who were drawn to its warm, sunny climate.

Ken and I left the office at 7 a.m. because the drive takes five hours. We had just gotten through Provo, and the mountains were speckled with stands of scrub oaks that had lost their burst of color and had faded to brown. I remembered that I wanted to ask Ken about Dr. John Flake's call. Dr. Flake was one of the West's most famous archaeologists, and I couldn't imagine why he would be calling Ken.

"Why did Dr. Flake call you last week?"

"John had a crew working in Grand Gulch and they noticed recent pot-hunting activities at the Turkey Pen site. They think the pothunters hit it more than once and might return. We're going to have our special investigator try to catch them. The site's a mess. The pothunters even burned beams in their fire pits, and they excavated a large pit in the middle of the ruin."

"The agency has a special investigator to catch pothunters? Is that all he does?"

"Nah, it's just one of his jobs. Lately he's been trying to catch some of the better-known pothunters who live in southeastern Utah. He infiltrated their sales channels to figure out who's buying the stuff. It's big business down in Monticello and Blanding."

"When I worked for ASC I worked with a reformed pothunter, Ben Edwards."

Ken chuckled. "Reformed my ass! Ben will never stop digging sites. Once it's in their blood, they can't stop."

"Ben told me he isn't going to pothunt sites any more. He's really a nice guy—not the sharpest tack in the box, but kind of sweet." I looked over at Ken and he was shaking his head.

"Time will tell. I bet he hasn't stopped. You know, we told ASC they couldn't use Ben anymore."

"Really? He just kind of disappeared one week and no one knew where he went. I thought he went back to school."

We rode in silence until we stopped for gas in Nephi. I bought coffee and hit the ladies room. When I returned, Ken was pumping gas with his field hat on. It was amazing. At the very least it was the most ridiculous hat that I had ever seen. He caught my expression of horror.

"You like it that much?"

"That has got to be one of the ugliest hats that I've ever seen. For God's sake, it's pink. What kind of archaeologist wears a pink fishing hat?" I walked over to get a closer look. His hat was faded pink plaid and made of a thin cotton fabric. The top was flat, and it had a blue hatband at the seam along the short brim. Sweat marks and stains were visible under the dozens, maybe even hundreds, of pins that covered the entire surface. Most of the pins were from vacation places related to hunting and fishing expeditions. I noticed a Lake Powell pin and one from Yellowstone.

"I love this hat. I'll never give it up, no matter what, and the pins make it heavy so it doesn't blow away."

I returned to the car, shaking my head. Ken got in next to me, smiling, obviously pleased with himself. "This hat has been with me for twenty years. It's lucky and has seen me through difficult times."

Ken then took off the hat and placed it on the dashboard right in front of me. I wanted to move it, but I was afraid of touching the years of accumulated sweat and grime. I tried to look away, but no matter where I looked, my eyes were magnetically drawn back to the hat. It sat there daring me to touch it.

"You're going to have to either move that hat or pull over and let me out. I am not staring at it for another three hours. No way. Is this some kind of a test?"

"You passed." He grinned at me and moved the hat onto his lap. Then he stared ahead at the road. "My wife won't touch it either."

"Good for her. It really is disgusting, you know."

Ken looked straight ahead at the road and cleared his throat. "Have you always been opinionated, or has it come later in life?"

"What do you mean?"

"You don't beat around the bush much. Sugar coating is not part of your approach."

I looked over at Ken, who was concentrating on the curves in the road. "I come from a long line of swamp Yankees who were tough as nails. We call it like we see it. I guess I grew up listening to women speak their minds." For some reason I had always felt timid and tongue-tied around Dr. Johnson, but around Ken I felt more assertive. Why was that? I wondered. Maybe it was because I didn't respect him?

"I can see that," said Ken, chuckling. "I feel sorry for your boyfriend."

"You don't have to be since there isn't one—or a serious one, that is."

The way Ken looked at me made me realize I probably shouldn't have told him I'd pretty much been single the last few months. Tom, it seemed, was busy with other things. Fortunately, Ken changed the subject and started talking about the antique collection that he'd been building since he was a teenager. I nodded now and then but basically tuned out. I could only take so much in one day.

We arrived at the Slickrock campground a little after noon. It was a beautiful fall day, warm and clear. The contrast between the deep blue sky and red sandstone cliffs reminded me how much I missed canyon country. The campground was nestled under five-hundred-foot high sandstone cliffs at the base of the Pine Valley Mountains.

"Where are we meeting everyone?" I asked.

"At the site. I helped with the excavation a few times so I know where it is."

We drove down a narrow paved road along a clear, shallow creek. We passed the ruins of a stone house, probably built by the first Mormon pioneers, and crossed the creek twice. Ken pointed ahead.

"The campground is up a ways, but we're going to head east to the top of that small knoll."

He pointed to a ridge off in the distance. I could see small figures moving around.

"I think I see someone working."

"They should be setting up."

We drove a few hundred more yards and then parked. I grabbed my hat and followed Ken up the ridge. A government truck had almost made it to the top. Next to the truck sat a small cement mixer and stacked bags of cement. Just ahead of the mixer, two guys stood and watched our approach. They were both about six feet tall. The older one had gray hair tied in a ponytail. He was as thin as the shovel he was leaning against, but his smile was broad and welcoming. The younger guy was dark and handsome— probably the first archaeologist I'd ever met that I thought was attractive.

Since Ken was talking to the older archaeologist, I introduced myself to Mr. Handsome. "Hi, I'm Ivy Jones, Ken's new slavette."

"So you're Ivy. I'm Greg Lehman from Hurricane."

We shook hands, and I had a funny feeling that I'd met him before.

"Have we met?" I asked. "You seem familiar."

Greg shook his head. "I don't believe so, but archaeology is a small world."

"Ivy!" yelled Ken. "Come and meet Gordon."

"Hey, Ivy, nice to meet you." Gordon's wonderful deep voice boomed out of his thin body. The rural Utah twang seemed more pronounced in person. We shook hands, and I instantly liked him.

"You're not what I expected."

Gordon laughed. "Let me guess. You thought I'd be big and burly?"

"Something like that. I guess it's your deep voice that created a big guy mental picture."

"Yeah, I get that all the time."

Ken interrupted. "So let's get to it. Greg, why don't you show Ivy the site while Gordon and I strategize?"

Greg smiled at me and motioned for me to follow him. We walked over to a deep pit lined with huge sandstone slabs. He gracefully jumped into the center, and the walls came up to his shoulders.

"We excavated this site two years ago." He pointed over to an area next to the cement mixer. "The site contains a string of linked storage rooms and these deep storage cists. There's also a pithouse in the center of the linked storage rooms, but you can't really see it now." Greg pointed to a depression between the storage cist he was standing in and the row of low masonry rooms. "The pottery decorations suggest that the site dates to the Pueblo I period, but the radiocarbon dates were all over the place—possibly an old wood problem."

"What's that?" I sat on the edge of the storage pit with my legs crossed.

"Juniper trees can live for over a hundred years and then they can lie around for another hundred or even two hundred years before they're picked up by someone and used as firewood. If the wood was two hundred years old when it was burned in a fire, then the radiocarbon date will be two hundred years too old."

"I get it. So what were the radiocarbon dates for this site?"

"Like I said, they were all over the place. I'd guess the site was used on and off throughout the Puebloan period."

Greg lifted himself gracefully out of the cist. I imagined trying to get myself out of there. The walls would come up to my neck, and I didn't think I'd have enough strength in my arms to lift myself up. I'd be stuck like a bug in an ant lion's sand trap. I followed Greg over to the shallow, oval-shaped masonry rooms. The walls were made out of cobbles and boulders, and the floors were slab lined.

"These linked storage rooms are characteristic of the Virgin Anasazi sites in this area. Sometimes there are so many rooms that they form a C-shaped room block. In the Puebloan II period the end rooms are often larger than the others, and they contain a central hearth. The hearth suggests that people lived in the larger rooms."

Greg stood inside one of the rooms. All that remained of the masonry walls were stacked boulders and leaning sandstone slabs. The walls were only about one or two feet high, and the floors of a couple of the larger rooms were lined with slabs. The rooms measured about six feet long and three feet wide. They were way too small to live in and had instead been used for storing food for lean years.

"We're going to make concrete out of the local sand and then cement these rocks together. It's easy. You'll get the hang of it in no time."

Gordon walked up to us. "Greg, I need your help with the mixer. Ivy, why don't you clean out the rooms?" He pointed to a dead bush that had blown into the structure. "Just clear all this stuff out while we mix the concrete."

The afternoon zoomed by. We started on the linked rooms. Ken and I worked in adjoining rooms, and Gordon made concrete. Greg hauled the concrete over and instructed me on the finer points of ruin stabilization. Since we were using the concrete slower than Gordon was making it, he and Greg took a break and helped us stabilize the rooms. I slopped concrete on the ground and then rebuilt the walls, placing concrete under and between the rocks. I learned to make the mortar look old by stippling it with a wet brush and throwing sand on the concrete when it was wet. I was pleased with my handiwork, but the lime in the cement was eating the skin off my hands. They were red, raw, and bleeding in places. We agreed to buy heavy rubber gloves in the morning.

"Tomorrow we'll start on the deep cists," Gordon said. "Let's call it a day."

Gordon drove home to Washington City for the night, but Greg, Ken, and I drove to St. George and checked into the local Best Western. The motel had tiny rooms but a gorgeous pool and Jacuzzi. With the way my muscles were feeling, I figured a soak was in order. The guys convinced me that it would be better to eat and then relax in the tub. After a quick shower, we met in the lobby and drove to a nearby Italian restaurant. I marveled over how much easier this was than camping out.

We had a better time in the restaurant than I would have thought possible. Greg had the same passion for archaeology that I did. We were definitely connecting, and I could see that Ken was annoyed with both of us. Naturally, he wanted to be the center of attention.

"Where did you go to graduate school, Greg?" I asked, noticing Ken checking out one of the waitresses.

"University of Ohio," he said proudly. "They have an excellent archaeology program. That's where I met my wife. She's a schoolteacher."

"Whatever possessed you to move here?"

"I did it for the archaeology, and my wife wanted to get away from the cities. Also, there weren't that many jobs available when I finished school. The Land Management Agency offered me a job, so here I am."

"How do you manage in a small Mormon community? Do you feel like you fit in?"

"It hasn't been a problem yet." Greg finished off his beer.

I remembered hearing in one of my anthropology classes that there was a large polygamous town right near here. "Do you have any dealings with that polygamous group in Colorado City?"

"I just did a survey there a few weeks ago. They want the agency to donate a parcel of land to the town for a park. It has a small site on it, but it looks like the sale will go forward. The people all dress funny, but they were nice enough." Greg moved his plate away and put his crumpled napkin on it.

"I drove past that town once and noticed some of the houses don't have windows. Isn't that strange?"

"Nah, they avoid property taxes by not installing windows. A house isn't considered completed until windows are installed, so they don't get taxed on it. Most of the people in Colorado City are on some form of welfare. They're all poor except for the leaders."

Ken had had enough of our conversation. "Living in a small Mormon town has its advantages and drawbacks. Things are orderly, and once the Mormons figure out that you can't be converted, they leave you alone. Once you figure out the liquor store system, it's not so bad."

Ken lived in a small town fifty miles north of Salt Lake City.

"What's the name of that town you live in, Ken?"

The waitress had come back to refill our water glasses, and Ken was leering at her. "Loran. Are we done here? Let's hit the hot tub. My back is killing me."

We all enjoyed the pool and hot tub, just soaking and drinking beer. Greg was a great Ken deflector. After an hour Ken realized he was making no progress with me so he left us to talk about archaeology. With Ken gone, Greg and I discussed anthropological theory, statistics, and regional culture histories. I was weak in practical knowledge, but had a pretty good understanding of the new processual archaeology movement. Since we were both about the same age and he was happily married, there were no leers like those I received from the Resources Division guys when they thought I wasn't looking.

We met early the next morning, hit the hardware store for some gloves, and then headed back to the site. The plan for the day was that there would be two seasonal employees to make the concrete, allowing the rest of us to work on the structures. Greg and I would start on the deep storage cists while Gordon and Ken finished the linked storage rooms.

"When you excavated these cists, did you find any evidence of how they were roofed?" I asked Greg out of curiosity.

"They were cleaned out except for blown sand and some organic material that probably blew in. We did take pollen samples from just on top of the slabs on the floor."

"What did you find? Any corn pollen?"

"There was a trace of corn, but there was also a lot of wild seed pollen, like rye and pigweed."

Greg slapped some concrete between two huge slabs. "We also floated some soil samples to recover seeds."

"What did you find?" I asked, looking over at Greg's concrete slinging technique.

"Not much. Rodents or termites got everything except for a few pine nuts and a kernel of corn."

"Well, that's better than nothing. How many samples did you process?"

"We only had enough money for a couple. It's pricey to pay someone to float out the organic materials and analyze the seeds. We had very little money for analysis, and what we did have, we spent mostly on radiocarbon dates."

"How do you think they covered these cists? Maybe with slabs and adobe? Or do you think they used wood?"

Greg pointed to a pile of sandstone slabs on the slope. "I think they covered whatever they stored with mud and sandstone slabs. Then when they retrieved the contents of the cist, they just threw the roofing materials aside. If they had never returned to retrieve the stored food, perhaps we'd know more about the roof construction methods."

I thought about this as I worked. The gloves were protecting my skin from the concrete's lime, but my hands were still red and peeling from yesterday, and there were places where sores had developed.

The day was warming up, and it was time to take off one of my several layers, which in the desert is the only way to dress. Fall mornings were usually cold enough for a T-shirt, a flannel shirt, and a sweatshirt or light jacket. I removed my concrete-covered gloves and took off my flannel shirt, throwing it onto a bush so it wouldn't get smeared with concrete too.

Greg was also down to his T-shirt. He was intently smoothing and stippling the concrete around the edges of a huge slab. I genuinely admired his work, but I was really checking out his muscles. This was the first time

I had found myself in the field with an attractive coworker, and before I realized it, I was lost in my thoughts and standing there like an idiot. Greg looked over at me and seemed to read my mind. His mustache twitched, his eyes twinkled, and then his whole face lit up with a knowing smile.

"Like what you see?"

I quickly turned my eyes to the concrete work and ignored his innuendo. "Yeah, I was just noticing that your stippling looks much better than mine."

Greg raised one eyebrow and smiled. "I'm sure that's what you were thinking."

I realized I was blushing, so I quickly turned away. I scooped up a glob of concrete with my gloved hand and slapped it in place, but I could feel Greg's eyes on my back. Oh boy, now what? I had discovered a whole new, unexplored problem with fieldwork.

The week zoomed past and we were driving back to Salt Lake City. Being back in the field had been so much fun, but I'd discovered muscles that I never knew existed. I felt exhausted, and the warm sunshine was lulling me to sleep. I suspected that Ken was mad because I had paid more attention to Greg, but I didn't really care. We were halfway home before he said a word to me.

"You seemed to get along fine with Gordon and Greg—especially Greg," Ken said pointedly, leering. "Did you get any sleep last night?"

I looked straight ahead. "That is none of your business."

"Too bad."

Ignoring him, I turned toward the window and went back to sleep.

Computers and Archaeology

"Ivy, you'll need to answer the phones and take over for me tomorrow. There's an all-day meeting I need to go to about the DX missile project."

Ken was clearing his desk and heading home. It was nearing the holidays, and everyone except me seemed to be arriving a little later and leaving a little earlier. My workdays, though, had gotten longer and longer as Ken realized I could do many of the jobs that he didn't particularly like. So far, I had taken over permitting, the publication series, and the contract to computerize archaeological site data. Of course I never got credit for doing any of these things.

"Do you want me to go ahead with the meeting scheduled for tomorrow with the university?"

"Oh, shit, I forgot about that." Ken grabbed his jacket and headed for the door. He looked over his shoulder at me. "You can handle it."

Ken never forgot a thing. He was definitely lying. He didn't even sound surprised, just annoyed that I'd remembered the meeting before he made it out the door.

I stacked the survey reports that I was still working on, grabbed my down jacket, and headed for the elevator. Salt Lake has an excellent public transportation system, so it made sense for me to ride the bus to and from work. It was snowing again, and the ski areas had just opened. I planned to spend the weekend at Alta. It had been way too long since I'd

been skiing, and I was looking forward to the new powder being promised in the forecasts.

My bus was at the corner when I arrived, right on time. I jumped on
and took a seat, my mind wandering back to tomorrow's 10 a.m. meeting.
Ken had contracted the anthropology department at Utah College to create a computer system for the agency's growing archaeological site data.
They had been hired to write the programs for a site database and then
encode the previously recorded archaeological sites in the northern half
of the state. Ken was bored with the project, so he had pretty much turned
it over to me.

Computers were still new in the late 1970s, and most were large mainframes that could only be programmed if you knew a language like Fortran.
Mini mainframes had just barely been invented, and user-friendly laptops
were only a glimmer in Steve Job's eye. With the goal of making computer
data more accessible to their employees, the Department of the Interior
had developed a relational database system called DEX. These databases
could be queried using English words to retrieve data. For example, I
could ask DEX how many sites and what kinds were known in a section
or even a quarter section area.

The main problem with computerizing the site data appeared to be
updating the system. Who would add new sites to the database? Currently,
every federal and state agency used a different recording form for archaeological sites. The state of Utah was mandated to maintain site records,
but hadn't yet agreed to update the computer system. I was trying to convince Ken that we needed to get all the agencies to agree on one site form,
and then it would be technically possible for the state to maintain the
archaeological computer system.

I reminded myself to be patient. I looked out the window at the
gloomy, cold day. In November, temperature inversions often develop in
Salt Lake, trapping a dense layer of fog and exhaust. These inversions can
last for weeks, smothering the valley in a pea soup of smog. The ski slopes,
on top of the mountains, rise above the inversion into the cold, blue skies.
I longed to go skiing and breathe fresh air. Perhaps I was even missing
fieldwork a little bit too.

"Ken was called to a meeting today, and he asked me to talk to you about
your progress on the project. So, how are things going?" I cleared my

throat, feeling unsettled. There were four of us in the agency's smallest conference room, a cold, sterile space. The contractors from the university included Mike Lamont, a computer wizard; Dave Wright, the project director; and Maureen Smith, a graduate student in charge of encoding the site data. I'd met Dave at Utah College, where he ran the contract archaeology program. Most of his projects were surveys and excavations for roads and highways. I'd never met Maureen before, but I had met Mike at two other progress meetings.

Mike was a nerdy version of Indiana Jones. Imagine Harrison Ford—bedroom eyes and crooked smile—but with a shock of black hair and solid, dark-rim glasses. He had a dry sense of humor and was wicked smart. Maureen, on the other hand, was insecure and ultra mousey. She had mastered the skill of never making eye contact, but I caught her sneaking enraptured gazes at Mike. Dave, dressed in standard professor attire—corduroy sport coat complete with leather patches—was almost finished with his Ph.D. His dissertation was on a large site that he had helped to excavate several years ago in southwestern Utah.

Dave answered my question. "In our last meeting we agreed on the data fields that we're using in the site database. I think you were there, Ivy."

His stare made me squirm in my seat. "Yes, I remember."

"Since our last meeting we started to encode the archaeological site forms and have hit some snags. For one thing, the oldest site forms are difficult to read because they are written in long-hand, and they often don't have useful information." Dave passed out a site form to each of us.

"This site form identifies the site as a prehistoric camp with a dense scatter of flakes and projectile points. The problem is that the form doesn't say how many of which types of artifacts are present, and the database only allows us to enter specific categories of artifacts, not subjective site types."

I hadn't thought of this. "I see what you mean. We all know what the archaeologist who recorded the site meant, but how do we translate it into the database?"

Dave reached over and picked up another form. "Here's another site form that identifies the site as a Fremont habitation. That's all it says, other than the general location and the setting."

"Could I see that form, Dave?" He handed it to me, and I noticed that it had been filled out by none other than Dr. Johnson. "But Johnson made us put tons of detail in our descriptions," I muttered under my breath.

What a hypocrite, I thought to myself. No big surprise, but I needed to focus on the problems at hand. "So what do you suggest we do?"

"We have two choices. We can add some interpretive site type categories, or we can encode the site and mark the categories in the database as 'unknown.' That way we have an unknown prehistoric site, which, if you think about it, is really all we do know about the site. These old sites aren't even well located. There's no township-range given, and the directions to the site are vague."

Mike picked up a stack of computer printouts and put it in front of me. He adjusted his glasses with his middle finger. "We have finished encoding three of the five counties covered by our contract. Here are the printouts. All told, we've entered 2,568 sites into the system. Around 200 of those sites were unclear and ambiguous, like the ones you just looked at. If we create a site recording form that is based on the computer system's data categories, all of these problems go away. And let's face it. How useful are the old sites when we can't even figure out where they're located?"

He was making a lot of sense. "I agree, Mike. There's no point in worrying about these old site forms, especially if the sites can't be relocated. Dave, I don't think we should add a site type field to the database. After all, one person's prehistoric camp is another person's habitation. I think the new site form should be descriptive and contain concrete categories of artifact types and numbers."

"Site types don't really tell us much in terms of details about the site composition," Dave added. "Plus, the meaning of some site types, for example, 'camp,' can change as we learn more about these sites. For example, our ethnoarchaeology research has shown us that a few flakes can be all that is left after four families camped somewhere for a month. We probably wouldn't even record it as a site. For a 'camp,' does there need to be ground stone, tools, and fire-cracked rocks? Most archaeologists would say that the latter is a camp, and the former is a lithic scatter. It's all very subjective. Quantities of artifacts are meaningful, but functional site types really aren't."

"I'll have to run this all by Ken, but in principle I agree with you," I said. "I think artifact categories are our best bet."

"I'm in," said Mike, removing his glasses and looking me up and down.

We spent the rest of the meeting discussing the categories and the new site form layout. This was beginning to get exciting. When I was doing surveys, it had been confusing to use different site forms depending on who owned the land. One site form for the entire state would save everyone a lot of trouble.

"Okay," I said. "I'll try to organize a meeting with the other agencies. Who would that be?"

Dave started rattling them off. "Forest Service, Water Resources Bureau, and of course the state."

"Do you think the state archaeologist will want to participate? If the state won't join us, I don't think the system will fly." I looked at Dave and Mike.

"I think he'll be okay," Dave assured me. "Brian is a reasonable guy, and he understands that the site records are a mess." Dave pushed the new site form toward me and slapped it. "I think we can get everyone to agree that this is a better form."

"How about if we hold the meeting after the holidays? It will take me a while to talk to everyone and find an acceptable date. I'll also need to do a little scouting to find out how everyone feels about using one site form." I pulled the form toward me and scanned it again. We all stood up. "Okay. Until next time. Thanks for coming."

As I walked to my office, I patted myself on the back for doing a pretty good job at the meeting. This whole government archaeology thing didn't seem to be that difficult. The worst part was putting up with Ken. He really was a jerk, and I'd begun to suspect that he had at least two girlfriends at strategic business travel locations. I couldn't imagine what the women saw in him, but perhaps one day I'd get to meet them and find out.

As it turned out, I already knew one of Ken's girls, and I'd watched their relationship develop for some time. It dawned on me one day that Sandy, who worked in records, was probably one of Ken's "friends with benefits." She was all boobs and legs, and she and Ken took breaks together twice a day, usually disappearing during lunch too. My suspicions were verified when Ken announced that the two of us, and Sandy, were going to the spring Society for American Archaeology meeting in San Diego. How weird would that be?

"What do you mean? All three of us are going to the SAA meetings? Sandy isn't even an archaeologist."

Ken and I were heading to the field to help Shaun White, the new Salt Lake regional archaeologist, with a survey.

Ken looked over to gauge my reaction. "Well, she's interested in archaeology."

"I think she's probably just interested in you. Look, have as many girlfriends as you want, but please don't tell me the details. Ignorance is bliss, and that way I'll never have to testify against you when your wife finally dumps you and takes all your money."

"My wife would never do that. She doesn't suspect us, and anyway she loves me."

"That's what all philanderers say."

It was a gray, bleak day, and we had about an hour's drive to where we were meeting Shaun. I'd met him just once, when he'd dropped off some reports for Ken. He was all sinew, very lean, and seemed like a sweet guy. I realized I was looking forward to the survey and getting away from office work for a while.

Ken was driving the government-issue truck. He had on his ugly field hat, scruffy jeans, and a work shirt that was frayed around the cuffs and collar. He was sipping coffee out of a large ceramic mug and steering with just one hand.

"When is the SAA meeting?" I wondered out loud.

"The second week in February."

"Are you sure you'll still be with Sandy then?"

"Of course. I'm the best thing she's got going."

I shook my head. "You have the most amazing ego. What makes you so sure you're the best thing going for her?"

"Her husband is an idiot, and she's trapped in a loveless marriage."

"Sounds like what your wife probably says to her lover about you."

Ken laughed. "Ouch! You really can be a bitch, you know?"

We both laughed. "I can be a bitch, but you really are an asshole. You know that, right?"

"And proud of it."

I decided to stop talking. Is this what adults do when they're married too long and sex gets boring? Or was he just monogamy challenged? I wondered in silence what it would be like to be married to Ken. Did his wife have a clue? Did she even care as long as she didn't have to work and had most of her days to herself? Ken bragged all the time about giving his wife a list of things to do each day. If I were her, I'd want to shove that list up his ass. How could anyone live with this disgusting man? But then he gives me a list of things to do in the office every day too....

My ruminations were interrupted by a coyote running across the road and Ken slamming on the brakes. He just missed it. The coyote loped down the embankment and looked over its shoulder at us.

About an hour out of Salt Lake we turned onto a gravel road. Ken grabbed a USGS map off the dashboard and asked me to figure out where we were and how far we had to go on this road.

I looked over the map. The survey area was marked in red, and I figured we had just turned onto the gravel road that led directly to our area. It looked right anyway. I counted the sections to our project area.

"It looks like we have about three miles on this road. Since you've been driving for a while, it's probably less than two miles now."

"Shaun told me there's an old corral at our meeting place. I think I see it ahead."

The road ran down the middle of a wide, sage-covered valley. It was cloudy and cold outside, but you could see forever. I could just barely make out what looked like a fence next to the road. As we got closer, it looked less like a fence and more like a cluster of posts. A green pickup was parked nearby, and a rail-thin guy was standing next to it with maps spread out across the hood. He looked our way, squinting slightly as he reached for his hat and planted it on his head.

"I think I see Shaun's truck."

"That's him," said Ken.

Ken parked and we visited with Shaun a bit before getting down to business. I enjoyed watching Ken interact with the regional archaeologists. He was a pretty good leader, even if he was a jerk. Shaun's short brown hair was covered by a broad-brimmed hat, and he wore a tattered ski jacket and tan field pants. He was just a few inches taller than me but all muscle. His gaze was deep and intense, and I felt his eyes on my back when I turned away to look over our survey area.

We walked transects most of the day. This was the first time I'd done a survey with Ken, and he was impressed when I found the first two sites. They were just lithic scatters, but Shaun pointed out a cluster of fire-cracked rocks that I would have missed. At the second site Ken found two Archaic spear points. In the afternoon we discovered a huge artifact scatter on a low ridge near a spring. Shaun proved to be very knowledgeable about ground stone. When he pointed out a large boulder with flat surface that had been ground smooth, I realized that I'd probably not noticed grinding slicks in the past. At the southern end of the site, I found a small cluster of brown sherds. After I showed them to Ken and Shaun, we examined them more closely and agreed that they were probably made by the Utes, who have lived in the area since AD 1400.

The day ended too soon, and before I knew it, I was back in the truck with Ken for the drive back. That exhausted, relaxed feeling coursed through my body as I sat in my seat. This was probably a good time to talk about developing a multiagency site form.

"So are you going to call everyone for the site form meeting in January?" I asked.

"You and I need to meet with all the agencies separately first. I'll call Jake at the Forest Service, Brian Franz the state archaeologist, and then there's Kurt with the Water Resources Bureau. I'm sure Kurt will go along with whatever we decide. Let's meet with Brian first. If he won't commit to one site form, then there's no point in calling Jake or anyone else for that matter. I think it pretty much hinges on Brian."

I looked over at Ken, momentarily impressed with what a good politician he was. No matter how much I disliked how he handled his personal life, I had to admit he was good at the intricacies of working the system to achieve his goals.

"Do you have any idea what kind of site form Brian would like to see?"

"Since Brian is a graduate of Utah College, I suspect he'll like whatever Dave and Mike come up with for the site database. Utah College folks all think pretty much alike."

"Does that include me?"

Ken looked at me. "Nah, field school doesn't count. You never went through Johnson's graduate program so you haven't been properly indoctrinated."

I had to think about that a minute. I'd been trained in field school, but one season of training had had less impact on my thinking than my contract archaeology jobs. I'd learned more about surveying in my former job than I had at field school.

"Johnson wrote me off pretty early on in field school. At first I thought it was because I wasn't smart enough, but when I asked him for career advice, he told me he figured I'd just get married, so his, or anyone else's, efforts to train me would be wasted. I didn't really believe he meant it at the time, but I guess he was serious."

Ken looked over and then added his two bits. "Johnson has been discriminating against women forever. What made you think he'd treat you any different?"

"He admitted other women into his graduate program. There was Penny, and another woman at Pint Creek was also his graduate student." This was so frustrating. Why didn't Johnson think I was worthy?

"Perhaps he just didn't like the color of your hair," Ken said. "Or maybe he thought you were too cute, and it would be torture to have you around."

"But Penny is gorgeous. Why would he let her in?"

Ken looked over at me to gauge my reaction to his next comment. "Maybe you're too opinionated. You know, what they used to call uppity."

"Are you kidding?" I shook my head. "Maybe I'm just not smart enough for him."

Ken looked over at me with another sly smile. "Nah, you're smart enough."

We drove the rest of the way home in silence. I felt like the fog enveloping the city was surround me as well. It had never occurred to me that roadblocks would be placed along my route to becoming an archaeologist just because I was a woman. What exactly did Ken mean when he said I was uppity? To me it's an old-fashioned way of describing someone who doesn't follow conventions and ignores directions for reasons of their own. Perhaps Johnson recognized that he couldn't be sure I'd follow the party line.

Ken pulled the truck into a parking space.

"What? We're here already?" I asked.

"And it's Friday. Are you going to join the gang for a beer?"

I visualized Ken flirting with Sandy, and me struggling to find something to talk about with Guy and Peter. The thought was depressing.

"I have plans tonight," I lied. "Maybe some other Friday." I escaped from the truck and headed to the bus stop.

"See you Monday," I said over my shoulder. I'd decided to let Ken turn the keys into the motor pool. I'd done enough of his work this week.

I went back east to spend the holidays with my family, and it was wonderful to see everyone and tell them about my archaeological adventures. My mom is a fantastic cook, and dinner is always a spectacular event. When I returned to Salt Lake, the inversion's gloom fit my mood, but in mid-January, the inversion ended with a huge snowstorm. The days were already getting longer, and I could imagine spring just around the corner.

Ken and I met or called all the agency heads, and they all agreed that a single site form was a good idea. We gave each of them a copy of the database categories and the draft form and scheduled a meeting to decide on the form's contents and organization for the last day of January—the thirtieth. I had just finished the agenda.

"Here it is," I said, handing a copy to Ken.

He read it over fast. "Why don't you give the introduction and take the lead?"

"You need to do that. You're the head archaeologist, and I'm just your assistant, remember? I realize I do most of your work, but I'm not going to do this."

Ken smiled and ignored my comment. "The agenda looks okay." He acted like I had just vaporized, so I figured that was my cue to exit stage right.

"Well, that takes care of that," I mumbled.

The day of the meeting arrived. I'd reserved the Land Management Agency's large conference room, which contained a giant round table made of dark, highly polished wood. For a few minutes I allowed myself to time travel again. I could see the table sitting in the banquet room of a damp, cavernous castle. I imagined the meeting participants arriving dressed in medieval attire: swords, chain mail, leather pants, rich fur-lined robes, and high leather boots. Since I had never met most of them, I visualized them as tall and rugged, with beards and long hair, and faces lit with rakish smiles. I saw myself attired as Ken's page, walking in just behind him and seated not at the giant table, but in one of the chairs placed around the edge of the room. My clothes were plain, and I had no sword.

"Ivy, why are you sitting over there?" Ken asked, motioning me to join him. "Come over and sit at the table."

I shook my head and returned to the twentieth century. "You want me to distribute the draft form now or wait until everyone arrives?"

"Wait. We don't know how many will come."

I sat with my pile of papers and looked at my watch. It was ten minutes to show time. I had butterflies in my stomach and felt a little queasy. I decided to check over the site form one last time. It was three pages long. The first page was for administrative information such as where the site is located, whose land it's on, whether it appears to be significant, who recorded it, and when the work was done. The second page contained environmental data such as the type of landform, depositional setting, closest water source, and vegetation. Archaeologists consider this information relevant because prehistoric people lived off the land and selected their camping and habitation locations based on the availability of food resources. For example, since pine nuts were an important food source, we would expect to find campsites in pinyon pine forests. The last page was devoted to the artifacts and features present at the site. On this page archaeologists would be able to record the number of stone tools, pottery sherds, grinding stones, ceramic types, and projectile point types plus describe any features such as rock piles, masonry structures, storage pits, and charcoal stains. I anticipated that most of today's discussion would focus on this page, and as it turned out, I was correct.

Jake Jefferies and his assistant, Doug Cloxton, from the Forest Service were the first to arrive and Ken introduced us. Jake was nothing like what I'd expected from talking to him on the phone. He was dark, with bushy eyebrows, and meticulous attire: dark slacks, a starched white shirt, and an expensive sweater—maybe even cashmere. His handshake was firm, but he spoke softly and never smiled. Everything about him screamed "perfectionist." His assistant was the polar opposite: blond, boyish, and open. His hair was conservatively short, and his jeans were short too. He gave me a goofy smile and limp handshake. I stood silently while Ken talked with them. I could tell that Jake did not take Ken seriously, and I sensed the meeting might turn out to be very interesting.

Brian Franz, the state archaeologist, arrived next with an entourage. He was possibly the smallest man I had ever met. Barely my height, he was cute in a boyish way, and his face brightened whenever he smiled. For once someone looked me straight in the eye. We were introduced, and Ken's warning not to judge Brian by his looks came to mind. As soon as he greeted me, I realized that what he lacked in height he compensated for with sound. His voice was deep and powerful. Words rolled out like a flash flood. I imagined God speaking down from the heavens. I was momentarily speechless but managed to mumble hello.

I was next introduced to John Steinberg, Utah's compliance archaeologist. He looked like he hadn't done fieldwork for years. His bulging belly was partially hidden with a well-fitted sport coat, but he couldn't hide his triple chins. I shook his warm, plump hand, and he introduced me to a bespectacled and slightly heavier version of himself named Clint Voss. Clint ran the Utah Historic Resources office, and his background was in historical architecture rather than archaeology. He wore a blue suit with a yellow polka dot tie. He certainly didn't look or dress the part—that is, like a frumpy archaeologist. I stood back and watched as everyone talked and selected their seats at the table. Dave and Mike had managed to sneak in while I was being introduced to the state folks, so I made my way over to ask Mike a few questions about the site form.

After we were all seated, Ken started the meeting by thanking everyone for coming. He told some lame joke and then launched into a discussion about why we needed a single site form. I was impressed. His argument was logical and compelling. Then, without warning, he turned the meeting over to me!

I turned bright red and mumbled a few platitudes of thanks. Then the words just magically poured forth.

"It sounds like we all see the need for a single site recording form and a computer database, so why don't we begin by reviewing a prototype of the form that Dave and Mike put together." I stood and handed stacks of forms to the people on each side of me.

"As you can see, we divided the form into three pages." Everyone's eyes followed me as I went page by page through the data categories. I finished and looked up. "Any questions?"

The spell was broken, and everyone started speaking at once. After fifteen minutes of this, Brian gained the upper hand and took control of the meeting. I made notes as he led the discussion of each data category. My head was pounding and my hand starting to cramp, but I kept going. Jake noted that we needed to add information specific to the Forest Service's system. Brian didn't like the physiographic regions and noticed that we had failed to include several ceramic types. I frantically wrote, trying to keep track of the decisions on changes to the form. After two hours we took a break.

I sat in a daze, looking over my notes to make sure I'd be able to understand what I'd just written. Mike joined me, grinning ear to ear.

"It's working, Ivy. I can't believe it." He pushed up his glasses and sat next to me.

"I know. Brian is amazing. This is the first time I've seen him in action." I flipped to the second page. "Can you believe he knew these categories off the top of his head?"

Mike smiled and nodded. "He's a brilliant guy."

Everyone straggled into the room, and the meeting resumed. Brian continued to take the lead.

"It seems we've made good progress on the site form. Now we just have to decide who will maintain the database and what we'll call it." Brian looked over at Dave.

"Why don't you explain how that will work, Dave?"

I was fading fast, but I kept up with the notes. The group decided that the State Historic Preservation Office would assume responsibility for the database once the contractors finished the data entry. Ken offered to obtain more funding to add all the sites in the state to the system. Before I knew it, everyone was getting up and the room was emptying out.

I realized that we hadn't named the system. Before I could stop myself, I said, "Wait! We need a name."

Everyone turned and looked at me. Mike spoke up for the first time today. "I was thinking we could call it the Utah Archaeological Computer System."

Jake shook his head. "That won't work. My Forest Service region covers Idaho too. How about the Intermountain Cultural Resource Automated System."

"Or CRAS," said Brian. "I like it."

There were murmurs of approval, some backslapping and hand shaking, and the meeting ended. I wandered back to my desk.

The Monday after the meeting I was back at my mundane tasks, plotting surveys and sites on the base maps. When Ken walked over, I was feeling bored and restless.

"Ivy, we're going to Grand Gulch next Thursday, just for the day."

"What for? And how will we get there and back in a day?"

"Rooster Pen Ruin in Grand Gulch got hit by pothunters. The rangers caught the guys, and we need to visit the site with the prosecuting attorney. We'll fly down for the day. You're coming because you know one of the pothunters, Ben Edwards."

My mouth dropped open. "What? It can't be Ben. He told me he'd given up looting sites."

Ken shook his head. "They never give it up. We've been trying to catch him for years. I still can't believe we let him work on the Utah Coal survey."

"What did he do to the site?"

Ken looked at his watch. "I'll tell you over lunch. I'm going to grab a quick bite at the mall. Let's go."

I put on my coat and followed him. "Hey, wait up."

I caught up with him at the elevators.

"Are you sure it's Ben?"

"Ivy, why do you like the guy so much? He dug big holes in one of the most important archaeological sites in the Gulch." We walked a short block to the nearby department store known as ZCMI. In the housewares department, they were trying to convince Mormon housewives of the value of microwave ovens by selling microwaved snacks for a buck.

"He's a nice guy. I spent a lot of time with him, and he told me that he was done with pothunting." I ordered my slice of homemade bread with a thick hunk of cheddar cheese. The bread was heated for a minute, and the cheese was bubbly and hot—a cheap and delicious lunch. Leave it to Ken to discover the best deal in town.

"And you believed him?"

"Well, he probably believed it himself at the time. Things change."

"Ivy, he was lying to you."

I rolled my eyes and reluctantly agreed. "All right, he probably was. But I still like him. How did he get caught?"

"The investigator told me that he hit the site a few weeks ago, and they set a trap for the guys. Ben was with one of his Monticello buddies. The ranger caught them walking out of the site, but evidence ties the recent digging to Ben. His footprints were all over the place, and he was carrying a shovel and screen. He must have stashed the artifacts somewhere, but they caught him with his digging stuff."

We found a bench in the mall that adjoined ZCMI and sat down to eat.

"How are we getting from the airport to the Gulch?" I knew from my maps that Grand Gulch was at least fifty miles as a crow flies from the closest airport in Blanding.

"I chartered a helicopter in Blanding."

"You're kidding, right?" I put the last crumb of bread in my mouth and threw my paper plate in the trash.

"If we don't rent a helicopter, we'd have to hike in. It's a five-mile hike from the nearest road. The helicopter should be able to land right next to the site. Have you ever been in a helicopter before? It's not bad."

I looked at Ken, who was leering at a group of young women walking toward us. One of the women had huge breasts that jiggled braless in her shirt.

"Nice puppies." Ken chuckled under his breath.

"What are you talking about?"

"Her boobs look like puppies in a sack. They're about the right shape and they wiggle."

I shook my head and chuckled. "That's a good one. I haven't heard that before."

"I made it up. Pink-nosed puppies!"

We stood up to leave. "Yeah, right. And you invented 'knock, knock' jokes too."

We walked back in silence. I was thinking about the helicopter ride, and Ken was probably thinking about puppies.

Ken spent the rest of the day on the phone coordinating our Thursday trip. I spent another couple of hours on the maps and then called it a day.

Monday and Tuesday dragged by, but by Wednesday I was getting really excited about our trip. We were to meet at the office at 5 a.m. and then meet the prosecuting attorney at the airport. We were taking the morning flight on a small plane to Blanding, where we'd switch to the helicopter. Ken told me to pray for good weather because the trip would be cancelled if storms were predicted.

It was still dark when I got to the office Thursday morning. The forecast was good, even though it had snowed in Blanding two days ago. Everything went as planned. David French, the attorney, was at the airport when we arrived, and the "small" plane turned out to seat twenty. When the sun rose, it revealed a perfect day: cold, calm, and cloudless. Ken spent most of the flight talking the case over with David, who was tall, thin, and sported a short, dirty blond Afro. He looked young, perhaps barely out of law school. After the plane took off, I gazed out the window for a while and then fell asleep. I awoke as we were flying over the Colorado River and descending fast toward a small town surrounded by soaring red sandstone. Junipers mixed with sand sage provided blotches of green.

We were herded from the terminal to a helicopter whose noisy blades were already whirring. Ken and David took the back seat and I sat next to the pilot. The entire front was glass, from ceiling to floor, with nothing else between me and the sky. When we took off, I had a moment of vertigo and then felt a wild exhilaration. We gained altitude and flew close to the ground over the edge of a mesa. As the earth dropped beneath me hundreds of feet, my heart nearly stopped. After a few more minutes my heartbeat returned to normal, and I grabbed the camera and started shooting pictures. I could see Canyonlands off in the distance, the hundreds of narrow slot canyons in the Maze, and the open tableland of Salt Canyon. South of Canyonlands, I saw a cliff dwelling tucked in a wide alcove. Click, click. I took pictures furiously. The pilot pointed out a tower in Beef Basin and then we entered the Gulch. He flew down the canyon, banking steeply in the winding curves.

I had spent lots of time backpacking in Canyonlands and four-wheeling in Beef Basin, but the terrain looked completely different from the sky above—vast and incredibly complex. The Maze District of Canyonlands is a labyrinth of steep, narrow canyons. From the air it resembles red tripe, fresh out of the cow's stomach. When I was young, my mom occasionally fed us pickled tripe, breaded and sautéed in butter. Since I was too little to understand what I was eating, I thought that it was pretty good—tangy and crispy when cooked just right.

"There's Rooster Pen!" Ken yelled over the roar of the helicopter. He pointed to a small alcove with a burnt beam stretched across a recently extinguished campfire. "Land us as close as you can and we'll hike down to the site."

The pilot turned the helicopter and hovered for a minute. "How is that clearing over there? Is that too far away?"

Ken shook his head. "That will be fine."

I held my breath as the pilot performed some delicate moves and landed the helicopter.

"Mind if I tag along with you? I've never seen anything like this before."

"Sure," answered Ken. "Ivy, grab the camera so we can take pictures. Bring a couple extra rolls of film."

Ken gathered his notebook and daypack, the pilot helped us out of the helicopter, and we started hiking, single file, toward the site. It was so quiet I could hear the blood rushing in my ears. I took a deep breath. The air smelled clean, with a hint of sage and pine, and an inch of snow blanketed the canyon floor. The ruin was tucked into a huge alcove on the canyon's west side. The alcove faced south, scooping up the sun's rays, which would have kept it warm in winter and would have protected the structure's inhabitants from the snow and wind. It was no doubt cold at night but would warm fast when the sun rose over the canyon's edge.

I could see that we didn't have far to hike, and I had a good view inside the alcove. There were no cliff dwellings, but along the alcove's back wall I saw a small masonry room. Next to it stood an enclosure made of reeds and branches. The standing branches formed a small fenced-in area.

"I see the rooster pen!" yelled Ken. "At least it's still intact."

We wove our way down to the canyon bottom, where a thin creek lay partially frozen and inert in a deep shadow. I looked up to the alcove and could see a path worn into the skirt of the talus slope. We followed the path, with me bringing up the rear. I could hear David marveling at the beauty of the site, and Ken swearing softly.

"Damn, they dug a pretty big hole."

I walked along the alcove edge to where Ken was examining a large pit. If I jumped into it, I'd barely be able to look out. The hole was just wide enough for the excavator to throw shovels of dirt up and out.

"I brought some pictures of the site from last summer." Ken reached into his pack and pulled out an envelope. "Here they are. Let's see if this hole was here then."

We crowded around Ken and looked at the photos as he shuffled through them.

"Here's the one I was looking for."

He held out a photo that looked like it had been taken from our present location. A small pot hole was visible in the corner of the photo, and a meter stick lay next to the hole.

"Yup, they enlarged the hole," said Ken, handing me the photograph. He set a meter stick in about the same spot as in the photo and then motioned for me to give the photo back. We all crowded around to compare the views.

"Wow, it looks about three times bigger!" I blurted.

"We paid Washington College archaeologists to collect the artifacts from the surface and remove a sample of midden from this pot hole. They were just here last summer." Ken walked around for a minute and pointed to some basketry fragments, flakes, and bone fragments. "This site was occupied before pottery was being made. It's one of the only sites that was lived in during the Basketmaker period and not during the later Pueblo period."

I walked around for a few more minutes, examining the alcove's sandy surface. "Wait, here's a spear point." My heart raced with excitement as I bent to pick it up.

Everyone took turns examining the almost complete spear point. "I guess Ben didn't think this was worth collecting. I still can't believe he would do this."

"You know Ben?" David asked in his deep, clear voice. I imagined him convincing the jury of Ben's guilt with his melodious voice and boyish smile.

"Ben and I worked together last fall. He swore that he'd given up looting sites. I liked him a lot. He's really funny, and he told us some great stories about his pothunting days." I shook my head.

"Ben admitted to pothunting sites in the past? Tell me more. I could use you as a character witness." David looked at me more closely.

"What? I'd have to testify against Ben?"

"It could be a big help."

"I don't think I want to do that. Are you guys sure Ben did this?" I asked. I put the spear point back where I'd found it.

"The rangers caught Ben and his friend with a shovel, but no artifacts. They traced their footprints back to Rooster Pen, where there was a campfire that was still warm. They searched everywhere for the artifacts without luck. Still, I think it's a pretty solid case."

I shook my head. "Yeah, that does sound convincing." Ben had lied to me. If he was capable of digging this famous site, he probably wouldn't hesitate to return to some of the untouched rock shelters we had recorded last fall. The idea that he would violate sites made me angry. What a waste.

"So the vandals left these artifacts?" asked David, pointing to scraps of cordage and a tiny piece of a woven basket.

"They only carry out the good stuff," said Ken. "These fragments can tell archaeologists a lot about cultural ties, and they can be radiocarbon dated, so we can learn how old they are, but to the pothunters they're just junk. They have no monetary value."

Ken walked over to the pole enclosure. "Looks like they at least left the Rooster Pen alone."

"Was that really an enclosure for turkeys?" I asked. "How do you know that?"

"The first artifact collectors who visited this site were the same local ranchers who found Mesa Verde, the Wetherill brothers. They kept pretty good notes on their collections and the sites they came from. They named this site Rooster Pen because of the large quantities of turkey dung and feathers that they found in this enclosure. The holes they dug have been backfilled so you can't tell the site was excavated."

Ken looked over at me. "Okay, Ivy, we don't have much time, and we need to document the vandalism. I'll record what we've found. You and David take pictures of the pot holes and fire pit using last summer's photos as a reference. Try to duplicate their exact orientation. After you finish photographing, you can collect the artifacts."

Ken pulled some small plastic bags and paper labels from his coat pocket. "Put the artifacts in the bags after you photograph them in place, and use these tags to document their locations on the surface. Ivy, give each artifact a point provenience number and plot them on this sketch map. The police already collected cans and cigarette butts from the hearth, but they decided to leave the artifacts to us." Ken took a sheet of paper out of his clipboard and handed it to me. "Use this to log the photos. Here's Washington College's map."

Ken sat and took notes while David and I scurried around collecting artifacts and taking photos. It was getting late, and the pilot told us that we'd have to leave in one hour. The days were short, and he wanted to get back before it got dark.

The flights home were beautiful. When we got back to Salt Lake, I felt like I'd traveled to a wonderland—to some far-off mythical place of the past.

The magic stayed with me until I checked my phone messages the next morning. One was from Jake, the Forest Service archaeologist. I called him right away and luckily he was in.

"Sorry I didn't call you back yesterday. We were in the field."

"That's just what I need, some real work," answered Jake. "Where did you go?"

I cleared my throat, excited to tell someone about our adventure. Jake was envious.

"So, what's up? Why did you call me?" I asked.

"I won't beat around the bush, Ivy, and I called you instead of Ken because I thought you might understand."

"Understand what?"

"I have decided that the Forest Service isn't going to participate in the CRAS system."

I only half listened while he explained his reasons. Because the Forest Service manages a huge chunk of the state's land, without their participation we would essentially be back to the old system of multiple site forms.

"So, you see, Ivy, unless the other states that I manage also join, I can't make my agency use multiple forms. It will be too complicated. Another problem is that we have information categories on our form that pertain to management units. There are about thirty of these units. How are you going to fit all of these categories on the form?"

"I see your point. Do you really need these management units on the form, Jake?"

"We use them every day in our planning process and ongoing resource management."

"Okay, I need to think about this. Why don't we meet for lunch next week? Oh wait, I'll be at the SAA meetings."

"Yeah, me too. Why don't we visit the week after. How about lunch?"

We arranged a place and a time. I hung up the phone, depressed that CRAS was proving so difficult.

I noticed Ken was off of his phone so I walked over to tell him the news. He had his cowboy boots planted on his desk and was looking intently at his nails. He watched me approach with a mischievous grin, which probably represented some filthy thoughts. I felt naked in his gaze.

"Jake has decided to bail on CRAS."

Ken hardly blinked. "No big surprise there."

"Why do you say that?"

"Jake's a loner. He doesn't want to have to rely on others."

"Is that it? He told me it was because the other states in his region didn't like the idea, and we don't have categories on the form that they need. Why are you being so cynical? I set up a meeting to talk it over with him after we get back from the SAA meetings. I'm not giving up so easily."

"Okay, Ivy. I won't give up yet either. You can work on him, but I really don't get along with Jake, so he's all yours."

I slunk back to my desk. Thank goodness it was Friday. Tom and I were planning to get away for a long weekend and head to Canyonlands. He'd been working for a tire dealer while waiting to hear from law schools, and we'd both taken Monday off. Since I wouldn't leave for the SAA meetings until Wednesday, I'd still have time to pack and get my stuff ready. I'd never been to the annual archaeology conference and was looking forward to it, but I was more than a little anxious about spending five days with Ken and Sandy.

I left work early on Friday so that Tom and I could start the six-hour drive that afternoon. We planned to camp out around Salt Creek Canyon and explore the Beef Basin area where I'd seen the prehistoric pueblo with towers out of the helicopter window—definitely an inspiring trip. Tom had recently traded his Volkswagen in for an old Toyota Land Cruiser, which can go anywhere. After a frenzied hour of packing, we hit the road.

I hadn't seen much of Tom for the past few months and I was glad to be spending a weekend camping with him. I took his hand in mine and squeezed.

"So, you haven't heard from any of the law schools yet? Which ones did you apply to?"

Tom squeezed my hand back and looked over at me. "I probably won't hear for another month. I applied to Utah College and Arizona State."

"Which one do you want to go to?"

"My family wants me to stay in Utah, but Arizona has the best Native American law program, and that's what I think I want to specialize in."

"What's happening with that Hopi/Navajo land claims case you got interested in when you lived on the reservation?"

As Tom launched into the case's details, my eyes started to glaze over: too much detail. I needed to change the subject fast or he wouldn't stop. "I copied the locations of the major Beef Basin pueblos onto a topographic map so we shouldn't have too much trouble finding them. Remember that time we tried to find those cliff dwellings in Canyonlands?"

The afternoon sun was low on the horizon, and I suddenly felt sleepy. Tom hadn't been distracted by my question and continued talking about the Navajo/Hopi dispute. His voice and the warm sun lulled me to sleep.

When I woke up, we were in Moab, and Tom was filling the tank with gas. Even with our pit stop, we made it to Beef Basin in just over six hours. It was already dark, so we wasted no time finding a sheltered spot to make camp. Tom set up our small pup tent while I built a fire and cooked dinner: a simple meal of beans and hot dogs. After an hour of sitting by the fire, we climbed into our warm sleeping bags.

The next day we explored several of the pueblos that I'd seen from the helicopter. Three of them still had standing walls, and the tower I'd seen from the air was a circular masonry room with six-foot-high walls. A rubble pile surrounding the tower's base indicated that the structure had originally been much higher—maybe two stories tall. The masonry techniques and pottery styles showed that the pueblos' occupants had cultural ties to Chaco Canyon in New Mexico. I had heard that these towers could be found in strategic locations up and down the area's mesas and canyons. Their function is unknown, but archaeologists speculate that they were signal towers.

The last pueblo we visited contained over fifty rooms, half of them badly vandalized. Craters where vandals had searched for artifacts riddled the partially buried rooms. Soil that had blown or washed into the abandoned rooms had been churned and rendered scientifically meaningless. Pots that had lain on the floor when the pueblo was abandoned were probably now sitting on someone's bookshelves. My thoughts turned to Ben, and I wondered if this was one of the sites he had looted.

The weather stayed clear and warm through the weekend, but Monday we woke to heavy clouds that threatened rain. Leaving my warm sleeping bag to face a cold wintry day wasn't easy, and we decided to pack up and go home. We stopped for breakfast in Moab rather than eat cold granola and yogurt. Denny's Grand Slam breakfast was the perfect antidote for a cold, gray day.

On the long drive home, I made a mental list of clothes and everything else I'd need for my San Diego trip. I had no idea what the meeting would be like and how archaeologists would dress. Ken had mentioned a trip to the beach, so I decided to pack my swimsuit in case it was warm enough. Ken told me that he could only stand one day of meetings, and he was renting a car so that we could see some of the local attractions. I knew just what I'd need for sightseeing, but I didn't have any idea what to wear for the meetings. Maybe Tom would know. He told me that he'd gone to the SAA meetings once when they were in Albuquerque.

"Tom, do you have any idea what people will wear at the SAA meetings?"

"Sport coats and dress pants."

"What? Are you teasing me? I don't want to overdress. What will the meetings be like?"

"Professional meetings are the strangest conventions. Imagine hundreds of completely self-absorbed scientists standing up in front of their peers and summarizing a year's worth of research in fifteen minutes. At the SAA meetings there are ten simultaneous symposia, and participants run from room to room listening to mostly mind-numbing talks. I noticed that the more senior archaeologists rarely went to hear any papers presented except their own. The rest of their time is spent holding court— you know, talking to students and peers about their work. It's all pretty strange when you think about it."

"I can't wait to hear the papers. Some of the abstracts sound really interesting. I'm hoping to learn all the latest—what's hot and what's not."

"I always said you were an optimist, Ivy." Tom smiled.

I liked Tom, but his family was very unhappy with him for dating a Gentile. I suspected that their disapproval had contributed to Tom's less frequent visits to see me. "Have your Mom and Dad stopped complaining about me yet?"

Tom looked serious for a minute. "Ivy, you know I don't really care what they think."

Taking his hand, I told him, "I hope you don't get into ASU and move away. I'll miss you if you go. But your parents would probably be glad that I'm out of the picture."

"They're so happy that I'm going to law school that they haven't said anything about us lately."

We drove in silence the rest of the way home. Tom had been a good friend, but I had to admit I wasn't passionately in love with him. Our relationship was based more on friendship and mutual respect. I doubted that we'd ever have gotten together if we hadn't both been lonely at field school. Tom and I were from completely different worlds, and it was hard to imagine a life with him. Deep down, I was pretty sure that he felt the same way about me.

The SAA Meetings

Most people associate San Diego with Shamu leaping out of the pool at Sea World or tanned surfer dudes bobbing like corks while waiting for the perfect wave. After my first trip to San Diego I associated the city with a darker, seamier side—Black's Beach, drunken archaeologists in stale bars, and naked hot tub parties. It was San Diego as seen through Ken's perverted eyes, and it was also the first time I realized that I should NEVER drink whisky.

Ken, his married girlfriend, and I left the office at noon to catch our flight. Before I knew it, we were sailing down a California highway in Ken's rented Mustang with the top down. Luckily I hadn't had to sit near Ken and Sandy on the flight, so I was spared their lusty, knowing looks. But now I was feeling like a fifth wheel—unnecessary and unwanted. I didn't even know why I was on this trip: I wasn't presenting a paper, and I had no work duties. Ken had said that it was all about training, but I wasn't so sure.

We checked into our downtown hotel, located about two blocks from the San Diego Convention Center, where the meetings would be held. My room overlooked a parking lot between two nondescript, boxy office buildings. It was late afternoon, and I had the rest of the day to myself, so I decided to walk to the convention center, pick up my registration materials, and catch a few presentations. As I got closer, I started seeing archaeologists, who were easy to identify: shabby sport coats, jeans or khaki pants, and cowboy boots. Like me, most of the archaeologists were blind, and their glasses were thick and out of style. Beards were definitely in vogue, and I saw two men with long hair tied back into thin ponytails.

Near the registration area, dozens of archaeologists milled about looking confused and slightly out of place. Men seemed to outnumber the women, who looked as frumpy as other women archaeologists I'd met: drab suits, outmoded hairstyles, no eye makeup, and untamed unibrows. In retrospect, my worries about what to wear seemed silly. I looked just fine—in fact, pretty good—in my new white shirt and taupe suit. I'd bought the suit at a small store in the mall, and its perfect fit made me look downright chic for an archaeologist. With my contacts and makeup, no one would even know I belonged here.

I stood in the registration line labeled "H to J." Two people were ahead of me. The registration clerk asked the first one his name and handed him a large white envelope. When it was my turn, I learned it contained a nametag, a book of abstracts, a schedule of papers, and a map of the convention center. Okay, I'd managed the first step, but now what? I walked over to a bench and removed the schedule of presentations. Thumbing through the program I noticed that many sessions were topical, with names such as "Current Views on the Paleoindian Period in the Great Basin" or "New Thoughts on Ground Stone Tools." Several symposia were general sessions organized by time period or region. I saw one titled "Southwestern Prehistory" and another on the "Archaic Period along the Eastern Seaboard."

It was 4 p.m. and I had just enough time to hear the end of the general session on Great Basin prehistory. Using the map, I found the correct room and snuck in the side door. The room was dark, and the presenter stood behind a podium. I'd missed five minutes of his paper, which examined modern experiments to replicate boiling liquids with fire-heated rocks. The presenter showed dozens of slides to demonstrate in excruciating detail how labor-intensive it is to boil water with hot rocks. Before ceramics were invented, all liquids were boiled with rocks, which were heated in a fire and dropped into baskets or wooden containers. The paper also identified the unique shapes that the rocks take when they break after repeated use.

The next paper traced obsidian sources in the eastern Great Basin based on each source's unique chemical fingerprint. This technique allows researchers to trace obsidian artifacts to their point of origin. Obsidian sourcing had opened whole new areas of research comparing source use through time. The last paper, on lithic scatters, was given by a nervous Utah College graduate student, and it was disorganized and boring. His rambling talk reminded me how much I hated speaking in front of a group. I dreaded the thought of ever presenting a paper.

After light applause, the room emptied, and I found myself riding a wave of strangers. I felt conspicuous and alone as I watched others talking in small groups or hugging long-lost friends. I walked past dozens of people laughing and talking at once, many quite animated and clearly on their second or third beer. I saw no one I recognized, so I decided my best bet would be to escape. With my head down, I made my way past the bar to the main entrance.

"Ivy!"

I scanned the crowd. The voice sounded vaguely familiar, but I still didn't see anyone I knew.

"Ivy, over here!"

I looked again in the direction of the voice. "Bob! Is that really you?"

Bob Vrey was standing with a group of graduate students, probably from his new school in Canada. He broke away and came over to give me a hug.

"How are you, Ivy? What is this I hear about you working for Ken?"

"I got tired of fieldwork and saw that there was an opening at the Land Management Agency, so…here I am."

Bob looked happy and healthy. I realized again how solid and stable he was. "What about you? You look great. How do you like Canada and your new Ph.D. program?"

"Let me buy you a beer and I'll tell you all about it."

"I'd like that. I don't know any of these people."

"Oh, you'll be surprised how many people you'll see who you worked with in the field. These meetings are all about seeing your friends."

"That's good, because the first two papers I heard were not exactly a positive advertisement."

"Yeah, you'll learn to pick and choose which sessions you attend. There are a lot of bad papers."

We found an almost quiet spot in a bar just outside the convention center. I told Bob about Ben's pothunting at Rooster Pen, and he was as shocked as I was. Eventually, Bob confided in me that life was much better without Dr. Johnson's torture.

The beer tasted good, and I was glad to see Bob. I ordered two more, and we looked around at the crowd. The bar was full, and most of the patrons appeared to be archaeologists. I spotted Ken and Sandy over in the corner talking to an uncharacteristically tall and handsome twenty-something guy. I also spotted Mike and a group of Utah College students, including two pretty grad students hanging on his every word.

"There's Penny." I waved at her, and she walked over.

"Hey, Bob. Ivy!" She hugged me, and I realized how excited I was to see her again and catch up on her feud with Johnson. She looked great, as usual.

"How's Dolores?" asked Bob.

Penny smiled. "I never went."

"What? I thought you'd decided to move on." Bob seemed very surprised. "I heard you had a bad time with Johnson the last Pint Creek session."

"Well, I did stand up to him, and I thought for sure I was out of the program. Ivy, you were there. It was bad, wasn't it? Then the strangest thing happened. Johnson and I were walking down the stairs after he'd been lecturing me on the macrobotanical samples I was analyzing from Pint Creek, and Jenny passed us walking up the stairs. Suddenly Johnson reached out and grabbed her boob, and Jenny retaliated by reaching down and squeezing Johnson's balls. It was surreal."

"What? Are you kidding me? Who is Jenny?" I asked, eyes wide with disbelief.

"Jenny is one of his M.A. students, and she's married to one of Johnson's favorite Ph.D. students. Both of them got their B.A. degrees two years ago."

"Johnson is such an ass."

Penny shook her head. "No, Bob, it was great that I saw him do that because it made me realize that I had been dealing with him all wrong. I needed to lose my respectful student attitude, stop letting him intimidate me, and treat him like the asshole he is. Once I started standing up to him, he magically backed down and let me take the lead on the write-up for the kiva site that we found at Pint Creek. Johnson is actually encouraging me to say it's Kayenta. Can you believe it?" Penny smiled and took a delicate sip of wine.

I looked around and noticed that Penny was one of the few archaeologists drinking wine. "So, Penny, is he going to let you go on for your Ph.D.?"

Penny shook her head. "He thinks I should go somewhere else. I plan to finish my M.A. this year and apply to the University of Arizona and Colorado for my doctorate. I hear that Edward Svenson in Arizona has no trouble with female students."

"Good luck with that," Bob said. "Johnson and Svenson are major rivals."

"Really?" Penny got that faraway look for a minute. "I guess I should talk to Johnson about the schools before I apply. I need his recommendation to get in. Maybe Colorado is my best option. I know Johnson gets along with the director of the Dolores project. Ivy, I heard you're working for the Land Management Agency. How is that going?"

I shrugged. "It's a job. But my boss is a sleazebag and I miss the field. I'm thinking of going back to school for an M.A. I just don't know where the money will come from. What do you think I should do, Penny?"

"Definitely get your master's. The whole field of archaeology is changing with new environmental laws. With a master's degree, you'd be very employable. Go for it!"

We talked for a while, laughing and sharing updates on everyone else at Pint Creek. I told them about Tom's plan to attend law school. It turned out that Susan had stayed on and had been admitted to the master's program.

One of Bob's fellow students appeared and suggested we do a little hunting and gathering for food, and so we did. The drinking and eating continued for hours, until I could barely speak clearly. Somewhere along the way we lost Penny, and then Bob walked me back to my hotel. We promised to get together again during the meeting.

I was sound asleep when my phone rang at 6 a.m. I reached over and grabbed it to make the ringing stop, but only reluctantly put the phone to my ear, wondering who would be calling me this early.

"Who was that guy you were with last night?"

"Ken, is this you?" My head was pounding, and I still felt fuzzy-brained.

"You were all over him."

"What? He's just a friend, and I wasn't all over him. And you know what? It's way too early for this."

"Sandy and I are coming by your room in half an hour. We're going to breakfast. Be ready."

Before I could say yes, no, or even fuck you, he'd hung up. What was that all about? Since when did Ken care who I hugged and drank beer with? I struggled to wake up, even though both eyes were open. I lifted myself to one elbow, sat up, then threw my legs over the side of the bed. Who had turned my brain into cotton candy? I dug through my purse for aspirin and staggered to the bathroom for a quick shower. The warm water perked me up enough so that I managed makeup. Hair was easy: long and straight would do just fine. As soon as I'd put on my shoes, I heard a knock at my door.

Ken strode in with Sandy in tow. "Let's go. We need to eat quickly so we can make the first papers at eight. There's a symposium I want to go to. Planning and CRM. You should go too."

I shot Ken one of my most powerful death-ray looks and grabbed my purse, program, and nametag.

Noticing the nametag, Ken asked, "You registered already? Were the lines long? Hurry up, let's hit it."

Words escaped me: too many questions at once for my pounding brain.

"Ivy, what is wrong with you this morning? Oh, I get it. You had a few too many."

I followed Ken out of my room and remembered my key too late.

"Shit," I said as I closed the door. "I forgot my key."

"You can get another one later. Let's go."

We walked a short distance to a small diner. Inside the air was thick with grease, and the place was colorless and dirty. I was reminded of a *Twilight Zone* episode in which several people were trapped in a diner just like this. It turned out the cook and waitress were aliens. We were herded to a booth with dirty windows looking out to a crowded street. Thick fog, like the one strangling my brain, blanketed the city. Sandy was chirpy and happy, and I imagined the aliens beaming her to another planet. Ken did his separate check and "fucking fish in the water" thing, and then we got down to ordering.

The waitress took one look at me and brought me coffee before I even asked. The menu was basic. How would you like your eggs? I decided that eggs might push me over the edge, and I couldn't imagine barfing in this restaurant's ladies room, so I ordered toast, coffee, and a large glass of milk.

Ken gulped coffee and looked over at me. "Today is our meeting day. We're going to hear papers and then go to the beach. I should be papered-out by three, so that's when we'll meet in the lobby. After the beach you're on your own for dinner."

I mumbled something like "sounds good" and sipped my coffee. It tasted delicious.

At least I wouldn't have to hear about fish fucking twice in one day. The restaurant may have been shabby, but breakfast was fast and hot, and we ate quickly. By the time we'd walked to the meeting, the coffee and aspirin had kicked in.

Because it seemed like the easiest route, I followed Ken to the CRM session, which was as dull as a lithic scatter without arrowheads. Looking over my schedule for something with more pizzazz, I spotted a session on ground stone (boring), another on Columbian prehistory, and a third on microwear. I'd heard from Bob that microwear patterns on stone tools was one of this meeting's hot topics, and I knew nothing about it, so I headed to the session. The huge room was standing-room only. A young professor was showing electron microscope slides of the edge of stone tools and explaining that wear patterns on the edges of stone tools vary with the materials cut. Cutting meat or plants produces smooth polish, and cutting wood produces dull, wavy striations. This new avenue of research was exciting but untested. I wondered what the pattern would look like if a tool had been used for several different tasks. Would that skew the patterning and render them meaningless? I figured lots of people would be asking the same question and only further study would solve the mystery.

The day dragged on, and by 2:30 I knew what Ken meant by "papered-out." I was there. My brain had gone into overload a half hour before and had shut down from the strain of listening too hard to boring papers and trying to look engaged. I headed back to my room to change into beach clothes and then remembered to go by the office for another key. It was still overcast. Definitely not a great beach day. I decided on jeans, a T-shirt, sweater, and sneakers. I combed my hair, applied a new coat of lipstick, and headed for the lobby.

Sandy and Ken were waiting for me, and after Ken mumbled something, the two of us followed him single file, like ducklings, out to the Mustang. We drove for about twenty minutes and then parked and walked a short distance. I inhaled the fresh salt air and felt my hair dancing in the breeze. Sandy and Ken headed in the opposite direction. I saw Sandy frolicking in the waves, but Ken was just staring out to sea. Left to myself, I decided to go for a walk. I gulped great breaths of sea air and scanned the sand for washed-up treasures.

The beach was like home to me. I'd spent a good portion of my childhood at Rhode Island's beaches. Every weekend during the summer months my family would pack up the station wagon and head to my grandmother's house in Snag Harbor, where we'd spend the long days making sand castles, riding the waves, and watching fishing boats return to the marina. I left the East Coast when I was fifteen, but the ache for the shore remains. There is no mantra more powerful, or lullaby more soothing, than the pounding of the surf—a rhythmic movement that matches the beating of our hearts in some ancient primal way. I'm reborn each time I walk the shore and hear the crash and roll—in and out, forever without end, like eternity itself.

This was my first visit to the Pacific Ocean. Immediately I noticed subtle differences: palm trees rather than wild roses, and cliffs covered with ice plants instead of sand dunes anchored by sea grass. Shells that I'd never seen before glinted in the sand. Yet, if I closed my eyes, the differences evaporated, and the sounds, feel, and smells transported me back to the beaches of my youth.

I was glad to see that the beach was practically deserted except for one lone soul sitting in a chair reading a novel. There was something different about him, but I was too far away to see what it was. I turned my attention back to the shells and sand, but as I got closer, I noticed the reader was showing a lot of skin. Maybe he was wearing one of those tiny Speedo numbers. It was way too cold and gray for me to imagine swimming. He could be one of those polar bear guys. A few steps closer, and it hit me: the guy was stark naked! His winkie barely peeked out of two folds of fat rolling down his middle like a high tide wave.

My mouth dropped open, and I think I gasped out loud. I also made the mistake of making eye contact. He smiled, lips wide, showing black in places where teeth should be. His hand lurched to hold his penis, and it started to grow. Oh no! Had my stare acted like a visual caress? In a panic, I looked away and increased my pace. Just my luck…The one person on the beach was a pervert. I scanned the horizon for a lifeguard, or cop, or anyone who could enforce public nudity laws.

Ahead I saw a couple playing Frisbee, and a little farther down the beach a few solitary sunbathers were stretched out on towels, watching the surf and reading. I noticed that there were no lifeguard chairs or red trucks. Nearing the couple, I came to a complete stop, as transfixed as a defecating horse. As the man leapt to execute a perfect Frisbee catch, I saw he was wearing nothing but a T-shirt. He landed with his feet slightly apart, dingle dangling. With a grin, he launched the Frisbee back to his partner. She was prepared to receive it, bent slightly at the waist, hands splayed on her thighs, and giant naked boobs swaying like lobster buoys on a choppy sea. She was naked from the waist up! What kind of a beach was this?

Looking ahead, I saw that the other sunbathers were completely naked too. Oh, my god! Ken had taken me to a nude beach. Stunned, all I could think to do was act as normal as possible and keep moving. I did my best to look straight ahead or out to sea. Play it cool, I thought. Maybe they won't notice my fully clothed state. No way was I going to join the fun. This wasn't my bag. I vaguely remembered hearing about a nude beach in Rhode Island. It was whispered about, and we had been warned that only perverts went there—rapists, kidnappers, and dirty old men. I realized these cautions were intended as scare tactics, but I suspected that people who frequented nudist beaches probably had ulterior motives. Didn't they?

After I'd passed a few more naked bodies, my beach stroll no longer seemed appealing. I turned around and did a fast walk to the parking lot. The people on the stretch of beach near the lot were dressed, so I waited there for Ken and Sandy. Were they planning on staying long? I had been so excited about seeing the Pacific Ocean for the first time that I'd forgotten to ask when we should meet back at the car. On a patch of sand in front of the lot were two people sitting on a bench, holding hands. From a distance it looked like Ken and Sandy. I kept my fingers crossed and broke into a slow jog. It was them, and they were laughing at me.

"How do you like my favorite beach?" Ken chuckled.

Unexpectedly, my blood boiled. Some switch had flipped in my brain, and I was raving mad. "You asshole! You could have given me a little warning! I should have known you would take me to a nude beach."

"Whoa, it's not that bad." Ken looked at Sandy, who had stopped laughing.

"You are such a jerk. You ruined it for me." I strode back to the Mustang and jumped in the back. Tears were rolling down my cheeks. I'm not against nudity, and naked bodies are not offensive to me, but what had made me so mad was that Ken hadn't had the decency to warn me.

We drove back to the hotel in silence. When we arrived, I jumped out of the car without a word and retreated to my room.

When I was in college, my first apartment was a dilapidated duplex within walking distance of school. For ninety-five dollars a month, I finally had a place of my own. Two days after I settled in, a calico cat who acted like she belonged there visited me. She stuck around for a couple of weeks, and then disappeared for a few days, but soon returned. After a month it was pretty clear that my duplex was her home too. I named her Saga because there was definitely a good story locked away somewhere in her tiny cat brain. She was a nice cat, but whenever I sat down, she'd jump in my lap, settle in, and drool. The more I petted her, the larger the pool of drool grew. One day she came home with a kitten, and then there were two drooling cats.

My archaeology career has been a lot like my first apartment, but instead of drooling cats, it has come with a series of defective men. Like Saga, they have annoying habits. Johnson was a dirty old man and a male chauvinist, and Ken was an oversexed egomaniac. Why me?

Being raised in a family dominated by women, I'd had little exposure to the ways of men. My dad was nothing like these two. He is a gentleman who might brag on occasion, but since none of us girls listened, he saved his exploits for more appreciative audiences. My father did try to warn us about men and the male attitude toward romance and sex. Basically he told us that sex for men is just like blowing their nose: it relieves an itch and "cleans out the tubes." I always thought he'd simply been trying to scare me away from sex—that is, until I saw a Nevada whorehouse. I imagined a quaint old Victorian house painted in rich colors and snuggled in among huge cottonwoods and lush beds of roses. Instead it was a double-wide trailer surrounded by a seven-foot-high chain-link fence—no lawn, no trees, just a huge sign advertising hot ladies. What was the fence for? To keep the men in and the women out—or vice versa? Most of the men I've asked about this never even noticed the fence. The pathetic condition of the whorehouse shocked me until I remembered Dad's nose-blowing analogy. Really, how many women would pay to have sex with a stranger in that ugly trailer?

Ken was the kind of guy who actually bragged about going to Nevada's infamous Chicken Ranch, and if I was going to continue to work for him, I had to figure out a way to deal with his sleazy side. Enough solitary rumination. I decided to hit the convention center bar and look for my friends. Perhaps it wasn't too late to join them for dinner. If I were forced to spend the evening alone, I'd watch the other archaeologists and figure out a way to cope with Mr. Sex Addict. My strategy for Johnson had been to avoid and outlive, but since I couldn't avoid Ken, and he was only forty, I needed to come up with a different plan.

I didn't run into anyone at the bar so I got takeout from Kentucky Fried and ate alone in my room. I slept like the dead and woke dazed and confused. When I smelled the salt air, I thought for a minute I was at my grandmother's beach house. The clock said it was 9 a.m., so I'd already missed the first hour of papers. I made coffee in the tiny pot, showered, and headed to the meeting.

I decided to attend a session on another trendy topic: ethnoarchaeology. After three hours I'd learned that archaeologists are learning from modern hunter and gatherers what archaeological sites mean in terms of behavior, for example, how artifacts and forager camps are organized. It seemed to be a promising avenue of research. At lunchtime I bumped into Ken.

"Are you over it yet? Look. Why don't I make it up to you? Dinner is on me tonight. A group of us are going to a Mexican restaurant in Old Town, then to a party at Lee Ann Morrow's house—you know, the famous Mojave Desert archaeologist. It should be great. Lots of famous people will be there. Meet me in the lobby at five."

He melted into the crowd before I had a chance to say anything.

"Ivy!"

I turned and headed toward the female voice.

"Susan! I didn't know you were here. What are you up to these days?" It was my field school roommate, smoking and standing alone. We hugged.

"You look great," I told her. "I've missed you. I heard somewhere that you started grad school in Johnson's program."

"Yeah, I started last fall."

Susan looked thinner and tanned, but there were little lines of sadness around her eyes.

"Are you and Kurt still together?" I asked.

Susan's smile melted. "No, we broke up. He's making my life hell, Ivy. He's bad-mouthing me to everyone in the department. I think I'm going to have to leave if it keeps up."

"You're tough, Susan. Hang in there. Don't let him get you down. But why did you break up? You two seemed great together."

"He dumped me. I think he's having an affair with Professor Green."

"Are you sure?" I'd taken a class from Green, and she was pretty amazing.

"No, I'm not sure." Susan smoked for a minute, suddenly pensive. "But they did an ethnoarchaeology field project together in Australia, and he broke up with me when they got back. It was sudden, although his letters did stop halfway through the summer."

"Susan, I'm so sorry."

"Now he's telling everyone that I got into the program only because Johnson is my dad's friend. For some reason he's trying to make me leave."

"Maybe he considers you a threat and suspects you know about him and Green."

"Everyone suspects that. So why is he picking on me?"

I remembered what a brown-noser Kurt had been in field school and realized that I wasn't the least bit surprised at this turn of events. Poor Susan. She never saw the bad in anyone. Another hopeless optimist crashes and burns.

"Come on, Susan, let's get a beer and you can tell me all about it."

Two beers and two hours later, my dislike of Johnson was retuning like a bad LSD flashback. Susan had earned the right to feel slighted, and Kurt was definitely a weasel.

I told Susan about my job and what it was like to work for Ken. She sympathized with me but didn't have any useful advice. It was almost five, so I had to get back to the hotel. I invited Susan to come with us, but she had other plans. We hugged and promised to keep in touch.

Back in my room, I quickly changed into Frye boots, jeans, and a peasant blouse that my mom had brought back from one of her Mexico trips. I combed my hair and added a dash of lipstick. Ken and Sandy were waiting for me. Sandy complimented me on my blouse, but conversation was strained.

Old Town was a surprise, like a time capsule hidden by the San Diego hills, a slice of the past nestled among tall trees and waves of fuchsia-colored bougainvillea. We entered the restaurant, added our names to the waiting list, and hit the bar. Several of the Land Management Agency archaeologists from Nevada, Wyoming, and Idaho were meeting us. I was happy to see that Jake from the Forest Service was already there. We talked about the good presentations we'd seen, and the problems with CRAS. As usual, I was the only female archaeologist in the crowd. I was beginning to suspect that Ken had brought me along as arm candy. With Sandy and me to either side, he could almost claim two-chicks-at-once bragging rights. Or maybe I was just being paranoid.

It took an hour before we were seated, and our food was slow in coming, but the pitcher of margaritas never went dry. My glass was the size of a small pool and seemed to be bottomless. I learned later that the guys refilled it every time I looked away. I don't usually drink hard liquor, but the margaritas were great, sweet and refreshing.

By the time we'd finished dinner and piled into the cars, I was having the time of my life. Being the only female archaeologist in the group, I was the belle of the ball. I was squashed in Jake's rental car between two archaeologists from Wyoming and Nevada. Both of them were young and handsome, at least by an archaeologist's standards. I have no idea which direction we went, but we drove for half an hour to a neighborhood with big lots and ranch-style homes. Fortunately, I sobered up some during the drive.

From the outside, Lee Ann Morrow's house was typical 1960s suburbia. We headed toward a solid oak front door and rang the bell. It was quickly opened into a large, poorly lit room. I saw candles, and walls lined with books, baskets, and other Native American crafts. As my eyes adjusted to the darkness, I noticed that the entryway was a raised platform in the center of the room. Several people milled below in jeans, sport coats, and work shirts. I spied a white-haired woman adorned with Navajo silver talking to a young professor-type in a suit.

At the other end of the room, an elderly woman looked our way and then swam through the crowd toward us. At least it seemed like she must be swimming because she was completely naked. She looked like she'd spent a hundred years doing archaeology in the desert. I'd seen Egyptian mummies that looked better than her. With a broad smile and outstretched arms she introduced herself and welcomed us to her home. She recognized one of us, the agency archaeologist from California, and I looked on in horror as they hugged. When it was my turn to be introduced, I tried not to stare at her sagging breasts and graying pubic bush. She greeted and hugged two of the other guys and then it was my turn. To fend off the possibility of body contact, I offered my hand.

Was this really happening? I looked more carefully across the room. This time I saw a naked guy sitting on the couch talking to a middle-aged woman who was formally dressed in a gown and heels. She appeared to be smoking a joint. Maybe I'd passed out and was dreaming. But no, the naked crone was now offering us drinks and reciting party rules: no swimsuits in the pool and hot tub, shower before entering, and no peeing in the pool.

I followed Jake in a daze toward the crowded kitchen. At the end of a long corridor I spied an island littered with liquor bottles, half-filled cups, and empty beer cans, floating in a sea of drunks.

"Jake, what is with this party? I feel like I've just entered a nudist colony."

Jake shook his head. "I'd heard about Lee Ann's wild parties, but I thought people were exaggerating. This is amazing. Did you see the naked guy on the couch?"

"And how about the lady next to him smoking a joint? How bizarre was that?"

Jake had brought a bottle of whisky and poured two shots into paper cups. "No point in sobering up now. To archaeology!"

We downed the shots and found a corner of the kitchen that faced the pool. I looked out the window and saw several people frolicking naked. All were young and athletic. I watched Jake checking out the women. After a few more shots I was feeling less conspicuous. Ken and a couple of agency archaeologists joined us.

"Where's Sandy?"

"She passed out in one of the bedrooms," Ken said. "How about a dip in the Jacuzzi?"

"I didn't bring my swimsuit."

Jake nudged my arm. "Didn't you hear the naked lady? Rule number one is no suit."

One by one, the guys agreed to hit the hot tub. And after two more shots, it didn't sound like such a bad idea. I was seeing double and laughing at some stupid story Ken was telling about a fish that bit him on a raft trip down the Green River.

"So we were taking a break and skinny-dipping in a small side channel when I felt something grab my dick. It was a large-mouthed bass," said Ken seriously.

"I'll bet it was just a minnow!" yelled Wyoming's agency archaeologist.

"Let's get in the hot tub. Come on, Ivy," coaxed Jake. "Here's your opportunity to convince all the western states to join CRAS."

"You know, that's not such a bad idea. Will you join CRAS if I can convince Idaho and Wyoming to join?"

"If you can do that, I'm in. Hell, I'm in if you just get in the hot tub with us."

I was never one to back down from a challenge, particularly after four shots of whisky and several margaritas.

"Okay, I'll try my naked powers of persuasion."

Next thing I knew, I was in the hot tub naked with the Land Management Agency archaeologists from Wyoming, Nevada, Utah, and Idaho—and Jake. I vaguely recall listening to the guys tell horror stories about contract archaeologists. Then Ken brought up CRAS. He was bragging about how it was going to be the next best thing to sex. Nevada and Wyoming sounded interested—at least they agreed to learn more if I would do the teaching. I remember offering to visit them and show them how the system would work.

Since I didn't drink in the Jacuzzi, I sobered up a little—at least enough to feel slightly embarrassed. We all got out after about two hours of soaking. I remember stumbling from the house into Ken's car, but the rest is a blur.

The next day I kept a low profile, attending only a few presentations, and prayed I wouldn't run into anyone from the party. Thankfully, after lunch it was time to go home. The conference had been educational after all. I'd learned something about hard liquor and myself: there are happy drunks, mean drunks, quiet drunks, sloppy drunks, and, like me, naked drunks. After a few whisky shots, soaking naked in the Jacuzzi had seemed like a fine idea. Now I wondered how I would ever live it down.

Clovis Points and Cowboys

After thinking about it on the flight home from San Diego, I had decided that the best course of action would be to tell Tom about my nude night in the Jacuzzi, and to my surprise he just shook his head. He'd been around archaeologists long enough to understand that my behavior was not all that strange within the context of the annual SAA meeting. Ken, on the other hand, proceeded to tell everyone who would listen how I had single-handedly sold CRAS to Nevada, Wyoming, Idaho, and the Forest Service by frolicking naked in Lee Ann's hot tub with half the archaeologists in the West. I must have heard him tell ten people the story over the phone. He also told all the guys at work, who were now convinced that I was fair game. I decided to stay out of the break room and skip the Friday pub parties indefinitely.

After a month everyone seemed to have forgotten about my SAA adventures. I'd been keeping busy implementing the CRAS system and helping the district archaeologists with surveys. This Monday morning I was driving a truck to southwestern Utah to help Cedar City's new district archaeologist, Joanne Dunn, do a survey. I was meeting her at the Circle K in beautiful downtown Delta. Joanne had just moved to Cedar City after finishing her master's degree in anthropology at the University of Illinois. Ken suspected that she knew next to nothing about actually doing a survey in the West, so he sent me to teach her the ins and outs of Utah archaeology. I planned to stay for a week in Delta's only motel. The spring weather was perfect, warm and sunny, and I was ready for a week in the field. The four-hundred-acre survey was necessary before the county could develop a gravel pit for road maintenance. The Land Management Agency had agreed to do the survey as a favor to the county.

It was 9 a.m. and I'd already been driving for three hours when I turned off the interstate into the ranching town of Beaver, Utah. I drove a two-lane road for another fifty miles. The survey area was just west of Delta on the edge of an ancient dried-up beach of Lake Bonneville. During the last great ice age, giant lakes had covered parts of Utah, Idaho, and Nevada. Lake Bonneville had filled all the valleys dividing the steep rocky mountain ranges. About 15,000 years ago, the lake retreated when a huge amount of water was suddenly discharged in a massive flood event in what is now southeastern Idaho. After that, sagebrush filled the valleys, and pinyon pines spread across the mountain ranges. Pine nuts became one of the most important foods of the Great Basin's Indian tribes. Because good crops of nuts are erratic, native people moved their winter camps to the most productive groves. The Ute and Western Shoshone, who lived in the region historically, processed and stored the nuts for the cold winter months. Family groups spent winters at their pine nut camps rather than in the valleys because of plentiful game, mild weather, and access to firewood. Even when temperature inversions trap cold, damp air in the valleys, the foothills stay sunny and warm.

I sipped my coffee and drove west until Delta appeared on the horizon, sitting on the flats at the edge of a huge valley. I saw a small cluster of pioneer homes and doublewide trailers, a grocery store, a hardware store, two gas stations, a motel, and a post office. I had no idea what had attracted the first Mormon pioneers to this arid, lonesome place. I saw no obvious signs of springs or other water sources. I'd read in the newspaper that a huge coal-fired power plant was being built nearby and was supposed to rejuvenate Delta with new jobs, but it looked to me like it would take more than a power plant to make over this town. I pulled into the Circle K for gas and noticed another white pickup truck with government plates pulled over to the side. A tall, dark woman was intently reading a book, her windows rolled down.

I walked over to introduce myself. "You must be Joanne. I'm Ivy." But she wasn't reading. She was sleeping. She looked up startled and slightly confused.

"Hi. I didn't expect you quite so soon."

"I drive fast. I couldn't wait to get away from the office." Joanne opened her door, extended her long legs to the pavement, and stood up. She offered her hand and we shook. Her smile was wide and her eyes sparkled with intelligence—maybe even a little mischief. Her otherwise attractive face was marred only by a nose that defies description, but a picture of a monkey I'd once seen in a textbook popped into my head. Its nose hung from its face like a giant appendage, long and thin, with a round, ball-shaped tip.

Joanne towered over me, but then most people did. "It's a great day to be outside. I'm so glad you could come and help. I haven't worked on any surveys out west, and I'm not sure how it's done."

Joanne pushed a long, frizzy strand of hair back under her bandana. Her dark brown hair complimented her beautiful olive-toned skin. She was dressed for the field—in a T-shirt, jeans, and work shirt—except for her footwear: worn-out sneakers. Her loose field clothes couldn't hide a figure to die for.

"How far away is the survey area?" I asked.

"It's only a couple of miles from here. There should be a dirt road just beyond town, and the gravel pit will be just off of it."

"Why don't we leave my vehicle at the motel and drive the rest of the way in yours?"

"Sounds good." Joanne squinted and pointed down the road. "That's our motel over there. Why don't you meet me there after you finish gassing up."

At the motel I transferred my daypack, lunch, and water into Joanne's vehicle. We drove another five miles down the main road before turning west onto a dirt road. I looked over the survey area, an expanse of dry lakeshore terrace covered with low sand dunes.

"Looks like a great place for a gravel pit. Are we expecting to find many sites?" I asked.

"I have no idea. Our site files don't show previously recorded sites, but I don't think any archaeologists have been out here before. One of the guys in the office had heard that this was a good place to hunt for arrowheads, so I suspect we'll at least find some stuff."

To my relief, Joanne then reached in the back of the vehicle and pulled out a well-used pair of sturdy hiking boots. No one could hike for long in the sneakers she was wearing.

"Your boots look like you've done some hiking. Did you do much survey work in Illinois?"

"Yeah, I did my master's thesis on a large survey of Mississippian period villages around Cahokia. I spent three months trudging through forests, fields, and thick stands of poison ivy. I swore after that I'd find an easier place to do fieldwork."

"How do you even see sites with all the vegetation?"

"We look for mounds, find clearings, or check in plowed fields. If all else fails, we shovel test. It was slow going, but my thesis turned out okay. So I heard that all we have to do here is walk and look for artifacts. It should be easy to see artifacts in sand dunes. How do you want to proceed?"

I liked Joanne already. She was smart and honest, and I was looking forward to my week in the field. "Why don't we look at the map and figure out where the project boundaries are? Then we can walk a compass heading from one end of the project area to the other."

Joanne spread out the USGS map on the hood of the truck. The project boundaries were marked in red. It was a square-shaped area that ran from the dirt road due west to a section line. I looked west and saw a fence running north to south.

"It looks like that fence probably follows the section line. What do you think?"

Joanne adjusted her glasses. "Yeah, my boss told me the gravel pit would be located between this road and a section fence. That must be it."

I looked at the map and saw that the corner of the section should be located due west. "If we're here," I pointed at the corner of the project area, "then we should find a section marker at the fence on our first transect." I explained about our survey methods. "We walk fifteen meters apart, and the person on the end flags the transect with toilet paper. Then the flagger follows the toilet paper line back on the return transect."

Although we hadn't flagged our transect lines in field school, just about everyone I knew had started marking them with toilet paper. It made the survey faster and more accurate.

"With the toilet paper flags, we can spend less time looking at the compass and more time looking at the ground for artifacts. It works great. On this first transect why don't you follow your compass heading due west and I'll flag first?"

I grabbed a roll of toilet paper and headed to my starting point. Joanne stood near the truck and used her compass to pick a point to walk toward.

The transect was just a quarter of a mile long, and we were at the fence before we knew it. On the return transect Joanne flagged and I walked fifteen meters away from my toilet paper line.

"Flake!" I yelled. "Another flake! Do you see any over there? Hold up while I look around." I circled the spot, which was sandy and bare, and spotted two more mustard-colored flakes and a rounded rock that looked like a mano fragment.

"Site!" I yelled. "Why don't you come over here and see what I've got."

We walked in circles, searching for the edge of the lithic scatter, which turned out to contain thousands of flakes and fragments of ground stone. Joanne found a spear point, and I noted a scatter of fire-cracked rocks, indicating the site had probably been a campsite. After marking the site boundaries with flagging tape, we drew the sketch map and filled out the forms. It was Joanne's first time using the new CRAS form, so the recording went slowly.

On the next three transects we found two more sites. The project area was loaded with flake scatters, and it seemed like we were having to stop and record every few transects. Several large spear point fragments told us the area had been used during the Archaic period. Today the area looked desolate, and I tried to figure out what had attracted people to this place. We took a break to move the car down the road to where we would finish our last transect. By the end of the day we had recorded five sites but had finished only a quarter of the survey.

"I think this whole area is one big site," I said. "At this rate, we won't finish the survey until Friday, and I doubt they'll be able to build the quarry because of all the sites. It's almost quitting time. I'm going to pee, and then let's call it a day."

I left Joanne to finish the paperwork on the fifth site and walked behind a low dune. Just as I pushed my pants down and squatted, out of the corner of my eye I saw a spear point sticking out of the sand. I bent over to retrieve it and saw that the tip was broken off, but a long flake had been removed down the center of the blade. It was a fluted point! My heart beat faster, and I yelped with excitement.

"Ivy!" yelled Joanne. "Are you okay?"

I put the point down to take care of business. After buttoning my jeans, I yelled out, "I think I found a Clovis point!" Joanne was already walking in my direction.

"Are you kidding, Ivy?"

I held out the point. "Look at it yourself. It's fluted and the edges are ground. The base looks like the right shape too." I let out another whoop. "I found a Clovis point!"

Joanne held the white chalcedony point in her hand, and I noticed for the first time how large it was. Although only two-thirds of it had been preserved, it nearly covered the palm of her hand.

"I can't believe it," she said. "It looks just like the pictures I've seen." She handed it back to me. "My first day in the field and we find a Clovis point. I think I'm going to like doing archaeology in the West."

I looked out over the project area. "These sand dunes probably were beaches along the edge of the lake 10,000 years ago. Do you think there could have been mammoths or bison here then? I'll bet it was more like a marsh."

My imagination was running wild. Clovis points were made by one of the first Native American groups to inhabit North America. The points are rarely found, and most of the time they're not associated with flakes or other tools. In New Mexico and Arizona, Clovis points had been found embedded in the skeletons of extinct mammoths. For decades archaeologists had believed that the Clovis were the first Americans. Isolated Clovis points are found everywhere in North and South America, but only in the southwestern United States have they been found with mammals.

"Let's mark this spot with flagging tape, and we can search the area tomorrow. I think we should collect the point. Ken is writing an article on fluted point finds in Utah, and he'll want to see this one."

I grabbed a small plastic bag from my backpack, and it already had a field specimen label. I wrote the project title on the label and gave the artifact a temporary site number and a field specimen number. Joanne flagged and walked the area while I labeled the point.

"I don't see any other artifacts, Ivy. It looks like it's an isolate."

"Too bad. But we'll look again tomorrow. It's getting late and the light is pretty bad."

We loaded our stuff into the truck and headed to the motel. While Joanne drove, I gave the Clovis point a closer inspection. The flake scars across the surface were smooth and worn, sandblasted from lying in the dune for thousands of years. The area where the tip was broken off looked like an impact fracture, and I imagined a hunter standing in the marsh on the edge of the vast lake, poised and ready to hurl a spear at a huge tusked mammoth. Several other hunters would have helped him isolate the giant animal from the herd and trap her in the marsh. As the mammoth wandered into deeper water, the men hurled their spears into her thick skin. Tusks raised, she bellowed with fear at the hunters' assault. Surrounded, she had nowhere to run except out to deeper water. The men knew they needed to bring her down before she waded out too far. One of the hunters threw his spear, and it struck deep into her chest. She bellowed again and fell to her knees. The most experienced hunter moved closer so that he too could thrust his spear into her chest. Trapped in the mud, the mammoth's eyes went wide with fear as the spear found its mark and a fountain of blood sprang forth.

I snapped back to the present and realized that Joanne was talking.

"This is so exciting. I can't believe we found a Clovis point on my first day. Maybe tomorrow we'll find a site nearby with channel flakes or maybe even another point. Let's go celebrate. Is there a bar in town?"

I suspected that our motel rooms wouldn't be the kind of place to spend time—except to sleep.

"I think I saw a small one when we drove through town. Let's check into the motel and clean up a little."

My tiny room had a double bed, a small closet, and a bathroom. The carpet was brown, and the walls beige. A television sat in the corner waiting to keep me company. Above the bed hung mountain scenes reminding me of my paint-by-number days. As long as the shower didn't resemble the one in *Psycho*, I guessed the room would do. After all, it had a real bed and plumbing, which was better than camping. I washed my face, changed my shirt, and combed my hair. Joanne knocked on the door.

"Ready, Ivy? The motel manager told me the bar also serves the best food in town, so we can drink beer and eat dinner there."

"Great. I'm starving."

The bar reminded me of Water Hole #1 in Escalante. It sat at the edge of town, off by itself. The outside screamed "cowboy bar," but inside it looked more like Salt Lake City's new fern bars. It was light and bright, with large houseplants scattered everywhere. I wondered if beer and smoke were the key to healthy plants. The scene would be complete with a row of yuppies lining the bar. Instead, occupying the bar stools were three fully accessorized cowboys, complete with hats, boots, Wranglers, and rodeo belt buckles. I guessed they represented the town's twenty-something, non-Mormon male population. They probably worked the large ranches on the outskirts of town. They stared at us as we walked in, and the shorter one tipped his hat.

We found a table at the other end of the room, and a few minutes later a middle-aged woman appeared with two menus. "Are you going to have dinner?"

"Ivy, should we have a beer first?"

I looked at the waitress. "We'll have a beer and then order. Are there any specials today?"

"Chicken-fried steak for $5.99 and it comes with mashed potatoes, gravy, vegetables, and a dinner salad. I make the gravy myself."

We ordered beer and checked over the menu. Joanne looked perplexed.

"Is chicken-fried steak beef or chicken?"

I laughed. "I never heard of the stuff before moving to Utah. It's actually a thin steak that's breaded and deep-fried. If it's done right, it's delicious. Try it. I'll bet it's good here."

Joanne spoke softly. "You sure? It sounds like a heart clogger to me."

"I know what you mean. My mom never fried anything, so I'm not big into deep fried stuff, but chicken-fried steak is the best, especially with mashed potatoes and gravy."

We drank our beers and got out the Clovis point to make sure we hadn't imagined the find. As we ordered two more beers, we saw two of the cowboys headed our way.

The short blond one spoke first. "Couldn't help but notice your arrowhead. I've got a half dozen whole ones at home. Did you find it out by the sand dunes west of town?"

Our eyes widened. Did the cowboy say six?

"We wouldn't have bothered with that broken one."

"Did the ones you collect have this down the center?" I asked, pointing to the thick groove running the long way down the middle of the point.

"Yeah, sure, a flute," said the cowboy. "They're Clovis points, right?"

"Do you still have the points you collected?" I asked.

The cowboy's long mustache twitched. "Sure. My mom likes to frame them and hang them on the wall. They look real nice when she finishes with them. Where are you gals from?"

Joanne spoke first. "I just moved to Cedar City from Chicago."

The tall cowboy nudged the shorter one. "Told you they looked like they're from back east."

The short cowboy looked at me. "Are you from there too?"

"Originally from Rhode Island, but I've been living in Salt Lake for a while."

"Mind if we join you two? This town is starved for good-looking ladies."

Before I could answer no, Joanne motioned for them to take a seat. "That would be great." Her face lit up with a warm smile. "Tell us about your arrowhead collection."

The tall one introduced himself as Gavin, and the shorter one was Marty. I got a better look at them as they went to retrieve their beers from the bar. Gavin was the Marlboro Man: tall, thin, and muscled in all the right places. My eyes traveled down his body, his wide shoulders tapering to a small waist and tight Wrangler butt. My eyes vacationed there briefly until I realized he'd noticed I was checking him out. His short dark hair was hidden under a beat-up cowboy hat shielding his eyes. I decided that although he was nearly perfect, his green eyes were his best feature. They reminded me of a deep forest stippled with glints of light.

Marty turned out to be extroverted, funny, and as easy to read as a neon sign. Right now the sign was flashing "young male needs woman bad." His blond hair was cut short and thinning slightly in the front. A clear complexion and ruddy cheeks suggested eastern European ancestry, and he was just starting to develop a small beer gut that hung over his Wranglers.

Joanne got right down to business. "So, boys, where did you find your Clovis points?"

Marty did most of the talking. "Gavin and I have been friends since we were kids. We've walked every inch of those sand dunes and collected dozens of arrowheads. How many would you say, Gavin?"

Gavin paused for a few minutes and took a sip of beer. "That depends on who wants to know. What are you two doing collecting a Clovis point? Are you archaeologists? If not, you shouldn't be telling everyone you collected government property."

Joanne chuckled and smiled at Gavin. "You're pretty smart for a Delta, Utah, cowboy."

Gavin checked his beer bottle to see how much was left. The glints in his eyes turned into pools of light. He stared at Joanne for a few seconds before he spoke, then smiled. "Since when was IQ determined by birthplace?"

"I didn't say it was," Joanne replied. "It just seems that someone who was smart enough to know it was illegal to collect arrowheads would also know better than to do it."

Marty started squirming in his seat, then shook his head, stood up, and headed to the bar.

"It isn't illegal to collect arrowheads. I've read the regulations, and there's no law against it. You show me where it says I can't collect and I'll stop."

Joanne's cheeks flushed. I'd just learned from Ken that Gavin was correct: arrowhead collecting was exempt under the new regulations. Gavin was well informed.

Joanne refused to back down. "If you collect all the surface artifacts, it's impossible for us to figure out how old the sites are."

"All you have to do is ask around. We all know that the Indians lived around the lake thousands of years ago."

Now she was starting to get annoyed. "How do you know that? There haven't been any excavations or surveys done in this area."

Gavin smiled again. "It's simple. The points are Clovis types, and the lake dried up during the Clovis drought. You didn't answer my question. Why are you two collecting arrowheads?"

"We're archaeologists for the Land Management Agency, doing a survey for a county gravel pit."

Marty returned with four beers and placed one in front of each of us.

"What'd I miss?" Marty looked around, sensing the tension.

"So what if we work for the Land Management Agency?" Joanne asked. "What's wrong with that?"

Gavin took another swig of beer. "You're new around here, aren't you?"

"How'd you guess?"

"The Land Management Agency isn't too well liked." Gavin leaned back in his chair to watch Joanne's response.

"Why not?"

"Let's see. Where do I begin? They determine when and where we can graze our animals, they require expensive NEPA documents before we can expand our mining operations, and they won't even let us cut down a Christmas tree without a permit. Anything you want to do, the federal government will have a reason for you not to." Gavin sat back and smiled.

Marty kicked Gavin under the table and gave him the evil eye. "Hey, ladies, Gavin doesn't mean you two, just the managers. You're just out here doing your job. Now let's drink some beer and have some fun. So, Joanne, what brought you out west?"

Effortlessly, Marty diffused the tension, and Gavin and I listened to Joanne's story of her move to Utah. The waitress reappeared, and we all ordered the special. Marty had decided that Joanne should see his arrowhead collection, and as they became more engrossed in their conversation, they found all kinds of things in common. Even I could see the chemistry. Joanne moved fast.

The door to the bar opened, and another cowboy entered. He was very thin and had a bad complexion. It also looked like his head was too big for his body. Gavin called him over.

"Ivy, this is my cousin Evan."

They talked quietly for few minutes. They seemed to be making fun of Joanne and Marty, but then their conversation turned serious. I couldn't really follow what they were talking about, but it sounded like a legal battle between their family and the Land Management Agency. It became pretty obvious that Gavin was the prosecuting attorney in the case.

"You went to law school?" I blurted out.

"Yeah. So what? Lots of people do."

"What are you doing out here with a law degree?"

"I graduated in '76 and then moved home. I live here." Gavin looked at me to see my reaction.

"So you practice law?"

"Now and then, when it doesn't conflict with my ranch duties. Mom and Dad still live on the ranch, but I do most of the hard work."

I was flabbergasted. No wonder he knew so much about law. I felt silly for assuming he was an uneducated cowboy.

Evan shoved Gavin's arm playfully. "And Gavin's a cowboy poet to boot. Tell her about your book, Gavin."

He shrugged and I believe he even blushed. "Shut up, Evan."

"Come on, Gavin, don't be so humble. Charm the ladies. Tell them about the reviews in that New York magazine."

My mouth dropped open. I looked over at Gavin, and his dark eyes sparkled. All the glints were gone. He picked up his beer, downed the last swallow, and then stood to get another.

"Gavin's the quiet and smart one in the family," explained Evan. "Hey, you aren't from around here. What are you doing in Delta?"

"Joanne and I are archaeologists for the Land Management Agency. We're doing a survey for the new county gravel pit. I guess you guys don't particularly like the agency."

"Well, see, the Land Management Agency hires outsiders like you who come here and tell us how to run things. No offense, but you easterners don't understand this part of the world. It ain't like back east. I did a mission in Boston, so I know a little bit about that."

"You did a Mormon mission? Then why are you here drinking beer with us?"

"Well, I kind of had a falling out with the church. When I got back from my mission, I fell in love with Mary. She's Paiute, and the church didn't approve. She's real active in the Indian Rocks band and doesn't have any interest in the Mormon church. She says they blamed the Mountain Meadows Massacre on her tribe, and the Indians had nothing to do with the massacre. Elders are still bitter about it. We're getting married soon, and she doesn't want anything to do with the church. I love her more than religion, so I said 'good-bye church.'"

"How about Gavin? Is he Mormon too?" I was more interested in Gavin than I cared to admit.

"We was all raised Mormon, but now we're Jack Mormons. We drink and smoke and only go to church at Christmas and Easter."

It reminded me of my own church upbringing. "I was raised a Baptist, but I can't handle all that arm waving and talk about God's wrath, hell, damnation, and all the rest. I guess I just never understood religion."

Gavin joined us again at the table. "Evan, haven't you learned you don't talk to pretty ladies about religion or politics?"

"Get real, Gavin. I'm out of here. I need to get home to Mary or she'll be worried. You two enjoy your date." Evan winked at Gavin and stood to go. "Nice to meet you, Ivy. Watch out for my cousin here. He's dangerous."

I looked at Gavin, who was shaking his head. As if on cue, our dinner arrived. Marty and Joanne were deep in conversation, so Gavin and I were left to our own devices. We ate in silence. The food was delicious, and I realized I was starving. The steak was fresh and cooked to perfection, the gravy was spiced with something I couldn't identify, and the mashed potatoes were puffy clouds of pure pleasure. Garvin was appreciating the food as much as I was.

"What was the Mountain Meadows Massacre, Gavin?"

"Well now, that depends on who you ask. The official church story is that the Indians killed a wagon train full of men, women, and children near Pine Valley. The U.S. government, the Indians, and most historians recognize that the perpetrators were Mormons from Cedar City, Harmony, and Parowan. The wagon train leaders taunted the Mormons about killing Joseph Smith. Probably another factor was that the wagon train was carrying a lot of supplies that the Mormons could badly use. The Mormons were dirt poor and often hungry. Probably it was complicated— revenge and hate over different belief systems, jealousy, you name it. A Mormon elder was tried and executed for the massacre, but most of the others involved never told their stories. I read an account once by Jacob Hamblin of visiting the massacre soon after it occurred. He found out about it after a wagonload of children who had survived arrived at his home in St. George. His young second wife tried to care for them but they all died. The Indians told Jacob where the children had come from and what had happened. When he visited the massacre site, bodies were everywhere, being eaten by wolves."

"That's horrible. I never heard of the Mountain Meadows Massacre before. Can you recommend a book about it?"

"There's a new one by Juanita Brooks, just out." Gavin dipped the last piece of steak into a smear of mashed potatoes and pushed his plate aside. "So, Ivy, what made you move to Utah, all the way from Rhode Island?"

"Old Westerns."

"Now what kind of answer is that?"

"No, really. When I was young I watched old Westerns and realized the West was for me. You know... wide open spaces, long, empty stretches of uninhabited deserts."

Gavin smiled and I felt self-conscious for a minute. "It's hard to explain, but I feel drawn to the West. It just feels like home to me."

"But Utah seems an unlikely place for you to end up."

"I picked Utah College because of its archaeology program and the great skiing. I just finished my B.A. in anthropology a year ago and started working right away. I haven't had any trouble finding jobs."

"Why the agency?"

My plate was still half full, but the conversation had become more inviting than dinner.

"I don't know. It pays well, and I get to learn all about cultural resource management. My boss is a creep, though, so I doubt I'll last long."

"How so?"

"He's so sleazy, he oozes slime. I feel dirty just being in the same room with him. He's married but has girlfriends everywhere."

Gavin sat back and watched me as I tried to eat and talk at the same time. His eyes continued to draw me in.

"How old are you, Gavin?"

"Almost thirty."

"I don't see a wedding ring. Why not?"

"Now that's a touchy subject. Usually I try to avoid it, but I guess I'll answer you straight. I returned from law school with the intention of marrying my high school sweetheart only to discover she'd been having an affair with a guy in Cedar City."

"How'd you find out?"

"Marty told me. The worst part was learning that everyone knew about it. No one had the guts to tell me."

"Ouch! I'm sorry."

"Since then I haven't met anyone. Guess the psychologists would say that I'm having trust issues."

"I don't blame you. People say that time heals all wounds, but I'm not so sure."

We sat in silence. Gavin suddenly looked like he was somewhere else. I finished my steak and tried to change the subject.

"So tell me about your ranch. I always thought it would be great to live on a ranch beneath tall mountains and miles from my nearest neighbor. You know that song, 'Give me room, lots of room, and the open skies above. Don't fence me in.'" My singing brought Gavin back to the present.

The glints in his eyes returned. "We own two sections, or around 1,300 acres, of prime grazing land. We also lease another 2,000 acres from the Land Management Agency. My great-grandfather settled this country before the agency took control, and he was first on the list when grazing rights were sold. I'm the fourth generation of Stewarts to hold the rights and run the ranch."

"I wish I had such deep ties to the land. I was raised in suburbia. There were lots of open spaces to play, but when the farm behind us was developed, it broke my heart. Do you come from a big family, Gavin? I always picture ranchers as having big families."

The sadness returned again, briefly. "Nah, just me. I was born in the ranch house. Mom couldn't get to the hospital fast enough, so my dad delivered me. It was a hard birth, and by the time the doctor arrived, it was too late to repair the damage, so I'm an only child."

Joanne's peals of laughter interrupted Gavin's second sad disclosure.

"What's so funny?" I asked.

Marty answered, and Joanne kept laughing. "I was just telling her about the time my younger brother fell into the pig pen. I didn't think it was that funny."

"Oh, Marty, you're a riot. Don't stop," coaxed Joanne. "I haven't laughed this hard in ages."

"It was pretty funny," Gavin said. "I was there."

"Come on," I said. "Tell me the story."

"I'll leave that to Marty." Gavin stood up and put on his coat. "I need to be heading home."

Marty waved and then launched into the story.

"Bye, Gavin. I enjoyed meeting you." I was sad to see him leave. He nodded and tipped his hat as he turned toward the door.

"Okay," Marty continued. "So we were bored and decided to go bother the hogs. Dad usually keeps one so that we can butcher it in the fall. We had two that year, and it was late in the summer and they were huge. We decided to tie their tails together and see what would happen."

"You can't tie hogs' tails together," I insisted. "That's ridiculous!"

"Okay, so we thought it over and decided to try duct tape. I went to get the tape, and Gavin had it all figured out by the time I got back. You see the hogs were sleeping next to each other. They were sisters. The plan was to duct tape them without waking them up. Gavin and I crept into the pen, and we each had the end of a single piece of tape. The hogs kept sleeping, and the tape stuck pretty well, but when we were almost done, they woke up confused and mad. My brother, who was sitting on the fence, started laughing when the hogs looked at their butts and realized they were tied together. We jumped out of the pen, and while I was scrambling to get onto the fence, I hit my brother's leg. He lost his balance and fell into the pen. The hogs were real mad and running in circles. My brother had sprained his ankle so was a little slow getting up, and the bigger hog ran right into him, knocking him down. When he got up, the second hog nailed him.

Finally Gavin jumped back in and grabbed him. The hogs managed to get the duct tape off their tails soon after, but it was so funny watching them."

Joanne was in hysterics again, but I was too tired to think it was that funny. I announced that it was time for this little piggy to hit the hay.

"Are you ready, Joanne?"

"I promised to check out Marty's arrowhead collection. He'll give me a ride back to the motel. I'll see you in the morning. Does eight sound like a good time to start?"

I stood to leave. "As long as I have time to get my coffee, I'm fine. See you, guys. I'm ready for a long nap."

As soon as I got into bed I fell into a dreamless slumber. My alarm went off at seven, but it still seemed pretty dark out so I opened the curtain to see what kind of day it was. It was dreary and overcast, and looked and smelled like rain. At least I'd remembered my raincoat.

I brushed my teeth, braided my hair, put my field clothes on, then grabbed my room key and walked across the street to the only restaurant in town that served breakfast. It was a small diner with lots of homey decorations. The cash register sat on a glass display case filled with souvenirs from the Far East, carved ivory and delicate fans. Mixed into the collection was an assortment of etched Styrofoam cups with detailed wildlife scenes: an elk with a huge rack, and a bear standing upright, ready to attack. The sign with today's specials told me to seat myself.

I looked over the room and noticed that I was the only woman in the place. About a dozen old men looked up from their cups of coffee or stacks of pancakes and stared. I grabbed a booth by the window and hid behind the menu, flipping my coffee cup over to signal I was ready for some.

A rail-thin woman with heavy lip liner soon appeared to pour me a cup.

"Coffee, honey?"

"Yes, please," I mumbled.

"What's it going to be?"

"Uh, I'll have the special. It's pancakes, right?"

"You bet. The best around."

I sipped my coffee and listened to the men around me. Two behind me, clad in overalls and work shirts, were talking about someone's new truck. The four elderly men at another table were talking about a tractor that apparently wasn't working right. All were wearing jeans and button-down shirts. Their hands were worn and bent from years of physical labor, and I noticed a couple of the men were missing more than a few teeth. Everyone was wearing either a cowboy hat or a ball cap. They joked with the waitress when she refilled their cups, and she called them all by name.

So this was what it would be like to live in a small town your whole life. It looked to me like this diner was the locals' equivalent of a Puebloan kiva, a men's meetinghouse—a place where the guys could get away from the women, eat whatever they wanted, and shoot the breeze.

The Naugahyde booth seats were cracked and worn thin, the paint was stained with years of grease and grime, and many of the blinds were missing slats. In typical Utah fashion, the coffee was weak, but at least it was steaming hot. My pancakes arrived before the men had moved on from the subject of the broken tractor. I poured syrup next to the stack and lost myself in cutting, dipping, and chewing. I ate every morsel and drank two more cups of coffee. It was almost eight, so I paid the bill and left a hefty tip. Back at the motel I gathered my daypack, lunch, and water for the day, making sure to pack my raincoat.

It was just after eight, but there was still no sign of Joanne. Her room was next to mine, and I hadn't heard her return. Slightly worried, I knocked on the door. Nothing. Not a peep. As I loaded my stuff in the vehicle, a huge truck, with Marty at the wheel, pulled up. Joanne, all smiles and light, gave him a good-bye kiss that made my toes curl. She jumped out of the high pickup with a Cheshire smile, last night's clothes, and bed head.

"Morning, Ivy. Isn't it a beautiful day?"

I shook my head. "Must have been fantastic arrowheads. Or did you even get to see his collection?"

"I most certainly did. They were a dream come true, and so is Marty. Right now I am the best-fucked woman on the planet." She hummed to herself as she pushed open the door to her room. Looking over her shoulder, she said, "Just give me fifteen minutes."

I went back into my room to watch the news while I was waiting. I'd never slept with anyone on the first date, and I wondered a little what it would be like. Marty certainly wasn't my type, but Gavin was another story.

Joanne was true to her word: clean and ready to survey in fifteen minutes. We drove out to the future gravel pit in silence. Joanne seemed lost in a pleasure coma. It started to drizzle after our first transect and rained on and off all day. By midday the temperature had dropped twenty degrees. By three we were soaking wet and freezing cold.

"I think I'm done here, Joanne. What do you think?"

"Stick a fork in me. I'm done."

"I'm thinking hot shower, beer, and chicken-fried steak—in that order."

I was soaked to the skin because my raincoat had only protected me for about the first two hours. My hat had prevented rain from getting into my eyes, but now my hair was stringy and plastered to my head.

"Ah, my feet are soaked," I whined. "I hate wet feet." I removed my boots and socks and rubbed my feet together under the truck's heater.

"I think I'm in love, Ivy."

"You can't be. You just met Marty. I'd say it's more like in lust."

"He's going to meet me at the bar after work. Round two."

"Don't you think it might be a good idea to slow down a little? Take your time?" I looked over at Joanne. She was driving in a daze.

"Why? I've never met anyone like him before. He's funny and sexy. You wouldn't believe what we did last night."

"I can only imagine."

"Mmm good. I'm all tingly just thinking about it."

I gathered up my boots and wet socks as Joanne parked the truck.

"How about we meet at the bar in an hour? I need to warm up in a hot shower. Damn, that's going to feel good."

"Not as good as what I plan to do later," Joanne said with a wink as she slipped into her room.

An hour later we were ensconced at last night's table, all clean, dry, and warm. The room was empty except for a couple sitting at the bar. I recognized the man from the diner. The woman, who was probably in her sixties, had a beehive hairdo, blue eye shadow, and pancake makeup so thick it looked like she'd put it on with a trowel. She was wearing a miniskirt and a low-cut tank top that hugged and accentuated her massive but sagging chest. They stood up to play pool, and I watched her rack the balls and prepare to break. Her shot moved more than the balls on the table.

"Hey, Joanne. What do you think of the couple playing pool?"

"Quite the advertisement for recreational opportunities in Delta," she said, laughing. The cowbell rang as the door opened, and Marty entered the bar, followed by Gavin a few seconds later.

I stared as Gavin strode in and felt everything around me stop, like a science-fiction movie. I felt like I was in a state of suspended animation, with only Gavin moving. His tall, muscular frame was swathed in a long brown duster that fell almost to his ankles. The chaps hugging his hips flapped loose around his legs. He smelled like sage and horses, and his spurs clanged softly with each step. His Stetson was perched low to shield his eyes, but when he smiled, our eyes met. I fell into them as if they were a broad valley with an infinite horizon moving farther out of reach with every step. For a second I understood what people meant when they said they could see their unborn children in someone's eyes. I blushed as Gavin pulled out the chair next to me. He sat down and stared at me with an intensity that made parts of me tingle.

Joanne and Marty had stopped talking. Maybe they sensed the magic.

Gavin leaned over and whispered into my ear. "Wanna see my arrowhead collection?"

The Habiliment Chart

After my week in Delta I felt disoriented—like I was watching the world move forward from some distant place, or I had entered a new dimension. Colors were a little brighter and sounds sweeter. Technically, I had not crossed the cheating line with Gavin, but I felt like something had happened that I shouldn't share with Tom. Oh, I told him about the bar and the cowboys, and even mentioned Gavin's name, but I kept my feelings a secret.

I had taken Gavin up on the offer to see his arrowhead collection—and his horses, his home, and the barn. After I met his parents, we saddled the horses and went for a moonlight ride. The storm had moved on, leaving the night clear and crisp. After our ride, Gavin drove me back to the motel—no kiss, no hug, just a handshake.

The next afternoon we quit a little early so that Marty and Gavin could take me and Joanne to see the Parowan Gap petroglyphs that Native Americans had carved into the black outcrops thousands of years ago. Exotic images of lines, circles, sheep, men hunting, and monsters covered the basalt cliffs. Marty told us that Mary's family believes that the glyphs were carved by little men who live in the cracks of the rocks and have special powers. According to the Paiutes, the petroglyphs shouldn't be messed with.

We finished the survey on Friday. On the drive home I'd decided it would be best to put the whole experience behind me. My life was complicated enough: I had a job, and I needed to stay focused on the moment.

The first week home I successfully pushed Gavin from my conscious thought, but at night he roamed my dreams—riding toward me through wide valleys, materializing out of the rain. In a couple of dreams he just sat across a table from me, smiling, but twice I awoke from particularly vivid dreams smelling sage and horse sweat.

The guys in the office had missed me—or, I should say, seeing me. The past few weeks they'd been paying attention to my attire. It started when I wore a sexy dress to work. I hardly ever wear dresses, and this one was hot. I have no idea what possessed me to wear it. I guess I was in the mood to look good. I'd also started to wear a little makeup and pay more attention to my hair. Some days I'd look like a polished professional, others like a hippie archaeologist. The guys in the office had become intrigued by my style swings, so during my absence they'd devised a new office game: a habiliment chart to record and rate my appearance each day. It was a monthly calendar taped to a wall with a line for each guy to rate me on a scale of one to ten. I made light of the whole thing, joking with the guys each day when my score came in, but deep down I worried about the attention and wished there was another professional woman in the office I could talk to.

When not running the habiliment gauntlet or blocking Ken's daily landslide of sleaze, I worked with the state and federal archaeologists to implement CRAS. The subcontractors were almost finished encoding the site data, and the Land Management Agency had started requiring contract archaeologists to use the new form. Soon the State Historic Preservation Office would issue regulations regarding the system's statewide use.

I was also busy managing a survey contract issued by the Land Management Agency to a small company in Nevada. The agency had hired them to survey ten percent of the coal-rich lands in central Utah. The site density data would be compiled as supporting data for an environmental impact statement. I was the contracting officer's representative, which meant I was responsible for tracking the contractor's progress and providing assistance. My main responsibility, though, was to monitor work quality, which meant visiting the survey crews and looking at some of the sites they'd recorded.

I left the office at 7 a.m. with a plan to meet the project's supervisor, Linda Redmund, in Emery at noon. I drove the same route through the mountains that we had taken to field school and then turned south toward Emery. Until coal had been discovered, it had been a small Mormon farming and ranching community. Located in the desert, the town survived on snowmelt and runoff from the adjacent Wasatch Plateau. The tree-lined main street followed a creek draining the mountains and was bordered on each side by hundred-year-old brick homes. Emery felt like a safe place to grow up. Newly planted fields surrounded the town and covered the floodplain spilling out the canyon. I'd learned somewhere that the first Mormon settlers found a network of prehistoric irrigation canals already in place when they first arrived. The Fremont had probably lived here, farming the land, more than five hundred years ago.

I arrived at our meeting place a little early, and Linda was nowhere in sight. Did I have the right place? I checked my notes and waited for a few minutes in the Dairy Queen parking lot. After thirty minutes I decided to check the motel, but she wasn't there either, so I went back to the Dairy Queen and waited. A few minutes later she pulled up in a battered Jeep Cherokee.

A towering inferno of a woman, Linda made me look like a midget. She was giant in every way: feet like snorkeling fins, breasts the size of soccer balls, Medusa hair—even her hands were massive. My hand disappeared in hers when we shook. Her halo of multicolored hair was like Saturn's rings, the color changing from dark brown at the roots to yellow to green. Her super-sized figure was squeezed into jeans and a T-shirt that were at least two sizes too small. She was a tower of power, the archaeological version of a roller derby queen. With her arms swinging, and one small hip nudge, I could imagine her opponent flying from the track, marginalized, crumpled, and whimpering in a corner.

"How's it going?" I asked. "What kind of sites have you found?" I remembered that beta primates smile a lot in the presence of the dominant alpha. I tried that.

"Mostly lithic scatters, but a few rock shelters," she replied, spreading out the map on the hood of the Jeep. "Here are the units that we've surveyed and the sites we've recorded so far. As you can see, most units have sites. This one has a big old site right in the middle. It's huge."

"Have you found any pottery?" I asked. The project area was close to a known Fremont settlement, where ceramics were common.

"Nah," she said, shaking her head. "Haven't seen a single sherd."

"That's strange. I'd expect there to be some. How about historic sites?"

Linda looked at me funny. "What do you mean? We're working in the middle of nowhere. I wouldn't expect any historic sites."

"Uh, just wondering," I stammered.

"Why don't you put your stuff in my vehicle and we'll head out and look at a few of the sites."

As soon as I'd gotten in and closed the door, Linda took off—or, rather, peeled out. She was the fastest driver I had ever been in a car with. With one hand on the wheel, she left Emery at speeds exceeding eighty miles per hour.

Linda looked over at me out of the corner of her eye. "These towns are great. I've already figured out where the cops are throughout the day. I just saw them at breakfast. My dad taught me how to drive fast. It gets into your blood."

As she turned off the main road, I could have sworn the Cherokee was up on two wheels. Linda seemed to know what she was doing, but it was scaring the shit out of me. Fortunately the gravel road was wide and straight. In seconds the speedometer hit sixty and continued to climb. That's when I noticed curves ahead. The Cherokee clung to the first wide curve, but the rear tires shimmied and skidded on the second one.

"Do you always drive like this?" I asked.

"Yeah, it keeps me in practice. I still race now and then. It's a blast."

Maybe talking would ease my anxiety. I wondered if she would notice if I just closed my eyes. "Did you learn how to fix cars too?"

"My dad and I took apart my first engine when I was ten. After five of them I got pretty good."

Although being stranded in the middle of nowhere was probably the least of my worries today, it was always a comfort to know that someone on the crew could fix cars. I was a mechanical idiot. I had no interest in machines or how to fix them. Even *Zen and the Art of Motorcycle Maintenance* hadn't erased my distrust of machinery. Most of my boyfriends had known about cars, and I sometimes wondered if I subconsciously fell for men who were mechanically handy.

The Cherokee caught a little air on a bump at the top of a low hill. Linda's eyes were wild, and she was smiling like a lunatic. I imagined myself trapped in a twisted, burning vehicle, miles from rescue and slowly losing consciousness.

Linda took her eyes off the road and glanced at me, her smile fading. "I always carry my tools with me. They're in the back."

That must have been what I heard clunking after that last hard landing. What a relief. I'd thought it was the vehicle falling apart. She hit another bump, and my butt left the seat. I looked up to grab the handle over the window and discovered the cliché was true—my knuckles were white.

We flew over a corduroy section of the road so fast that the shocks were too slow to respond to each bump. Linda banked another turn, and I swear I heard the Jeep groan. Without slowing her speed, she continued our conversation as if we were chatting over tea. I was too scared to respond and just nodded periodically, smiling like an idiot.

Linda turned onto a two-track road and slowed down a little, but we were still traveling at twice the speed I would drive. Small junipers flew past as we headed down a narrowing canyon.

"We're in one of the survey areas now." Linda took one hand off the wheel and pointed. She didn't slow down. "That hill over there is in, and the flat valley bottom is out."

I noticed an old coal mine on the hill. "That old mine must be in then. Right?"

"Uh, I guess so. Why?"

"It looks like it's probably at least fifty years old, which means it's considered historic. Shouldn't you record it?"

"It's just a pile of spoil dirt and a broken-down head frame. What's the point?"

I looked over at Linda. "Well, the regulations say anything historic needs to be recorded as a site."

A steep stretch of road loomed ahead. I wondered if Linda would slow down for it. I grabbed the handle over the door again and closed my eyes. Mercifully, the Jeep slowed, and I opened one eye for a peek.

Linda was looking at me and smiling. "I guess I could slow down a little for this stretch of bad road. The sites I want to show you are at the foot of the hill, in the open area."

Linda stopped at the bottom of the hill, and I swear, this time the Jeep audibly groaned. I breathed a sigh of relief and sat there for a moment, trying to regroup. The stress of the drive had momentarily paralyzed me. I suddenly noticed that it was blissfully quiet and still outside, but in a flurry of motion Linda was out of the car and putting on her backpack. She was a bee swarm of activity, and I wondered if she ever really stopped. She gave me a funny look, so I opened the door and stood up. My legs were stiff from nervous tension, and I had to restrain an impulse to kiss the ground.

"Load up your stuff. We need to hike for a half mile to the site. There's no road to our section." Without waiting for me, she took off.

I had to run to keep up with her. Linda's legs were as vast as the rest of her, and she moved like a gazelle. How could a woman that big move with such speed and grace? My breath was coming in gasps and my side was hurting when Linda abruptly stopped.

"Here it is. Let me see if I can relocate some of the projectile points that we found." Linda took off again, but I knew she wouldn't go far.

I paused a minute to catch my breath and get my bearings. We were on a low hill in the center of a wide valley. A quarter of a mile to the east I could see sandstone cliffs, and to the west were low hills covered with a dense stand of pinyon pine and juniper. There'd been no sign of water for miles. The area was traversed by dozens of intermittent creeks, but they only flowed briefly during summer downpours. I wondered for the thousandth time how people lived out here without water nearby. I reminded myself that the area seemed so remote because modern people consider a place remote or not according to its distance from roads and towns. In prehistoric times, there were no roads. Before people farmed the land they journeyed from resource patch to resource patch. In the fall families would gather nuts in pinyon groves, where deer were plentiful. In the spring the band would travel to lower elevations where edible greens were sprouting, agave was ripe for roasting, and cactus flower buds were hiding a rich supply of calcium. Summer was a time of plenty: sweet strawberries, cactus fruit, and meadows thick with seed-bearing plants. Fat rabbits and other rodents were everywhere and easy to trap.

I began to circle in search of artifacts. Flakes of red, white, and gray chert littered the ground. I looked up, wondering what had happened to Linda, who had disappeared. She was probably just making a pit stop.

I became lost in the search for tools and arrowheads, and immediately spotted a large fragment of a sandstone metate and the tip of a point. The small tip was triangular, but without the base I had no way of knowing how old the point was. I walked a little farther and hit a dense concentration of knives, mano fragments, and even a drill. Then my eye caught the tell-tale shape of a point. I reached down and picked up a perfect Elko

Corner-notched spear point made of red chert. Its translucent finish indicated that it had been heat-treated during manufacture. I was marveling over its size and perfect shape when I heard my name. Linda was calling and waving me over.

I grabbed a piece of flagging tape to mark the location of the point and walked over to Linda. She had turned her attention back to the ground, intently searching for something.

"Ivy, here it is." Linda handed me another perfect Elko point, this one notched on the sides rather than on the corners of the base. The people who made side-notched points would have occupied the site about 8,000 years ago, during the Early Archaic period. The corner-notched variety is not time sensitive, meaning it never went out of style. In fact, it was made for thousands of years. Even after the bow and arrow came into use around two thousand years ago, the Elko Corner-notched points continued to be used.

"I found a point too," I told her, "but it's corner-notched."

We compared the points and continued to walk in circles, looking for more. I spied a gray, unnaturally flat object and reached down to pick it up. "Just as I suspected—pottery!"

I called Linda over for a look.

"Yup," she said, "and here's another." She reached down and picked up another sherd next to her foot. "Guess we missed that the first time around."

"It happens," I said, offering consolation.

"Seen enough? Let's go to the next site. It's the best rock shelter we've found so far."

The thought of getting back in the Cherokee filled me with dread. "How far away is it?"

"About five miles that way." Linda pointed north, toward open bottomland.

We loaded up and headed out. Linda was driving a little slower, but only a fraction so. Five miles wouldn't be so bad, I told myself.

"So, Linda, where did you get your master's?"

"Arizona State." She took her eyes off the road to check the maps.

"Did you like it?"

"It was okay, but I like doing contract archaeology better than going to school. Open road, sunshine, and fresh air. I tried museum work, but I couldn't stand being inside all day. How do you like working for the government?"

"I'm learning a lot," I offered, trying my best to be positive. "I'm not comfortable with the power though. I think I'd rather do archaeology myself than tell other people how to do it."

"I'm with you on that one."

We drove for a while in silence. We passed another Jeep, and Linda informed me that her crew was working on a unit nearby. The road turned and dropped into a canyon. Linda was taking it slow and careful for once. She stopped the car and looked at her map.

"This is the place. We have to hike a little ways down the canyon from here."

We packed up again and started walking. Linda was moving at a slower pace so I was able to keep up. The slope was steep, and she wasn't as agile as I was from years of skiing. I saw the overhang a short distance ahead. It was like the dozens I'd recorded during my year of contract work.

"There it is," said Linda. "It doesn't look like much from here."

She was right, but it looked more interesting as we got closer. We had to bend down to enter the shelter through a small opening. It was dark inside, and Linda pulled out a flashlight.

"I had to buy this so we could record the site." She flipped on the light and pointed it toward the center of the cave.

I first noticed a fragment of a basket, what looked like a piece of cordage, and a dense scatter of artifacts. The soil was blackened from a thousand years of campfires. There was also dung from some large animal, maybe a bear.

"Wow, and I thought I'd seen a fair share of cool rock shelters," I said. "This one takes the cake. It's the first dry shelter I've seen with cordage and basketry on the surface."

I could barely see Linda's grin. "I know. It's great. Look at this depression." She pointed to it on the floor. "See the slabs lining the perimeter? I'll bet this is a food cache, and it doesn't look like it was emptied. It may still hold whatever was stored."

We both walked over to have a closer look. Cedar bark that had been carefully shredded stuck out along the edge near one of the slabs, and a thick layer of mud covered the cedar bark.

"I excavated one of these on the Navajo reservation for the Cedar Mesa project," Linda said. "It looks like a Basketmaker cist. The one we excavated was lined with slabs and filled with corncobs and pine nuts.

Shredded bark and plants covered the food, and then a layer of mud was plastered over to keep out the critters. Just like this one."

I looked over at Linda. "Can you believe that no one has looted this cave?"

"Guess the outside appearance wasn't enough to attract pothunters. Hope word doesn't get around. I already told the crew not to tell anyone in town about it." Linda reached down and picked up a cane arrow, the stone point still hafted on the end. "This is pretty cool." She handed it to me for a closer look.

"Wow, that's an understatement." The arrow was painted with different colored parallel lines, and a feather clung to the notched end.

"Look at this, Ivy. I've heard about this but never seen it." She was standing next to a large crack in the back of the shelter wall. As I walked closer, she pointed to chunks of red and yellow ochre that had been stuck into the crack.

"This must be a sacred cave," she said solemnly. "These are offerings."

"How do you know that?" I asked.

"I grew up in Oklahoma, and most of my friends are Indians. I picked stuff up. I'd guess this was probably a song or medicine cave."

Linda removed a Marlboro from a pack in her T-shirt pocket and rubbed it between two fingers, breaking the paper and scattering the tobacco.

"What are you doing?"

"Taking precautions. This here cave has juju. I'm leaving an offering, and tobacco is the best thing."

"You're kidding, right?"

"Nope. I've spent enough time with Indians not to take precautions. Science can't explain everything."

I had to agree with her. "This cave does feel a little creepy."

Linda announced it was time for lunch and a cigarette break. We found a large boulder on the slope in the sun and plopped down. I retrieved my sardines and crackers while Linda smoked one of her Marlboros. She popped open a Coke and rested her back against the rock, staring at the sky.

The view was spectacular: twenty miles of unsettled wilderness of canyons and mesas, and thirty miles to the west, the Wasatch Plateau. I could still see patches of white on the highest peaks. It was a blue-sky day, warm and sunny. I wolfed down my lunch and basked in the sun like a lizard. Linda polished off a can of deviled ham and opened a can of peaches with a huge hunting knife. She stabbed the top of the can, cut a cross in the metal, and peeled back the flaps with a spoon.

"I always carry my knife and spoon. I love peaches." She finished them in a few bites and lit another cigarette.

"Why does smoke smell so good out here in the middle of nowhere and so bad in a bar?" I asked.

"Funny you should mention that. I've often wondered that same thing. It seems stupid to drag my fat ass up these hills all day and then smoke, but it tastes extra good out here. I can't figure it out."

Linda stubbed out her cigarette and stored the butt in the rear pocket of her jeans. "I don't litter. Let's go see another rock shelter. Come on. It's getting late."

We took a quick look at a smaller rock shelter and then picked over a lithic scatter. By day's end I'd decided Linda wasn't so scary. I actually admired her and had even begun to trust her driving—or maybe I was too numb or tired to care. I wasn't going to stay in Emery overnight so I still had a four-hour drive ahead of me. I managed to take a catnap, and before I knew it, we were back in Emery. We shook hands, I wished her luck with the rest of the survey, and off I drove. My twelve-hour workday ended with a hot bath and a frozen chicken pot pie.

I was still tired the next morning when I dragged my ass out of bed to make a pot of coffee. What would I wear today? I groaned at the thought of the habiliment chart. What could I wear that would be innocuous? It seemed that no matter what I wore, it was open to scrutiny and discussion. I hadn't done laundry in a while so all my regular clothes were dirty, and my closet was nearly empty. I'd worn my last pair of clean jeans yesterday, and the shelves for my pants and shirts were empty. All that was hanging in my closet was a gray wool skirt, two blouses, and the dress that had started the whole problem. That gave me little choice, so I grabbed the skirt, a red blouse, and a pair of black tights, an outfit that won me an average point rating—that is, a mean of seven. The mode was six. Chuck hated the skirt and gave me a two. Another guy liked it and rated it an eight. Go figure.

I was sitting at my desk plotting surveys onto the master maps when Ken stopped by my desk.

"How did the site tour go?" He was holding his new coffee mug—a woman's naked upper torso. Her arm twisted around to form the mug's handle, and she was headless. Ken apparently hadn't noticed the irony of this image.

"Great. They seem to be doing a good job. Did you know that Linda is a racecar driver? She drives the Jeep like she's racing to stay in practice."

Ken was staring at my skirt, and I realized that it had worked its way up too high on my thighs. I pulled the hem down to my knees.

"I noticed an old coal mine in one of their units. Shouldn't they record it?"

"Let's check the maps." Ken headed back to his desk to grab the set of USGS maps with the survey areas plotted. He shuffled through the stack for a minute and sat down. As I walked over to his desk, Ken pointed to one of the sample units. "Yeah, I remembered seeing a mine marked on one of the survey units. Here it is. What about it?"

"They didn't record it. Linda didn't seem to think it was that important."

"Why not?" Ken tended to talk faster when he was irritated or frustrated, and words started spewing forth. "They're required to record everything older than fifty years. Is the mine that old?"

"I didn't get a close look, but it seemed pretty cool. The head frame is in place, and I also saw what looked like a stone building."

"For sure it's fifty years old then. More recent mines use concrete, not stone masonry. Did she say why she didn't record it?"

Ken grabbed the phone and looked over at me before dialing. "I'm going to set up another site tour when they finish the survey." Realizing Ken was done with me, I returned to my boring tasks.

A month later I was headed back to the field with Ken and Linda. I'd warned Ken about Linda's driving, so he'd decided to take a four-wheel-drive vehicle big enough for the three of us. He put on his ugly pink hat and got behind the wheel. It was early, and I was only half awake, but I was dimly aware of a sick, yucky feeling in the pit of my stomach—like I'd done something bad and was waiting to get caught. I liked Linda and hoped everything would turn out okay, but my gut was sending me warnings.

We picked Linda up at the Dairy Queen and headed out to the survey area. I immediately noticed that Ken was acting differently around Linda than he did around more attractive women. After watching them for a few minutes, I decided that he was treating her like one of the guys. Interesting. . . .

After about half an hour, the coal mine was in view. Linda pointed in that general direction, at a low hill abutting the mine. "That's one of our survey units. We found a few artifact scatters but nothing to write home about."

"What is that spoil pile?" Ken asked, slowing down.

"That's an old prospect. It's just a pile of waste rock with some trash and boards scattered around. There's a lithic scatter just upslope that we could look at."

"Let's go see the mine. I'm writing a book about bottles that I collected from an old dump in Denver. It was being bladed for a new office building, and I collected as many bottles as I could. I've got five hundred intact ones, and many still had labels."

"Why were so many bottles intact?" Linda asked.

"I wondered that too," said Ken, "so I checked the Sandford maps and found out that there had been a pharmacy there in the late 1800s. I suspect the bottles were dumped in the back yard, probably in a pit made for that purpose." Ken rubbed greasy sunscreen across his face.

"What are you going to do with all the bottles?"

"I'm going to build a museum someday and display them. But first I've got to finish my book. I sent a draft to Academic Press, and they're interested in publishing it."

I could tell Linda was feigning interest. She was into prehistory and Native American sites. Like me, she found historical archaeology pretty dull, but she was trying to be polite.

"Your book sounds like it will be real handy for historical archaeologists." The wind was blowing Linda's hair wildly around her face. She made an effort to control it, then put her pack on and started toward the old mine. I grabbed my pack and did my best to keep up.

We walked the short distance to the spoil pile and remnants of a head frame. Ken circled the mine like a wolf around its prey. Periodically he stopped to pick up some glass fragments. I walked over to see what he had found. His hand held a few shards of purple and aqua glass.

"Do you know why this glass is purple, Ivy?"

"Someone told me once, but I'm afraid I can't remember."

Linda had come over to see what we were talking about.

"The glass is purple because manganese was added to make it clear after the Pure Food and Drug Act was passed in 1906," Ken explained. "The manganese turns purple when it's exposed to ultraviolet rays. It's called sun-colored amethyst. This is an embossed medicine bottle that dates to the 1880s. Everything else I've seen here—the nails, white ware pottery, and hole-in-cap cans with hand-soldered seams—tells me the mine dates to the late 1800s. You need to record this site, Linda. Everything older than fifty years needs be recorded, so why didn't you record this?"

I could tell Ken was annoyed because his face was blank and he was talking a little too fast.

"Well, it's right on the boundary of the unit, and besides, we didn't think it was old enough. But if you say it's over a hundred years old, we'll certainly record it as a site. No problem."

"Do you have someone on your crew with experience in historical archaeology?" Ken asked.

"My assistant crew chief did some work back east excavating historical sites. I'll send him over here."

"Make sure he records everything and researches the General Land Office maps and mining records. Let's go see that prehistoric site."

We hiked over to the lithic scatter and walked around looking for tools. It was a typical scatter without points or tools—lots of waste flakes and little else. Ken and I pointed out some ground stone that the crew had missed, and then we walked back to the vehicle to see sites in other units.

Later we found two other historic sites that Linda hadn't recorded. They were both small prospector camps, boring in every way, but Ken insisted that they be recorded. I wondered how many more historic sites they'd missed. Ken stayed good-natured, but I could tell he wasn't happy about the missed sites. We saw a rock shelter that Linda had found since my last tour, and we showed Ken the one with the basketry. He was jazzed about that site and decided that the perishables should be collected before someone else found the site and looted it. After four hours of touring sites, we left Linda at the Dairy Queen and drove home. Ken didn't wait long to vent his frustrations at me.

"What kind of archaeologist doesn't know how to recognize a historic mine?"

"Not everyone knows as much about historic archaeology as you do," I said. "Most of us were trained to record prehistoric sites. I learned nothing in field school about historic sites. No one ever said anything about how to distinguish fifty-year-old sites from more recent ones."

Ken shook his head. "That's the problem with archaeology training programs in the Southwest. No one studies historical archaeology, and no one considers it important. That's particularly true of the major universities. I came out of one of the best programs, and yet I didn't learn a single thing about historical stuff either. I taught myself."

I took off my hiking boots and put my feet up on the dashboard.

"That feels better," I said, sighing. "You know, I'll bet we missed historic sites on the surveys I did when I worked for ASC. In fact, I don't remember recording any historic roads or mines."

"What? Don't tell me that. Those projects are a done deal. There's nothing I can do about it now."

Ken continued ranting about everything related to historic archaeology, but I'd stopped listening, only tuning in after he'd convinced himself that he should force Linda to redo the entire survey. I groaned, thinking of the part I'd played in the drama. Poor Linda. I held my tongue and stared out the window. Ken told me he would take over managing Linda's contract, so at least I wouldn't have to be involved in the resurvey negotiations.

I fell asleep near Provo and woke just as Ken pulled into the government parking garage. We said a hasty good-bye and I headed for the bus stop. It was late and dark, but I wasn't too concerned. Salt Lake City was a safe place in the early 1980s.

That night I slept fitfully, probably because I felt responsible for Linda's troubles. I dreaded hearing the phone calls Ken would make the next day. I knew I'd have to listen to him all morning repeating the same story over and over again. These projects were not that lucrative, and redoing the survey would mean Linda's company would probably lose money on the job.

I struggled out of bed and brushed my teeth. What to wear? Would this shirt provoke special attention? How about these pants? I'd come to the decision that consistency was my best bet: boring and professional. Still, it was awkward to be under scrutiny every day and scored like a beauty queen or show animal. I selected a pale blue sweater and black slacks, loafers, and a gold necklace that my sister had given me for Christmas.

I made it to the office on time and noticed that Ken was already gabbing on the phone.

"Yes, I know you'll lose money on the survey, but that's not my problem. I want you to make sure that all the historic sites are recorded. No, forget that. I want it done right."

The conversation continued to go on like that, so I went to the break room for a cup of coffee. Today I'd planned to work on a brochure I was writing about the agency's cultural resources, but I couldn't seem to get focused. The brochure included a description of the cliff dwellings in Grand Gulch.

I walked back to my office thinking about Tom and his decision about grad school. I suspected that he was leaning toward ASU, and I wondered when he would tell me.

We were planning to go backpacking down Coyote Gulch, near Escalante, and had agreed to take two extra days off to make it a long weekend. I'd invited my college friend Jeff and his girlfriend to join us, but only Jeff was up for a long hike. We'd drive there Friday night and camp out at the top of the canyon.

On Sunday I woke to sunshine and blue sky. Tom was lying next to me, wrapped like a mummy in his down bag. He snored softly, letting out little puffs of breath. I sat up and looked around. He'd told me during the drive that he had decided on ASU. I still felt a little sad, even if it wasn't really a surprise.

We'd stopped last night at the entrance to the canyon, off a dirt road running down the center of a wide valley. The sun had risen only a sliver above the horizon. The earth was glowing red, and the sky was brightening into a perfect blue. Little tuffs of sand sage dotted the spaces in-between. The air was crisp and smelled of damp earth. Jeff's sleeping bag was empty, but I didn't see any coffee activity.

I scooted out of my sleeping bag and headed toward Tom's beat-up Land Cruiser. I rooted around in my backpack and retrieved a small gas-powered backpacking stove, a pan, coffee, and some water. Just as I'd finished setting up the stove, Jeff materialized over a low sand dune. His short, dark hair was a tangled mess, but his crooked smile and mischievous grin told me he was in a good mood.

"It's a fine morning," he said, plopping down next to me in the sand and lighting a cigarette. "What's for breakfast?"

I heard Tom moan and looked over to see his sleeping bag writhing like a snake shedding its skin. "What time is it?" he asked no one in particular.

"It's time to hit the trail," answered Jeff. He stood up, walked to the Land Cruiser, and grabbed an ice-cold beer. "There won't be any of this where we're going, so you may as well have it now." Jeff threw Tom a cold Coors, but he didn't react fast enough to catch it. The can whizzed past his head and landed in the sand with a dull thud.

Unperturbed, Tom snatched it up and popped the top. "Um, um, good. Vitamin B. Just what the doctor ordered."

Jeff opened a beer for himself and settled back in the sand.

"How can you two drink this early? You'll be dead by noon."

"I wish you could hear yourself, Ivy. You sound like my mother."

"Thanks, asshole. At least I'll still be full of energy at noon."

"You're always full of energy."

"Yeah, a regular energizer bunny," added Jeff.

The guys each downed another beer, and I watched in horror as Jeff filled a bowl with cereal and added beer instead of milk.

"That's disgusting," I said, munching a granola bar.

"Breakfast of champions." Jeff belched so loud that I heard it echo across the valley.

Tom crumpled his beer can and threw it toward the trash bag. He grabbed his mummy bag and stuffed it into a tiny sack, then rolled up the pad he'd used under his sleeping bag. With his usual mastery, he quickly and neatly tied both to his pack.

Tom's hair had gotten long, and during the night it had become a tangled web in the back. His flannel shirt was wrinkled and frayed. He found his toothbrush in one of the pockets in his pack, and I watched as he brushed and spit. Then he walked toward me and leaned down. After planting a kiss on my forehead, he moved his lips to my mouth. His breath smelled sweet and clean, with only a hint of beer. His eyes twinkled, and he nibbled my ear.

"Coffee, tea, or me?" I joked.

"Since we have company, I guess I'll have to settle for coffee."

"Get a room, you two." Jeff went through girlfriends like I skied through perfect powder: with precision and abandon. Ah, perfect powder—deep and weightless, like a cloud. Jeff was currently madly in love with a woman from his hometown who had moved to Salt Lake to be with him. Maybe this one would last.

I finished my coffee, rinsed out the pan and my cup, packed the stove and dishes, and stuffed my sleeping bag. After strapping it to my backpack, I hefted the pack to check the weight. The guys were busy checking the USGS map for our route.

"I'm ready," I announced. The guys looked at me briefly and then went back to their discussion. I started toward a side canyon that dipped down and disappeared. The guys would follow eventually. A canyon wren greeted me with a single note that dropped down the scale, one long note at a time, then faster, like water cascading over the canyon wall. With the exception of the wren, the canyon was still, like the world had stopped. Even my footsteps made no sounds. It felt so good to be back in the world of complete silence. I'd forgotten how much I love the stillness.

For almost an hour I traveled alone, deeper and deeper into the canyon. The walls grew from two stories, to four, and then they were skyscraper tall. Giant boulders littered the floor and sides of the canyon. Half of the canyon wall was a sloped bench littered with boulders and debris. Above the bench, canyon walls rose straight and shear to the deep blue sky. Where the bench and walls met, I could see small alcoves and masonry storage rooms.

"Ivy, give it a rest," I reminded myself out loud.

"Who are you talking to?"

Tom and Jeff had finally caught up.

"I guess to you, since you're here. There are storage structures in the alcoves, and I was just reminding myself that I'm on vacation and don't need to explore them."

"Where are they?" asked Jeff.

"Everywhere, if you know what to look for." I pointed to a low overhang high up the canyon wall. "I think there's one there."

Before I could finish speaking, Jeff had shucked his pack and sprinted up the slope toward the alcove.

"Ivy, you better supervise him," Tom said. "I doubt he has the good sense not to touch." Tom had removed his water bottle and was taking a swig. "Let's go."

I put my pack down and followed Tom. Jeff had disappeared inside the alcove.

"Wow, it's a little room!" Jeff yelled, his excitement obvious.

Tom and I struggled up the slope. I caught a good view of the masonry structure and could see it was just like the ones we had recorded during our weeks of survey and camping at Pint Creek. A triangular figure had been painted on the upper wall. His body was capped with a square-shaped head. Horns erupting from the figure's head probably represented a mask. Jeff picked up a piece of pottery from the alcove floor and walked toward me.

"Don't even think of keeping that," I commanded.

"Why not? You don't own this place." Jeff sat and lit a cigarette.

"No, but you're with a government archaeologist who knows it's illegal. If you or anyone pockets artifacts while with me, I could get into big trouble. Besides, if everyone takes just one sherd, someday they'll all be gone. Let me see that."

Jeff reluctantly handed me a small fragment of gray pottery with black painted lines.

"It looks Fremont to me, and so does this rock art."

"Is she always like this?" asked Jeff, looking over at Tom.

"Yeah," answered Tom.

"Okay, CBIC, I won't take anything." Jeff returned the sherd to where he'd found it.

"What is CBIC?" I asked.

"Chief Bitch in Charge."

Tom laughed. "I like that. I'll remember that one." He had seen enough and started down the slope.

"Someday I will be in charge," I said over my shoulder, following after Tom.

We hiked down the deepening side canyon. After three hours it connected with Coyote Gulch. A small creek wound down the canyon bottom in a narrow bed of fine red sand. The vegetation changed from scraggly stands of sagebrush, prickly pear cactus, and Mormon tea to lush thickets of willow, watercress, and horsetails. Bright green ferns dotted the steep canyon walls where water dripped from seeps. The air smelled of damp earth, fresh herbs, and life. I crossed the inches-deep creek again and again until we all decided to trade our hiking boots for sandals. The gnats weren't out yet, but deer flies were buzzing around my head. After two bites on my legs, I changed into jeans and a long-sleeved shirt. The guys didn't seem to notice the flies and continued past me when I stopped to change.

We hiked until early afternoon, then stopped and made camp in an alcove off a side canyon. We'd traveled about six miles. In the morning we planned to hike to the confluence of Coyote Gulch and the Escalante River, and then continue down the Escalante a few more miles. Now, though, I was content to rest. I changed into a swimsuit and walked downstream until I found a deep pool of clear water. I cooled off in it and then flopped in the sand. The canyon wrens and dripping seep were the only sounds. The guys had disappeared.

I lay in the sand and stared at the dark blue sky, thinking of everything and nothing. After a while I fell asleep and dreamed of days long past, when the world was quieter, without machines. In my dream I was running down the canyon, my long hair was brown, and I was wearing only a grass skirt and woven sandals. I was running in fear, away from something and toward an unknown destination. I woke to Tom's soft lips caressing mine.

"Hi there." I blinked and stretched. I'd fallen asleep on my arm, and it was aching and prickly. "I guess I dozed. Where did you guys go?"

Tom took my hand and we headed to camp. "We hiked up that side canyon. We were looking for a more direct route back to the Cruiser."

The next two days passed like a dream. We saw no one and talked little. But that all changed the last day on our hike out. We were resting near a small seep when a troop of Boy Scouts invaded, or so it seemed. They swarmed and joked, churning the silence into chaos. Like us, they had decided to take a break, and we were asking them where they were from and where they were going. Suddenly two more hikers appeared, walking toward us from the canyon below. As they got closer, the Boy Scouts' chatter ceased. One by one they simply stopped talking and moving and just stared in the direction of the hikers.

Tom and Jeff were also mesmerized, mouths slightly ajar, so I squinted my eyes to get a better view. As the hikers got closer, I realized why all the males around me were transfixed. One of the hikers was a goddess. Almost six feet tall, she was a vision, and the most luscious woman I had ever seen—Barbie goes to Coyote Gulch. Tiny triangles of fabric struggled to cover her huge, frolicking breasts. Her perfectly tanned legs rose for miles to her just plump enough butt, which was barely covered with the teeniest pair of cut-off jeans I'd ever seen. I swear I saw one of the Boy Scouts drooling. Tom's smile had morphed into a Cheshire cat grin, but Jeff continued to stare, open mouthed. The goddess smiled and flicked her long blond hair out of her eyes with a practiced movement of her head. I marveled at the perfect symmetry of her face as she paused to take in her appreciative audience.

"Hello, boys. Where are you all from?" She spoke with a slight southern accent, in a deep sexy voice.

Silence. Everyone was dumbstruck. Eventually, their leader found his voice.

"Ah, we're from Escalante. You know, the nearest town. We're working on our hiking badge."

"Oh, that's sweet," she cooed.

She sat down, removed her water bottle from a waist pack, and took a long drink.

The troop's leader seemed to remember his manners and asked the woman and her hippie companion where they were from.

She stood, winked, and said, "Vegas." Then, without another word, she and her partner resumed their hike.

21

Trapped in the Rooster Pen

There is no prerequisite body type for an archaeologist. As long as you're fit enough to hike or dig for eight hours a day, and have a high pain threshold, practically any shape or size will do. Being short and slightly pear shaped had its disadvantages, but I managed. Still, after we'd left Barbie behind in Coyote Gulch, I couldn't stop wondering how different my life would have been if I looked like her. Would I have ended up being an archaeologist? I think if I had Barbie's body, and could pick any job I wanted, I'd be a Dallas Cowboys' cheerleader. Think about it. You spend your days around hunky rich guys wearing tight pants. You go to dozens of NFL football games, work outdoors, get plenty of exercise, and then there are the pompoms. All girls have a thing about them, and some of us never grow up. I could picture myself jumping up and down after a touchdown, waving and shaking my pompoms with total abandon, smiling like a drunken fool.

Although I still loved archaeology, I was beginning to realize that I wasn't cut out for government work. There were two main reasons for this—well, three if you counted Ken. First, I wasn't actually doing much archaeology; I was overseeing it. There were no opportunities to conduct research projects, I wasn't participating in excavations, and without research data, I would never be able to publish anything. Second, I was frustrated daily by the snail's pace of government work. Today, for example, it had taken two hours to write a few letters and it would take two more days to get them in the mail. Why? Because all my managers had to read, approve, and sign the letters first.

So what now? Back to contract archaeology? Or onto graduate school? I had no idea what I should do, and I was weighing the pros and cons of graduate school when Ken walked up.

"Ivy, the district attorney wants you to testify against Ben at his trial next month." As usual, Ken had his ugly coffee mug in hand.

"What?" My heart was racing, and I flashed on Perry Mason cross-examining a witness until she broke down and confessed in a torrent of tears. "What can I contribute?"

"The attorneys decided that Ben's stories about his pothunting days would demonstrate a history of these activities. It wasn't his first time."

"Do I have a choice?"

"Nah, they'll just subpoena you."

Ken strolled back to his office, leaving me to stew. Most people don't realize I suffer from almost pathological stage fright. Talking before an audience makes me physically ill. I get so anxious that I can't sleep, or eat, and as soon as I stand in front of a crowd, my mind goes totally blank. Although I know public speaking is one of the most common human fears, that doesn't make it any easier.

My phone rang. "Ivy Jones."

"Ivy, I'm here."

It was Gavin. My heart kicked into overdrive. "Hi."

"How about lunch today? High noon in front of your office? We'll decide then where to eat."

Before I had a chance to say anything, he'd hung up. For a few minutes I just sat and stared. I looked at my watch; three whole hours before noon.

Time dragged like a slug crossing dry pavement. Feeling particularly annoyed about the habiliment chart this morning, I'd dressed frumpy and dull. No makeup, my hair was straight and stringy, and my shoes were scuffed. I've always thought that shoes reflect a person's character. Those who wear beat-up white sneakers suffer from low self-esteem. Highly polished, crisp loafers indicate the wearer is organized and caring. Pointy designer heels suggest a narcissistic social climber. Gavin always wore no-nonsense cowboy boots, further proof that he's practical and secure. If I'd known that I was going to lunch with him, I would have worn my Frye boots with a fresh coat of polish. Instead I was wearing the absolute worst thing: an old pair of Earth shoes, those ugly shoes that were popular then among environmentalists and hippies. Cowboys and environmentalists mix about as well as Nixon and war protestors.

What was I doing? Hadn't I convinced myself to forget Gavin? Why should I care what I had on if I didn't need to impress him? But no matter what I told myself, my morning continued like this—the angel and devil Ivys battling it out. At quarter to twelve, I ran to the rest room and primped as best as I could without special equipment.

When I exited the elevator on the first floor, there he was, wearing Wranglers and a crisp white shirt. Tall, dark, and handsome—every girl's dream. My heart was beating so fast I felt slightly out of breath.

"Hey," he said with a smile, mustache twitching just a tiny bit. I caught a whiff of fresh air and sage.

"I didn't expect to see you again," I said. Standing next to him, I saw he towered over me, and he looked even better than I remembered.

"Is that what you wanted or what you hoped?"

"I don't know. You make my life complicated. Let's get out of here. Where do you want to go?"

"This is your town, Ivy. What do you suggest?"

"I know just the place—a no-frills sandwich shop with an outside patio. It's a bit of a walk though."

It was a warm June day, and the leaves were still that bright new green. The city looked fresh and clean. Gavin stole a sideways glance at me and smiled again.

"What brought you to Salt Lake?" I asked, just to make conversation.

"I wanted to see you again."

"Yeah, right. You know that's not true. Why are you here, really?"

Gavin raised one eyebrow. "I filed some papers in court. My family is suing the Land Management Agency over some grazing leases they took away."

"Why? Oh, maybe you shouldn't tell me. After all, I work in the enemy's camp." I realized I'd been grinning like a clown, so I tried for a more sophisticated expression.

"Speaking of the court system, I just found out that I have to testify against someone I worked with who is being tried for vandalizing a cliff ruin. All I know about the legal process is what I've seen on television. How nervous should I be?"

"What's your involvement in the case?"

"None really. I'll be a character witness for the prosecutors. I worked with Ben, the guy on trial, in contract archaeology. He swore he was done with pothunting, but he told us plenty of stories about his digging days. I really like Ben, though, and I don't want to do this."

"Why don't you tell the prosecutor that?"

"Do you think he'll let me off the hook?"

"Probably not, but it's worth a try."

We were walking down Main Street. Several old buildings had been renovated, and "For Lease" signs hung in a few of the windows. The sidewalks were busy with lunch hour traffic. People seemed harried and preoccupied. We turned down a side street that was closed to cars. Grass, flowers, and young trees replaced the pavement and parking meters. Just ahead was a cluster of tables and chairs in front of a restaurant named Annie's Apple. Most of the tables were occupied by small groups of suited business people.

"We order inside."

Our orders were up fast, and we carried our trays outside. We sat and talked about Ben's case for a while. After I finished my turkey sandwich, complete with cranberry sauce and dressing, I looked at the small red apple on my plate.

"I have another legal issue. The guys in the office have created this chart that they use to rate me every day on how I look. It's getting old, and I don't know what to do." I sounded a little whiny, even to myself. "Any words of wisdom?"

"After lunch go back to the office and quit your job. You can work the ranch with me." Gavin said it so matter-of-factly that I almost believed him. Then he gave me that sexy smile.

I felt myself blushing and had to fight an overwhelming desire to say yes. I really wanted to ride off into the sunset with my Marlboro man. "And what about my present boyfriend? Go home and dump him?"

"Yep. You said he was moving away to graduate school anyway, right?"

"I know, but he doesn't leave for two more months."

Gavin gave me a skeptical look, eyebrows raised. Then he did something completely unexpected. He reached over and cupped my chin in his calloused hand, lifting my face so our eyes met. "I've missed you, Ivy."

My heart skipped a beat and my eyes began to water. I thought how nice it would be to leave the Land Management Agency behind and be taken care of. Like Cinderella, my prince had come, and I would live happily ever after.

I swallowed a lump in my throat. "Gavin, I can't. I have a job, and I love archaeology. I can't work if I live on a ranch in Delta."

He dropped his hand and smiled. "Oh, you'd probably make a lousy cowgirl anyway."

"I'd be a great cowgirl, but that isn't the point. I can't just up and leave my job and expect you to support me. I know we could have a great time together, but I hardly know you. I'm sure that this whole attraction between us is nothing more than chemistry, some type of primate pheromone thing."

Gavin said nothing for a while. I bit into my apple. It was crisp and sweet, and it gave me something to do. I wondered what it would really be like to live on Gavin's ranch, to wake up with the sun and work outdoors each day—to give up my dream of being an archaeologist and live hours from the nearest stores and ski areas.

"I need to get back to work," I said, feeling as sad as an abandoned puppy.

"I'll walk you back."

Walking back to the office, I felt lousy, like I had PMS and the last chocolate bar in the world had just been given to someone else.

"I have some legal advice for you about that silly chart, and also about testifying against Ben." Gavin's long legs set a fast pace, and once again I was struggling to keep up.

"I need all the advice I can get."

"Most government agencies have an EEO officer who handles workplace discrimination. Your coworkers have made the office uncomfortable for you because you are a woman. The chart is a way for the guys in the office to make you feel unwelcome. You are a victim of sexual harassment."

"You really think so?"

"As women enter the workplace and compete with men, the men often feel threatened. Sexual harassment can be anything from your boss making sexual advances to all the men singling you out for what you wear. A group of women just won millions of dollars in a harassment lawsuit against a big brokerage firm on Wall Street. A jury agreed that this was a form of discrimination and the women's employers had made no effort to stop the men's behavior."

"That fits my situation, and I am the first professional woman in the Resource Division. What I should do?"

"Document the problems and take it to your EEO officer. If he or she fails to do something about the situation, well, then you can hire me. I'd love to sue them for you."

We were almost back at the office. I really didn't want to go back. Perhaps I could claim I was sick.

"Now about that trial. My advice would be to not say one word more than you absolutely have to when you answer the attorneys' questions. Don't offer anything, and answer as simply as possible."

We stopped in front of the office and faced each other. I felt awkward. Gavin smiled at me, and I suddenly felt like it was Monday morning and I was stuck in the field, lonely and exhausted, for another week.

"Thanks for lunch," I said. "It was great to see you again. Call me next time you're here."

He raised his hand to my chin again and made me look into his eyes. "Maybe."

Then he squeezed my shoulder and walked away.

I was sad and grouchy for a week after our lunch. I kicked myself a thousand times for not getting Gavin's phone number—just in case. Seeing him had made me think more about my future, and made me less comfortable with my present situation. I could go back into contract archaeology, but without a master's degree, I'd be right back where I started: a lowly technician spending my work week in the field. I love fieldwork, but being in the field all the time gets old. What I really wanted was to be in charge, to supervise and write reports. But that would mean I'd have to go back to school. Then there was the problem of having a career in archaeology as well as a normal married life.

My thoughts of graduate school faded as Ben's trial neared. When the prosecuting attorney summoned me for a dry run through my testimony, I had tried to convince him not to use me in the trial, but he turned my argument around and convinced me that my testimony was critical. If he was so good at changing my mind, maybe it would be okay. The trial was scheduled to begin on Monday, and Ken and I had decided to watch the proceedings. Since I'd never seen a courtroom except on television, I was curious, but also nervous.

The courtroom was large and stark. Ben sat next to his attorney, cute and sad. He looked absolutely miserable—nothing like his former happy-go-lucky self. I tried to remind myself that he had lied about pothunting and had destroyed a really important site, but I was tormented. I really liked him.

The first day of testimony left me terrified. Ben's attorney had twisted everyone's words until he'd convinced even me that digging in a site wasn't a crime. He pointed out that no one had ever caught Ben taking artifacts from Rooster Pen, and there was nothing in the new Archaeological Resources Protection Act that said digging in a midden or trash deposit is a crime. The law covered artifacts, not trash deposits. This was not going well for the prosecutor. Wracked with anxiety, I decided to stay away from the trial until it was my turn, but there was no escape. I was due to testify the next day.

After a restless night, I got up and dressed as professionally as possible, applying makeup liberally to hide the dark circles under my eyes. Once at the courthouse I was instructed to wait outside the courtroom, and I felt small and vulnerable sitting on the hard bench.

The courtroom door opened and I heard the prosecutor say, "My next witness is Ivy Jones."

I felt numb as I walked to the front of the room. With everyone's eyes sticking into my back, I felt like a pincushion. I raised my hand and swore on the Bible to tell the whole truth and nothing but the truth.

"Ms. Jones, how do you know the defendant?"

"We worked together as archaeologists."

"When was that?"

"Two years ago."

"How much time did you spend with Ben?"

"We worked together for several weeks."

"Is it true that your employer hired you to survey for archaeological sites?"

"Yes."

"And was your work location so remote that you had to camp out?"

"Yes."

"So you spent days and nights with each other, sitting around the campfire at night, eating meals together, and working all day. Did Ben ever talk about looting archaeological sites?"

"Yes, he told me a few stories about digging sites illegally and almost getting caught."

"Objection," said Ben's attorney. "The witness is making a legal judgment and has no basis for a legal opinion."

"Sustained."

"I'll rephrase the question, your Honor. Ms. Jones, could you tell us one of Ben's campfire stories about digging in an archaeological site?"

"Well, Ben told me that he was digging with a friend in a rock shelter near Canyonlands Park. Ben and his friend parked several miles from the rock shelter and hiked in to avoid detection. Despite their precautions they narrowly escaped capture and had to hide without food or sleeping bags for several days until the authorities gave up the chase."

"Did Ben tell you what types of things he found when he went looting sites?"

"He said his family had a large collection of pots, baskets, turquoise beads, sandals, and more. He told me his grandfather had learned to excavate when he worked as a guide for museum expeditions around the turn of the century."

"Did he ever talk about digging up human remains?"

"Yes, he said he was the best in his family at locating Indian burials. He used a special probe to locate the skull, and he said he could tell by feel whether an object struck by probe was a pot or bone. He seemed to take special pride in finding and digging graves. He told me that the best artifacts come from graves."

"Did Ben tell you he had turned over a new leaf and was no longer looting sites?"

"Yes, when I worked with Ben he was studying anthropology at Joseph Smith College. He told me he was done digging illegally, but I guess that was a lie."

"Thank you, Ms. Jones. That will be all."

I felt a surge of relief. That hadn't been so bad. I started to stand when the judge motioned me to sit back down. I remembered with dread that I wasn't done. It was the defense attorney's turn.

"Ms. Jones," he began with a smile, "where are you from?"

"I grew up in Rhode Island."

"So, you never spent time in the West until recently?"

"Um, yes, I came to Utah to attend college."

"I see. Did you ever go arrowhead collecting back east?"

"Yes."

"Do you consider collecting arrowheads wrong?"

"Not then, but I do now. When arrowheads are collected, archaeologists can't tell how old sites are."

"Is that so? If I have a site on my property, and I collect arrowheads from it, is that wrong?"

"Yes."

"And Ms. Jones, would it be wrong for me to excavate a site located on my property?"

"Yes. Excavating sites for artifacts destroys the context and renders the sites meaningless."

"So even on my own property, it is wrong to remove arrowheads or artifacts? Would you say it is against the law?"

"Um, without professional training it is wrong to destroy a site and desecrate graves."

"Ms. Jones, the law is clear about private property. I'm afraid that it is perfectly legal to collect arrowheads, pots, and other artifacts on your own property or on someone else's property with the owner's permission. As a professional archaeologist, shouldn't you know this?"

"Yes, but there is the moral issue."

"Were the sites that Ben described in his campfire stories on private land?"

"I don't know."

"So it's possible that Ben had been digging legally, yet you have assumed he was looting sites illegally. Or maybe you assumed he was breaking the law because you have made a moral judgment about non-professionals excavating sites."

"Ah, maybe . . . I'm not sure." I was starting to feel confused and angry at how my words were being turned around. I looked over at Ben, and he was smiling at me. His eyes seemed to be saying, "Silly girl, got you!"

"And is it also possible that the family's collection of artifacts came from their own land, and that they have every right to own them?"

"I suppose so."

"Thank you, Ms. Jones."

My face burned red from embarrassment and anger. I walked back to my seat feeling sick to my stomach. Why hadn't I made the legal distinction between private and federal land? The attorney had made me sound like an eastern environmentalist who considered picking up arrowheads a federal offense, which would make a lot of westerners criminals.

As I sat down, Ken avoided eye contact with me. The rest of the trial was a blur. In his closing argument, the defense attorney pointed out that I was a sweet but misguided easterner who didn't understand the West and believed that collecting arrowheads was a criminal offense—even though it is perfectly legal. He said Ben's stories were just flirty entertainment, nothing more than fireside chat to impress a cute young woman. He reminded the jury several times that Ben may have poked around a little in prehistoric trash deposits, but according to the new Archaeological Resources Protection Act, that was not a crime.

In the end the jury sided with the defense. Ben was convicted only on the charge of destroying government property, a misdemeanor. He paid a fine and walked out. I felt responsible, even if it wasn't my fault.

Ken tried to cheer me up on the way back to the office, but it was pretty hopeless. As a consolation prize he told me we were heading to northeastern Utah next week to help the district archaeologist with a survey.

I spent the weekend sulking and puttering around my apartment—watching old movies on TV and petting Saga and her kitten, the drooling cats.

On Monday morning Ken and I drove east across Utah to Vernal. I was happy not to be going to the office. It would have felt like walking back into my fourth grade classroom the day after I'd thrown up. The janitor had cleaned up the mess, but I'd still had to face everyone in class. Ken seemed happy and talkative, and I thought he might be trying to cheer me up.

"This survey is going to be great. We're helping Decades Archaeology survey some units as part of their contract to build a site location prediction model. Remember that contract selection meeting you sat in on for oil and gas leases?"

I looked over at Ken and noticed that he'd already donned his ugly pink hat.

"That one in February?" I remembered Decades' proposal.

"Yup. Fieldwork is almost done, and we're going to help survey the last units and then tour some of the sites. I brought you along because you're going to review their report and evaluate their site prediction model."

"Where is the survey?"

"It's just east of Roosevelt, in the oil and gas lease areas. We're doing the survey so that the oil guys only have to have an archaeologist survey the high probability areas."

"Has Decades found many sites?"

"There haven't been that many, and we didn't really expect many except around springs and in the few thin stands of pinyon."

"What percentage of the area are they surveying? I forget what the proposal said."

"They're doing twenty percent of the area, around four thousand acres."

"Are you sure that's enough?"

"Time will tell."

Ken had changed the subject and started blabbing about his antique store and his bottle book, so I only half listened. I was thinking about where I'd like to go to graduate school—somewhere out of Johnson's reach. The University of New Mexico and the University of Arizona had great archaeology programs, but Johnson didn't get along with Arizona's premier archaeologists, and I doubt he could stand the chair of New Mexico's program. He was considered a "new" archaeologist, meaning he cared more about science and theory, and less about culture history. While their theoretical philosophies were diametrically opposed, I suspected that their rivalries revolved more around alpha males vying for territory. Both schools were highly rated, and I would try for the best program I could get into, with or without Johnson's blessing. I'd have to take the GRE exams before I could submit an application. It was already late summer, but if I applied this fall, maybe I could start in the spring rather than a year from now.

"Here we are," announced Ken.

"Already?" I looked around. There was nothing as far as the eye could see but low hills covered with thin grass and stubby sage—except for an empty Jeep Cherokee with magnetic signs advertising Decades Archaeology in big red letters.

"Where is everyone?" Ken wondered out loud. "We're right on time."

"What's the plan?"

"We were to meet at 10 a.m. sharp."

"Just relax. They're probably out surveying and running a little late." I scanned the horizon for a line of archaeologists—nothing.

Ken opened the door. "Guess I'll go water the plants."

"You do that."

About half an hour later four archaeologists appeared on the horizon, resembling marching ants. When they reached us, greetings were exchanged, and the crew apologized for being late. Their transect had had more sites than anticipated. We talked with them for a while and then lined up to start surveying.

We surveyed for the rest of the day but found little of note. Since the crew was staying in Roosevelt, and our hotel was in Vernal, we said our good-byes at the end of the day. Tomorrow we were going to look at some of the sites Decades had found, and the next day we planned to help survey in the morning before driving home.

After checking into the motel, Ken and I parted ways to shower and change. We agreed to meet for dinner across the street in the town's one decent steakhouse. My room had the usual western painting over the bed—mountains, sunset, elk adorned with a giant rack. The mud color of the carpet couldn't hide two large stains between the double beds. The walls were painted dingy beige, and I could smell the last guest's cigarettes.

I set my overnight bag on the suitcase rack and checked out the bathroom. A protective strip of paper indicated the maids had sanitized the toilet seat, but I couldn't say as much for the bathroom floor. Several short, black, curly hairs hovered in one of the corners, like a black widow waiting for a victim. The towels looked clean, though, and the sink was only slightly marred by a deep cigarette burn. I threw a towel over the dirty floor and undressed. In contrast to the rest of the room, the shower scored a "10"—clean and hot.

I dressed, caught a few minutes of news, and headed to the restaurant. I was ten minutes late, and Ken had already polished off half a glass of Seven and Seven. He was sitting at the bar flanked by two twenty-something women. How did he do this? In less than ten minutes he had managed to capture the attention of two women who from a distance weren't half bad. Up close was a different matter.

"Ivy, meet Sue Ann and Geri Lynn."

"Hi," they said in unison.

"They're sisters," explained Ken. I could see he was maxing out his charm-o-meter.

I smiled and said hello, then sat down and ordered a beer. The sisters didn't look like they had any DNA in common. The blond was tall with big hair, big boobs, big everything. The other woman was small, with short brown hair, tiny hands and feet, a tiny waist, and mosquito-bite boobs. Even her teeth were tiny, and also pointed—sort of reptilian. I'd never met any prostitutes, but I had my suspicions. Was Ken really that stupid?

I sipped my beer and watched Ken in action. Plenty of TV shows weren't half this entertaining. He preened and bragged, trying to convince the girls that his work required him to be a cross between Luke Skywalker and Indiana Jones. I was thinking his skills were more along the lines of the doctor in *Lost in Space*. After the girls tried to coax Ken to party with them at their place, I saw a little lightbulb come on in his head. He announced that he'd kept me waiting long enough, and he motioned for me to walk with him to the restaurant side of the establishment.

"That took you a while, Ken."

"Damn, how did you know?" He shook his head and chuckled.

"Well, they didn't exactly look like sisters, and nice girls in Vernal don't dress in miniskirts, transparent blouses, and three-inch heels. What was your first clue?"

"The blond was hot, too."

"Does your libido ever give you a rest?" I was really curious about his answer, but he completely ignored the question.

"Too bad, too, I was kind of thinking a threesome might be nice."

"Could you keep those thoughts to yourself?" I pleaded. Unbidden, the mental image of Ken and those two gals rolling in bed, naked, popped into my head. Gross. Ick. I left our table and went in search of the bathroom.

Ken stared at me as I walked back to our table.

"What? Don't look at me like that, Ken. You really are a slut, you know that?"

A waitress appeared and we ordered steaks. I asked for the smallest one, and Ken ordered the largest. The meal included potatoes, salad bar, and Texas toast.

"Ken, we need to talk about work."

"What about it?"

"I want you and the guys to give the habiliment chart a rest. It's not funny anymore."

"We think it's funny."

"Well, it isn't, and I'm sick of it. If you guys don't throw the chart away, I'm going to have a talk with the human resource folks."

"Huh? Why would you do that? It just our way of telling you we like you."

"No, it's not, and you know it. If any of you really liked me, you'd understand how I feel. Are you going to tell them or what?"

"I'll think about it. Hey, I need you to do something for me tonight. I'm going to buy an old Mustang convertible in a town just over the border in Wyoming, and I need you to drop to me off after dinner so that I can drive it back."

"In the government rig?"

"Yeah."

"Isn't it against the rules to drive a government vehicle across state lines when there is no work reason? It's just a personal purchase, right?" I couldn't believe he actually expected me to be a partner in crime.

"Yeah, so what? No one will catch you."

"What if I get stopped for speeding?"

"Just drive the speed limit. Ivy, this isn't a capital offense. It's just dropping me off in another town."

"No, it's against the rules. I don't want to."

Our salad plates arrived and I got up to fill mine, even though the salad bar looked like someone had stolen the two-day-old discount sign. I settled for the iceberg lettuce and cherry tomatoes, then poured on a liberal helping of ranch dressing. We ate in silence for a while. Ken had sampled a bit of everything at the salad bar, apparently oblivious of the risk he was taking.

"Okay, Ivy, I'll have the guys quit it with the habiliment chart if you drive me over to pick up the Mustang."

"That is what this trip was all about, right? You could care less about Decades' contract. You just figured it offered you an opportunity to collect your car. For a minute, I actually thought you planned this trip to make me feel better about Ben's trial."

"Everything isn't about you, Ivy."

"No, Ken, it's about you."

Silence again. The steaks came, and we continued to eat without talking. I wasn't much of a steak person, but after walking all afternoon, I was hungry, and it hit the spot. I ate most of my baked potato and all of the bread.

Ken wiped his mouth with his napkin and looked ready to leave. "Let's get going. It's getting late."

I shook my head. "One last thing, Ken. Dinner is on you."

"You drive a hard bargain." Ken collected the bill, but since he was a known cheapskate, I offered to leave the tip.

The Mustang caper went as planned, with no one ever the wiser. I stewed the entire way, saying little and feeling used. Ken either hadn't noticed my mood or didn't care. What an asshole. I got back to the motel around eleven, crawled into bed, and slept a dreamless sleep.

Chirping birds woke me at dawn, so I dressed and found a diner occupied by the usual batch of wrinkled men escaping their wives' morning prater. I didn't care what Ken's breakfast plans were, and anyway, he had his own transportation. He showed up and joined me after all, uninvited, chatting happily about what a great deal he got on the Mustang.

During the drive to Vernal, Ken had told me about his new girlfriend in one of the agency's district offices. He bragged for an hour about his skill at keeping his wife and girlfriends in the dark. I couldn't help but wonder if this was normal behavior for a married man going through a midlife crisis. I looked closely at Ken and realized that, even ignoring the pink hat, he disgusted me. Sick and tired of hearing him brag and lie, I made up my mind right there to quit my job. I just couldn't stand looking at Ken anymore.

Tomorrow I'd apply for a job at an archaeology company that Avery Green, one of Johnson's Ph.D. students, had just started. I'd met him in the anthropology lab, and he seemed like a pretty normal guy. Ken had recently told me that Avery had won a large data recovery contract with an oil company. They would be excavating ten prehistoric sites in the way of a proposed pipeline. A technician job on a dig sounded just fine at this point.

Sheepherders and Antelope Traps

Avery hired me on the spot for an excavation that was scheduled to start in two weeks. The pay would be lousy, but I'd actually be doing archaeology! So far eight people had been lined up for the crew. We were going to live in rented house trailers in Lyman, Wyoming, near the dig, and would work ten days straight and then have four days off.

Tom supported my break from the Land Management Agency, and he was moving away in a month anyway. Our relationship had never been that serious, and we seemed to be drifting apart more and more.

How would Ken take the news? I suspected that he'd care only because it would create more work for him. Instead of spending his days working on his stupid bottle book, he'd actually have to do his job or train someone else to do it. I took secret pleasure in the thought that his book would have to be put on hold.

It was Monday morning. I planned to break the news to Ken first thing and then calmly hand him my resignation letter. No muss, no fuss, right? Wrong. It was the first day of the month, and the guys had posted a new chart on the bulletin board. Some switch in my brain flipped. Months of torment made me suddenly and inexplicably angry. Adrenalin coursed through my veins. I tore the charts off the bulletin board and headed for the personnel office. Ken saw me but merely shrugged and returned to work.

I charged down two flights of stairs, taking two at a time, to the personnel office, off in a protected corner of the building. I pushed open the door and saw a middle-aged secretary with a bland smile guarding the personnel czar's door.

I willed myself to stay calm. "Could I speak to the EEO officer?"

"John is on the phone right now. Why don't you have a seat? He shouldn't be too long. What's your name?"

I told her and then sat in one of the two comfortable chairs flanking the entry. The reading material included a pamphlet on the Department of the Interior's natural treasures and a two-year-old *Good Housekeeping* magazine with an article on Utah's federal lands. I read both before Ms. Bland asked me to follow her.

"John, this is Ivy Jones. She would like to discuss something with you."

John was the only African American employee at the Land Management Agency, and possibly one of only a dozen people of African descent that I had ever seen in Salt Lake City. The Mormon Church had only recently stopped discriminating against them. In the 1960s the church president had a vision about racial equality, but before that, African Americans were never eligible to be elders of the church, even if they completed two-year missions.

"Hi, John. I'd like to talk to you about my coworkers in Resources."

"Sure, Ivy, have a seat." John waved at a wooden chair facing his desk.

I sat down and laid two of the charts on his desk. He listened carefully as I explained the rating system. Periodically he nodded and shook his head.

"How long has this been going on?"

"It started in March. I thought the guys would get tired of it, but they never did. I just want someone to put a stop to it. I asked my boss to talk to the guys about it, but he never did."

"Who's your boss?" John asked.

"Ken Blink."

"Ivy, I wish you hadn't waited so long to tell me about this."

I couldn't believe my ears. He was making it sound like it was my fault.

"Look, I'm the victim, here. Don't get on my case for not reporting it sooner. Ken should have done something about the chart when I asked him to stop it."

"I understand, but in an organization of this size, it's difficult for us to know everything that's going on. Now that we're aware of this, we'll take immediate action."

I wondered who the "we" was. Did he mean himself and his secretary? As far as I knew, he was the only one in Personnel. I noticed that sweat had broken out on his forehead, and he seemed a tad defensive.

"That's fine, but I'm leaving the agency in two weeks. I have a new job. I just wanted you to know what's been going on in case another young woman joins the staff. I don't want this to happen to her."

"That sounds reasonable. Rest assured it won't happen again. I wish you would reconsider leaving."

"No. I'm positive that I'm done here."

I said good-bye and left. That was easy, I thought. As I walked into my cubicle, I felt a wave of relief. Then I saw Ken headed in my direction.

"So what did he say?"

"He said he'd take care of it. And by the way, I'm quitting." I looked to gauge his reaction.

"Yeah, I know. I just got off the phone with your new boss. He filled me in. Archaeology is a small world, Ivy. Don't forget that."

What? He'd already heard? Before I could say anything, he turned and walked away. I sat there stunned for a minute. How had he found out so fast? I should have known that Mr. Gossip would figure out what I was up to. Screw it. There was no point in beating myself up over a done deal. Now I just needed to look forward.

That was easier said than done. My last two weeks at the agency were hell. Ken sulked because I had had the audacity to take a job without his consent—as if I needed that. Mr. EEO raised hell, and by Friday all the guys in Resources had discovered my betrayal. John had interviewed each of the chart participants and signed them up for mandatory sexual harassment training. And if that wasn't bad enough, he put disciplinary letters in their personnel files. I was public enemy number one. I felt like a Puritan being locked in the stocks, on display, for the public to humiliate me. Obviously, no good-bye parties or luncheons were held in my honor. Good riddance! I thought, closing the door on my way out.

I had three whole days off between jobs to decompress. On Tuesday morning, at 7 a.m., Tom dropped me off at Avery's downtown office. I left my suitcase in the lobby and found the office on the second floor. I knocked on the door and let myself in. A thirty-something, paunchy, balding guy looked up at me. He was stuffing pin flags into a tube. A younger woman, who was counting pencils, looked over and smiled.

"Hi, I'm Ivy." I offered my hand and we shook. They introduced themselves as Tim and Mary Sullivan.

"I'm one of the supervisors," said Tim.

"And I'm an archaeologist in training and wife extraordinaire," said Mary, looking at Tim with a shy smile.

They act like newlyweds, I thought to myself. I noticed a mound of gear piled in the corner and suspected it would all have to be hauled to the vehicle. "What can I do to help? How about if I start carrying that gear downstairs?"

"That would be great," said Tim. "Stack it all down by the curb in front of the building and I'll pull the truck around."

I decided that having an archaeology business on the second floor of an old downtown office building with limited parking wasn't terribly practical. Lucky for me there was a small elevator so I didn't have to deal with the stairs.

After three trips up and down, I noticed that a middle-aged woman had materialized in the office. She must have used the stairs. Dora was a housewife whose kids had left the nest. I'd later learn that she was trying on new careers for size. She looked the part of a bored housewife: frumpy, slightly overweight, and in desperate need of a makeover. Despite her physical shortcomings, she seemed nice enough. She grabbed some gear, and we hauled the rest of the stuff downstairs.

Just after we made the last trip, Tim pulled up in a beat-up old van. Perfect, I thought. I hope we make it there. All of the gear, including excavation equipment, easily fit in, and the four of us rode in the front two seats with room to spare. I was guessing that the site would be accessible by decent roads since the van had no four-wheel drive and minimal clearance. I mumbled a quiet good-bye to city life as we began the three-hour drive to Lyman, Wyoming—home of cowboys, sheepherders, oilmen, and soon, eight archaeologists.

During the drive I learned that Tim had been an air traffic controller at Chicago's O'Hare Airport. When the controllers went on strike, he lost his job. Before that, he'd been a contract archaeologist. As I had correctly surmised, Mary and Tim were newlyweds of just a few months. Mary had recently been accepted to graduate school to study history. Tim and Avery were old friends, and when Avery had offered him the job, he and Mary had decided it would tide them over until Mary started school in January. We were all hoping the snow wouldn't fall until we finished the excavations in November.

I fell asleep about an hour from our destination and woke to miles of rolling hills. We left the interstate and drove a few miles down a state highway to a small cluster of dilapidated homes and vintage house trailers in various stages of decay. A row of brick buildings housed a grocery store, a hardware store, a drug store, and a boarded-up store advertising sports equipment and hunting licenses. Two gas stations occupied the corners at each end of the row of stores. A sign in the window of one station simply said BAIT. In flashing neon, the more modern gas station advertised coffee, beer, snacks, and cigarettes. We drove to the edge of town and parked between two sad-looking house trailers.

We stretched our legs and followed Tim and Mary over to the smaller but newer trailer. Since I'd never been in one, I was curious to see what they looked like. A young, thin woman with shoulder-length hair and a pretty face opened the door.

"Hey, you made it. I'm Jill."

She reached and shook each of our hands and ushered us in. Just inside the door a long-haired, bearded guy introduced himself as Jack. Jill followed us into the trailer and put her arm around Jack's waist, but I didn't see any rings on their fingers.

Just as the "Jack and Jill" rhyme popped into my head, Jack announced loudly, "Anyone who makes Jack and Jill jokes will be given the boot. Got it?" He said it with a crooked grin, which I would later learn was the closest he ever got to a smile. His voice was raspy, and his face scarred by acne.

"I hate that fuckin' rhyme," said Jill. She shook her head and smiled. "We almost broke up after the tenth time one of our friends couldn't stop themselves and started reciting it."

Jack nudged Jill. "Who was that?"

"Uh, I think it was Avery. I was surprised he still wanted to hire us after I ripped him a new one."

"He's onto you, Jill. He knows your bark is worse than your bite."

I couldn't help noticing what a cute couple they were, but despite the admonition, the rhyme kept going round and round in my head. "Jack and Jill went up the hill to fetch a pail of water. Jack fell down and broke his crown and Jill came tumbling after." The introductions had continued, and I suddenly realized everyone was staring at me.

"Uh, I'm Ivy Jones." I offered my hand to a plain-looking woman who introduced herself as Barb and who looked about my age. Her short, brown hair emphasized her square face in a bad way, and she spoke with a twangy western accent. I later learned that she was from Cheyenne and had just finished her anthropology degree in the spring. Like me, she was struggling with the lifestyle of a contract archaeologist.

A scrawny guy who reminded me of the Scarecrow from *The Wizard of Oz* introduced himself as Dave. He didn't make eye contact with me at all. Shy perhaps? He had also just finished his degree. When I discovered that Barb and Dave had driven to the project together and were sharing a room, I assumed they were a couple. I became really confused when Barb told me how hard it had been to leave her boyfriend for this job.

"I have an announcement!" Jill yelled. "Attention!"

We quieted down.

"This trailer is where Jack and I will live. The small one next door is Tim and Mary's. Three trailers down is a pink doublewide, and that's where the rest of you will stay. Our trailer will also serve as an office, lab, and storage area. If your stuff isn't in the van, throw it in, and Tim will drive you over. We'll leave here after lunch, around one, and we'll tour the sites and set up the grids. I have two local kids meeting us here at one. Hop to it."

Avery hadn't explained the organizational structure to me, but it didn't take a rocket scientist to figure out who was in charge. I wondered how Jack and Jill had hooked up with Avery.

Our trailer was larger than Jack and Jill's, but it was in worse shape, a throwback from the era of green shag carpeting and dark cabinets. The inside was damp and dingy, and everything was covered with a fine coat of grease. The bathroom turned out to be the best looking and cleanest room in the trailer. It looked like the shower and toilet had recently been replaced. The living room was furnished with a brown plaid couch that sagged badly in the middle, and a swivel La-Z-Boy chair that had probably been blue but had faded to a nondescript gray. The walls were paneled with dark imitation wood, and the windows were covered with dirty blinds.

Maybe this place wouldn't look so grim if I opened the blinds. I walked over to the largest window and pulled the cord. The blinds crashed to the floor in a puff of greasy dust. I struggled for a minute to pick them up before Dave came to my rescue.

"Great view," he said.

Barb walked over for a look. Our window looked into our neighbor's side yard. A huge, one-eyed pit bull was staring back at us. He was chained to a metal fixture that had been screwed into the ground next to a rickety doghouse. The bare ground was littered with several months' worth of dog shit. As we contemplated the brutish beast, he started to bark.

"I can't stand barking dogs," said Barb. "Get the antifreeze."

"Antifreeze? What's that for?" I asked.

"Where I grew up, that's how we cope with barking dogs." She made a cutting motion across her neck. I thought for a minute that she was joking, but she seemed very serious. I made a mental note not to cross Barb. She didn't look like a dog-killing homicidal maniac, but who knew?

Dora and I took the smaller bedroom near the back of the trailer. Barb and Dave claimed the larger one in front. Neither room had a stick of furniture. I unloaded my meager belongings—sleeping bag, air mattress, pillow, duffle bag, and dig kit. I was happy that I'd had the forethought to throw in an air mattress. Dora looked upset when she realized that she'd have to sleep on the floor unless she could buy a mattress or cushion. She seemed a bit whiny, and I wondered how she would handle physical labor. If this was her first dig, she was in for some big surprises.

Our first afternoon was one of the most pleasant I'd had in months. The sun was warm, and a slight breeze lifted my long hair in an endless caress. I'd forgotten how good it felt to let my hair blow free. The temperature was a comfortable 78 degrees, and it was too late in the season for bugs. My crew had been assigned to dig a site perched on top of a low, grassy hill. The grass had turned golden, and I could see forever across an endless sea of gold. Rabbitbrush had been blooming in Utah, but not here in Wyoming. Maybe I'd be spared my allergies here.

Driving back that first day I experienced a sense of well-being, what the Navajos call "horzo." Peace and beauty surrounded me again, and I was happy for the first time in almost a year. No commute downtown, no cubicles, and no Ken. Perhaps office work just wasn't for me. Too confining, I thought, as we drove the fifteen miles from the site back to town.

Before heading home we were going to stop at the grocery store. I mentally planned my menu: Swanson fried chicken TV dinners, meatloaf TV dinners, pot pies, and Cheetos. Breakfast would be toast and coffee. Lunch was easy—canned seafood and crackers. I'd brought some food in case we didn't make it to the store right away, but I hadn't bothered with a cooler so everything I had was dry or canned.

With my menu planned, I turned my thoughts to the dig. I was on Tim's crew with Barb and one of the local guys, named Joe. Tim had been trained in Texas, where the supervisors dig beside crewmembers, and he informed us he would continue digging just like the rest of us. That was a good thing because it looked like we had a lot of dirt to move, and not many people to move it.

On the surface the site was a typical lithic scatter—waste flakes, a few spear points and scrapers, and some fire-cracked rocks. The unique style of one of the points suggested the site was between two thousand and five thousand years old. The prehistoric Indians who had lived in the region hunted antelope and rabbits, and gathered grass seeds and other edible plants. The fire-cracked rocks and pieces of burnt bone hinted that hearths or roasting pits might be buried at the site.

The weather stayed perfect for the first session. We moved a lot of dirt and were rewarded with the discovery of a well-preserved prehistoric campsite. We had started digging in the center of the artifact scatter and soon found flecks of charcoal, pieces of bone, and burnt rocks. Most of the charcoal and bones were buried more than a foot below the ground surface. Every couple of days someone would find a spear point or some other interesting tool like a stone drill or a bone awl. The bones scattered everywhere made the digging slow. Each level of bones had to be carefully excavated, mapped, and sketched, then wrapped and bagged.

Tim explained that the site's occupants had probably killed a large number of antelope and then butchered and cooked the carcasses right where they lay. By counting the number of mandibles, he estimated that at least twelve animals had been processed at the site. A faunal analyst would be able to determine exactly how many antelope of what ages had been consumed here.

I excavated five one-meter units at the eastern edge of the grid. In the center of my excavation area I uncovered a conical-shaped pit filled with partially burned bones. I wasn't certain yet if the bones had been thrown into the feature after the meat had been removed, or if the carcasses had been pit-baked in the feature. The faunal analyst would probably be able to tell after examining the bones.

On the last day of the session we covered our excavation units with plastic and left at two for the drive home. I was ready for a real bed and my own apartment. It would be lonely without Tom, but I knew he was busy at law school.

The break flew past. Before I knew it, Tuesday morning had arrived. I took the bus to the meeting place and waited at the curb for the van. Everyone except for Mary, Tim, and I had opted to stay in Wyoming—or at least that's what I'd thought.

A truck pulled up and out jumped Russell, the incompetent crew chief I'd abandoned in Bryce Canyon. He proceeded to unload a pile of gear.

"Russell, what are you doing here?" I knew he'd probably been hired to help with the dig, but I hoped it wasn't true.

When he recognized me, his pupils grew smaller and his mustache twitched. "I didn't know you were working on this project."

"Did Avery just hire you?"

"Nah, he hired me a while ago, but I couldn't make the first session. My other job didn't finish up until last week."

"So how have you been?"

"Can't complain."

I couldn't believe that this was happening. How could Russell be working on this project? What a nightmare. I'd thought I was done with him.

We waited in silence for the van. I decided not to say anything about our fight. Maybe no one would find out. Was I going to run into people like this for the rest of my career?

Russell did look better than I remembered—tan, tall, and well proportioned, maybe even thinner and more muscular.

"So what have you been doing? Still working for ASC?"

"No."

I loved talking to this guy. He was so articulate, like every interviewer's worst nightmare.

Dora arrived and I introduced her to Russell. Then the van pulled up, and we headed back to Lyman. I slept most of the way, and during the last half hour I decided to treat Russell like everyone else. He wasn't my supervisor this time, and maybe as a coworker he wouldn't be so bad.

After six days of digging, all the guys starting looking good to me. I guess something about sweaty men makes my thoughts turn to sex more often than usual. Even Russell started looking hot. You'd think that the hard physical labor would tire me out and crowd out any thoughts of wild sex, but that just wasn't the case. I was muscle sore and exhausted, but I was also ready to rock and roll.

Day seven I woke to six inches of snow and went right back to sleep. Two hours later, loud laughter coming from the kitchen woke me up. My fingers and back were stiff and sore. After flexing my hands about ten times, they almost felt normal. I threw on some sweatpants and an old turtleneck and headed to the kitchen. Coffee, coffee, coffee! Living with other people in a trailer was like being back in a college dorm. People came and went, and there was no such thing as privacy. You quickly got to know everyone really well under such conditions, whether you wanted to or not.

Dora and Barb were drinking coffee at the small table in the living room and comparing notes on the dig's male crew members. Dave was frying bacon and watching a tiny television perched on the counter. He seemed to be ignoring the gals. I made myself a cup of instant coffee and joined Dora and Barb.

"So what do you think of Russell?" asked Dora.

"Well, there's a tricky one," answered Barb. "He isn't my type, but I'll bet he'd be good in the sack if you could get his garments off."

"What's that?" Dora asked.

"Mormon underwear," Barb said, chuckling. "Don't you have any Mormons living in Denver?"

"Yes, but I don't know any well enough to have had a heart-to-heart conversation about their underwear." Dora leaned back in the old La-Z-Boy.

"We have lots of them here in Wyoming," explained Barb. "When I was little, most of my friends were Mormon. Then in junior high they figured out that they couldn't convert me, so I was dumped like smelly trash."

"So what are garments?" prodded Dora impatiently.

"Garments are special underwear that all adult believers wear under their clothes."

Dora looked perplexed. "What do they look like?"

Barb smiled. "Uh, they're like old-fashioned long underwear. You know, like the ones you see in old westerns, but thinner and lighter. Garments are one-piece numbers that cover the entire torso. The sleeves are short and the legs go to mid-thigh. I think they come in different styles for hot and cold weather, but I've never seen summer garments. The amazing thing about them is that Mormons are never supposed to remove them except to put on a clean pair. They're even supposed to wear them during sex!"

"Are you making this up?" Dora asked. "Tell me you are. That is just too weird." She had stopped rocking and was listening carefully.

"It's true, Dora," I said.

After making another cup of instant coffee, I'd lifted myself up to sit on the kitchen counter, and my backside was against the cabinets.

Barb grinned at me. "See? I'm not making it up."

"Not all Mormons wear them, but the faithful do," I explained. "You can tell who wears them because they make a bump or line across their thigh where the garment ends under the pants."

Dave had stopped watching TV and was listening to our conversation. He might be a man of few words, but he paid close attention to everything going on around him.

"Russell wears them," said Barb. "And you didn't tell me what you think about him, Dora."

"He's not my type. Anyway, all the guys here are too young for me. My son is their age, for cripe's sake."

"How about you, Ivy?" asked Barb.

"I haven't thought about it," I lied. In fact, I'd thought about it a lot. I just didn't want to admit that I was physically attracted to Russell of all people. I looked into my coffee cup so that Barb couldn't see my eyes.

"Come on, Ivy. You're fibbing. I've seen you two together. You're attracted to him."

"Well, maybe a little," I admitted.

"So, Ivy," Barb continued, "tell us what you think. Good or bad in the sack?"

I'm not a shy person but this was not a conversation for people who like to keep their private lives private. "Okay, I agree with you, Barb, he probably would be good in the sack."

"See?" Barb said with satisfaction. "I knew it."

The trailer door opened, and Jill entered carrying a giant coffee cup. "Hey, what's happening?"

"Nothing. we were just trying to figure out who's the sexiest guy on this dig," answered Barb.

"Damn, that's an easy one. Jack, of course. He's the best fuck for sure."

"No fair!" yelled Dora. "You can't include anyone that you've actually slept with."

Jill plopped down on the couch with abandon, like a man who had just finished mowing the grass and had the rest of the day to watch football. "Okay, so who are we talking about?"

"Russell," said Dora.

Dave must have decided that he'd had enough because he left the trailer. I felt kind of guilty for driving him off, but not too sorry to stop our girl talk. We were behaving as nasty as Ken, but at least there were no men around.

"Hmmm. . . Russell. Let's see." She pushed a strand of brown hair out of her face and took a deep drink of coffee. While she was thinking, there was a knock at the door, and Mary stuck her head in. "Hey, am I missing the pajama party?"

"Come on in and join us," said Jill, waving her in.

Mary took the recliner and joined in the conversation. We speculated about each of the guys except for Jack and Tim. We laughed and drank coffee, and had a great time. Finally, the conversation turned back to Dora's son.

"Do you have a picture of him?" I asked.

"Sure, let me get it." Dora disappeared and returned with her wallet. She removed a small photo and handed it to Mary.

"He's handsome," she said. "How old is he?"

"That was his graduation picture. He was eighteen. He's twenty now."

Mary handed the picture to me. I agreed he was a handsome guy and passed the picture to Jill.

"Oh, yeah, I'd fuck him," said Jill. "He's a cutie."

I turned bright red, but Dora didn't miss a beat.

"He is handsome," she said, looking at her son's picture with a smile.

How could Jill have said that about Dora's son? If anyone had said that about my son, I would have felt embarrassed, but not Dora. It was fun working with women again. It reminded me of my sisters on that rare occasion when we were all home for the holidays. This was nothing like my previous fieldwork projects in Utah or, for that matter, field school. Everyone was too stressed out at field school to have much fun, and after that I'd worked mostly with men. It felt so good to be back with women, joking and laughing, and doing what women do best—talking.

The snow had melted by the end of the day, but the dirt roads had become muddy quagmires with the consistency of baby poop, and the van slipped and slid several times. Fortunately, we had covered everything with plastic the night before so our digging areas had stayed dry.

We dug for two more days, and then I was back in Salt Lake City—to my bathtub and privacy. Another weather front moved in over the weekend, but the days stayed warm and the storm brought rain instead of snow. I prayed the snow would hold off just a few more weeks.

The excavation turned tedious during our next session. We made no interesting discoveries, and mornings were cold. Screening and digging with gloves added a new dimension of complexity. I had to take them off and put them on a hundred times a day. During the entire session we found only a few projectile points and a hearth. The good news was that the bone bed had played out, so the digging went faster.

At the halfway point of the project, we decided to break the tedium with a trip to the site of a Native American antelope drive. No one knew how old it was. A cowboy professor in Wyoming had identified dozens of these sites across the state. The first Europeans entering the region wrote about the traps, but archaeologists had only recently started recording them. I had never seen one before and had no idea what to expect.

We quit digging a little early and loaded everyone into the van. The drive took just a half hour, and we were definitely in the middle of nowhere. Grass-covered hills rolled across the horizon as far as the eye could see—no houses, no roads, and no trees. We parked the van and walked a hundred meters to a messy row of juniper branches and logs piled along the edge of a ridge. When we got closer, I could see that the makeshift fence extended for hundreds of meters.

Without a word we all took off in the direction of the juniper row. Like a small herd of antelope, we followed the line down the ridge until it stopped at the edge of a sheer cliff. Twenty meters below I imagined a group of women waiting for the animals to fall to their deaths. Broken and twisted bodies would have been swiftly butchered and the flesh hung to dry in the dry Wyoming air. Just back from the cliff edge, I noticed a second row of juniper branches leading back from where we had just walked. The two fences stopped at the edge of the cliff, forming the bottom of a V. Jill explained what the archaeologists had discovered buried below the cliff.

"Dyson, the cowboy archaeologist, and his students excavated some units at the base of the cliff. On the ground surface all they saw was a couple of flakes and a few bifaces, but once they started digging, that picture changed. In each test trench they found hundreds of antelope bones. The deposits were stratified in layers, and the oldest layer, buried six feet below the surface, dated to around four thousand years ago. The most recent was deposited about five hundred years ago."

"So how did the trap work?" asked Dora. "Did they scare the animals into running along the fence until they fell off the edge like lemmings?"

"Pretty much," answered Jack. "Antelope grazing on the ridge were probably scared by hunters hiding along the fence at strategic locations. If the animals got too close to the fence, the hunters could jump up and scare them to keep them running forward. Dyson thinks that hunting antelope in traps was a communal activity involving several different bands. They may have monitored the herd so that half could be killed without decimating them all. In the fall, when the animals were healthy and fat, and the weather cool enough so the meat wouldn't spoil too fast, the hunt began. I think it probably would have taken about twenty able-bodied men, women, and older children to pull off the drive. Probably one person would hide behind the brush every hundred meters, and since the trap follows the ridge for at least a kilometer, that's ten people manning each side of the fence. The fence was probably pretty substantial when it was in use. I'll bet if you put in test units, you'd find staining in the soil from decomposing wood."

With difficulty we followed the other side of the trap back to the van. Large segments of the fence were completely missing. There was no way I would have recognized the trap for what it was if I had been surveying the area. I would have never guessed that these tree branches represented a site. During our walk the air had grown colder, and clouds were blowing in from the north. By the time we reached the van, the sky had turned flamingo pink.

The portable radio was blaring that Pretenders song with a refrain about a chain gang, inspiring Barb to climb to the top of the backdirt pile, dancing and lip-synching. Joe followed, and then we all joined in, dancing and singing that we were "back on the chain gang."

Jill drove up just as the song ended but she'd seen us dancing.

"What's going on here? No fun allowed," she joked.

As we headed back to our excavation units, Jill walked over to take a look at mine.

"What's that?" she asked.

"Huh?" I didn't know what she was talking about.

Jill slipped her trowel out of her back pocket and knelt down for a closer look.

"You've got a stain there."

I looked down and saw a couple flecks of charcoal and maybe a slightly darker color in the corner of the unit. Jill scraped the darker spot.

"I'll bet it's a hearth. Why don't you open the next unit over and take it down to this level, Ivy."

"You want me to stop at this level and cover the stain?"

"That works for me." Jill stood up and headed over to Barb's unit. She had found a small scatter of bones that didn't look big enough to be deer or antelope.

"Barb, looks like bunnies were on the menu at this site." Jill stepped down a foot into the five-by-five-meter unit, where Barb was carefully removing the dirt from a scatter of a dozen small bones.

"These bones are burned, and I think this one has been carved to a point."

Jill took a closer look. "Yup, looks like it."

"Bahhh, bahhh!" Joe, the local high school kid who screened all our soil, had dropped the screen and was watching a small herd of sheep round the hill.

"Hey, babies, come to Papa," he crooned. "I got something nice for you."

Jill ignored him, but I couldn't help myself. Joe, who was tall and thin, and wore a bad case of acne with grace, had climbed onto the dirt pile and was making sheep sounds. "Sheep, beautiful sheep, come here!"

"What are you doing, Joe?" demanded Jill.

"Looking for a date for Friday night. See that one there?" He pointed. "She's the one. Look at her fine, thick coat and sexy backside."

Jill laughed and Joe continued his monologue. "Over here, honey! This way! That a girl. Oh, you make me so hot! I got a nice spot for your hind legs right in my boots."

I'd had enough. What the hell was he doing? "Joe, what are you talking about?"

"In these small towns there just ain't enough bad girls to go around, but we've got plenty of sheep."

"Oh, gross! Are you talking about a romantic relationship with a sheep?"

"I love the way they squirm when I put their back hooves in my boots." He made a thrusting motion with his hips, and we all burst out laughing. Then he danced off in the direction of the sheep, talking dirty and trying to coax them away.

Jill was laughing so hard she fell down, and Barb was doubled over, but Tim was shaking his head with a disgusted look on his face. Joe's display had definitely bordered on repugnant, but I could see the humor too.

Joe kept walking toward the sheep, but they weren't having any of it. When he got close, they'd move away. We all kept laughing, watching him try to catch his "date," and he continued to chase the flock until a guy on horseback made an appearance. Joe mumbled a greeting and gave up the pursuit.

We worked hard, and the sessions flew past. I was sick of our living conditions, but I never tired of my fellow crewmembers. It seemed that each day was more fun than the last. Even Russell, who had moved to our site to help knock out some excavation units, turned out to be funny. I hadn't seen that side of him when he was the supervisor. I guess responsibility had robbed him of his sense of humor. I ended up screening Russell's dirt for a whole day, and we talked about everything. I didn't apologize for walking out on him, but I did admit to being burned out on survey work. He said he understood.

The dig had started winding down, and we had just one site left when we got word that Avery had a survey for us in Delta. Of all the places in Utah, why did it have to be Delta?

Delta Dawn

As we lined up to begin our first transect, Tim yelled, "Everyone ready?"

No one answered, but he motioned with his arm for us to move forward. The sky was overcast and the air felt thick and heavy, with that cool, damp, indescribable smell of snow.

We walked a mile to the west, stopped, and walked back the way we came. I stepped over low sagebrush and skirted prickly pear cactus as I kept my eyes on the ground, looking for a flake or sherd. My thoughts wandered despite my best efforts to concentrate. The dig had ended last Thursday, and here we were in Delta walking transects. I was with some of the same crew from the excavation: Tim, Mary, Barb, and Dave. But Dora had moved back to Colorado, Russell had taken a job somewhere in Arizona, and Jack and Jill were working in Salt Lake City on the excavation report. They had rented a furnished apartment and planned to stay for the winter.

Avery had decided that the rest of us should do the Delta survey before washing the artifacts from the dig. He wanted to get the fieldwork done before the project area became buried under snow. After the survey Barb and Dave were going to Arizona to work on a large project they'd just been hired for. So it would be just me and Mary washing artifacts until the holidays, when Mary and Tim were moving so she could start graduate school.

It would probably take a week to survey this project area for a state land sale. I wondered if there would be many sites. The area was located in the center of a wide valley. Low sagebrush covered the valley floor, and there was little else in the way of plant variety. The surrounding mountains were already snow covered, and soon the snow line would creep down until it covered the valley.

I wondered if I'd run into Gavin. I had no way to contact him, but he'd probably hear that I was in town—news travels fast in Delta. I'd called Joanne, who said she would meet me for dinner Tuesday night at our old watering hole. She had stopped seeing Marty regularly, but they were still friends. I couldn't wait to see her.

Suddenly I saw a flake, then another. I stopped to look around. "Site!" I yelled.

Everyone put down their packs and came over to check it out. I wandered around until I spotted a triangular-shaped flake. Sure enough! I gave a little yelp. "Point! It's a nice obsidian one too." It covered half of my palm and was notched on the corners.

"Let's see," said Tim, holding out his hand.

"Elko Corner-notched. Johnson's cave excavations tell us they were made for seven thousand years. That won't tell us how old the site is."

"Well, we can probably say it was Archaic, can't we?" I asked.

"Nah, Powell collected these from the Southern Paiutes when he did ethnographic work in Utah, so they were still using these in the late 1870s. No one knows if they were making the points or just reusing ones they found. Unfortunately, they're not temporally diagnostic. They don't help much."

"Too bad." I started looking for a more temporally sensitive projectile point. "Last time I worked in Delta we found a Clovis point."

"Lucky you," said Tim. "I've yet to find one. Okay, everyone, let's find the site boundaries and get the paperwork done."

We did find another point, but it was missing the base, so we couldn't tell how old it was either. We also found a scraper, two bifaces, and a couple of mano fragments. We used pin flags to mark the locations of the tools, took photos, drew a sketch map of the site and the topography, and then filled out the site form. It took only half an hour to record the site.

We found two more sites that day. Since they were large, it took us a couple of hours to record each of them, making for a long, tiring day.

Daylight was fading by late afternoon, so we had to quit a little early. We just couldn't see anything.

We were staying at the cheapest motel in town: the Clown. The clown theme was everywhere. Even my bathroom had a small picture of a clown. And I hate clowns. To me they're not the least bit funny. In fact, they seem evil, but I have no idea why I feel this way.

We agreed to meet in an hour for dinner, and I took a deep breath before opening the door and plunging into clown hell. My mom once told me that fear of clowns is a legitimate phobia recognized by psychologists. In New England, where I grew up, we were taught to tough out any mental problems; only weak people couldn't cure themselves. For me, clown avoidance had worked just fine—until now.

In the tradition of New Englanders, I needed to deal with this. The pictures couldn't be removed, so I draped towels over the largest ones and removed the clown bedspread. After I'd covered the bathroom picture with a hand towel, I could breathe again. That will do, I thought, unlacing my heavy hiking boots and peeling off my filthy clothes. The shower was heaven.

As we were driving to the Watering Hole, I was wondering if Gavin would be there, and my eyes found him the minute I walked through the door. He was standing at the bar talking to Joanne. I felt my willpower drain away, and I tumbled like a boulder off a cliff, under his spell again. This time I knew I was lost. Without a word he wrapped me in an embrace and looked deep into my eyes. Joanne hugged me next, and I introduced everyone.

"Joanne tells me you left the agency," Gavin said. "Good for you." His mustache was a little longer than last time I'd seen him, but otherwise he looked the same—deliciously sexy.

I felt all hot and tongue-tied. "That stupid chart finally did me in. The guys just wouldn't stop, so I turned them all in for sexual harassment."

"Good for you." He patted me on my back.

We talked and joked, and drank beer. After filling our tanks with chicken-fried steak and a couple pitchers, Joanne and I were gabbing like long-lost sisters. She decided to head home around eight, and everyone else got up to leave. I'd promised to have dinner with Gavin at the ranch the next night.

Maybe it was the clowns, or maybe it was Gavin, but I hardly slept that night. I fell into a fitful sleep sometime after 3 a.m. and dreamt about a Hopi kachina clown. His body was painted with alternating black and white stripes, and he was making fun of me for my crush on Gavin. Was he warning me of the consequences if I veered from my destiny? I kept asking myself what he meant by that, but he would only point at my heart and tell me I knew. Frustrated and sweating, I woke at six and decided to read for a while. At 6:30 I pulled on my dirty field clothes and opened the door to signal that I was ready to head out for breakfast. We were all half asleep, and the weak coffee did little to help.

The weather turned bitter cold that day, making the day seem longer than normal. We found a few more lithic scatters but little else. Finally the sun set, and Tim announced we were done. Even the short drive back to the motel seemed to take forever.

Since I didn't have a car, Gavin had said he'd pick me up at six. I showered, shaved my legs, and put on some mascara. Checking out my image in the mirror, I thought, Not bad. My hair was clean and shiny. I had on my best jeans, a white turtleneck and green sweater, and Frye boots. I took a deep breath to calm my nerves when I heard his knock.

"Hi."

"Find any arrowheads today?"

"No, not a single one."

"What's with all the towels covering the paintings?"

"I was kind of hoping you wouldn't notice."

For some reason I was feeling shy. I checked my purse to make sure my room key was there and closed the door.

"You sure you want to know?"

He smiled. "Let me guess. You don't like the art."

"Sort of."

"You don't like the clowns looking at you."

"That's closer."

He started the truck and looked over at me. "I give up."

"Well, okay. I sort of have a fear of clowns."

"You're kidding, right?" His face lit up with a wide grin.

"Don't make fun of me. It's serious. There are two things that scare me: clowns and bears. I can't decide which is worse. I guess I'm more scared of bears, but clowns make me feel sick. When I'm around real clowns, I feel nauseated and dizzy, like I'm going to hurl."

"Even rodeo clowns?"

I had to think about that for a minute. I'd only seen them on television. A mental image popped into mind of a cowboy in makeup and a red yarn wig. "You know, I'm not sure. I've never been to a rodeo."

We drove in silence for a while. His ranch was only a few miles outside of town at the base of the mountains. He looked at me and smiled.

"What's for dinner? I'm starved."

"Elk steaks, salad, and baked potatoes. My mom and dad are on a cruise, so it looks like you'll have to put up with my cooking tonight."

Uh-oh. No chaperones.

Gavin turned off the paved road and headed north on a graded road running along the edge of a grove of pinyon pines. The ranch was just as I remembered it: a one-story stucco house with a wood shingle roof and two large stacks of hay standing guard next to the barn. A corral holding a few horses, and a cluster of old trucks, tractors, and horse trailers. Gavin parked next to the house, and I followed him inside. Inside a large black Lab and an Australian shepherd greeted me. Their tails wagged, and their back ends wiggled with excitement. I took turns petting one and then the other.

"I thought ranchers didn't let dogs in the house."

"These two are my mom's babies. She spoils them rotten." Gavin busied himself in the kitchen.

"What can I do to help?"

"Nothing. Just sit and keep me company. Tell me what you've been doing since I last saw you."

I climbed onto a bar stool next to the kitchen counter. "Let's see. Okay, after you left, I fell completely apart thinking I'd never see you again. I ran away from Salt Lake and lost myself in a dig in Wyoming."

He'd stopped what he was doing to stare at me. For a second I could tell he wasn't sure what to think and then I saw he realized I was joking.

"Yeah, me too. I started walking in my sleep and lost twenty pounds. I was pining away."

We laughed. Gavin took two Coors out of the fridge and handed me one. He opened a cupboard next to the sink for a tall glass and put it down in front of me.

"Okay, what really happened is that I blew my testimony against the pothunter, I decided I couldn't stand Ken for another minute, and I realized I wanted to do archaeology rather than shuffle paperwork. So I quit and went on a dig in Wyoming. I'm back in contract archaeology again, but this time for a non-Mormon outfit."

"What is it with you and Mormons, Ivy? You seem to have a chip on your shoulder. What is it about them that irritates you so much?"

"I don't know. I've given it a lot of thought too. I guess it has something to do with the way Mormon men treat me. I always feel like a second-class citizen. They act so patronizing and superior."

"Is it just the men, or the women too?" Gavin had put two steaks in a bowl to marinate and was gathering ingredients for a salad.

"Can I help you cut stuff up?"

"Nah, just relax. I'll bet you worked harder than me today. It's been pretty quiet at the ranch. Things slow down here this time of year."

"Well, to answer your question. I don't know many Mormon women, and I've only worked with one. I got along with her great, so maybe it is just the men." I thought about it as I watched Gavin cut up a pepper and a tomato.

Gavin paused a moment and looked up at me. "The Mormon Church teaches women to be obedient to their husbands. They also teach them that having children and keeping house is their primary job. Did you know women can't get into the highest heaven unless they're married in the Temple and their husbands call them by their secret names to join them in heaven? You probably haven't been obedient, Ivy." He said it all serious and patronizing. For a second I wondered about him, and then he broke into a big grin.

I gave him a playful punch in the arm and started laughing. "You are kidding me, right? Tell me you just made up the secret name thing."

"It's true. Cross my heart."

He assembled the salad in a glass bowl, and it looked great.

"Voilá! Shall we head into the other room and start a fire?"

"Sure. I'm so glad I didn't have to spend this evening with those evil clowns." I visibly shuddered.

Gavin led the way into the living room. The ceilings were high, and the outside wall was made of local stone. Two large Navajo rugs covered the hardwood floors, and a leather couch and chair faced each other in front of the fireplace. The room looked like it was right out of a western decorator's magazine. Gavin knelt to build a fire, and I sat down on the floor in front of the couch. I decided to tease him about living with his parents.

"Aren't you getting a little old to still be living with your mommy?"

He stopped stuffing newspaper under the logs and turned around to see me smiling.

"Good one. Almost got me," he said, returning to the fire.

"How old are you again?" I asked—not that I'd forgotten.

"Older than you."

"Come on, tell me."

"Twenty-nine. I turn thirty next month. How about you?"

"Twenty-three and my biological clock is hardly ticking yet. I've got lots of time. But I did visit my oldest sister recently and had a great time with my nieces. I decided I might want children someday."

"I know what you mean."

He lit the fire and joined me on the floor. He took my hand in his and kissed the inside of my palm. Then he held my chin, looked into my eyes, and pulled my lips to his.

As it turned out, I never had to sleep with the clowns that week. I checked out of the motel the next morning and moved over to Gavin's. He delivered me each morning to the motel in an altered state of euphoria. I floated through my transects, and when Gavin asked me to move to Delta on the last night of the survey, I didn't even hesitate. I just said yes.

I gave a month's notice on my duplex, helped wash the Wyoming artifacts, and packed my stuff. Considering that I'd been living on my own for five years, my pile of possessions was pretty small and fit easily into the back of Gavin's pickup.

My sisters tried to talk me out of moving to Delta. They reminded me that I don't like small towns, I hardly knew Gavin, and I'd be several hours away from the nearest airport. They were right, but none of their arguments worked. I was in lust and determined to move on. Archaeology was not going to work if I wanted to have a husband and a family. At least with Gavin I could spend lots of time outside and learn how to work a ranch. I had no idea what I'd do for money, but Gavin had offered to pay me for helping out with chores.

Soon after I'd settled in, it snowed a foot of wet, sloppy crud. We were trapped. Gavin's parents were wintering, as they did every year, in a small house in St. George, so we had the house to ourselves. St. George is less than three hours away, but twenty to thirty degrees warmer than Delta, and temperatures there hardly ever dip below freezing. Snow is unheard of. Gavin's parents wouldn't be back until early May, so we had time to figure out what to do about living arrangements. Until then, we were more than content in the ranch house.

At first we spent most of our days tending the cattle, exploring the countryside on horseback, hauling hay out to the fields, and feeding the few chickens that Gavin's mother kept for fresh eggs. Gavin thrived on the routine, but I started growing restless. Despite the never-ending chores, we still found time to read, laugh, and play. At first I felt relaxed and happy like never before. Gavin was everything I'd ever wanted in a man: smart, funny, kind, yet mysterious in ways I was only beginning to sense. But although we had a love of books in common, we had little else. He'd grown up in a small remote town, and I was a product of eastern suburbia. He was a Mormon, and I hadn't belonged to a church since I'd left home. The side of his personality that I had the most trouble relating to involved sociability; he was a loner, and I needed lots of human contact. I missed my friends' parties, but I also realized I missed civilization: restaurants and pubs, the mall, concerts, and movie theaters.

I struggled to adjust to the isolation of the ranch and the small-town atmosphere of Delta as winter dragged on. Snowstorms were interspersed with warming spells that raised false hopes until it snowed again. I went cross-country skiing alone, but I missed the speed of the downhill slopes and the company of my Alta friends.

There weren't many people in town my age, so I had a difficult time making friends. Luckily, Joanne lived less than an hour away. She was happy to have me nearby, and I helped her with surveys when the weather permitted. Surveying gave me a welcome break from ranch chores, and the Land Management Agency was happy to have volunteer help.

Gavin's extended family accepted me, even though several of the older members thought we should get married before living together. Gavin did offer to marry me, but I told him I wasn't ready, and he didn't seem to mind. He understood this was all new.

A month after moving in I started having the kachina dream again. I'd be surveying until I found a large rock shelter where the kachina lived. Despite an overwhelming sense of foreboding, I'd enter his lair. Sometimes he shunned me, and other times he poked fun at me, telling me I was being foolish and warning me that time was running out. I'd wake up anxious and out of sorts.

Tom wrote to me from Phoenix. His letters were filled with stories about the difficulty of law school, and the excitement of living in a new place and meeting other students. I realized that I was envious. I was starving for new challenges and bored out of my mind. After much hand wringing, I decided to go ahead and apply to graduate schools, and I just barely made the deadline at the University of Arizona in Tucson, the University of New Mexico in Albuquerque, and the University of Nevada in Las Vegas. I didn't tell Gavin, although I think he suspected.

I'd also decided to go to the SAA meetings in New Orleans in April. And since I'd already be halfway across the country, I'd decided to follow up with a visit to Rhode Island. I think Gavin was looking forward to having me out of his hair for a few weeks. I tried to convince him to join me, but spring is a busy time at the ranch, and he'd have to stay and tend the animals. I hated to admit it, but I couldn't wait to escape.

The Big Easy

It snowed three days before I left for New Orleans. The daffodils had just bloomed, and their bright, sunny flowers had filled me with hope—until the storm squelched it. Once the sun came out, the snow melted fast, but many of the daffodils had fallen, their stems bent and flowers crumpled.

Gavin was quiet as he drove me to the airport, but I was chattering like a four-year-old. I was so excited to be going on an adventure that I felt like my old, optimistic self again. I couldn't wait to see some of my friends and former coworkers, hear papers on new topics, and enjoy New Orleans' great food and music. And after the meetings, I'd be reunited with my family.

I took a bus into New Orleans from the airport, and through the window it seemed like any other city: busy highways, tight rows of houses, strip malls, and gas stations. I had booked a room at the meeting hotel, which was located next to the French Quarter and near the river. Spring had come to the city, and the trees all had new, fresh, bright green leaves. Magnolias bloomed and flowers were everywhere—none of them damaged by winds and snow.

The bus dropped me off right in front of my hotel. As I entered the large, airy lobby, I heard my name.

"Ivy, is that you?"

I turned to see Jack and Jill standing near the registration desk. They were drinking beer and wearing welcoming smiles. We hugged. I was so happy to see friends and be away from Delta that my eyes filled with tears.

"Hey, Ivy, you can't be that happy to see us. What's up?"

I dabbed my eyes with a tissue and explained. "Delta winters are a little too long for me. Even with the hottest guy in the West."

"You mean second," said Jill with a throaty laugh. I caught her flashing Jack a special look.

"Okay, if you say so, second. I'll just have to agree. Is anyone else here from our project?"

"We're giving a paper on our dig, and Tim is giving one too. I haven't seen him, but I know he's here with Mary."

Jill, wearing a navy blue T-shirt and jeans, looked like she'd just walked off a dig. Jack, in contrast, was all dressed up. His long hair streamed down his back, and he was wearing a dress shirt with a button-down collar.

"When is your paper?" I asked. "I haven't had time to pick up my registration materials. Jack, you look kind of dressed up. Are you presenting soon?"

"You guessed it. We were just heading toward the session." He looked in the direction of the hotel conference center.

I wondered for a second how he could drink beer just before giving his paper but then remembered that I was with archaeologists. Beer drinking is a staple at the SAA meetings. Those who weren't beer drinkers before becoming archaeologists learn to be in field school.

"Let me check in, and I'll head right over. What room is it in?"

I threw my suitcase down in my room, quickly used the bathroom, and raced to hear Jack's paper. The session was in a smaller room, and only half full. I saw Mary and Tim sitting together near the front. Jack's paper focused on the nuts and bolts of the project: who, what, when, where, and how. The site's radiocarbon dates indicated that the sites had been occupied between six thousand and four thousand years ago. The jumble of bones I'd excavated represented over ten adult and juvenile antelope that had been butchered and roasted in the earth oven. They had probably been thrown in after the flesh was consumed. Jack speculated that the bones were disposed of there for later use as fuel; however, the site's occupants never returned.

Tim's paper was next and examined our discoveries within a regional context. Five thousand years ago, large game had roamed what is now

Wyoming in thick herds, and wild grass seeds had been plentiful. Native Americans hunted antelope and bison with spears and game traps, supplementing this diet of meat with green plants and grass seeds. The artifacts suggested that the local Archaic hunters and gatherers were not completely isolated. They had worn beads made out of Pacific shells, and they had made projectile points using obsidian that had come from several distant sources, including some in Utah. Tim hypothesized that the trade goods had moved into the region from down-the-line trade rather than direct travel to these far-off locales. I stayed for the rest of the session and then promised to meet everyone in the lobby at five.

I picked up my registration materials before heading back to my room to brush my teeth and change my clothes. Black jeans and a tight, low-cut black shirt would be perfect for a night on the town. I put on comfortable shoes and the dangly turquoise earrings that Tom had given me before he left. He'd bought them from a Gallup pawnshop, and I treasured them. I checked myself in the mirror and decided I looked pale but otherwise okay. I grabbed my purse, checked for my room key, and headed out.

The lobby was already packed with hundreds of drinking and smoking archaeologists, elbow to elbow, connecting with field school friends, fellow students, former professors, and coworkers. I heard that each keg of beer lasted just one hour. The crowd's noise rivaled any I'd ever heard. How would I find Jack and Jill? I waded through the lobby, spotted Johnson out of the corner of my eye, and quickly turned the other way. Heading toward the cash bar, I saw Bob standing in the center of a young crowd.

I walked over and gave him a hug. I thought he looked thinner.

"Hey, I'm supposed to meet some friends in a minute," I explained. "Are you giving a paper?"

"Tomorrow afternoon."

"I'll find you there."

I wove my way to the spot where I'd first run into Jack and Jill, hoping to find them there.

Perfect! There they were. We talked while we waited for Tim and Mary. After they arrived, we walked over to the French Quarter. It was blissfully quiet outside the hotel, and Tim led the way to a small restaurant he knew of that served fresh crawdads and shrimp.

To a small-town New Englander now residing in rural Utah, I felt like I'd been beamed to another planet. New Orleans's buildings are old, like Rhode Island's colonials, but the resemblance stops there. Everything in the French Quarter is fancier, more posh, almost lush, like the back-drop of a French-themed masquerade ball. Puritans had definitely not settled this town. Houses were decorated with overdone woodwork, and hotels were topped by mansard roofs. Many were painted pink, red, and orange, and some were gaudy enough to fit in a Barbie doll village. Even the wrought-iron fences sported curlicues, circles, and spikes. New Englanders—thrifty and practical—would shake their heads and sigh, quietly disgusted with the waste, the decadence, the irreverence.

Like a bear waking from hibernation I suddenly felt starved for every-thing—food, drinks, fun! New Orleans was alive, and the French Quarter lay at its heart, with pumping music, food, drink, and people cruising up and down Bourbon Street. Stores along the street were stuffed with masks, beads, boas, sequin-covered high heels, party clothes, and sex toys. Black magic also had its place, with voodoo dolls, Tarot cards, and crystals lining the shelves. Bars without walls teased the crowds in with live bands blaring blues, rock, and jazz. Tourists roamed in and out, wide-eyed, clutching mugs of beer, cylinders of margaritas, and tropical umbrella-clad flasks. I peeked into some of the bars and spied couples dancing like plumed jun-gle birds, in choreographed mating steps. We lined up at a corner bar and ordered another round of drinks. I opted for a multicolored slushy mar-garita—to go.

A few blocks later the crowds thickened, and men were throwing beads to the people below. I looked up and heard loud drunks goading women on the street to bare their breasts, accompanied by cheers and taunts from the crowd. I drank and watched, entranced by the sweat, heat, and sounds. I could smell popcorn, cigars, beer, perfume, and hot bodies. The pleasure zones of my brain lit up like Vegas neon, like a slot machine, its bells, lights, and colors rolling. I wanted to do everything at once. More, more, more!

The restaurant Jack took us to was a crowded local's bar on the edge of the French Quarter. Our food was served in steel buckets, and we were also given an empty one and a roll of paper towels—silverware appeared optional. The buckets were filled with steamed crawdads and boiled shrimp. We drank, peeled, sucked, and dipped until our arms were slick with butter and crawdad slime.

Jill made us laugh till our stomachs ached with a story about her first boyfriend and their awkward attempt to make love in a car. Overzealous cops on patrol had thwarted their fumbling. Her bawdy story of failed love seemed perfect for this place and this time.

After two beers and one very large margarita, my buzz had turned me brazen, and I decided I wanted beads. Lots of beads. And I knew how to get them. We cleaned up as best as we could and moved our small herd back to Bourbon Street, where the party was in full swing. Apparently what I'd seen earlier had been just a prelude; this was the symphony.

A woman selling multicolored drinks in test tubes stopped me and offered a special two-for-one deal. Who could resist? Two were better than one, so why not? As we pushed our way through the crowd, I focused on the men throwing beads to the throngs of people yelling and laughing below. A woman pulled down her top, floppy breasts bare, and was rewarded with a hailstorm of beads. She caught two strands and recovered another from the street, and these she proudly donned. An idea popped into my head.

"Jill," I said, grabbing her arm to get her attention. "Do you think they'd throw us beads if we pulled out our shirts like basketball hoops?"

"Not if you have a bra on," she laughed.

"Got that covered—or I should say, uncovered." Jill smiled.

"Well I haven't got a bra on either. Let's do it!"

"One, two, three!" I yelled drunkenly. We pulled out our shirts, exposing our breasts to the guys upstairs armed with beads. They snapped to attention, then elbowed each other and aimed. The beads flew, and Jill and I danced around collecting them, then did it again. The basketball jocks among the revelers couldn't resist.

Jack and Tim, who had been talking with Mary, paused to see what was causing such a loud commotion. By now Jill and I were being goaded by the crowd, all chanting for us to do it again. Jack looked confused for a minute, not sure why the crowd was yelling at us, until Jill pulled open her blouse. Her breasts bared, the beads rained down. Jack's look of amazement became tempered by something that just might have been lust, but it passed in an instant. Then he grabbed Jill's arm and mine and dragged us away, into a bar that hummed with music and warm, gyrating bodies. Jill broke away, and we joined the dancing throng. Whatever was in those test tubes coursed through my brain. More, more, more!

The last thing I remember before passing out was Jill throwing up in the alley on the way back to the hotel. Magically, a man appeared with a Windex bottle in hand and proceeded to clean her up. What seemed even more amazing was that Jack had the presence of mind to tip him. It was all surreal. Too much. Then the lights, bells, and whistles in my brain short-circuited, and Mary and Tim half dragged, half carried me back to my room.

I woke the next morning fully clothed with a brassy band clanging in my head. I struggled awake and looked in the mirror to make sure that the pounding wasn't actually visible. I took off my clothes—including my huge trophy bead collar—washed down some aspirin, stumbled into the shower, and headed back to bed—so much for the morning sessions. When I woke again I felt a little better, but troubling images kept floating through my brain: Ivy drinking, Ivy baring her breasts, Ivy dancing, Jill sick, Windex Man. I convinced myself that it had been dark out, and with the exception of Jack, Jill, Mary, and Tim, no one else had seen me in action. For that matter, once my brain stopped hurting, I could go back to the meeting and make believe nothing happened.

Wrong. The first person I ran into was none other than Ken. He stopped me and smiled in that sleazy, knowing way.

"Did you get the beads I threw down to you last night?"

"What are you talking about?" I tried playing dumb, which was pretty easy considering my condition.

"Don't even try it, Ivy. I threw at least three sets of beads into your hoop. I made some pretty good shots, if I do say so myself—cute little breasts."

"Argh...." I stammered, trying to jump-start my brain. Nothing happened. "You must be thinking of someone else."

"Don't bullshit me, Ivy. I know it was you. Don't act like you don't remember dirty dancing with me later."

"What?" I really didn't remember that.

Overload. Some distant voice in my head yelled, "Captain, she can't take anymore! The transporter has malfunctioned. You can't beam back up yet." Too bad. Nothing short of beaming up to the starship could save me from this humiliation.

"Okay, Ken, it was me, but under the influence of whatever was in those test tube things."

He chuckled and walked off. Looking over his shoulder, he said, "You really shouldn't drink hard liquor."

By late afternoon I felt a little better, but I ordered chicken soup in my room and hid out for a while. At dusk I took a walk, away from Bourbon

Street, enjoying the warm breeze and the smells of the river. I found an open-air cafe that sold chicory-flavored coffee and some warm powdered sugar confections that were delicious. Couples strolled by, arm-in-arm, window-shopping and admiring antiques displayed in quaint storefronts. For the first time I missed Gavin, but I didn't miss Delta. I wasn't even sure that I could force myself to go back. Tears welled in my eyes. I hated to leave Gavin, and I cried at the thought of having to say good-bye.

I wandered back to my room and went right to bed. I wanted to get up early to attend a symposium by a group of students from the University of Arizona. A professor there had taken the lead in a new topic: the study of modern refuse disposal habits. He'd been able to obtain funding from the American Can Company and various other packagers and distributors to learn about discard habits. These archaeologists were arguing that their study could be applied to prehistoric behavior, but I had my doubts. Although I didn't particularly want to spend my graduate career studying garbage, especially in Tucson's climate, I'd applied to the University of Arizona and wanted to hear how the project was going.

The session was surprisingly interesting. By interviewing people about their trash disposal habits and then comparing their answers to the actual trash, they had discovered that people are not necessarily honest about what they throw out. For example, the tendency to lie about how much alcohol is consumed appeared universal. The researchers also discovered that when meat prices skyrocketed, people tried to economize by buying cheaper cuts. Unfortunately, they often didn't know how to prepare them, and the result was higher rates of discard. The presentations grabbed my attention and even provided a few laughs when pictures were shown of students going through trash after it had been sitting outside in the Tucson heat. I crossed that field school off my list.

The last paper ended at 10:30. The next symposium I went to was on optimal foraging in the Great Basin. This theory was all the rage, so I needed to get caught up. For some reason, Johnson was the session's discussant. In this role he would review the papers and comment on their adequacy and accuracy. I'd heard him make disparaging remarks about the topic, so I couldn't wait to hear him rip the papers. I expected fireworks.

The first paper reviewed the theoretical underpinnings of optimal foraging theory. The theory was first developed in the 1960s in biology and ecology as a way to understand the relationships between caloric values and consumption times, and their role in a predator's diet. Application of this model to hunter and gatherer cultures had helped anthropologists predict how forager populations used food resources given different environmental conditions. The theory assumes that human decisions are made to maximize food-energy capture, and that foraging behavior responds to natural selection. Other papers presented models or the test results of those models.

The first paper used the diet breadth model to predict what resources a forager will take if encountered. The author evaluated the resources available to foragers in an area of Nevada and ranked those according to search and handling costs. He had discovered that large game was the best caloric bet for the effort, and small seeds the lowest. Next was a paper that looked at resource patches to determine at what point a forager decides to move from one to another. A few of the papers looked at the detailed composition of certain food nutrients and the caloric values of the food groups. There was one really interesting paper on tubers and how man-made fires promoted their growth.

Johnson's review of the papers was more positive than I expected. He said that it was helpful to know what foods provide the greatest buck for your bite. However, he felt that all of this theory was more likely to be confusing rather than helpful. In his opinion, new kinds of archaeological data, especially those discoveries made by careful fieldwork or through analytical techniques such as radiocarbon dating, are far more important than theory. I sort of agreed with him because I could see the many problems with applying optimal foraging theory to the bulk of the archaeological sites that make up the prehistoric landscape. How does a lithic scatter fit into a foraging system when you have no idea what period the site dates to, and what resources were available to the people who lived there?

My mind was racing when I left the session and headed to the ladies room. I stopped for a drink at the water fountain and, busy thinking about the papers I'd just heard, barely missed backing into Dr. Johnson.

"Dr. Johnson," I stammered. "How are you?"

I saw recognition in his eyes. "Old," he glowered.

What could I say to that?

"I heard that you stopped doing archaeology at that bad private firm and the Land Management Agency." His lips curled back in a sly smile. "You left for some guy, just as I predicted."

"No, you're wrong. I'm just taking a break from work and staying with a friend. I've applied to graduate schools for the fall." My quick response surprised even me. I guess I really was going back to school after all. "I don't know how I'll afford it, but I'm applying for financial aid. I'm hoping something comes up."

"Where'd you apply?"

"Arizona, New Mexico, and Nevada—Las Vegas."

His eyes bore into me as he lit a cigarette. "Forget New Mexico. That's Winford. He'll eat you alive. I doubt you could handle Arizona. Las Vegas might work, but Reno is better. Try there. I'll talk to Carl."

"You mean Carl Wright?" Who hadn't heard of him and his wife, Marie? They were both big-time famous. They'd gotten their start on the Glen Canyon project working with Johnson.

"Carl and Marie, yes, I think that would work," he said, more to himself than me. "My advice is get out of Utah."

He put his cigarette out in a large standing ashtray and walked away. I watched him go and actually felt a little sad. Had I misread Johnson, just as Penny confided? Oh well, that was water under the bridge. One way or another, I was going to graduate school. Now all I had to do was break the news to Gavin.

Moving On

Gavin met me in baggage claim with a hot kiss and a warm hug. He smelled of horses and sage, and looked as handsome as ever. His smile told me I'd been missed, and his mustache tickled my upper lip. I almost lost my resolve right then and there.

He collected my bags, and we headed to the ranch. In the two weeks I'd been gone, spring had arrived for good. Snow still covered the mountains, but the valleys were green and the trees had finally leafed out.

There was no sense in beating around the bush. It wasn't going to get any easier to tell him. After our first rush of conversation had ended, he held my hand and we sat in silence.

"Gavin, we need to talk." He looked at me with soft eyes, and I realized he already knew.

"I know, Ivy. You need to leave Delta, right?"

"Yes, but it's not you that I want to leave. I love you. I just can't live in Delta. I won't be happy here, and I don't want to give up archaeology. I've decided to go back to school in the fall."

There was a heavy silence. Gavin squeezed my hand and concentrated harder on the road ahead. I'm sure that over the winter he'd come to realize that I wasn't cut out for the life of a rancher's wife, but that he and his ranch would make some other woman very happy.

"Maybe you could come with me?"

He shook his head and his eyes bore into me. "I can't leave, Ivy. You know that."

"I know, but I don't want to lose you. Please come." I started to cry and looked out the window, hoping he wouldn't notice. Sometimes the emotions that turn my eyes into a faucet can be easily turned off. At other times, grief overwhelms me—tears flow, my throat tightens, and a huge block of angst travels slowly to my heart. This was one of those times. My tears rolled down my cheeks and fell onto my coat, and that block lodged in my heart.

I glimpsed at Gavin and saw he was frowning and shaking his head. We sat in silence for the rest of the drive home.

While I'd been away, I'd received letters from the University of Arizona and the Las Vegas and Reno campuses of the University of Nevada. Arizona turned me down cold. Reno had accepted me but offered no financial aid. Las Vegas, my least favorite option, offered me a research assistant position that would pay my tuition and give me a small monthly stipend. Las Vegas, here I come!

Spring quickly turned to summer, and by mid-May Delta was as green and lush as it gets. I'd decided to find a summer fieldwork job and move out of the ranch house before Gavin's parents returned from St. George.

Fortunately for me, the Land Management Agency's controlled burn in the Mineral Mountains the previous fall had gotten out of control. Twelve hundred acres of scrub oak had burned, revealing a treasure trove of pristine prehistoric sites. Since the agency had no money to hire a private company to record the sites, they had decided that Joanne could spend the summer surveying the burned area and recording them. She had convinced management to hire a temporary archaeologist to help, and of course, she'd hired me. Since the burn area was in a remote part of Beaver County, the agency had arranged to have a trailer moved to the project area so that we wouldn't have to make the long drive each day. It gave me a place to stay where I could live, work, and put some distance between Gavin and me.

The fire had burned off the oak leaf litter to reveal hundreds of archaeological sites, giving me the opportunity to discover what they looked like before they'd been visited by local arrowhead hunters. The sites were littered with hundreds of tools and projectile points, most of them made out of obsidian from a nearby source. Soon after we started recording sites, we caught two people hunting arrowheads. After shooing them away, we decided to collect all of the points so they would end up in a museum rather than on someone's wall.

Halfway through the survey I started to wonder if the Indians had camped in this locale primarily for the acorns or for the deer that ate the acorns. Since Joanne traveled back to the office fairly often, I asked her to find out from the biologists which animals eat acorns, and if the Utes and Paiutes were eating acorns from the oaks that had burned. If the prehistoric inhabitants were eating the acorns, they would probably have used special tools to process them. Joanne offered to bring me her textbooks on California Indians because I couldn't remember much about acorn processing, but I knew that the California tribes had supported large populations on acorns and other gathered plants and animals. But what kinds of tools had they used?

I read Joanne's books cover-to-cover as soon as they arrived and learned that the California Indians had processed acorns using pestles and mortars. After the acorns were ground, they were washed to leach out the tannin. Then the remaining flour was dried and stored, and it can be stored for long periods of time. We hadn't found any mortars or pestles yet, so it didn't seem that acorns were the food source. What we did find were hundreds of projectile points, scrapers, and bifaces—all typically used to kill animals and process the meat and hides. Because there were so few grinding tools of any type on the sites, I decided that the Indians who'd camped in the burn area had probably been there to hunt rather than collect acorns and seeds. Once I had an opportunity to study the styles of projectile points, I'd be able to infer how long the campsite had been used. Spear and arrow points were present in large quantities, and their styles hinted that Native Americans had camped here for the last few thousand years.

I tried not to think about Gavin. Instead I spent time plotting a path forward through the land mines of family and career. I decided that with a master's degree in anthropology, I could get an archaeology job with a private company and juggle motherhood if I married the right man. If I married someone who'd be willing to share household tasks and child rearing responsibilities, then it might be possible to have it all. I needed someone who wouldn't mind if I had to be gone for days or even weeks at a time.

I spent a few weekends in Joanne's guest room back in civilization, if you can call Cedar City that. Toward the end of the summer I discovered Joanne's collection of Edward Abbey books. I read them over the rest of the summer and fell in love with *The Monkey Wrench Gang*, the story of a misanthropic group of characters who become crusaders for wilderness and Mother Earth. The book's cast of characters includes a disillusioned Vietnam vet, a river-running Jack-Mormon polygamist, a wealthy divorced doctor, and his beautiful young receptionist. The gang travels some of the Southwest's most awe-inspiring countryside in a doomed quest to stop the encroachment of civilization.

Abbey's books not only got me through the rest of the summer but inspired me to buy a Jeep with my summer earnings and some help from my parents. After finishing the burn survey, I spent my last two weeks in Cedar City hunting for the perfect one. I finally located my dream vehicle on a used car lot in St. George. It was jacked up and loaded with extras, like the one owned by Hayduke of the Monkey Wrench Gang. I felt invincible as I rolled out of the lot in my shiny blue V-8, complete with winch, hard roof, fog lights, cassette tape recorder, and ski rack. In appreciation for Joanne's help over the past two months, I offered to take her on an all-expense-paid camping trip to the Deep Creek Mountains.

I'd never been to the Deep Creeks, but I'd heard of them, on the western edge of Utah in one of the most remote places in the country. By remote I mean that you have to drive at least a hundred miles of dirt roads to get there from any direction. In the grand tradition of the Monkey Wrench Gang, we planned to calculate distances by six packs and spend our days exploring the mountains by Jeep and backpack. We took the top off, loaded up sleeping bags, camping gear, dried and canned food, coffee, and two cases of ice cold beer, and hit the open road. As soon as civilization lay far behind, we put down the windshield, cranked the volume up on the Pretenders, and cracked open beer number one.

Our trip was one of those experiences I'll always remember. Everything felt surreal—too perfect: the cloudless sky, temperatures in the low eighties, the smell of sage and cedar, a warm breeze like a caress, and no bugs. As we neared the mountains, the sun fell low on the horizon, creating a thousand shadows interspersed with soft, shimmery light. We hadn't seen another car all day, and I popped open beer number five as we started climbing the mountain. If my counting was accurate, Joanne was on six. Higher up the canyon, new smells assailed me, and I felt a tremendous sense of well-being as the sky darkened and the air cooled.

In no time we found an ideal camping spot in a wide meadow next to a creek. After building a fire, we threw some hot dogs and beans on the grill and settled into chairs around the fire.

"I've got something for us." Joanne smiled and walked over to the Jeep. Reaching into her backpack, she brought out a flask of tequila. Holding it high, she said, "Voilá!"

"You know I can't drink hard liquor," I said, but my mouth was salivating.

"Come on, Ivy. It's just us. So you get too drunk. What's the worst that can happen here? No one will see you if you take your clothes off."

We toasted to Clovis points and passed the bottle back and forth.

"Joanne, do you think it's possible to be an archaeologist and have a normal life, with a husband and kids?"

"You know, Ivy, that's a good question, and I wish I had an answer. I've been thinking about it a lot lately because I'll be thirty before you know it." She waved the bottle at me and looked sad for a minute. "I don't seem to be having much luck finding the right guy in Cedar City. It's real easy to get them into the sack, but none of them seem to want to marry a career woman. I make it pretty clear that I'm not going to quit my job for them— or for a family."

She stood up and moved her chair away from the fire, then settled back in. "I'm thinking I need to move out of Cedar City if I ever plan on finding a man. Cowboys and Mormons aren't doing it for me." She giggled. "Well, actually they're doing lots, but I don't like any of them enough to tie the knot. You know what I mean. I just can't see myself married to any of the guys here. Look at you and Gavin."

Joanne peeked over at me, perhaps to see if the mention of Gavin had ruined my mood. I nodded sadly.

Joanne continued. "My mom keeps reminding me that my clock is ticking, and she's right. I've decided to transfer to a Land Management Agency office in another state. Maybe I'll have more luck finding the right guy in California or Arizona. What do you think, Ivy?"

"That sounds like a good plan." In my drunken state my thoughts kept returning to that sweet, handsome cowboy in Delta. "I miss Gavin."

"Yeah, he's hot. I don't know if I could have left him." Joanne took another swig.

"Do you think I'll find someone in Vegas? I want it all—a career, a man, and some kids. I'm not giving up, Joanne."

"We can do it, Ivy." She held up the bottle. "To career and family."

Things got a little crazy after that. Joanne popped in a Doors tape and cranked up the volume, and as the stars lit up the sky, and the full moon rose over the mountains, we danced around the fire—wild, reckless, laughing, singing, and hopeful for the future.